THE
SCHOOL
OF
MIRRORS

A NOVEL

EVA
STACHNIAK

WILLIAM MORROW
An Imprint of HarperCollins*Publishers*

To the memory of my mother

P.S.™ is a trademark of HarperCollins Publishers.

THE SCHOOL OF MIRRORS. Copyright © 2022 by Eva Stachniak Literary Holdings Inc. All rights reserved. Printed in the United States of America. No part of this book may be used or reproduced in any manner whatsoever without written permission except in the case of brief quotations embodied in critical articles and reviews. For information, address HarperCollins Publishers, 195 Broadway, New York, NY 10007.

HarperCollins books may be purchased for educational, business, or sales promotional use. For information, please email the Special Markets Department at SPsales@harpercollins.com.

Originally published as *The School of Mirrors* in Canada in 2022 by Doubleday Canada.

FIRST U.S. EDITION

Library of Congress Cataloging-in-Publication Data has been applied for.

ISBN 978-0-06-311960-4

22 23 24 25 26 LSC 10 9 8 7 6 5 4 3 2 1

Paris 1793

SHE RUNS AFTER THE TUMBLING CART, her heart tripping, racing, tripping again.

The morning is crisp, the sky robin's-egg blue. The streets are empty. Houses are shuttered, doors locked. Here and there chimneys belch plumes of thick smoke. Traitors are burning their sins, she has heard. Madame Guillotine is not swift enough.

The cart, pulled by a single horse, sways. The man on the cart, his once-black hair streaked with gray, is holding fast to the side. His eyes follow her, not letting go, not for the shortest of moments.

On the quai d'Orsay, slippery from the night's rain, she glimpses an old bony woman huddling in the doorway. On the pont de la Concorde, a hunch-backed beggar, a bulging sack flung across his chest, is poking through a pile of rags.

In the place de la Révolution, the·cart slows. Around a scaffold, a small crowd has gathered. A child wails and is quickly hushed. A dog barks.

She catches the glint of the blade and stops.

Part One

Versailles, 1755–1757

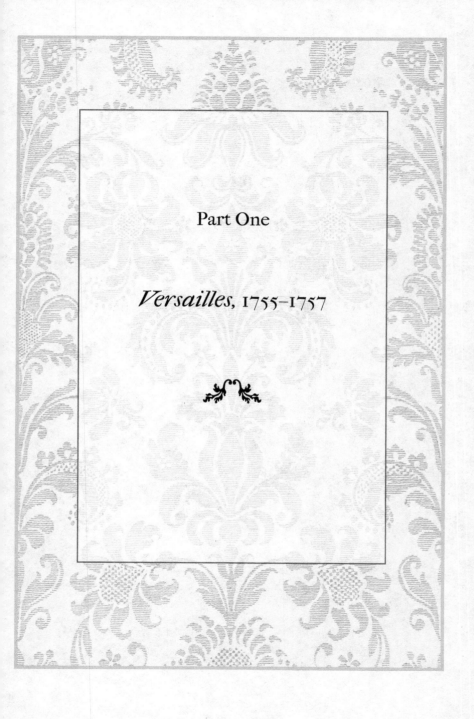

1755

MY MOTHER DIDN'T tell me much.

I would have to go into service, she said. It is not what my late father or she had once hoped for me, but it is how it would have to be. I might still do well for myself, if I learn fast, that is, and if I learn to please. At all times, not only when it suits me, willful girl that I am, eager to listen to everyone but my own flesh and blood.

Should I have guessed what bargain she had struck for me? Perhaps, but I was still a child, even if I had turned thirteen already. I didn't know how to spot danger in the silence between words. I didn't know the sequence of steps in the dance of sacrifice and betrayal.

Used women's clothes was my mother's trade. Old taffeta dresses frayed at the hems, underarms rotten with sweat; fancy court robes once embroidered with silver and gold now deprived of adornment; the torn, muddy skirts of suicides fished out of the river. I hated it when she brought them home to sort and mend, soaked through with the stink of their previous owners, filthy, infested with fleas.

We lived on rue Saint-Honoré by then, on the fifth floor of a building overlooking the Quinze-Vingts market. In our old house, on rue des Jardins, Papa had his own printing shop, where he printed and sold pamphlets and books, and we all lived in an apartment above it. Here our rented room was divided with strings on which I hung laundry to dry. We slept on folding beds: my brothers on one, Maman and me on another. We ate on Papa's rickety workshop bench, which doubled as a sewing table. We cooked our meals in the communal kitchen downstairs, with its smoking fireplace and damp, moldy

walls, a place of constant quarrels over firewood and cooking space, and sometimes of blatant thievery. The very day we moved in, I learned its basic rules:
Turn your back and your wooden spoon will disappear. Leave your pot unattended and your food will vanish.

Marcel was eleven then, Eugene ten, Gaston eight. They no longer attended the parish school but ran chores for the carpenter or the butcher, who
had their stalls in the inner yard. Marcel claimed that the carpenter's wife
would let him touch her pink tits. Eugene called him a brazen liar. Gaston
followed his older brothers in awe. They only came home to eat and sleep.
Sometimes when I collected their clothes for washing, in their pockets I discovered dice, stones or dead mice.

What would Adèle be like had she lived?

Children, I often heard Maman say, happen. Then they happen to live or
die. God, who has called my sister to His side, is inscrutable. He can take you
because He loves you or because He wants to punish you for your sins.

Lying in bed beside Maman at night, I thought about Papa and Adèle,
wondering where they might be. Adèle I pictured enveloped in light, joyful in
her Heavenly bliss as she worships around the Heavenly throne, God's faithful
and beloved servant. I imagined Papa there, too; although sometimes, remembering that he was not a child and may have sinned, I saw him in Purgatory,
restless in the eternal queue of souls awaiting their time of release.

On the day my fate had been settled I was in the kitchen, warming up a pot
of bean stew, stirring it all the time to prevent it from burning while I also
kept an eye on my brothers. The fireplace was smoking as badly as ever.
Gaston was running in circles, shouting as if possessed by demons, stopping
to inhale and starting again, his voice shrill and loud: "Here, doggy, here!
Sit! Paw!"

"I'm a hawk," Marcel screamed, throwing himself at his little brother.

"Get him, get him," Eugene urged him on.

I yelled at them to stop and was threatening to whack them with the spoon
if they did not obey me when Dame Rambeaux's chambermaid—of whom
people whispered that she had drowned her bastard in the Seine—rushed in.
Maman wanted me upstairs, she said, right now.

Catching Marcel's arm as he ran past me, I made him swear he would stop teasing Gaston. When he did, I told Eugene to mind the pot and hurried upstairs.

"Where are your manners, Véronique?" Maman asked as I entered the room, hot and breathing hard. "Keeping our honored visitor waiting like that!"

That is when I saw him, a tall, thin man dressed in a purple velvet frockcoat, a walking stick in hand. The dusting of face powder deepened the web of wrinkles on his cheeks, making him look like a corpse. The mossy scent around him I would later learn to know by its name: ambergris.

"Is she the one you meant, Monsieur . . . ?"

"Durand." The man finished Maman's sentence.

Haughty I thought him, for when Maman implored him to take a seat, pointing at the only armchair that had survived the move from rue des Jardins, he looked at it with disgust. Was it because of the pile of dresses next to it, set aside for mending?

"Is this who you meant?" Maman repeated, motioning me to step closer. Smooth your skirts, girl, her eyes ordered. Stand straight. Stop panting like a chased dog.

I pulled on the gray russet, tightened the chiffon fichu around my neck. It was stained with brown spots that wouldn't wash out and was therefore not worth selling. I forced myself to quiet my breathing.

Monsieur Durand rapped on the floor with his walking stick.

I had a vague feeling I had seen him before, but I didn't think much of it. Men often trailed me then, teased me with their foolish talk. How I had struck an arrow right through their hearts; how they would die if I didn't give them a kiss. I was a rare beauty, they said, a jewel to behold.

Some beauty, Maman scoffed. Gangly, she called me, all bones and sharp edges. It didn't take much to turn my head, did it?

Fat Nanette who lived in a room next door said Maman was jealous. Dainty I was and lissome, fine-featured, like a china doll. My figure had such a soft line to it that even my coarse dresses could not spoil it. My eyes were a rare mix of grayish blue, my eyelashes long and thick, my skin radiant. Just look at these auburn curls with their copper tint, Fat Nanette would say, so silky to the touch. She would've killed for such looks once, when it still mattered. Alas, youth doesn't last forever.

Monsieur Durand drew a sharp, impatient breath. His eyes passed over me as if I were just one of the objects in this cluttered room.

"Yes, Madame Roux," he said. "She is the one."

Maman's voice hardened. I was a good, dutiful daughter, she declared, her favorite and beloved child. I had a quick mind and deft hands. I could learn anything fast. A treasure, she called me, an adornment to any household.

Monsieur Durand cut my mother short. "I possess a mind capable of forming my own judgments." Then he turned to me.

"Can you keep a room neat and clean?"

I nodded.

"You can perchance also speak, can you not?"

"I know how to keep a room clean," I said.

"Do you know your letters?"

"I do. Papa taught me."

"Well enough to read aloud?"

"Yes."

"Write in a good hand?"

"Yes."

"Not too modest, are you?"

He ordered me to take a few steps to the right and to the left, though this had nothing to do with knowing my letters. I did what he asked, rather clumsily, forgetting about the loose board that always made me stumble.

"I've seen enough, Madame Roux," he said, turning back to Maman.

"Leave us, Véronique," Maman said.

I was happy to obey. I had already decided that Monsieur Durand didn't like me and that I would never see him again.

Downstairs in the kitchen, Eugene, Marcel and Gaston were sitting on the floor, shoulders touching. Glancing over their heads I saw that they were holding sticks, poking them into a piece of honeycomb and licking off the honey.

They didn't steal it, Eugene told me. It was a gift from someone they were not to mention.

Sticky fingers, lips, vests, breeches, I thought. More laundry. More ironing. Why do I have to be the eldest? And the only girl?

Maman didn't say anything when we returned to our room with the pot of bean stew. If it weren't for the lingering scent of Monsieur Durand's perfume, I could've pretended he had not visited us at all. But as we sat down to eat, Maman didn't complain that the stew was slightly burned and even let us all have second helpings. She did not chastise me for fiddling with my hair, or Eugene for talking too much; and when it became dark, she lit two candles, not one.

After my brothers climbed into their bed, after the kicking and elbow punching ended, after I had picked up and folded their clothes and emptied their chamber pot into our slop bucket, Maman motioned for me to sit at the table across from her and cleared her throat.

Monsieur Durand, she said, wished to take me into service. She said it quickly, with a frown.

"To work in his house?" I asked, staring at my hands, fingers pricked so many times that the skin was tough as leather, red knuckles, chilblains from doing laundry. There was a scab where I had scorched myself on the hot edge of the frying pan. A beautiful sweet child you still are, Fat Nanette had sighed often enough. A screaming shame.

"And what would be so terrible about that?" Maman snapped.

My mind was reeling with everything Fat Nanette had ever told me about being a servant in her youth. About the attic where she slept with other maids, cold in the winter, baking hot in the summer. Not even a bed to lie on but a prickly mattress infested with fleas. A brood of children even more unruly than my brothers to clean up after. A mistress who went through her things, to make sure she didn't steal anything. Another one who called her a slut and refused any advance on her wages.

Maman's eyes narrowed, her fists clenched.

What other grand prospects did I have? she asked. Who else was knocking on our door offering to take me off her hands? What was wrong with going into service at a big house? Learning some manners? Earning my dowry, too, so that I could get married to someone with a future? Or was I, perchance, aware of some other brilliant opportunity?

I felt tears rise to my eyes.

"Answer me, Véronique!"

I shook my head. I had no other prospects.

"Then it's high time you earned your keep," Maman said.

I was hoping she would tell me more about this house where I would live and work, but what followed was Maman's familiar lament. A woman's lot . . . a vale of tears . . . a bitter cup . . . How when she was still young and pretty, her parents implored her not to marry Lucien Roux. How she wouldn't listen, pigheaded as she was, refusing to look behind empty promises. She meant Papa's printing shop that never prospered. She meant Papa's debts that she was still paying off. She meant a pile of books no one would buy from her, crammed under the bed, gathering dust.

"Don't you dare disappoint me," she said. "Don't get sent back here. I have enough mouths to feed as it is."

Some calculations are simple. Sons trump daughters. Three children trump one.

Deep in my heart, I had already decided that nothing could be worse than the life I had. That my mother would always put my brothers ahead of me.

That the wrong parent had died.

⚜

Dominique-Guillaume Lebel, *premier valet de chambre du roi*, commands the realm of the king's most intimate pleasures.

How hard could this be? his rivals ask. Louis the Well-Beloved requires mistresses? Plenty of those around. Court ladies sneak into his private rooms, drunk on the very thought of his wine-soaked breath. Parents push their ripening daughters into his path. What else is there to do but direct the traffic and pocket the rewards? Ha, Lebel would say, were it only that simple. Do those who aspire to replace him know just the right hint of coarseness under a thick veneer of polish that appeals to the king of France and Navarre? The precise combination of innocence and sauciness? A tang of ignorance spiced up with a subtle taste of the gutter? Do they know that self-sacrifice inflames his sovereign's heart more strongly than any bedroom antics might? Or that any trait or word reminding him of the queen, of any of his daughters, or of Madame de Pompadour will kill the king's ardor in an instant?

Lebel knows his king the way he is, and not the way he appears to be. Or should be. Or even—during his rare flare-ups of uncertainty and remorse—desires to be. Lebel also knows how much his master—locked in a maze of identical days, chained with etiquette, hounded by the expectations of others—craves variety. If the royal mistresses—noble or common—keep changing, the king doesn't have to. He can tell the same anecdotes, offer the same gifts, which come so much cheaper if ordered by the dozen. Besides, as the duc de Richelieu likes to remind the king with a knowing wink, there is nothing like novelty to produce "the desired result."

Yes, Dominique-Guillaume Lebel knows how to delight and how to appease, what to say and what to keep to himself. After all, he is a son and grandson of Versailles servants; the court is in his blood. He senses boredom or annoyance long before it surfaces, rejection before it creeps into the dark blue royal eyes. He knows which lines not to cross, whom to placate and whom to ignore. Should Louis wish to be an unseen spectator of his own court, Lebel can offer a secret passage, a room equipped with double mirrors, a staircase that leads all the way to the palace roof. This is why, he would tell his rivals, no one can take his place, especially now with the latest shift in the royal kingdom of pleasure.

No, this is not the profound shift that the court still so foolishly expects after the day, five years ago, when Madame de Pompadour renounced her place in the royal bed. No noble beauty who has since been admitted to that bed has managed to oust Madame from her place at the king's side. Nor have any of the "little birds" flocking through the palace corridors in their flashy dresses, their bourgeois mothers in tow. Not even that Irish hussy, O'Murphy, who believed herself irreplaceable only because the king kept sending for her even after she produced a bastard.

The shift in the royal pleasure is of a different kind. The king of France, tired of courtly intrigues, has become a connoisseur of innocence. He abhors guile and artifice. He detests rouged cheeks, gaudy dresses, and saucy talk. The "little birds" Louis wants in his bed now must be unspoiled, which, on the royal lips, means willing to please but not yet knowing what pleasing a man entails.

Pleasing a man, not the king, is of the essence here, for Louis wants to be desired for himself, not his crown.

Since such girls cannot be conjured up at a moment's notice, Lebel has to plan well in advance. This is why his scouts are always on the lookout for a suitable candidate. "Unripe and unspoiled, with that innocent look the king favors now," he demands. "From a family with few prospects, willing to take a chance when it presents itself, but not searching for one." The pretty daughter of a small merchant or artisan down on his luck, he suggests.

If his scouts locate such a girl, Lebel will inspect her. If the girl passes muster, Lebel will make his first move.

Introducing himself as Monsieur Durand, the trusted servant of his noble master, Lebel will approach the girl's parents. He will be blunt. Their daughter has caught his master's eye, he will say, and thus might have a chance to make something of herself. *Might*, he will repeat in a solemn voice, because his master is a man of taste and discernment for whom beauty by itself, however striking, is not enough. His master demands impeccable manners and the ability to divert him. Here Lebel will mention dancing or playing an instrument, which of course requires training he is willing to provide. He will use words like *thespian*, *sophistication*, *ingenue*.

Such manner of speech, too, he will signal, is a desired skill.

If pressed for the identity of his master, Lebel will tell them of a Polish count, a distant relation of the queen, who frequently comes to Versailles and is thus in need of pleasing company. He will call him His Lordship Casimir Boski, the name decided upon after one of the queen's servants told him that in Polish *boski* means divine. An honorable man, he will say, ready to secure the girl's future when the time is ripe.

As proof of his master's good intentions, Lebel offers to pay any outstanding debts the family might have, provide for everyday expenses, make an investment in the family business. For the girl herself, he promises ample gifts of dresses, fine linen and precious jewelry, all hers to keep. He hints at a good marriage for which a decent dowry will be secured. His offers are carefully calculated to tempt but are never too big, for he knows the dangers of inflated expectations fueled by greed.

If the parents accept the offer, Lebel will swear them to secrecy. Not a word to the neighbors, he warns, or to the girl herself. Tell your daughter she is going into service. Tell her she has a chance to become a lady's maid, if she is agreeable and quick to learn. Tell her I demand absolute obedience. Tell her she will depart right away. Tell her she doesn't need to know anything else.

And if the parents refuse his offer? Or if they hesitate or bargain or ask too many questions?

The world is full of pretty "little birds" with no money and few hopes. Dominique-Guillaume Lebel will just move on to the next girl on his list:

> *Véronique Roux, thirteen years of age. A rosebud, impossibly gauche, lacking in style but with a fetching look of languor and still utterly unspoiled.*

For an avid hunter, Lebel thinks, the king of France is surprisingly averse to the pleasures of the chase. He wishes his human quarry flushed out of the thicket, presented to him for the perfect and easy shot.

Véronique Roux, gauche, languid and utterly unspoiled, might very well do.

___

How predictable my days, I had thought then, how harsh. Rising at dawn, serving breakfast, scrubbing the floors clean until my hands bled, taking out the slop bucket. Minding the stall when Maman left to fetch yet another batch of clothes for sale, which I would later have to darn and brush, and make presentable.

Maman sold her clothes at the very edge of the market from a shack cobbled out of broken planks. She kept it ill-lit on purpose, to make stains less noticeable, colors more deceiving. To tempt a hesitant buyer, she would cluck her tongue and remove the robes from hooks crudely fashioned from nails.

Lifted up, shaken to bring back their lost luster, the dresses took on a new life, fitting Maman's outlandish stories. Duchess so-and-so got tired of this one for sea green was—imagine this—no longer à la mode. Or Marquise so-and-so got too stout on too much pastry with cream to fit into this one. "Our good queen herself owned it," I once heard Maman whisper while pointing at a petticoat from which all lace had been hastily and carelessly removed. "Touch it!" she urged a would-be buyer. "Feel the quality! Fine as a butterfly's wing."

All lies, of course, but it could've been worse. In the stall next to us the Widow Goutier was trading in battlefield bargains: jackets rent with bayonet cuts, breeches stained with blood and excrement, smashed pocket watches and, for select clients, freshly pulled human teeth.

On the day before I was to go into service, Maman pointed at the pile of clothes on the floor as if nothing else mattered. "These need mending, Véronique," she said. "Bring them to the stall when you are done."

I watched her pin up her hair, adjust her fichu, bite her lips to make them look fuller. The period of full mourning had ended three months before, yet she was still wearing her widow weeds. "Good for business," she said, but I believed she liked how the black lightened her complexion. I thought her old, spent and bitter. I thought she pursed her lips to hide her rotting teeth, as if she could fool anyone.

I watched the door open and close. I heard Maman's steps descending the stairs.

My brothers were already gone, having wolfed down their breakfast and left the dishes for me to wash. Adèle would have helped me, without being asked. I recalled sitting beside my sister at the edge of the bed, the two of us wiggling our toes, giggling with delight. We had folded a piece of paper so that it could be opened, with fingers and thumbs, like a bird's beak. Forward or out to the side. Playing fortune, we called it, for inside each opening we inscribed words of destiny. *Hell*, or *Heaven. Damnation*, or *Eternal Bliss.* "Your turn first," I said, and Adèle pointed at the direction she wanted me to open the paper beak. Seeing the word *Heaven* inside, she smiled. "I can die now, then," she said, and for a moment she looked like a carved statue of herself, a figure of translucent white marble. "Don't say that," I warned her, but I was too late.

I picked one of the skirts from the heap, torn at the waist, caked with filth. It had been maimed by what Maman called drizzling, the pulling out of all the silver and gold threads for which goldsmiths paid far more than she could ever afford.

Maman had forbidden me to talk to anyone about my leaving, as if our building could ever keep secrets for long. Everyone knew that the carpenter was jealous and took his razor strap to his wife, who was carrying on with the butcher. Or that Dame Rambeaux's chambermaid—whose nose Fat Nanette called "a badger's snout"—cried every time she got news from home. Or that Master Deveaux would raise our rents in the new year. I could imagine the whispers gathering already: *Going into service after all . . . Fat Nanette can say what she wants . . . Beggars cannot be choosy.*

The torn skirt fell to the floor. A moment later I was out the door, the building, the market, rushing to the bank of the Seine, where the water was murky and brackish, its depths invisible. Once there, I didn't stop but continued walking toward rue des Jardins, a few streets away from the pont Marie.

⋙⋘

The Versailles apartment where Dominique Lebel charts his moves, keeps his records and receives his many deputies is right above the king's. Lebel has furnished it not merely for elegance but also for comfort. Mahogany tables are small enough to rearrange if needed. Chairs have curved backs and padded wings for elbows to rest on. In Lebel's study, his writing table has two columns of drawers, where he keeps his most important records. The back of his *fauteuil de cabinet*, upholstered in leather, is high enough to protect his head from the drafts he detests.

It is in this study, in October of 1755, that Lebel attends to the latest improvement in his kingdom of the royal pleasure, a new house he has recently bought on the king's behalf. The house is in the town of Versailles, on rue Saint-Médéric where it crosses rue des Tournelles. Named Deer Park after the old royal hunting grounds it sits on, the house is close enough to the palace for convenience—a brisk fifteen-minute walk to the Stag's Courtyard but far enough away not to attract attention from nosy courtiers.

There are four rooms on the ground floor of Deer Park: six smaller ones on the floor above and two low-ceilinged ones in the attic more than adequate for the servants' quarters. There is also a carriage house where the night watchman sleeps and a good-sized paved yard, all well hidden behind a stone wall high enough to stop prying eyes. In short, a perfect place for the "little birds" to perch as they await the king's summons.

This recent purchase has ended long months of scrambling, putting up with most unsatisfactory arrangements. Now Lebel has a permanent place to keep the "little birds" until he needs them, a place where order can be maintained, absolute secrecy demanded and enforced. No longer will his own Versailles apartment be referred to as a "birdcage," nor will his personal servants be tempted with bribes from thrill-seeking courtiers daring to poach the king's game.

Lebel has furnished the house himself, buying most of its contents from the former owner, who offered him an excellent bargain. This purchase, however— his informers tell him—did not please Madame la Marquise de Pompadour, who has called it hasty. The truth is that Madame la marquise, who prides herself on her decorating skills, would have preferred to furnish the house herself. In spite of her assurances that she and the king trust Lebel's judgment: "Univocally," she has said, "without reservations. In all matters." Lebel will have to think of an offering soon. A rare flower for her garden, perhaps? Or—this is a much better idea—an account of some touching moment testifying to the king's high regard for her precious friendship. Something no one else has told her before.

Lebel didn't ruffle anyone's feathers in his staffing of the house, though. Deer Park has a housekeeper, Madame Bertrand, a former abbess grateful for rescue from accusations of embezzlement and a few other venial sins. Having turned fifty, Bertrand cherishes her soft bed, the delicacies from the king's table delivered daily from the palace and the decent wine cellar that Lebel keeps replenished. All of it a reasonable guarantee of her loyalty and discretion. And if it fails, the Deer Park cook will make sure Master Lebel is the first to know.

Apart from these two, Lebel has hired a governess to watch over the two girls currently in residence—there were three, but one has recently been sent back home—and provide what he refers to as their "schooling." Two chambermaids keep Deer Park in good order. The night watchman and two hefty lackeys are ready to deflect anyone trying to force himself inside. And if they fail, the regiment of French Guards on avenue de Paris has standing orders to intervene at the slightest sign of trouble.

His Majesty may think of his servants as mere automata, hands and legs powered by some clever internal mechanism he has no desire to fathom, but Dominique Lebel, who is both servant and master, knows that servants, like all people, are ruled by their own interests.

Considering that the kitchen is well supplied with the leftovers from the king's table and that Marquise de Pompadour sends her cast-off dresses to Deer Park to be altered for the girls, Lebel scrutinizes the Deer Park expenses carefully, demurring when they are inflated above the acceptable 5 percent. So far, he has questioned one fanciful account of many long evenings spent reading or embroidering that supposedly required a hundred candles. He also demanded to know why the Deer Park seamstress received forty livres while Gaspard, his own *valet de chambre*, assures him one can be found for half that amount easily enough.

This is why, in his study, Lebel now underlines another item in the accounts ledger—twenty-five livres for the washerwoman—flagging it for further investigation. *Unreasonable*, he writes beside it. *Demand a receipt.* Frequent scrutiny, he believes, is the best strategy for keeping servants honest and diligent.

In the corridor, subdued whispers. A visitor? Now?

Gaspard, who should've made sure no one disturbed him, pokes his head inside and raises his hands in a gesture of supplication. It's Madame Bertrand, he says, begging to be admitted on an important matter.

Lebel sighs but nods. The Deer Park household is still too new, too untried, to let him loosen his vigilance. Besides, he does want to ask about that washerwoman.

"May I seek your advice, Monsieur Lebel?" the housekeeper asks.

Raising his head from the accounts, Lebel notes that she has placed two fingers on her lips. About to announce some earth-shattering news or merely to cover the black mole on her chin?

"Is it about the governess?" he asks, waving at her to sit down, which she does stiffly, a sign that she has corseted herself too tightly.

"Why . . . yes," Madame Bertrand says, her eyes darting toward the pages spread on his desk. Lebel doesn't bother to cover them. Without her spectacles, she won't see what he has written but will know that he is scrutinizing accounts.

"What about her?" he asks.

Mademoiselle Dupin, the governess in charge of polishing the girls' manners and keeping them occupied, is quite distressed over Marquise de Pompadour's last visit, which Madame Bertrand calls "a proper circus."

"Not only do we have to call the girls *élèves*, but Mademoiselle must prepare them to display their accomplishments. As if we were running a school here!"

Madame Bertrand paints a picture of an unannounced arrival during which the masked and gloved marquise took her place in the back of the drawing room, insisting the lesson be conducted as if she were not there. Mademoiselle Dupin, in spite of Madame Bertrand's assurances to the contrary, concluded that the marquise thinks her incompetent. A conviction made stronger when la marquise, before leaving, had her lady-in-waiting instruct the girls in her name: Idle hands conjure up mischief. Loyalty is the highest of virtues. Modesty becomes a woman more than the most costly of jewels.

Madame Bertrand scrunches her face as she pours out her indignation. Lebel closes his eyes. He has just noticed they are smarting, reddened no doubt. His sister likes to say that reading at all hours will ruin your sight, and alas she is right.

She has saved the worst of her wrath for "that unbearable du Hausset," the marquise's lady-in-waiting. "The gray mare" with her plain dresses and long teeth. Not only pompous, du Hausset is also an unbearable snoop. Lingers about the kitchen, eavesdropping on the servants. Even the chambermaids complain that she follows them around, demanding to see this or that girl's room, or asking why there are still unpacked crates in the kitchen.

This blatant spying is troubling but not unexpected. Marquise de Pompadour has always kept an eye on her rivals, no matter how insignificant they might appear. She knows that the world is not run by those who trust but by those who foresee trouble well before it is conceived. Such alertness Lebel admires. The two of them may have had their share of friction when she first arrived at the palace, but by now he is firmly on her side. The last thing this court needs is a new, untried royal mistress determined to make her mark.

Madame Bertrand is quite absorbed in her story, and Lebel lets her talk even though he has pressing things to do. The thought of the governess lingers in his mind, leaving a thin film of pleasure. The ease with which she carries herself, the flashes of witty malice no Versailles courtier would be ashamed of. "Madame la marquise believes in herself the same way she believes in God, without explanation or discussion." "What do you do for company, Monsieur Lebel?" she asked him once with a fetching smile and a flicker of her fan. "Not what I ardently wish, alas," he answered, for he has learned the pitfalls of mixing business with pleasure. "Ah, what a pity," she said, biting her lip.

"Speaking of chambermaids," Madame Bertrand continues. "I find that two are not enough. What with the third girl you mentioned coming— pardon me, *élève*—the cleaning of two floors, the running about."

"Do the maids complain?" Lebel asks. The Deer Park staff are paid well above the going rate. The maids were hired at eighty livres per year, twenty more than they would get anywhere else.

"No, but I do."

Madame Bertrand bends forward, as if she were delivering some invaluable secret. One of the chambermaids, Marianne, she tells him, might not stay at Deer Park long. The girl is being frugal, never asking for an advance on her wages, no doubt saving for her dowry. There is a fellow in the picture, too, a former groom of la marquise who has just opened a shop in Aix, selling lace and ribbons for liveries. In short, the housekeeper wants to hire a maid-of-all-work. Test her, and train her to replace Marianne when she departs.

Lebel leans back in his leather chair, grateful for its accommodating curve. This is not an unreasonable request. "Do you have anyone in mind?" he asks, sure that she does. Probably pocketed a bribe from the supplicant, maybe even spent it already.

"Yes. A daughter of someone I knew quite well. A friend."

A friend from long before her convent days, it turns out. The girl is from

Buc, a few miles south of Versailles, where she ran into some nasty trouble with a smith's son.

"What's her name?"

"Elisabeth Leboeuf."

Lebel frowns. Too grand a name for a maid-of-all-work. "Lisette will do," he says. "At forty livres a year, half of Marianne's pay, until she proves herself capable of replacing her."

Madame Bertrand heaves a deep sigh of relief and leaves him to his work. As she closes the door behind her, he realizes he didn't ask her about the washerwoman. Next time then. He turns from the accounts to the extracts from old police reports that Berryer, the Lieutenant-General of Police, has just sent him. They are of far more importance now. In any negotiation, preparation is half the battle.

Lucien Pierre Roux, a printer, tall, with a distinguished-looking face and auburn hair. A very honest physiognomy that has turned out to be quite misleading. He leases a house on rue des Jardins, a few streets away from the pont Marie, but pretends he owns it.

He arrived in Paris at nineteen from Bordeaux having inherited a printing shop from his uncle. While still in Bordeaux he wrote some pretty pieces in verse, which even brought him passing praise from Voltaire. Here, in Paris, he would've prospered and made a name for himself had he not foolishly married an unimportant girl who had neither birth nor wealth and who burdened him with children in quick succession.

Children: two girls, Véronique and Adèle, both exceedingly pretty, having taken after their mother, were followed by three boys: Marcel, Eugene and Gaston.

I have not ascertained when Lucien Roux turned to printing illegal pamphlets and smuggling forbidden books, but by the time his apprentice provided proofs of his master's dealings, most of his profits came from this illicit trade.

Confronted with indisputable evidence of his crimes, Lucien Roux has agreed to supply me with regular reports on his clients. He also promised to reveal the source of the latest vicious verses pertaining to His Majesty and Madame de Pompadour that are circulating in the streets.

The rest of the report contains names and addresses of clients and sources, pleas for patience as Lucien Roux struggles with falling sales. A journeyman has left. An apprentice has demanded a raise, has been denied and left threatening revenge.

A few pages later:

Lucien Roux died at his house, leaving little but debts. His widow has sold whatever she could and turned to peddling used clothes. His younger daughter, the more beautiful of the two as I've been assured, followed him to the grave two months later, having suffered from the same weakness of the lungs.

The report is appended with a few pages from Lucien Roux's old almanacs, which he began selling in order to repair his finances: calculations of eclipses, predictions of the weather. On one of them these proverbs:

The cat in gloves catches no mice.
The bird that sits is easily shot.
The end of passion is the beginning of repentance.
The royal crown cures not the headache.

I didn't think you would find them particularly useful, Berryer has scribbled in the margin, *but you must agree that, given the current circumstances, they are quite amusing.*

It was still early in the day but cool already. I walked along the river, its bank littered with discarded bones, fish heads, rotting fruit, crushed mussel shells, and broken bottles. Some barefoot children were skipping stones on the water's surface. A little girl with a dirty face scooped out a handful of mud from the river, spat on it and kneaded it as if it were dough. I walked past boatmen unloading their barges, who whistled at me and begged for a kiss until the women washing clothes told them to cut this foolishness out. One of the women inquired about my mother, promising to come by to see the newest batch of clothes she had for sale. Another complained about Eugene being rude to her, cheeky bastard that he was. "Tell your mother to mind him better," she said. "Teach the boy some respect."

Walking faster to get far enough so no one would recognize me anymore, I pictured Papa's shop, its printing press nailed to the floor in the corner, where Henri, Papa's apprentice, who Maman always said was stealing paper, was pulling the press bar, which he called the devil's tail.

I recalled Papa smelling of woodsmoke, his fingers stained with ink, bending over the wage book and account ledgers, telling us that almanacs were selling well. Or kissing the top of my head when I brought him his midday meal while La Grise, our cat who was supposed to hunt for mice and not beg for food, was rubbing herself against my leg, purring, insisting on a treat.

Papa, who taught Adèle and me to read and write "like true printer's daughters" and never said I was mouthy or gave him a headache with my prattle. Papa, who made Marcel practice his additions and subtractions and showed Eugene how to spread ink evenly on the form with ink balls while Gaston watched in awe. Papa, who read to us about rhinos, elephants and camels, promising to take us to a menagerie one day so that we could see these wondrous creatures with our own eyes.

"Papa," I muttered, gathering my breath, imagining all my pain bleeding into the ground.

Lebel sleeps in the state bedroom on a folded cot close beside the king's bed, a piece of silk string tied around his wrist so that the slightest pull from his royal master would raise him to his feet. Called or not, at dawn he puts on his sea-green velvet frockcoat, slips on his red shoes with the sparkling diamond buckles and waits.

As soon as the king of France awakes, Lebel appears at his side with a glass of red wine and a perfumed handkerchief to wipe the royal mouth.

"Another gloomy day ahead, Lebel. Isn't it so?"

"Melancholy, Sire, is best chased away before it descends," Lebel says as his royal master holds the glass to his nose for a sniff. The wine smells much better than the doctor's bitter nerve tonic and delivers the same result.

One royal sip, then another, followed by a deep sigh.

The royal body holds no secrets for Lebel. He is as familiar with the sound and color of his master's piss, or the stains of semen on his sheets, as he is with his moods. Lebel knows that the king of France thinks himself a shackled man in a cage for anyone to stare at. Beseeched to grant endless favors but forbidden to do anything that pleases him. Praised to his face for everything he does, behind his back condemned.

"How long before it starts?" Louis asks, referring to the *grande levée*, the official getting out of the royal bed, attended by courtiers, that awaits him. Like a trained monkey, Lebel heard him complain to Madame la marquise. A barely tamed lion, she retorted, the king of the beasts.

"Three-quarters of an hour, Sire," Lebel says, taking the empty glass and putting it on a side table. The king is sitting up in the state bed by then, ready for his dressing gown and his chamber pot, both warmed up.

The duc de Richelieu once said that Lebel's eyes possess the alertness of a snake. Not the highest example of Richelieu's wit, as Madame la marquise rightly pointed out, but the image stuck. That hissing of yours, Lebel, the king has said on numerous occasions, that slithering.

They go back a long way, the king and Richelieu. Friends mostly, but sometimes foes. "Too old not to pay for love" is the court's latest verdict on the duc, who has been parading his bejeweled new mistress, just shy of fifteen. This, Lebel thinks, should bring a smile to his master's lips, take his mind off the *grande levée*.

It does.

"There is no fool like an old fool, Lebel."

"How very true, Sire."

A swarm of good-for-nothing courtiers is already gathering in the antechamber outside, reeking of perfume, squabbling over trifles, jealously guarding their right to hand their king his shirt, his stockings, his jacket. As always, Lebel follows his master to the small cabinet off the bedroom where he will give the king his morning shave so that later some idiot courtier breathing rot in his face can pretend to administer an official one.

"Don't move, Your Majesty, please." Never a nick, all these years. Another source of pride. He wipes the soapy face with a warm cloth soaked in rose water. A touch of almond milk follows, then *eau de toilette.*

How scarce these moments of royal solitude, how precious. It is Lebel's mission to preserve them.

"The king is the most handsome man in France, Sire."

"Who says so?"

"Madame la marquise."

"Ah."

"And the duchesse de Guide, who has been begging me for permission to approach Your Majesty."

The mirror reflects an unsmiling face, a firm chin, dark blue eyes. Sapphire, some say; the king's color. At forty-five Louis is still trim and agile, his posture excellent. Still believes that horseback riding shakes the insides, stirs up the liver, cultivates alertness. During a hunt he can easily overtake a man half his age, of which fact Lebel takes care to remind him regularly.

"Again?"

"This was my very thought, Sire. The duchesse is a persistent woman."

"Even if discouraged?"

"Particularly when discouraged. A trait of many, I am afraid. Illusion, they say, is the king of the human heart."

"That's rather well put, Lebel."

"Thank you, Sire."

A last spray of perfume, and some *eau vitale* to rub on the palms of the royal hands, to bring forth a surge of *vitalitas*, life force. "It's almost time, Sire."

Time to relinquish the dressing gown, time to get back into the state bed for act one of the *grande levée*, which will begin, as it always does, with the court doctors taking the royal pulse and poking around in the contents of the royal chamber pot.

A few heavy steps, the give of the mattress, the drawing of the bed curtains, the weighty feel of the inevitable. Time to bend over the royal body and whisper, "Permit me, Sire, to tell you why women would never make good soldiers."

Permission granted, Lebel clears his throat.

"Because every one of them would want to serve under a colonel."

What satisfaction, knowing how to lift his master's spirits. What pride.

~❧~

As I approached the pont Marie, the riverbank became less muddy and marshy. Just before the bridge I climbed up the embankment and walked toward rue des Jardins. It was a market day and vendors tried to catch the attention of passersby with loaves of bread, onions, firewood piled up on racks. A coffee man, his big coffeepot perched on a layer of bricks, was arranging tin cups around it. An apple seller bending over a wicker basket tried to stop me, but I was ashamed of not having any money so I quickened my steps. "Don't think you'll find better apples anywhere else, you hussy," she cried after me.

From the street where we used to live came the fierce barking of the potter's mangy dog. Maman used to complain about it, and about the foul air from the river, and about prying neighbors. Everyone in this wretched part of Paris, she said, was sticking their noses into other people's business. Whenever Papa promised to move us to a better part of town, Maman snapped, "As if I needed another of your empty dreams!"

I hastened my steps, turned the corner and there it was, our old house, with its slate roof, looking even more narrow than I recalled. The upstairs windows our maid used to clean with old rags were covered with the same thick purple curtains, but the front door, which used to be dark blue, was now painted an ugly shade of brown. Was a chink still missing where Eugene had tried his pocketknife on it?

My eyes lingered on the front step where Adèle and I used to sit and play with La Grise, and where that one terrible morning we found her mangled body dressed in a paper skirt as if she were a doll. I recalled how hard we cried and how Papa said that some people were worse than wolves.

The printing shop was still there, but the window where Papa once displayed his almanacs was now occupied by elegant volumes bound in leather and embossed with gold leaf. I couldn't resist peering through the glass. Inside, shelves were filled with reams of fresh paper. Two journeymen were bending over the tables, composing sticks or ink balls in hand. Papa's old printing press stood in the corner now, dwarfed beside a big cast-iron one. A round-faced apprentice was pulling its devil's tail.

Watching the newly printed pages being hung on strings to dry, the bound ones arranged in even stacks by the wall, I blinked hard, unable to ward off the image of Papa, on his sickbed, coughing up blood. A strand of his hair, auburn just like mine, was plastered to his forehead. How small he looked under the covers, flat on his back, melted into bedding. "Who put this heavy stone on my chest?" he asked me, fever slurring his words, his breaths loud and raspy. "Was it Henri?"

When Papa died, the catafalque with his coffin on top was placed on the ground floor, in the printing shop. The candles were tallow, not wax. Papa's burial clothes were made of paper, stained to look like the fabric Maman said she couldn't afford. "The burden of life has been lifted from his shoulders," visitors muttered, crossing themselves. "Such is God's will." One by one, we children kissed Papa's folded hands, rosary beads wrapped around them. I placed my kiss quickly, for I didn't wish to remember their coldness. When I lifted Gaston, who was two then, he giggled with delight. Adèle said he must have seen Papa's soul hovering over us.

I stood in front of the building for a long while, as if such persistence could return me to the time when Papa was still with us and La Grise would curl up for her midday nap in the shop window.

I thought no one was paying attention to me. I was wrong.

The door of the house opened, and a woman in the kind of dark blue dress merchant wives favored came out. Elderly, slightly humped, she gave me a suspicious glare. "Move on, girl," she shouted. "Or I'll call the gendarmes."

There was nothing left to do but turn around and walk home.

It is past seven o'clock, another October dawn angling through the gap in the curtains, when Lebel's royal master returns to the state bedroom, forcing his breath in and out, signaling his displeasure.

Lebel doesn't have to be told what a disaster the duchesse de Guide was, but he will be. All that rubbing of her leg against her king's while they play at cards, whispering of her longing for the royal touch! The duchesse of calculated hints, she turned out to be, as if the king of France needed to be guided to his pleasure. There was a stain on her front tooth, too, and a sour note to her breath.

"How could you have not known that, Lebel!"

Royal anger rises from the royal groin, surges through the body parts that Louis is always keen to describe: intestines, stomach, esophagus, larynx, pharynx. All illustrated in his beloved book of anatomical drawings. The truth under the skin, as the king likes to put it, skin and muscles revealing their hidden layers. If the king of France could choose another life for himself, he would've become a doctor or a surgeon. He would have learned how to restore the harmony of the body when illness upsets it.

"I'll take care of the duchesse, Sire," Lebel says.

He will send her off to her country estate with some appropriate trifle. A snuffbox decorated with the royal portrait that she can gush over for years to come, contemplate how much she has lost.

"No more about her, Lebel."

Anger dissolves slowly, but it does, like salt in water. It is enough to stir the beaker long and hard. The mere twirl of the liquid makes the crystals smaller.

"Here you are, Sire," Lebel says, handing his master a glass of red wine and presenting a quick account of the latest news. Silverware has been stolen from the royal governess's rooms, fifty-four plates and three dozen place settings. No suspects, although a maid saw a masked man nearby, taking him for a reveler on account of his excellent clothes. The dauphine is heavier with each day, the new baby should arrive any moment. The queen has begun to fast in preparation for All Souls' Day, which she consecrated for the peace of the princess Henrietta's soul. No meat, no wine, and—perhaps the greatest of her sacrifices—no oysters.

On a lighter note, the warden has reported sightings of ten-point deer and Marquise de Pompadour has sent a reminder of tonight's theatricals. "A delightful evening is all I am allowed to say without spoiling the surprise, Sire."

Madame la marquise also sent a private note for His Majesty. Folded and sealed.

"Not now, Lebel. How much time do I have?"

"A good hour, Sire. Enough time for a rest. I have warmed the bed. October nights can get quite cool."

In bed, the king spreads his legs, testing the boundaries the bed warmer has charted. Satisfied, he turns on his side, pounds the pillow to make it fit the space above his shoulder and closes his eyes.

When Lebel returns to whisper in his master's ear that it is time for the *grande levée*, the king shudders. He had a bad dream, it turns out. Fought against a mesh of rotting roots clinging to his leaden feet, preventing him from walking forward. A horse was neighing in mortal fright. Shadowy figures slunk behind him. A tree was lit by lightning. "We'll march on Versailles," someone yelled. "We'll set the palace on fire!"

A moment ripe for some rousing news? Anticipation that will heighten the pleasure?

"A new girl will soon be coming to Deer Park, Sire."

In the courtyard cart wheels squeal. A dog howls. Another one answers.

"Does she have a name, Lebel?"

"Véronique."

"Pretty?"

"Exceedingly. A rosebud, she has been called."

"Yet another rosebud, Lebel? Can you not try harder? Whatever happened to all other flowers on God's earth? Consider peony, perhaps."

"Exceedingly helpful, Sire."

"Or cherry blossoms."

"Yes, Sire."

No more royal suggestions? Might this be the time for Madame de Pompadour's note?

My dearest, I'm mortified by the thought that I've lost track of where you are each day of the week. Please make me a list of places where you sleep. I want my thoughts to keep you company.

The smile is back on the king's lips, which will please Madame la marquise quite a bit when she hears about it.

It is only when the king departs for his council meeting that Lebel can catch up with the more mundane but pressing business at hand.

The two Deer Park lackeys, Michel and Saint-Jean, are both from the Dauphiné region, where winter hunger drives young men into service. They are sturdy and strong, hardened by mountain treks, their senses sharpened by guarding sheep. No intruder—and there have been a few in the past—would easily have an upper hand with these two around. They are also fast with a sedan chair whenever Lebel needs to bring one of the girls to the palace.

They stand before him now, in his Versailles apartment, eyes opened wide to hide their unease.

"You have been spotted at the local tavern, fleecing peasants at card games," he tells them. "Are you not paid enough?"

"We haven't done anything wrong," Michel declares.

"Just a friendly game of cards," Saint-Jean echoes.

Lebel keeps detailed records of everyone who has ever served under him. A month ago Saint-Jean's fiancée married a neighbor's boy—news the lackey received with quite obvious relief. Michel nurses a grudge against a fellow countryman, who has called his mother miserly. They both miss the Alpine air and the mountains, though why they would, Lebel cannot comprehend.

"Low stakes, *patron*, just to make it more interesting."

"They pester us to show them a few tricks."

"Then they complain."

"No harm, *patron* . . . a bit of amusement . . ."

There is no scheme or intrigue Lebel has not seen before. Lackeys learn card tricks from other lackeys, in the idle hours when they wait for their masters. How to rig a shuffle, cut the card deck where they want it cut. Learning how to cheat comes with the territory.

He opens his folder and reads aloud: *The servants of Count Boski . . . observed at the Golden Goose . . . hiding cards in their sleeves . . . always dealing themselves the best cards. Rudely telling the tavern keeper to stick his nose into his own rat-shit business or else.*

The sums mentioned, one or two livres, he tells them sternly, may seem paltry but are significant to those who have lost them.

They stare at their large, strong hands now, muttering excuses. They had a drop too much to drink. Perhaps they were a bit too forceful with a few fellows, too. But those were cutthroats, ruffians, who got what they deserved.

Lebel does not wish to appear too angry. He has already done his calculations, and the result pleases him. In the town of Versailles, some timely gossip about the servants of the Polish count who has just bought a house there may offer a useful distraction. His decision to order special Count Boski livery, purple with silver braid and shoulder-knots—not too flashy but made of excellent quality cloth—is clearly paying off. However, he doesn't want disgruntled peasants knocking at the Deer Park door, wailing that they have been cheated.

"Enough."

The two exchange uneasy glances. Michel lowers his head.

Lebel slides his hand inside his pocket and takes out his watch. It is three thirty. He has wasted enough time already.

"Listen to me, you two," he says in his official voice of displeasure. "I'll say it once only."

Deer Park, he impresses upon them, is like a fortress under siege. Any crack will be pried open, any indiscretion repeated. "The tavern keeper—"

"A liar," Michel interrupts.

"Waters his wine," Saint-Jean adds. "Thinks we cannot tell."

"Didn't I say, enough," Lebel thunders, fist landing on the table, making it rattle. "Any plans to get back to Saint-Christophe soon? Just in time for winter?"

The mention of Saint-Christophe brings the two to their knees.

This is what always happens, Lebel thinks, in spite of the mawkish talk of Alpine air and mountain views. At first, they all dream of going back home, to show off their smart new clothes, impress everyone with their stories. But those who go come back filled with warnings. Nothing is the way it was.

Their new clothes look out of place. Their stories, repeated too often, bring envy, not admiration. You have left, they hear, so you must be rich. Give and then give some more. Relatives you have never heard about emerge from the shadows. Leeches all, hungry with greed.

The lackeys shift on their feet, eyes to the ground. Michel clears his throat with an annoying hark, as if he were getting ready to spit on the floor, a Saint-Christophe habit he cannot shed.

They are mine to direct, Lebel reminds himself. I'm their master. It behooves me to teach them. Direct their impulses. Remind them of a larger canvas on which their lives are just tiny lines.

"Get up," he orders. "Smarten yourselves. Look beyond today."

They know what he means. He has made provisions for all servants who are still at Deer Park at the time of his death. Each lackey will get three thousand livres in addition to an annuity of three hundred livres, not to mention objects of value they have already received and will receive in the future. Unless they are dismissed beforehand, that is. Which will happen if they cross him.

He lets the numbers float in their minds, transform into farmland purchased, livestock, equipment, a good marriage.

"We beg your forgiveness . . ."

"Never again, *patron* . . ."

Before he lets them go, Lebel hints at a much better way of multiplying their money than cheating at card games. There exists a thriving network of lenders and borrowers at Versailles, and he knows them all. Right now, one of Madame de Pompadour's new drivers, Gourlon, or Bruiser as he is called in the stables, is in debt to a wine merchant. The merchant is getting impatient. And so are the merchant's two sons, well known for their short tempers and hard knuckles. Besides, Gourlon's wife knows nothing of the debt and our Bruiser would like to keep it that way.

The man is quite desperate to borrow. He would agree to 4 percent or more if handled well. If they wish, they can entrust their money to him, just sit back and watch it grow.

It was almost evening when I got home, sweaty and tired from all that walking. Anticipating Maman's fury I rushed upstairs, but she was not there. The pile of clothes she had given me to mend was gone. She must have also given my brothers their dinner, for dirty plates were piled up on the table, flies buzzing around them. The room still smelled of meat stew, so the butcher must have given Maman a good deal on today's scraps. And the water carrier had come, too, for our bucket was filled to the brim.

I cleared the table, swept the floor and scrubbed it clean with a hard brush dipped in soapy water. Then I carried the slop bucket downstairs and out to the backyard, expecting our neighbors to warn me Maman was furious with me and I would get it when she got back home. But instead everyone wanted to know about Monsieur Durand's visit. Who was he? What was his business with us? "Let the girl catch her breath," the tripe vendor said, handing me a bowl of hot tripe soup. Humpback Lily offered me some of her roasted meat. She even wrapped the morsels in the chicory leaves that Master Deveaux grew in the cellar—in the dark they grew very pale and thus less bitter. I ate hungrily, praising the tripe soup and roasted meat, confessing to the little I knew. I would go into service at Monsieur Durand's grand house. No, I didn't know where he lived.

Fat Nanette saved me from further questioning. Pulling me aside, she said Maman was in a good mood. She must have received quite an advance on my wages, too, judging by how much she had spent already. Did I know about it? No, Nanette didn't think I would. It might still work out for the best for me, though if anyone asked her, grand house or not, she would not have sent her own daughter into service. "No one asked me, though," she said with a comic sigh that was meant to make me smile.

By the time I climbed the stairs back to our room, the taste of roasted meat lingering in my mouth, empty slop bucket in hand, my brothers had returned and wanted to know where I had been all day.

"Walking."

"Where?"

"Along the river."

"Walking alone?" Eugene asked.

"Alone."

"Did you get us anything?" Marcel asked, and I saw that his breeches were torn at the knee. He was growing fast, his face becoming longer, losing its oval shape. He had just one big tooth in front, the other one just coming through.

"Enough," I said, ordering them to wipe themselves clean and Marcel to hand over his breeches, wondering when I would see my brothers again. Gaston must have wondered that, too, for he asked me if—when I live in a grand house—I would let them visit. He wanted to learn to ride a horse. He was sure it wouldn't be hard to gallop.

I was still darning Marcel's breeches when Maman came home from the market. She did not mention my absence, but she was not in a good mood, either. A woman tried to steal a fichu, she said, just before she was to close the stall. Grand-looking, too, all sweet talk and sticky fingers, screaming bloody murder as she fled.

Maman paused and looked at me, expecting me to say something, but I didn't feel like talking. I fixed her supper: a slice of cheese, all that was left of the bread and a glass of flat ale. When she asked if I wanted to eat with her, I said I was not hungry. I did not mention the roasted meat and the tripe soup, suddenly ashamed of eating it all by myself.

"Suit yourself," Maman said and sat down at Papa's workbench, kicking off her shoes. Not the scuffed ones she always wore to the market, I noted, but high-heeled ones, made of blue damask with what looked like a silver buckle.

It was only after the boys were in bed that Maman set about emptying a small trunk with a cracked lid and lined it with parchment paper.

"Time to get you ready for tomorrow," she said.

I didn't have a lot to put inside. Two shifts, two petticoats, the fichu with the brownish stains. Apart from the gray russet dress, which I intended to wear for the road, I had one other of plain cotton. I didn't like it, for Maman had altered it for me from her old one and it had never fit me well. My only precious possession was the book I had saved from the bailiff, which I now retrieved from under the bed, wrapped up in a velvet cloth. La Fontaine's *Fables*, beautifully bound in calfskin leather, Papa's gift for my eleventh birthday. Not fairy tales but parables, Papa said when he gave it to me, each a lesson about the ways of the world. The lion in love with a peasant's daughter agreed to have his claws clipped and teeth filed only to be killed as soon as he had lost his power. The upright royal oak was felled by a gust of strong wind, while a blade of grass that bent low survived the storm.

I quickly leafed through the pages with their intricate drawings of animals and plants before wrapping the book back up and slipping it under the plain cotton dress.

Maman went behind the partition and I heard her rummage there, telling my brothers not to mind what she was doing but sleep. A moment later she was back. "There," she said, clearing her throat.

I looked up from over the trunk and saw that she was holding a white muslin dress. "Don't you recognize it?" she asked.

I did recognize it. I remembered trying it on at the stall a few days before Monsieur Durand's visit, for a fussy customer who could not make up her mind. I remembered thinking how beautiful it was and how I would never have a dress like this.

"I didn't sell it. I kept it for you," she said, clearly expecting a leap of joy, or at least my gratitude, but words that scraped in my throat refused to come to my lips.

If Maman was disappointed, she hid it well. The dress was not quite ready yet, she said. She would have to mend the tears in the hem, gather the skirt a bit at the back, add a new ribbon.

I closed the trunk with a thud. A mouse scurried along the wall.

"It'll be ready for tomorrow," Maman said. "Go to sleep."

I wiped my face and hands clean with a washcloth, undressed and slipped into bed. Behind the partition, candlelight formed a flickering circle on the ceiling as Maman worked on the dress. I saw her shadow bending forward, her hand pushing the needle in and out. The last I recall before drifting off to sleep was Fat Nanette saying that she would not have sent her own daughter away like that but, perhaps, all will still work out for the best. Then for a moment I felt Adèle's hand in mine as we ran along the street. "Faster than the wind?" she asked, gripping me tight.

I woke up at dawn to the sound of grinding teeth, a sure sign that my brothers had worms again. Maman was snoring beside me. Her breath smelled of rot.

There was a new sagging to her chin I hadn't noticed before. I lifted my hand and placed it on her shoulder. The snoring stopped.

From the yard came the familiar sounds. A rooster crowed, delivery carts heading for the market clattered on the cobblestones, porters groaned hauling merchandise to the stalls, one calling another a halfwit. A dog barked, then whimpered. A horse neighed and snorted.

I slipped out of bed. The muslin dress was lying on Papa's workbench, folded neatly and tied up with a new purple ribbon. I undid the knot and put the dress on, wondering if it would fit me, for Maman had not measured my waist.

It did.

Maman emerged from behind the partition then, still dazed from sleep, scratching her arms. No amount of washing the bed frames with vinegar ever rid us of lice and fleas. Just watching her scratch made the skin on my head itch.

"White is not a good color for traveling," she said.

She was right. It had been raining all night, and the roads would be muddy. The old russet dress would fare much better. But I did not want to listen to her, not then, not anymore.

I shrugged.

"Do as you wish, then," she said.

I had a feeling she wanted to say more, but my brothers were up, hungry, demanding breakfast. My imminent departure excited them even more than yesterday. Jealous of my carriage ride, they planned their own daring exploits. They would sneak into the Jardin des Plantes and ride an elephant. No, a tiger. No, a rhino. Holding it by the horn. Making it jump through a hoop, like in a circus.

"What if a guard finds us?"

"We'll run away."

"Climb the railings!"

"Like monkeys."

I could not eat anything that morning, and only had a few sips of the coffee Maman brought from the kitchen herself. Real coffee, I noted, not chicory. She was unusually quiet, too, leaving my brothers to their foolishness unchecked.

We were still sitting around Papa's old workbench when the butcher's apprentice knocked on our door to tell us that a big black carriage was waiting and that I must hurry. The driver was blocking the street just as the market sellers were arriving. We were not the only ones in this world, were we?

"This is it, then," Maman said.

As I stood up, she began fiddling with the muslin folds that flared out from my waist, adjusting them for a better fit. There was no mirror in our room, so I could not see myself, but Maman said it was just as well. Modesty was my best adornment. Then she threw her own traveling cape over my shoulders and tied it at the neck.

Too tight.

Just before the hall clock strikes five, Elisabeth Leboeuf—Lisette as she is called now—wakes up in the attic room where she sleeps with Rose and Marianne, all on one mattress. In the room next door, the two lackeys and the night watchman share a proper bed.

Rose and Marianne are still asleep when Lisette washes her face and hands and heads downstairs, mindful not to fall. The attic can only be reached by the service stairs, which are narrow and uneven, especially at the top, where Lisette has tripped a few times already and scraped her knees.

In the kitchen she starts the fire and wakes the scullery maid, who curses her and refuses to get up until threatened with a beating. Together they bring pails of water from the pump in the yard and prepare the servants' breakfast. The lackeys demand thick chunks of roasted beef, followed by pastries and candied fruit. The cook is satisfied with a cup of hot broth and a slice of bread with butter. Rose and Marianne want soft-boiled eggs. The night watchman, back from his duty, demands an omelet, which, thankfully, only the cook is allowed to prepare for him.

It is her third week at Deer Park and she no longer finds it odd to be called Lisette.

She knows many things by now.

She knows that Deer Park is smack in the middle of the town of Versailles.

The noise of hammering and of weights dropping to the ground is that of construction; a few streets away, the new church of Saint-Louis is being built. The big palace of Versailles, where the king and queen live, is farther away, but some of its outbuildings are scattered all over town: the king's kennels, the tennis court, the queen's stables and the townhouses of some of the courtiers. Marianne and Rose say that at night, if Lisette strains her ears, she might hear the royal orchestra playing for the king's guests, but what Lisette hears is the squealing pigs and bellowing cattle being led to the royal abattoir.

When the servants' breakfast is over, Lisette waits on Madame Bertrand, whose morning wishes include wine, bread, a bowl of jam and coffee with frothy milk, all on a tray, with no spills. At eight o'clock, Lisette rushes upstairs to rouse the two *élèves*, empty their chamber pots, and lay the breakfast table for them and Mademoiselle Dupin. This is a protracted affair with silver cutlery, good china, serviettes, and there is a lot of washing up afterward. Then Lisette helps the chambermaids with their chores, cleaning the fireplaces, dusting the rooms and making the beds. The chambermaids never praise her, but Lisette doesn't mind. It's enough that they call her La Jeune, The Young One, ask if she has a fellow waiting for her back in Buc and laugh when she protests that she doesn't.

For the rest of the day, a maid-of-all-work is at everyone's beck and call. Sometimes she sweeps and scrubs the kitchen floor, the hall and the doorstep; sometimes she runs errands for the cook or the chambermaids; sometimes for Mademoiselle Dupin or even for Madame Bertrand herself.

Lisette doesn't complain. She does what she is told to do, fast and with diligence. She knows to clean the grate first and take the ashes out before dusting and sweeping. She shuts bedroom doors when she cleans the corridors. She doesn't leave smudges on the windowpanes when she washes windows. She is also good with needle and thread, knows how to take a garment in or darn a tear so it is almost invisible. She knows how many chocolate pastilles she can take from each room without raising suspicions. None if they are artfully arranged. One or even two if the *élèves* themselves leave a messy pile.

Her only enemies are dust, soot, rust, insects and the bad smells for which she has an acute nose.

Deer Park may not be as grand as the château her mother told endless stories about, but it has its share of schemes and intrigues. Marianne and Rose talk of hiding bonnets or fichus. If they are missed, they will retrieve them with beautifully enacted triumph, garnering praise for their good eyes. If they are not missed, they will disappear for good. Madame Bertrand has a deal with a wine merchant who trades the good bottles from Deer Park cellar for lesser ones and pays her the difference. The night watchman who began working for Monsieur Lebel ten years ago has just bought a house in Paris, for 3,450 livres, and is renting rooms for 15 livres a month. Where he got that kind of money is a compelling and frustrating source of much speculation.

Madame Bertrand has been kind to Lisette. She has twice given her a sou to buy herself a ribbon and a string of red beads—for her mother's sake, she said, for the good times they used to have together. She has also given Lisette things she no longer wants: a bonnet only slightly torn, a chipped china platter with a gilded rim and a hat pin with a beautiful crystal top.

"Keep your head on your shoulders, girl," Madame Bertrand says, "and you will not go wrong here."

Madame's dove-gray dress is Lisette's favorite. One day it will be yours, Lisette, Madame has said three times already, though never with Marianne or Rose present so it might not count for much. As she is helping her mistress dress in the morning, Lisette always puts a bit more rouge on her cheeks. To blend with the reddened skin, she always says, the result of Madame falling asleep on the balcony and getting sunburned. I call it the result of having a drop too many, Rose has said.

The two *élèves* at Deer Park believe that their master is a Polish count who keeps rooms at the palace on account of the queen, but Lisette, like all Deer Park servants, knows that is all a sham. Their true master is the king of France, King Louis himself, who came to Deer Park only once, masked and wrapped in a black cloak, thinking himself invisible, though Michel spotted him in the service corridor upstairs, peering into a room Lisette had cleaned and dusted that very morning.

Rose and Marianne, who have been at Deer Park from the very first day, say that Catin, the *élève* who was dismissed just before Lisette arrived, was particularly dim-witted and believed that the count was going to send her across the ocean to New France. "Little birds, little brains," Rose said.

Marianne pointed out that she had to work for ten years to save eight hundred livres, while Miss Élève, even if dismissed after one summons, might pocket two thousand. "Not that dumb, are they?"

On the day His Majesty visited Deer Park, Lisette also saw him, walking down the stairs. Just before she turned her eyes to the wall, the way she had been instructed, she managed to catch a glimpse of his fine narrow nose and the curve of his full lips and sniff the scent of citrus and ambergris.

When the king was gone, Lisette found a kidskin glove in the service corridor, soft and smooth like a horse's muzzle. It is now one of her most valuable possessions, and she takes it out of her trunk only when no one is around to feel how soft it feels on her skin.

The journey took many hours. At times I was convinced the carriage was traveling in circles, passing by the same cluster of trees, but this—I thought—had to be an illusion. "Where are you taking me?" I asked the driver before we started, but he snapped at me to be quiet. This unprovoked rudeness made me so angry that I vowed not to have anything to do with him. No, I wasn't hungry, I said when he asked me sometime later, at our first stop. Not thirsty, either. "Better for me," he said. "Just don't tell anyone later that I did not ask."

It was just past noon when we entered what looked like a small town. We turned into an ordinary narrow street and continued along a brick wall with shards of broken glass on top until it stopped at a double gate. My disappointment grew when the gate revealed a rather narrow courtyard and a modest house, its entryway crowned with a stone carving of a stag.

I did not expect any civility from the driver, but he held out his gloved hand to me as I stepped out, my legs wobbly after the ride, my head aching from the rattling of wheels. The day was clear, the air crisp. I drank it, filling up my lungs.

A stout older woman emerged from the house and walked toward me, limping slightly. Delicious scents of vanilla and chocolate floated about her, reminding me that—in spite of my high-minded refusal of refreshments on the way—I hadn't even had breakfast. Her dove-gray dress was simple but made of good velvet lined with silk. It would easily fetch fifty livres, I thought, hoping she took note of mine.

"There you are, at last!" she said, looking me over. "You had us all waiting, Véronique!" Her cheeks, I noted, were touched with rouge.

Taking her for Monsieur Durand's wife and thus my new mistress, I addressed her as such, making her laugh hard enough for tears to moisten her eyes.

"Just Madame Bertrand, thank you very much," she said when she got her voice back. "I'm the housekeeper here, and that is plenty of honor for me. You'll call me Madame."

Still laughing, she motioned me to follow her into the house.

I looked at the carriage, where the trunk with all my possessions in it was roped to the back, only to be rebuked that I had not come to a den of thieves but to a well-run house where servants knew what was expected of them. Mindful that I had offended her already, I vowed to be more careful with what I say in the future.

"This way," Madame said, leading me into a foyer paneled with embroidered silk of dusty pink. On one wall was a row of pictures, each illustrating a scene from a hunt. Riders mounting their horses; a pack of hounds chasing a deer; a big stag just slain, its horns resting on the ground, a gushing wound in its side; a hunter resting his right leg on the animal's bleeding flank. From the foyer, rooms opened to the right and left, revealing a table with a shining top, a clavichord, a bouquet of white lilies on a mantel. My spirits lifted. No matter how ordinary it looked from the street, it was an elegant house after all.

A stifled giggle from above alerted me to the presence of a girl hanging over the landing banister to see me better. Spotted, she drew back. Madame shook her finger in her direction and continued walking into the back of the house. The kitchen had to be close by, for I heard pots banging and a girl's frightened voice moaning an apology.

Madame asked me about my journey and if I was hungry, perhaps, or thirsty, or could I wait to eat after my bath. Resolved not to offend her again, I said I was not that hungry, and I praised the comforts of the carriage. "Not a complainer, are you then," she said, clearly pleased with my answer. "Though still in need of a good scrubbing."

In the scullery, where I was relieved to see my small trunk pushed against the wall, three maids in white bonnets were busy with towels, jars, bottles and brushes, placing them all on a low table. A copper bathtub stood in the middle of the room, steam rising above it. Even in our old house, where Maman made sure we bathed every Sunday before church, we never had so much hot water to spare or flakes of soap that smelled of lemons.

I was a lucky girl, Madame announced. Monsieur Durand was not, in fact, my new master but merely the *valet de chambre* of a Polish count whose name I did not catch. The count was obliged to keep an apartment at the palace, as he was a relation of the queen. This house was his as well; it was called Deer Park. He was a good master.

Hope stirred in my heart at these words.

Generous, kind, beloved by all, Madame went on. Thanks to his generosity, I, Véronique Roux, whose father died penniless, whose mother traded in rags, had a chance to better myself, learn my manners and perhaps, one day, improve my lot. Which was more than many girls in my situation could ever hope for. Only if I am good enough, that is. Only if I please. Which I might not do after all. Not many do, in the end.

The feeling of hope grew: the laundresses who lived above us on rue Saint-Honoré often said that the master of the house was always easier to please than the mistress. Though the words *to please* were vague in my mind. I took it to mean being cheerful, willing to be of use and doing what I was told. None of it too hard, I thought.

Madame went on speaking while, to my surprise, two of the maids began to undress me. Their hands were rough, impatient. I felt a tug before my fichu, crumpled, landed on the floor, a pull as the muslin dress slid down my legs. I bent to pick it up, but Madame slapped my hand. "Lisette," she ordered the third maid who had just emptied the last vat of hot water into the tub, "burn these rags when we are done here."

It was my best dress, I pleaded. Worn only once.

Madame rolled her eyes. I could not keep it because it was infested with fleas. Besides, it looked gaudy and cheap. Could I not see it? I must be the only one then. Everyone else needs just one look to know where this rag came from. Surely there was a lot I had to learn. I was being difficult, too. That was not a good sign, was it?

"Hands up," I heard, and my chemise joined the heap of clothes on the floor. I stood naked on the tiled scullery floor. If it weren't for the warmth of the bath awaiting me, I would've shivered.

Madame examined the flea bites on my arms and legs, the chapped, reddened hands, the broken nails. The scab on the spot where Eugene had hit me with a stick when I scolded him for spitting on the kitchen floor. The patch of my scalp scratched raw. My mother could learn a thing or two about raising children, she announced. Luckily for me, her apothecary was well supplied with salves and goose grease. Soon I would be as good as new.

In the tub, warmed to the marrow in my bones, I was soaped and scrubbed, my hair was raked over with a wooden comb, tearing on my tangled curls. Lice fell into the water, and Rose—the shortest of the maids—scooped them up, one by one, and squashed them between her fingernails.

Madame kept talking through all these ministrations and, as she did, the details of my immediate future began to take shape. The house I was in, Deer Park, was where I would live. Not as a servant but as one of the *élèves*, learning the finer skills befitting my new prospects, which required being properly trained. There would be daily lessons in deportment—sorely needed, Madame said with a knowing scoff—music and dancing.

I would be watched.

I would be judged.

I was not the only *élève*. Francine was another, and there was little Claire. There had been one more, Catin, but she was gone. Was I wondering why? No? But I should! Catin had been dismissed because she had been both ungrateful and plain stupid. And she wouldn't be the last. If Madame could have a livre for every silly girl who would be sent back where she came from, she would die rich.

The count, our master, His Lordship as I was to refer to him, had strict demands for his household. The girls in his service had to be of good character and disposition. With impeccable manners. This is why lying would not be tolerated. Or putting on airs. Or vulgar gossiping. Utter loyalty and discretion is what our master demanded above all. For a moment Madame's eyes become sharp and doubtful. As if I had been brought here into this house by mistake. As if I were the one destined to fail. But the moment passed, and Madame continued.

"You'll be sharing a room with Francine. Mind you, there must be no loud talking, ever. No running about, either. Proper behavior, fitting for a modest young girl wishing to improve her lot in life. Decorum is important. Do you know what it means?"

I was just about to say that I knew when I saw the maids exchange quick mocking looks and thought better of it.

"I didn't think so," Madame said. "But you will learn soon."

The water was cooling fast. By the time I was allowed to get out of the bath, my teeth were chattering. Wrapped in a big towel I sat on a round stool while the other maid, Marianne, smeared my head with turpentine to kill the nits. "*Terebintha resina* is made of the resin of the terebinth tree," I had learned from one of Papa's almanacs, but this, too, I kept to myself.

This is when the scullery door opened and a tall, lanky man with a black leather bag walked in. Monsieur le docteur, Madame addressed him with much reverence. He refused an offer of coffee, asked if her headaches had improved with the tonic he'd given her and only when she assured him that they had did he point at me.

"A new one?" he asked.

"Just arrived," Madame said, rolling her eyes.

I clutched the edge of my towel where it was tucked under my chin.

"Monsieur le docteur will examine you now," Madame announced. "We cannot have anyone drag diseases in here."

"I don't bite," the doctor said. "At least not after a good breakfast."

Behind me Rose tittered.

Even now, as I recall this moment, I can feel the doctor's cold fingers pressing the skin behind my ears, on my neck, my wrist. "Open wide," he said, pointing at my mouth. "Wider," he said, probing my gums, tugging at my teeth. The handle of the magnifying glass with which he examined the skin on my hands, wrists, forearms was made of horn.

I grasped tightly at the towel I was wrapped in, clutching it to my chest when he pulled at it. He called me a silly goose. He said, "Do you think, young lady, you might be in possession of anything I haven't seen before?"

My cheeks flushed red as I let go of my flimsy covering. My chest was still quite flat then, although there was some swelling around my nipples, which the doctor pinched at the way women pinch hens at the market.

"I take it she hasn't bled yet, has she?" he asked, turning to Madame Bertrand.

I felt a flash of shame at this question, thinking of Maman's monthly "visitor." Days marked with bloodstains on the sheets, rags soaking in the bucket, my brothers holding their noses with disgust. A woman's cross to bear, Maman had said, not a girl's.

Madame pouted her lips. "Not yet, I was assured."

What happened next was swift, incomprehensible. Madame gestured with her eyes at the maids. Before I realized their intentions, I was lying on the day bed, pinned by two pairs of strong hands, unable to move. The doctor was pushing his fingers inside me, feeling about. To stop me from screaming, Rose clamped my mouth.

"Good." I heard the doctor's gruff voice. "Intact."

Released from the maids' grasp, I burst into tears. Madame called it "theatrics." Had no doctor ever seen me? she asked. Is that why I was acting like a proper savage? She must've been wrong about me after all, which was quite a shame for she was beginning to think I might do.

I was still sobbing when Monsieur le docteur pronounced me healthy and clean, though in dire need of regular purgings to balance my volatile humors and avoid future troubles. "An enema and bloodletting, weekly" was all I retained from his recommendations. And a bitter taste of some tonic he made me drink. Best remedy for overexcited nerves, he said while all I wished for was to hide in shame as if his fingers were still inside me.

Rose said that crying would only make my eyes puffed up and my nose red and swollen. Besides making Madame angry to boot. Which I wouldn't want, would I?

No, I wouldn't.

I wiped the tears from my eyes and Lisette took me to the kitchen, where the cook gave me a plate of fish soup and a thick slice of light soft bread that tasted like nothing I'd ever eaten before. I ate fast, starved as I was, while Lisette chatted with the cook, whom she called Master Jacques. Someone they called Madame la marquise had a little monkey who sat at her knee at table. Nasty thing known to bite if you as much as touched it. Or piss on you when you held it. Then the conversation shifted to a certain Monsieur Lebel. "Is he really counting the bottles of wine in the cellar?" Lisette asked. "Who says that?" the cook wanted to know. "The lackeys?"

I was hoping they would speak of the Polish count, but they never mentioned him at all.

I wiped my empty bowl with the last of that lovely bread. I was just about to ask for more when Lisette said I'd had enough for now. The food here was not what I was used to, and I wouldn't want to wake up in the middle of the night with a bellyache. "Don't worry," she added as she escorted me upstairs to what would be my room. "No one goes hungry here, ever."

Madame de Pompadour delights in the way the rays of the sun pour into her salon, bouncing off the gilded curves of armchairs and table legs. Louis has often told her that when he was a child, all the rooms in Versailles seemed grim and scary, suffocating him with a grief he thought would never dissipate. Mother, father, brother all dead within weeks when he was still in his leading strings. It still haunts him, the empty loneliness of those days, the pitying looks that froze the blood in his veins.

This grief is still there, but over the past ten years Madame de Pompadour has watched a veneer of acceptance grow over it, like moss over an ancient rock. Death may be a stalker, a ruffian on the back stairs, plunging a dagger into your heart when you least expect it, but it is also a manifestation of God's will. The same divine will that made her beloved king.

Look at him now, seated in his armchair, sipping the Burgundy wine she keeps especially for him in the cabinet by the service door. He drops his left hand and lets Inez and Mimi, her two little Phalènes, lick the inside of his palm, their silky tails wagging.

Madame de Pompadour has perched herself on the other armchair, her back perfectly straight. Her chatter spills into the room, effortless, witty, drawing him in. Nothing in it is ordinary, no visitor or petitioner merely boring. "Oh, I do respect the comtesse de Polignac for making me aware of how often she was obliged to stop the carriage to have her wheels greased," she is telling him now. "For you know, my dearest, how *deadly* serious I am about carriage wheels and a good layer of grease . . . Richelieu did come by, just as you warned me he would. I was as nice to him as his bad breath would allow."

Louis kicks off his shoes.

She will tell Lebel to get rid of this pair; they must be pinching his toes. Inez, having abandoned the king's hand, is sniffing inside one of them with growing intensity. What can the dog smell? Blood?

Her voice flows easily, meant to soothe whatever fresh hurt he has brought with him. For the king of France is the target of malice. The lowest of his subjects feels entitled to judge him, spit after his carriage, blame him for every misfortune under the sun. Those who once called him Well-Beloved now call him a Herod. Or a kidnapper who sends his subjects in chains to till the land in the faraway French colonies or defend them from savages. Or a lecher who bathes his rotting skin in their daughters' first blood.

Mere words? The inconsequential debris of feeble minds? The dregs of sick thoughts, thrown to the wind? Madame de Pompadour does not think so, and neither does Berryer, the Lieutenant-General of Police, who calls himself her devoted friend and who, every Sunday morning, in her presence, delivers his weekly report to the king.

Berryer pays his spies well and keeps them busy every day of the week mingling with the crowds; lingering around tollbooths, churches and markets; trailing beggars and street singers; writing down everything they have heard. But since ignorance and malice also dwell in the townhouses of the merchants and the châteaux of the nobles, Berryer's clerks open all letters entrusted to the post and copy all extracts of interest, no matter how trivial.

For words do matter. Spoken or written, they travel, multiply, infest listeners' minds, spreading disease, like vermin. Gossip, draped in the mantle of truth, can lead anywhere. To stones hurled at police. To angry crowds marching on the palace.

My weekly dose of smut, Louis used to call Berryer's reports, until she objected. Your window into the true nature of your subjects, a peek under the covers.

You are a wise woman, he said.

This is her wisdom: sin reigns in the kingdom. Husbands surprise unfaithful wives in bed with other men. Mothers sell their daughters to the highest bidder. Servants cheat their masters, sell their furs and clothes and pocket the money. Or leave back doors unlocked for thieves.

People will harm you a lot to please themselves a tiny bit.

"Listen to this, dearest," she says, opening the latest of Berryer's reports.

> *The marquise de Piercourt, who conceals her ignoble connection with the son of a shopkeeper, has bought a fresh supply of letter paper.*
>
> *The street is so noisy I cannot sleep. Geese, dogs, beggars. There is a procession of bakers making a racket in front of my windows. I've sent the servant to ask what this is about, and she tells me that they are at war with the barbers.*

Her voice is clear, deftly slipping in and out of voices. She can sound like a gossipy lady's maid or a pompous courtier. In the mirror above the mantel, the diamonds in her hair sparkle every time she moves her head.

> *Madame de Beauharnois was at the Opera-ball with the colonel of the Soubise regiment. They absented themselves during the space of three hours, and next day the lady's waiting-woman declared that when she undressed her, she found both of the colonel's socks in the lady's stocking.*

Louis chuckles at this entanglement of hosiery, while she points out the maid's delight at the story she has thus uncovered. Sold, too, most likely to one of her mistress's enemies. There must be a whole ledger of such transactions, prices determined by the juiciness of the betrayal.

Lebel will know how much this one might have brought.

"Good man, Lebel," Louis says. "Loyal, above all."

Mademoiselle Muress goes every day to the Comédie-Française to lay traps for foreigners. There is not a night when some of them do not offer to conduct her home. Her lover, M. de Varenne, waits for them there; they turn to card playing, and are generally so fleeced that they have nothing left to promise to their mistress.

Madame de Pompadour turns her radiant face toward her king, parting her lips to reveal her small teeth. She is all soft pearly glitter. Thirty-four years of age but she knows she is as pleasing to him as on the day she let him spot her: in her blue muslin dress, hair loosely tied, gathering flowers in the meadow. Maybe she is a bit more rounded now, but Louis always says this suits her rather well. He hates the way some women become angular, edgy.

No longer lovers, but more in love than ever, she embroidered on a silk cushion she handed to him five years ago. A teary moment of renunciation, though also gratifying in its gravity, her voice quivering as she said, "Because I can no longer be what you, the monarch of my heart, need and deserve."

More in love than ever? Louis foresaw nothing but awkwardness, bitterness, regrets. Malice woven into the dispatches addressed to the monarchs of Europe, repeated at the taverns: Behold the French king, who fucks neither his wife nor his mistress. Now he agrees that it has all been for the better. Not that the shift has been painless. There have been a few lapses, always disappointing as the anticipation and the performance never match, but there is a new understanding between them now, a sense of easy comfort. She doesn't have to fear the hot ring of pain inside her or suffer yet another bloody miscarriage. He no longer has reason to wonder why she, always so warm and vivacious, freezes stiff in his arms.

Mademoiselle Deschamps has within six weeks cost the duc de Richelieu upward of twenty thousand livres, but the expense was shared by a certain Monsieur Bazin.

Inez has given up sniffing Louis's shoe and is now lying on the carpet beside Mimi. Creatures of the salons, these dogs have never been farther than their mistress's garden. How long could they survive in the woods? A few hours perhaps, she thinks, foreseeing a shadow pouncing on these tasty morsels of flesh, the crunch of breaking bones.

She will not think of death. Not when Louis is here, with her, smiling at his own thoughts.

"Shall I continue, dearest?" she asks. "Now that we have a solid proof that Richelieu's craving for variety comes at such a steep price?"

"Do continue," he says, the smile fading already.

She lifts a page up and gives a little gasp, a sign she has found something that will particularly delight him.

> *Monsieur de Guerigny is now breaking a little filly of Burgundy, between thirteen and fourteen years old, at his private lodge on rue Carême Prenant: if she were fifteen, he would have nothing more to do with her.*

She pauses, raises her head from the dossier and their eyes meet. She believes she can read his thoughts, his moods, his desires. Only yesterday she brought tears of gratitude to his eyes when she said he deserved every consolation for the cage he is forced to live in, for the chains that bind him. "Poison and its antidote," she had said. "Opposing forces that have to be brought together, necessary for life to continue."

"Another glass of wine?" she asks now.

"No, dear heart," he says. "Water." A moment later he sips the cold well water, with its scent of mint and a few drops of lemon juice, bracing himself back to attention.

Her dress today resembles a flowering bush, her colors dark pink and dusty whites. The pearls around her neck are too tight, though. Her fingers tug at them from time to time, but gently. If she pulls at them too hard, they will spill to the floor.

That would annoy him.

Pearls grow because of irritation. Each a cover to hide a foreign body. A tiny rock, a grain of sand. The jewelers who come to Versailles always wax poetic about this miracle. "Beauty born out of imperfection. Note, Madame, the differences of shade and texture. Note the sheen."

"A little filly of Burgundy," Louis repeats. "What's her name?"

"Berryer does not know everything, alas."

"Lebel might."

The smile is back.

"Shall I ask him, dearest?"

"No, don't bother."

"As you wish."

From what Lebel has told her, the last girl was a disappointment. Pretty enough at first sight, but . . . Lebel didn't need to finish. She can imagine the girl well enough. Shy, silent, picking at the skin around her fingernail, tugging at it. Armpits sliding with sweat. Every word having to be coaxed out of her. "Indeed, Your Lordship . . . No, Your Lordship . . . By no means, Your Lordship . . ."

Not the worst of Lebel's mistakes, though, she thinks. That O'Murphy girl was far worse. The brazen hussy dared to call her, the royal mistress, an old cocotte. Asked Louis, "What do you still want with her?" Which, as Lebel never fails to repeat, was the last thing the O'Murphy girl ever said to the king and she can now reflect on her stupidity every day until the end of her natural life.

"Good man, Lebel. Loyal."

"Yes."

"I've said that before, haven't I?"

"Because it is important."

"So it is. He even walks like me, they say."

"That it amazes your sensitive soul, my beloved!" She laughs. He who is emulated by everyone can never fully understand the desire to reflect even some of the borrowed luster.

They talk of everything and nothing. The musty smell in the state bedroom for which no one can figure out the reason. The plans for rebuilding Trianon she is still not ready to show him. His grandson, Louis-Auguste, a plump baby and very content. His older brother is calling him a toad.

They talk of their plans for the rest of the day. His council meeting, which he detests; her prescribed walk in the garden, which she would much rather take with him than alone.

"Alas."

"Alas."

It is only when Louis rises to leave that she mentions Lebel again. From Berryer she knows that the *premier valet de chambre* has just ordered a new pocket watch from the royal watchmaker. Not an ordinary pocket watch, either, Berryer said, but a repeater, which signals the hours, quarters and minutes at a press of a button so that its owner can tell the time discreetly without taking it out of his pocket. Such watches cost a small fortune and are all the rage at Versailles, which is not at all surprising.

"For how would a courtier check the time otherwise, my dearest, without annoying his beloved monarch with his impatience?"

⚞

My first memory of Francine is of a slender wisp of a girl, warming up by the crackling fire, her black hair let loose over her shoulders. When I came into the room, she jumped up and then, as if remembering something she should have heeded, clasped her fingers over her lips. How pretty she is, I thought. Still teary, I was already taken by her liveliness, her black eyes shining with excitement.

"So you are Véronique," she said as soon as Lisette left the room.

"Yes," I said.

"Just Véronique?"

"Véronique Roux."

"This is your bed, Véronique Roux," Francine said, pointing at one of the two alcoves.

The bed looked inviting, and I wished to slip under the cover, curl up and fall asleep. But Francine was starved for company.

"Do you snore?" she asked.

I shook my head first but then admitted, "I don't know. I don't think I do, but I might."

"Ah, well." Francine sighed, resigned. "Catin snored, too. I had to tickle her feet to make her turn on her stomach."

Catin, the *élève* who had been sent back home, was trouble from the start, Francine announced with a funny twitch of her nose. A simple girl, a fishmonger's daughter. She spit on the floor when she first arrived, though that, thank Heavens, didn't last long. She also ground her teeth and sleep-walked. Downstairs, into the kitchen and, if anyone left the door open, into the yard. In her nightgown! Madame ordered the maids to tie her legs together at night. It didn't help, for Catin would crawl on the floor. But that is not why they sent her back.

"Why then?"

"She put a firecracker under Madame's bed."

What a mimic Francine was! Just a few gestures and a grimace was enough for me to see the exploding cracker, hear Madame's frightful shrieks, watch her clasp at her heart and take nip after nip from a bottle. "As if the devil pinched her you know where," Francine said as I burst out laughing.

It was in this lighter mood that I examined what would become my room for the next few months. "Feel how soft it is," Francine said as I approached the bed, which, I suddenly realized, would be mine only. With what Francine called a "palliasse mattress," stuffed with wool, not straw. "You can also draw the curtains if you want," she added as I ran my fingers over the pale green brocade drapes trimmed with golden ribbon.

There was more to delight in. The ceiling was covered with paintings of frolicking monkeys. There was a vase adorned with birds and flowers on the mantel. A china basket on the table was filled with what looked like small packages. "Chocolate pastilles," Francine said, unwrapping one for me and making me sniff the scent of vanilla and cloves. "What are you doing?" she chuckled when I took a bite of it and thought it quite delicious, if slightly bitter. Didn't I know that chocolate pastilles required boiling milk or water to make a drink with?

I didn't. I liked them the way they were.

"Then," Francine said, "you are a perfect little savage after all."

I knew I would like her. Like the laughter, the teasing, the joy in her voice when she told me that the five candles in the silver candleholders were wax, not tallow. That the armchairs were gilded, that a dressing table drawer hid scent bottles with real perfume. That we had a whole jar of beef marrow pomade with orange blossoms for our hair.

And then there were the dresses. Four for each of us for now, with more promised for the autumn. Dresses we placed against our bodies, posing in front of the big silver framed mirror on the wall. Hair up. Hair down. A bow, a curtsy. On tiptoes, without a quiver or totter. Francine's eyes seeking mine. Her upturned nose making me giggle. We argued about what colors suited us best. Red or sea green? Dusty pink or royal blue? One of the dresses had a bodice of real Alençon lace, another had sleeves lined with soft yellow velvet. There were no stains on the pink taffeta of the skirts. No one had removed the silver and gold from the embroidery. The memory of the white muslin dress evaporated, its loss a trifle not worth dwelling upon.

"Have you seen him?" I asked the question burning in my mind. "His Lordship? The Polish count? What does he look like?"

Francine shook her head. "He is in Poland now," she said, quite sharply, dropping the satin dress she was holding to the floor. "Didn't they tell you that?"

"Madame Bertrand?" I asked, picking up the dress, shaking it to save the satin from creasing. "Or Monsieur Durand?"

"Durand! Do you want to know what I call him?"

"Yes."

"If you promise never to tell anyone."

"I promise."

Francine giggled and bent toward me. "A fuckwit."

"Why?"

"Because he struts about with his fat notebook. Because he looks like a scarecrow. But most of all because he thinks he is Saint Louis himself."

When I laughed, Francine told me that our Madame, of the foul breath and nips of heart tonic, had once been an abbess in a convent. Until she had been expelled. Such was the grand house I had come to. "Disappointed?" she asked.

I didn't know what to say, so I nodded.

"Poor you. What use shall I have of you now? Can you sing?"

"Yes."

"Play the harpsichord?"

"No. Why was Madame expelled from the convent?"

"For setting fire to the privy."

"Is it true?"

"No, silly."

"Why are you joking then?"

"Because I feel like it. Go to sleep if you don't like me."

"But I do like you."

"Thank dear Almighty God for this unexpected favor!"

The sound of approaching footsteps made Francine lower her voice. We had a real governess, she whispered, Mademoiselle Dupin with dagger eyes. Finicky, a stickler for her stupid rules. Did I know that every little thing was worth doing well? No? Who raised me then? And which pigsty was it?

I should also watch out for little Claire, the other *élève*. A tattletale who sleeps in Mademoiselle Dupin's room, cannot keep her mouth shut and who will never miss a chance to make me look bad.

There was more.

A grand lady they all called Madame la marquise came here the other day to check on their progress. First she demanded that Francine read aloud from the book her maid had brought with her. It was a very hard book with many long words, Francine said, which is why she didn't do very well and made Mademoiselle Dupin really angry.

"Claire, too?" I asked.

But Francine lifted her nose in the air and pursed her lips. "For Claire," she said in an imitation of someone's voice, "reading is as easy as pissing the mattress."

That evening, curled up alone in my soft, unfamiliar bed, I could not fall asleep, my thoughts racing ahead and retracing themselves. The rattling of the carriage, the first glimpses of the house, the taste of the fish soup and Francine's teasing blended with the memory of the doctor's probing fingers.

I could hear the night watchman in the yard, calling his dog to heel. I heard his dog whimper and yelp. But it was the absence of Maman's body next to me, the ins and outs of her breaths, that made me sit up and put my arms around my knees. I didn't know what terrified me more. The darkness of this unfamiliar room? The unknown shapes of my future? Or the threat of being sent back where I came from, like that Catin who had occupied this same bed only a few nights before.

❧

Lebel says, "Even if they think him merely a foreign count, Madame, they all expect feather beds. Or quilts of swansdown." These words are meant to soothe, although he knows that Madame de Pompadour does not believe she requires soothing. Unlike the queen, she has not ceded her place in the king's heart.

She has received him in her golden boudoir, which is filled with the muted light of early afternoon. Seated at her tambour frame, she is pecking at the fabric, pulling the thread through.

"How is the new girl settling down, Lebel?" she asks, eyes fixed on the hook gliding in, turning, coming out.

The girl, Madame la marquise still refers to her, not Véronique. A significant omission. An indication that this time Lebel has made the right choice and that she already resents him for it.

The tambour frame is black, the fabric stretched out on it creamy white. The thread Madame is pulling out so tautly is sea green.

"Well enough. Once we got rid of the fleas, that is."

Madame lifts her face toward Lebel, her lips turning into a slight grimace, which quickly dissolves into a pearly smile.

There was a time, long past, when Lebel suggested, vaguely, that perhaps Madame la marquise should spare herself any concern with these girls, only to get rebuked in return. Was he questioning the strength of her devotion to His Majesty, perhaps? Her vigilance on his behalf? Her desire to give him what he needs and wants and so amply deserves? The man who carries the weight of the whole of France on his shoulders, she said. Who has renounced his own most cherished dreams out of his sense of royal duty. Who is forced to perform, day after day, like a trained lion in front of uncouth crowds.

Does Lebel—a mere servant after all, as Madame la marquise put it tersely—wish to keep secrets from her?

Of course he keeps secrets from her. Of course he tells her he doesn't. Just like His Majesty himself.

Before coming here, Lebel resolved to turn the events of recent days into an amusing story, filled with tidbits that, even if they fail to amuse her, Madame la marquise can later repeat to the king. He accepts the necessity of keeping her well supplied with anecdotes. Making His Majesty laugh is not an easy feat.

The story starts with broad strokes. A description of the Quinze-Vingts market, which fully deserves its seedy reputation: women in gaudy robes followed by their maids, men's eyes trailing after them long after they have passed. Parading in the street as if they owned it. Showing off their buttoned-up shoes. Silk stockings. Finest white doeskin gloves.

The girl, Véronique, pays him no heed, but from inside the stall her mother casts an uneasy look in his direction. The buxom Widow Roux, Lebel calls her, pink-faced and with shrewd eyes, who swears her rotting dresses come straight from Versailles, pilfered by scheming maids who know how to make good use of a pumice stone.

There could be many reasons for her caution. The scouts may have been less invisible than they thought themselves to be, or the Widow Roux is worried about plainclothes constables itching to search her stall for illegal pamphlets or books. Considering what Berryer has reported on the late Lucien Roux, she should be, even if she doesn't sell them. An eager policeman will always spot some infraction or other. Or demand a bribe for not spotting one.

Madame de Pompadour bends over the tambour frame. The hook catches the thread underneath the canvas, pulls it through. Absorbed in her work she may be, but she has not missed a word of his story.

To assure the buxom widow that she is not the target of his interest, Lebel heads for the stall next to hers, with military jackets on display. From there he observes as the Widow Roux tends to a chatty woman in search of a wedding dress. Her youngest daughter is marrying a bird seller. Parrots are in great demand in Paris. So are canaries and turtledoves. Only yesterday, her future son-in-law sold a pair to the Lieutenant-General of Police himself.

"From the queen's wardrobe. Suitable for any important occasion . . . elegant and yet modest," the Widow Roux coos, taking a cheap muslin dress off the hook and giving it a light shake. "Given a new ribbon, that is."

"Is that why no one has bought it yet?" the customer asks in a mocking voice. "On account of this modesty?"

"Put it on, Véronique," the mother tells Véronique, who stands at her mother's side, scratching the top of her hand. "Let Madame judge how well it shows."

At this point of his story, Lebel hesitates for a brief moment.

Madame de Pompadour does not have to know that when Véronique finally emerges from the back of the shack having freed herself from her shapeless gray russet, she is transformed. The muslin dress may be plain white and quite ordinary, but she is beautiful and she knows it. For why else would she adjust her bonnet, releasing a cascade of curls over her neck? Making them catch the rays of the sun and shine like copper?

Madame's tambour hook flashes. The sea-green thread has been replaced with gold. A Turkish pattern most likely, for all things Turkish are much in vogue at Versailles now. Harem pants, all manner of Turkish turbans, cashmere shawls. Every day, Lebel's valet assures him, yet another court lady falls victim to the Ottoman craze.

"The Widow Roux, Madame, knows how to haggle." Lebel resumes his story.

"Turn around," she tells the girl, all along pointing out how well the dress flows, how much better muslin is than silk, especially for a wedding dress.

"How much?"

"Fifteen."

"You must think me a fool. No more than ten."

Madame gives him a look of impatience. He is taking her precious time with trifles.

The girl, Lebel concludes, does have rosebud lips. She does have an air of languor. She is small and lissome, with that innocent look the king so favors, an air of graceful reserve or shyness. Her pale complexion is without blemish, her face perfectly oval. Her hair, a darker shade of auburn, is always neatly tucked inside a bonnet.

Guileless, he calls her. Unassuming.

Madame de Pompadour returns her attention to the tambour frame. "They all like to seem guileless when they first arrive," she says. "Just make sure that this time there is no trouble."

Lebel bows, places his hand on his heart. "I'll do everything I can, Madame."

She nods, knowing he has given her the only answer he could.

I woke up not knowing where I was.

Rose was pushing the shutters open with a crunch and a squeak while Lisette poured hot water from a jug into a porcelain basin.

The memory of the doctor's fingers inside me came first, followed by the lost muslin dress, but then Francine jumped out of bed and came over to me. "Is that how your maman raised you?" she asked in a funny voice, poking me with her elbow. "Which pigsty was it, again?"

I giggled.

"Enough of this tomfoolery. Up, both of you. The water is getting cold," Rose said, clapping her hands.

Francine and I washed quickly. Rose tightened our stays, brushed our hair and pinned it up. I liked the way she had with ribbons, deftly weaving them in among our tresses to make them thicker. Just before she helped us put on our morning dresses, she made us rinse our mouths with a sage tincture Madame Bertrand had made herself. Foul breath, Rose said, is reason enough for dismissal.

Francine and I cupped our hands over our mouths for a sniff and laughed.

"Thick as thieves already, you two?" Rose asked.

At the bottom of the stairs Mademoiselle Dupin was already waiting for us.

In her plain gray dress, a black ribbon tied around her neck, she looked as strict as Francine had described her, but her voice when she spoke was kind and almost playful. Did you sleep well in your new room? she asked. Yes? Then I was ready to begin my first day as an *élève*, which, like all other days at Deer Park, started with the morning inspection.

Our appearance had to be flawless at all times, she explained for my benefit, as she gave Francine and me a long searching look. Not a hair out of place, not a smudge of dirt on our hands, fichus modestly tucked in.

Thanks to Rose's ministrations, Mademoiselle Dupin found nothing amiss that morning, though she decried the sorry state of my hands and told me to be thankful for Madame Bertrand's remedies. In the breakfast room where we followed her, Claire, the tattletale in Francine's warnings, was already waiting, and now made a step toward me. A child still, I thought her, all plump softness, her hair a beautiful shade of hazelnut, set off by the yellow trim of her morning dress.

"Welcome to Deer Park, Véronique," she said rather too quickly.

Mademoiselle Dupin frowned. "Try one more time, Claire," she said. "This time with as much grace and genuine feeling as you can summon."

"Welcome to Deer Park, Véronique," Claire repeated, holding out her palms as if she were handing me some invisible gift.

"Thank you," I said.

With Mademoiselle's permission, we took our seats. Lisette had been right when she assured me I would not starve at Deer Park. I had never seen that much food all at once. The breakfast table, covered with pink damask cloth embroidered with white lilies, was filled with platters. There were pâtés, thick slices of roasted meat and chunks of different cheeses. A silver bowl full of hard-boiled eggs stood next to a porcelain basket with fluffy white bread and a tub with butter. To my right I spotted a tiered cake stand with layers of puff pastries topped with cream. It was only thanks to Francine's well-aimed kick on my shin that I restrained myself from reaching for one right away.

This abundance, Mademoiselle Dupin said, looking at me as if she guessed what had happened, had been placed in front of us for two good reasons. First, to remind us of the need of gratitude. Second, to prepare us for the temptations of the world we were being trained to join. This is why no matter how hungry we were, we couldn't eat before she gave her permission. Or pick and choose what we liked, leaving what we disliked on our plates.

"Should I repeat these words, again, Véronique?" she asked.

"No, Mademoiselle," I said.

Francine's eyes flicked at me. I lowered my head just in time not to giggle.

In the days that followed, I learned a lot about the cardinal virtues of perseverance, obedience and acceptance. Every moment in a day brought a chance to display good manners or acquire ones we still lacked. And we had much to learn, to erase the petty bourgeois pretenses of the haberdasher, the stink of used clothes, the language of the butcher shop. Even the simple act of walking around the room required attention. Steps should be short, gliding, achieved by moving our feet to the left and right, without ever lifting them off the floor, to give the impression of flowing.

As for me, Papa may have taught me to read and write some pretty fancy words, but my handwriting was merely good enough to make lists of old dresses for sale, not to write the elegant letters my future position might demand. I might read fluently enough, but reading aloud to a discerning ear was another matter altogether. I had much to learn, Mademoiselle Dupin stressed, about proper inflection, clarity and feeling, before I would not reveal my lowly origins every time I opened my mouth.

Women, Mademoiselle impressed upon us, had special duties in life. We were to be pleasing, trustworthy, devoid of artifice and dissimulation. Emotions had to be controlled at all times. Anything vulgar had to be strictly avoided. Eating fast and too much, running, jumping, stomping our feet, shouting, cursing, showing either sadness or joy. "News of a death or a proposal of marriage," she repeated, "must be met with equal composure. Always smile, whether you are happy or not. Make your eyes sparkle, no matter what you are thinking of." She reinforced these lessons by letting us make mistakes and then pointing them out. Asking me a question, for instance, just as I took a huge bite of brioche and tried to answer her with my mouth full. Had I taken a small bite, Mademoiselle would point out, I would've had the time to swallow before speaking, rather than make a display first of my greed and then, when my face turned beet red, of my shame.

I have always been a fast learner. After only a few days of practice, I managed the gliding steps with grace. My handwriting, too, began to improve, and my recitations became more fluid. The music master pronounced me highly musical. My singing, he said, naturally good already, would greatly improve as soon as I learned the power of stage breathing, which he would teach me in no time at all. I learned to pay close attention when Mademoiselle Dupin took us to Mass on Sunday, to know the answers to the questions she would ask after we returned home.

"You are rounding up nicely, Miss," Lisette said when she was obliged to tie my stays more loosely. "And look at your hands healing already! And your nails so shiny now. Nothing like goose fat and rose oil every night, just as Madame told you."

I often wondered what Adèle and Papa would have said, if they could see me then, but whatever words I came up with didn't seem right. Their faces were already fading in my mind, and I didn't know how to bring them back. For what did I have left of them? A few memories from the time long gone? A book of fables with calfskin binding and gilded edges that lay at the bottom of my trunk?

～⁂～

Queen Marie has charted her territory. These rooms only, these cabinets, corridors, stairs. Her paths lead to the chapel, to the children's rooms, along the side allées of the palace park—always away from the crowds of courtiers. And always back to the window from which she stares at the horizon, the edge of Versailles, sometimes bright, but mostly gray and unyielding.

Don't burden the king with your feelings, Maruchna, her father has written. *Be patient. Most of all refrain from blaming him. It is so churlish to complain, even to yourself.*

Maruchna, her childhood nickname. After ten children of her own, four buried already, still a daughter, not a queen.

The diamond necklace weighs on the back of her neck, pinching the small hairs there. The boned bodice rams into her flesh. There will be marks and bruises where it is tied too tight. She is wearing a court robe of embroidered silk, over a petticoat and a skirt. Sea green, they call it. Toad green it looks to her.

The cat has claimed her favorite place on the chaise longue. "Growing old too, are you?" the queen asks, smoothing Nutka's thick gray fur. "But not bald! Not you!"

Nutka purrs, narrowing her eyes into two slits. The Polish name, meaning a small musical note, is hardly fitting since Nutka put on weight. If she ever had to pounce on a mouse, she wouldn't have the agility or strength for a kill.

The maid who has followed the queen from the chapel curtsies. "Does Your Majesty still need me?"

"Make sure the refreshments are brought in as soon as the king arrives. Leave the wine to breathe. Don't forget candied cherries this time."

"I won't, Madame."

A nice girl, the queen thinks, quiet, pleasing. Plain, too, just as she prefers them, hair hidden under her bonnet. No need to multiply her husband's temptations. Even at the price of being thought dull and unfashionable.

During today's Mass, the queen prayed to be a better steward of God's gifts, to make use of what brings her closer to God and to detach herself from what doesn't. Choose charity over jealousy. Love over bitterness. In the quiet moment after taking communion, she summoned the image of a fuchsia bush, its teardrop flowers, red and purple. Bees flew to the open ones, ignoring the closed, yes, but without judgment, without resentment. It can be that simple: a bee, an open flower, a task at hand. Just as God wishes us to tend to His creation.

"I've been spared precious little of sorrow," her own mother said the last time she visited Versailles. They were here alone, in this very room, when she said it, meaning the lost Polish crown, the years of exile, her husband's unending string of mistresses. "One cannot turn away fast enough not to see," she also said, her chin trembling. But she did not add, "as you well know, my child." Dead three years now. Buried in Nancy. *Passerby*, the inscription on her gravestone requests, *say a prayer for her soul.*

Is restraint a woman's duty alone? Is obedience? Is turning a blind eye?

These are precisely the thoughts Queen Marie shouldn't be having now when she awaits her husband's visit.

Sophie and Adelaide, both in white silk, arrive first, bestowing fleeting kisses on their mother's cheek. Sophie lifts Nutka, belly up, and rocks her as if she were a baby. The cat squirms and wriggles to free herself. There are tufts of gray hair on the chaise longue. The maids must be reminded to brush it clean.

"Off you go then." Sophie concedes defeat, releasing the cat.

Louis-Ferdinand comes alone, his wife begging forgiveness for her absence, which has been expected and requires no forgiveness. God has not spared the dauphin and his wife their crowns of thorns. Stillborn sons, a daughter breathing her last only two months ago, her body racked by convulsions no doctor could stop. Not yet five, the sweet child. Though, as the queen reminds herself, there have been blessings, too. Two healthy heirs to the throne, and if their prayers are answered, the third will join them soon.

Victoire and Louise walk in together, holding hands. Or rather Victoire is holding Louise's hand, even though she is older by four years. All in their chapel finery, five perfumed clouds blending into a combination of jasmine, hyacinth, rose.

Henrietta, who left them for the better world almost three years ago now, would have sneezed.

Victoire and Louise whisper into each other's ears and giggle. Asked to share the amusing anecdote with everyone else, they describe some silly fracas involving Victoire trying to read aloud with her mouth full, almost choking on a piece of raisin cake she smuggled into the music room. Louise trying to create a diversion, pretending to see an ostrich burying its head in the flower bed, making their governess look out of the window.

"Mama, what a face she made."

"For there was no ostrich. Just a squirrel."

"Another of God's creations, I said!"

"Equally magnificent!"

"Mama? Are you listening?"

Stay like this, the queen thinks, smiling, carefree, shielded from disappointment. "I'm listening," she says.

How they chatter, her brood, tease each other. "Thunderstorm?" Victoire asks abruptly, glancing out the window, just to make Sophie shudder and reach for her hand in fear.

"Charity and kindness, Victoire." The queen forestalls the incipient outburst. "Just rain. There are no thunderstorms in October, Sophie!"

For ten years she prayed for such moments.

The day four of her daughters were taken to Fontevraud to be raised by the nuns, Louise was still a baby. Not even a year old, crawling on her knees, milk on her tongue. Such sweetness! And Thérèse only two, fascinated by the sparkling rubies on her mother's neck, not knowing she would never see her parents again. Only Victoire and Sophie were old enough to ask her why they had to go away when their brother and elder sisters were allowed to stay at Versailles. "Is it because I ate all the candied plums, Mama?" Victoire asked with such remorse. "When you told me to save some for the next day?"

As soon as the carriage left for Fontevraud, she—their mother—came here, to this room. Sat on the chaise longue, shivering, even though the day was warm. Swatting at the thoughts that chased her like angered wasps. Her daughters will grow up without her. She won't be there to soothe their cries. Share their laughter. Sing with them. Pray.

"Why?" she asked Louis, startling him with her question.

"Why what?" he asked to gain time.

"Why did they have to go to Fontevraud?"

He stiffened, offended already. "The Daughters of France need a proper education. Away from the court," he said curtly and then left.

The following day, he didn't come to see her. When she asked to see him, she was told that His Majesty had pressing matters to attend to. And all this time whispers grew louder around her. How it was her own fault. How she gave birth to too many girls. How if her daughters stayed at Versailles, each would require her own retinue, her own teachers. And who, pray, would pay for that?

Is this what it was about? Money? Was France a beggarwoman forced to give up her children because she couldn't feed them? Were her husband's mistresses and their bastards less costly?

A closed flower, she reminds herself. Leave it where it is. Fly to the open ones. Taste their sweetness.

Adelaide turns toward the door, where the king will appear any moment now. She is still her father's favorite. Loque, he calls her, "Rag," because she liked to throw herself on the floor when she was little. She, too, would have been sent away, had she not clung to him crying. "I couldn't live without seeing you every day, Papa." Maybe—and this is a thorny, prickly thought—if she, their mother, instead of asking why, had learned how to soften her husband's heart, he would've agreed.

"His Majesty, the king!"

She turns her eyes toward the opening door to greet her husband of thirty years. Her eyesight is not as good as it used to be, and all she sees at first is a cinnamon-colored silhouette, a flash of embroidery. Every step he takes creates ripples in the room. The children stir. Adelaide is the first to throw her arms around her father's neck.

"Just one embrace, Loque? Why such stinginess? . . . One more? Better! . . . Eating again, Coche? . . . I don't see Graille anywhere! Has she finally managed to disappear?"

Coche is Victoire, a pig because she eats too much. Graille is Sophie, a scrap, for she eats too little. Amiable enough, this teasing. The jokes are always the same and are always greeted with the same peals of laughter.

"You look so handsome, Papa."

"Do I?"

"You know you do."

Small voice, big smile, followed by questions about the last hunt. Whole minutes can pass listing quarry: hares, partridges, deer. Or describing an ambush, a surprise appearance, a perfect shot right in the neck, someone missing his mark, someone else turning at just the right moment for a perfect shot.

"Papa, will you take me hunting with you?"

"You cannot even ride properly."

"Oh, but I can."

"Liar. See how you blush."

"I do not."

It should delight her, the greediness with which her husband wicks up their daughters' love. But she cannot help seeing how Louis-Ferdinand tenses his jaw, how he drops his gaze and looks away.

She rises to curtsy, for her husband has finally turned to her, but he stops her. No ceremony, not here, he orders. He bends over to place a tiny kiss on her cheek. The only time they touch now, skin to bare skin. The brush of his lips feels like touching cobweb, spun at the entrance of a deserted vault.

Their conversations are stiff but always polite. Rain, heat, cold. Allow me . . . if you please.

"The next one would kill you, Your Majesty," the doctor said after Louise, the tenth, not counting the miscarriages and the little angels God took to Himself. Still she was ready to do her duty, if Louis only wished. As soon as the doctor pronounced her healed. But he didn't come to her and soon the palace gossips began their assault. The queen has closed the doors to her bedroom! The queen has let herself go! The queen has nothing but complaints! As if the king didn't have a mistress already.

Settled on the chaise longue, having shooed Nutka away, Louis has stretched out his legs, the buckles of his shoes glittering with diamonds. He is close enough for her to touch the sculpted line of his jaw, if he only would welcome it. His face as handsome, as expressive as when she saw him for the first time, his eyes the same stunning dark blue. Even if he were not king, he would draw looks. A lion among beasts.

Adelaide has claimed the place beside her father and lifts his hand to her lips. When he asks her what the matter is, she whispers something into his ear.

"Really?" he asks, and she nods.

A pang of jealousy pierces the queen's heart. Or is it the pain of exclusion? The first a sin, the second merely a reminder that she is human. Don't do it, child, she'd like to warn Adelaide. Secrets, even the innocent ones, have a life of their own, and in the end, they always turn back to bite you.

"Marie." Louis turns his eyes at her. "Adelaide tells me you've been painting again."

"A landscape, but it isn't finished yet," she says, ashamed of herself now for adding the sin of false accusation to her list. She points at the covered canvas, by the window. Marie, Queen of France, she will sign it. In spite of Adelaide's entreaty, her husband won't ask to see it, but she is proud of it. A cottage with a thatched roof, a flock of birds resting on it before taking flight. A birch tree by the river. A place she remembers from childhood, at the edge of her parents' estate. Her painting master sketched it for her, from the description she gave him. She intends to insert two figures, girls in white summer dresses, seated under the tree. She and Anna, her older sister whose death at eighteen, after two days of high fever, broke her father's heart. "Promise me, Maruchna, never to say her name again in my presence."

A promise she has kept.

The refreshments arrive; this time nothing is amiss. Skewers with quail eggs, and pheasant tidbits. Oysters, pastries, walnuts dipped in honey. A bowl of apple slices kept from browning with lemon juice. Candied cherries.

Adelaide, still at her father's side, is telling a story about a courtier whom she surprised spitting into a garden pond. "I'm making bubbles," he said when she demanded an explanation.

"Making bubbles, Papa?" she asks with a comical grimace. "Have you ever heard anything more droll?"

The voices ripple, erupt in laughter, like sections of a fugue. Even Louis-Ferdinand joins in, recalling a childhood foray into the Hall of Mirrors, at night, with his sisters. Making funny faces at their own reflections, pretending they were ghosts. Hortense giggling as she slid on the parquet floors in stockinged feet. Big sister Babette trying to climb one of the marble figures, landing on her backside instead.

"And what did you do, son?" his father asks, much too sharply. "Hold the candle?"

What is it about fathers and sons? The current of resistance that flows between them? Her husband keeps mistresses, some younger than their daughters. Her son is faithful to his wife. Her husband hunts. Her son abhors hunting. Her husband refuses to take the sacraments, even at Easter, which counts as mortal sin. Her son takes communion every Sunday. "His temper is *polonaise*," the king once told her, when they still talked about their children. "Hasty and changeable."

Why is it always her fault? Because, as her confessor reminds her, it's human to blame the one you've hurt.

Two weeks later, after breakfast, Mademoiselle Dupin ordered Francine to go upstairs. "To get ready," she said.

"For what?" Francine asked, only to be told to please restrain her curiosity as she had been taught.

Francine blushed and looked down. Mademoiselle Dupin announced that His Lordship who had been away all October had just returned to Versailles from his Polish estates. Francine had been chosen to greet him. "Go get ready, Francine. It's your time to show how much you have learned."

I tried to catch Francine's eye, but she turned away too quickly. All I saw was the laced back of her dress as she climbed the stairs.

A moment later Deer Park was all a bustle of preparations. A carriage arrived from the palace delivering a new outfit for Francine. "Hurry up," Madame Bertrand yelled as Lisette ran up and down the stairs, now with Rose's sewing kit, now with Marianne's brushes and irons.

During my lessons, I kept picturing Francine admiring her new finery in front of our mirror, until Mademoiselle chastised me for being careless. Given maxims to copy, I had written the same one twice:

Ingratitude calls forth reproaches as gratitude brings renewed kindnesses.

It was getting dark when the lessons finally ended and I was allowed back into our room. Francine had already left, and the room was in disarray. The table was pushed against the wall, covered with snippets of ribbons and lace. Pots of rouge and creams had been left open. A box of beauty spots was lying on the floor, next to Francine's crumpled morning dress. The scents of jasmine, rose, musk in the air made me sneeze.

I was picking up the dress from the floor when Lisette walked in. "Let me do it, Miss," she said brightly. She gave the dress a good shake and hung it in the wardrobe. "I'll be done in no time."

Only I didn't want her to hurry. "Will Francine be back soon?"

"Don't know, Miss. Best to wait and see, Miss."

"What if the count doesn't like her? Will they send her back home?"

"Best not to talk about such matters, Miss. What if Madame Bertrand hears us?"

Lisette worked quickly, picking up the box of beauty spots from the floor, wiping jars and bottles with the edge of her apron, arranging them on the toilette table in a neat row, from the tallest down. "There," she said, giving the room one more glance. "All nice and tidy. I'm all finished, Miss."

"Don't go, please," I begged her.

"I have to, Miss. I'll get into trouble."

I picked up the bowl with chocolate pastilles.

"Take one," I said. "You don't have to make a drink out of it. It's good as it is."

Lisette looked at me as if I were trying to trick her but took one pastille, unwrapped it carefully and put it in her mouth. A big smile told me that she liked it as much as I did. Then she licked her fingers so that no trace of chocolate would go to waste.

"Take another one," I urged. "We are allowed to have as many as we want."

I didn't have to ask twice. When the last traces of the second pastille were all gone, Lisette agreed to sit down for just a few moments. And only if I promised not to ask her about the count.

I promised.

Lisette told me she was from Buc, not that far away from Versailles. She called it a mean place, hinting at some trouble not to be dwelled upon. Her mother knew Madame Bertrand from the time past, and that's how she came to Deer Park. Lisette did not intend to be a maid-of-all-work forever. Marianne, who had come from Madame la marquise's household, had an agreement with a fellow in Aix. She has already saved six hundred livres for her dowry, and at least two hundred in *hardes*: a feather bed, a silver candleholder and a dozen linen shifts. Once Marianne married, Lisette would become a proper chambermaid.

I let her talk, grateful for her presence. There was no sign of Francine, and I did not like the thought of Lisette leaving me alone in the now-dark room.

She must have noted my growing unease for she tried to cheer me up with a story of a parrot. It had red and green and yellow feathers, and the sailor who brought her to the tavern in Buc let the children come close and touch the bird's hooked beak. When it was Lisette's turn, the parrot cocked its head, opened its beak and squeaked, "Get the fuck out! Get the fuck out!"

Wasn't it really funny?

It was.

"One more chocolate?" I tempted.

Lisette took another pastille but didn't eat it. Instead she hid it in her pocket and said she had to go. The new scullery maid broke the good platter, Madame

Bertrand's favorite, and the cook was in a foul mood. The cook had tripped on the hole in the yard the night watchman was supposed to fix and strained his ankle. There would be accusations; there would be blows.

When she left, I got into bed and lay there, listening to the sounds of the house. Michel and Saint-Jean climbing the stairs to the attic, the yelp of the town dogs, one responding to another. Closer to the house a shriek, then a cat's meow.

I was about to fall asleep when I heard the squeak of the door opening, followed by hurried steps and candlelight. Francine rushed in, sobbing and gasping for breath. Just behind her Rose was telling her to stop such tomfoolery, before it gets all out of hand.

"This has nothing to do with you, Véronique," Rose snapped as I lifted myself up on my bed, asking what was wrong.

She helped Francine wiggle out of her outer robe and put it on the armchair. When she wanted to take off Francine's stays, Francine slapped her hand. "Suit yourself then," Rose said and left.

"What happened, Francine?" I asked, but she didn't answer. A moment later I heard her retch into the chamber pot, then spit, then retch again.

Outside our room, doors opened and shut. Footsteps descended the stairs. Madame Bertrand was loudly cursing someone for getting underfoot. In the room next door, Claire was begging Mademoiselle Dupin not to leave her alone in the dark. Mademoiselle said something in reply, but I could not make out the words.

"Tell me what happened, Francine," I pleaded.

"Go away."

I got out of bed by then. The room was lit by a single candle Rose had left on the mantel. The air smelled of vomit and of something singed. Francine was sitting on the edge of her bed by then, rubbing her right arm. Had she been hurt? Come up too close to the count's fireplace, perhaps? Mademoiselle Dupin had often cautioned us about such recklessness. A dress or a shawl catching fire, a girl burned alive before anyone could douse the flames.

"Francine, please."

"Shut up, Véronique."

I sat beside her. Again, I asked her what had happened, but she would not tell me. I tried to smooth her hair, but she pulled away. I sat for a while longer and then went back to my own bed. I didn't know what else to do.

I thought I wouldn't be able to sleep but I did.

The garden walk doesn't begin well. Madame de Pompadour almost steps on the dead bird, a tit. It must have flown into the freshly polished windowpane, fooled into thinking the sky it reflected was real. Smashed against it, broke its neck. And yet the small blue and yellow body, so light and delicate in her hands, looks untouched.

What you don't see cannot harm you, they say.

Fools.

Her heart is beating fast. Flecks of darkness float before her eyes. Mercifully her head gardener sees her and rushes to relieve her of the burden, apologizing profusely for the omission, promising to chastise the garden hands who have not spotted it, as they should have. That new boy he has just hired. Halfwit and two left hands. He will send him away.

"Don't."

"Madame has a good heart. Too good, if I may be allowed to say so."

"We all need forgiveness."

The gardener nods, his blue eyes blinking. There is a drop of yellow pus in the corner of his right eye. Dr. Quesnay should take a look at it.

"Such are the unintended consequences of too-clean windows," the gardener continues. "Would Madame care to rest?"

She would. The stone bench is right here.

"Should I call for your maid?"

"No. Please. No fussing. Have you managed to get rid of the snails?"

Alas, the gardener sighs. Snails have been especially destructive this summer, and especially for the dahlias. He has tried all his most trusted remedies. Set beer traps, sprinkled coffee grounds around the roots. Still every morning he has to pluck out the shredded leaves, naked stems covered with slime. "Even at the close of October, they are still at it, Madame. Winter won't kill them, just put them to sleep."

The snails are indeed brazen. One is even crawling along the edge of the stone bench. Alexandrine used to pick them up, put them on her palm and hum, coaxing them out of their curled shells. If humming didn't work, she would whisper, "Snail, snail, show me your horns. I will give you . . ." Here she came up with a myriad of lures. A piece of cheese. A giant strawberry. A bowl of cream.

"You'll find a way," she tells the gardener, rising from the bench, still a bit wobbly on the heels of her shoes but determined to continue on her walk. "You always do."

The gardener nods. Tomorrow he will replace all the dahlias with the China asters he has been growing in pots. All clean of snails and in perfect bloom. "You will be pleased, Madame."

"What colors?"

"Red, pink and white."

She used to think of her garden as a canvas, a clean slate upon which a new picture was conjured every day, an interplay of colors, intercut with paths of changing scents. Close your eyes, she would whisper in Louis's ear. Smell your way inside! But a garden is a battlefield, a set for bold invasions and shameful defeats. No matter how diligent the gardener and his army of helpers, not all fading blooms can be removed, not all chewed-up stems cut away. Death and rot always find a way.

A pulse of pain cycles up and down her spine, the memory of her daughter's last request: "May I, please, stay with you a bit longer, Maman?" To which she replied that the good nuns at the convent school were waiting, that duty was more important than pleasure. Alexandrine gave her such an angry look, pushed a clock off the mantel and broke it in half. A beautiful ormolu clock, Louis's gift smashed, and Alexandrine just stood there staring at the floor.

"Fanfan! Apologize right this minute!"

There was an apology, stiff and crooked. There was a shrug she pretended not to notice.

The first message from the convent was not alarming. *Indisposition, upset stomach, slight fever in the evening.* Fanfan was still angry, she thought, vying for attention. She would've done the same when she was her age, made her mother come to her side, in fright.

The second message mentioned agitation, hands cold and damp, tongue coated with white slime. The doctor advised bloodletting and fasting but was confident that the indisposition was a passing one.

Peritonitis, the third message said. *We are all praying for God's mercy.*

By the time she arrived at the convent, Alexandrine was already in her coffin, a victim of rampant inflammation, the nuns told her. So small her child, she thought, so unfinished, her cheeks sunken, her eyes rimmed with purple.

Death robbed her daughter even of her beauty.

She tried to be brave. She kissed Alexandrine's lips, her waxy hands with a string of rosary beads wrapped up around them. She crossed herself and fell to her knees. She prayed for her daughter's soul, now at peace, with God.

Grief was stronger, though. It choked her. It turned her into a demented woman, an ancient mourner howling in pain. The nuns held her, begging her to stop, but how do you keep silent beside the body of your only child? How do you stop yourself from shaking her, summoning back the departed soul, forcing it to live out its life beside her mother, be her comfort? How do you relieve the leaden heaviness of grief, the paralyzing feeling of waste and the aimlessness of life? How do you stop asking why bother . . . why force myself to wake up each morning . . . for whom?

For me, Louis had said, his hand clasping hers.

For him.

Later, after the funeral, Dr. Quesnay told her that inflammation was not the purposeless calamity the nuns believed it to be, but the body's defense against the unrelenting progress of some other deadly irritants. No, he didn't know what they were. All he knew was that Alexandrine's body was desperately trying to fight them off. Peritonitis did not kill her daughter. Trying too hard to fight it off, giving up too much, did.

Whatever it was, it was all God's will, Mother Superior said.

Is this God's will, too? Madame de Pompadour asks herself as she walks slowly back to her salon. Grief refusing to let go, seeping deep inside the bones. Her thoughts insisting: Such is the end of everything. Nothing will be left of you. There will be no grandchildren. No future.

"Is anything the matter, Madame?" Nicole du Hausset, who has been await-ing her return, asks.

A faithful soul, Nicole, a kind one. One of her blessings. Even if she asks unwanted questions.

"The snails are eating the dahlias, Nicole," she says. "The gardener is all flustered about it."

"Oh, is he?" Nicole laughs, relieved, removing the soiled shoes, bemoaning the soaked-through satin tops that will shrink, lose their shape. The second pair this week!

"Never mind the shoes, Nicole!"

Her maid, chastened, colors slightly and offers the latest gossip instead. The gardener, it turns out, is a frequent visitor at Lebel's garden. "On account of proximity," the man always says, but Nicole has it on good authority that he is curious about the red fish that recently arrived from China. A few of which Lebel offered as a gift for Madame's pond, if only Madame would allow it. The fish are supposed to be hard to breed, but the gardener doubts it. "I've seen them chasing each other plenty," he has said.

"Another of Lebel's gifts, Nicole? What is it this time? Enticement or apology?"

"He says it is merely a token of his gratitude for Madame's kindness."

"Enticement then."

The gardener also reported that Lebel had commissioned a portrait of himself. Pastel, Nicole says with well-studied bewilderment and a dollop of ill-concealed envy. "There have been three sittings already, Madame, and it is almost finished. I heard it will hang in his salon, above the oak console table, for every visitor to see."

No love lost between these two, Madame de Pompadour thinks. Just a truce, stewed in gossip. Tedious, really, though it is worth remembering that Louis will delight in the story of his valet's pastel portrait. And her maid's jealousy.

"The likeness is quite remarkable," Nicole continues, describing the picture. Lebel seated, eye turned toward the window, through which a glimpse of the palace gardens is offered. In front of him, the book of accounts, an inkwell, a watch and a key. "Oh, Madame, I don't know what to think of such pride."

How disappointing, the petty dreams of little men who think themselves big. Louis is right in preferring animals to people. No pretense, he says, no artifice, no grieving over what could've been but won't, no fretting over the future.

But how does one escape from oneself?

Francine did not get up in the morning. She didn't come down for breakfast either, and Mademoiselle Dupin told me to stop asking questions about matters that did not concern me. I had no choice but to go about my day. At midday, from the music room where I was practicing a new song, I heard Monsieur Durand's voice in the hall and Madame Bertrand's nervous answers. Rose ran up and down the stairs. Lisette averted her eyes when she saw me. In the evening, when I was finally allowed to go upstairs, our room smelled strongly of valerian and lavender, and Francine was fast asleep.

I got into bed and closed my eyes. The next thing I remember was the door bursting open. Startled and only half awake, I peered through my bed curtains and saw the two lackeys, lanterns in hand. Madame Bertrand was bending over Francine. "Get up, you ingrate," she snarled. "You are leaving."

"What has she done?" I asked.

"Go back to sleep, Véronique," Madame Bertrand snapped at me and ordered the lackeys to put the lanterns on the mantel so that she could see better. She didn't intend on killing herself by tripping over someone's chamber pot.

In the courtyard horses neighed. The big clock in the hall struck five.

The lackeys dragged Francine out of bed, holding her up when she tottered as if about to faint. Madame Bertrand pulled a dress over her shift. "You are lucky not to go in the same rags we took you in from the butcher shop," she yelled. She called her a disgrace. A savage girl who never learned when to keep her mouth shut. Good for sweeping floors, if her father would take her back, considering how eager he had been to get rid of her.

Francine lunged forward, and Madame yelped with pain. "You viper," she screamed, holding her hand to the air, looking for blood. A slap followed and then it was Francine who wailed and cursed. "Pox on this house. All of you! Servants of the devil."

By then she wriggled free from the lackeys' grasp. With one sweep of her hand she sent the porcelain basket on the table flying, crashing on the floor. The candelabra followed with a thud. She had no chance, though. The lackeys grabbed her hands, twisted them behind her back. Madame slapped her again, declaring that she had had a bad feeling about her all along.

A few more scuffles and curses later, Francine was out of the room.

I jumped out of bed and rushed to the window. It was still quite dark outside, but I could see the lackeys drag Francine into the courtyard. They pushed her inside the carriage; she managed to fling the door open. Fuckwits . . . morons . . . she yelled. Go to hell, all of you!

In the end the driver had to help them. The last thing I saw was him climbing back up to his seat, flicking his whip and the horses taking off.

I returned to bed, teary and bewildered, feeling sorry for Francine and for myself, still unable to shed the hurt of her distrust. I wondered if I missed doing something Francine expected me to do, if I let her down somehow, though in what way I could not fathom.

I was still sobbing when an hour or so later Lisette came in and opened the shutters. "Time to get you ready," she said, perching at the edge of the bed.

"Where did they take her?" I asked, the sound of Francine's curses still in my ears.

"Home, Miss. No need to worry about her."

She patted the coverlet over my feet when she said it, making me flinch in pain.

"What's wrong, Miss?"

When I did not answer, Lisette lifted the coverlet and screamed. "What have you done, Miss!"

My feet were swollen and smeared with blood. I must have stepped on the porcelain shards without feeling it. Madame Bertrand came running and declared me both careless and foolish. Armed with tweezers she removed the shards one by one, while Lisette fetched the plaster box and moistened linen strips with vine vinegar.

When my feet were cleaned and bandaged, Madame Bertrand collected everything Francine had left behind, her embroidery hoop, her stays and a jar of her hair powder. Later, she said, Michel and Saint-Jean would come to take Francine's bed away.

A new girl, she said, was expected tomorrow, but she would not stay with me. From now on, on His Lordship's strict orders, every *élève* would have a room of her own.

～⁂～

Queen Marie has been in a state of anguish ever since the duchesse de Luynes first brought her the news. An earthquake had struck the city of Lisbon. Then, forty minutes later, came a tidal wave, so big and so fast that even those on horseback couldn't outrun it. As soon as the waters receded, fires erupted.

Destroyed: the Lisbon Cathedral, the Basilicas of São Paulo, Santa Catarina, São Vicente de Fora, and the Misericórdia Church. All of this on All Saints' Day, while the queen was in the Versailles chapel, praying for Henrietta's soul.

The latest dispatches report hundreds, no, thousands, dead. Whole quarters of Lisbon are flattened, roofs are still falling down, walls are still crumbling, flames licking the walls. Groans of pain coming from people buried alive. There have been cases of cholera and smallpox.

Grave questions ambush the queen's thoughts, infringe on her prayers. Why Lisbon, always faithful to God? Why on All Saints' Day? Why at the time of high Mass, when thousands crowded the churches? What sins demanded such punishment? What transgressions? What has angered the Almighty that much? He who leaves so many other sins unpunished?

She, a queen without power, has taken Lisbon's tragedy to be God's call to duty. To answer it, she has postponed the annual move to Fontainebleau for the winter and has transformed her private apartments into a headquarters of mercy. She has sold two of her diamond necklaces and is personally supervising the purchase of supplies, bargaining with merchants to bring prices down. Her ladies-in-waiting are busy accepting donations of goods and collecting money for the victims. As a result of these efforts, cartloads of provisions of all kinds are leaving Versailles for Lisbon every day.

Charity is hard work. Baskets of linen and of medicines are stacked against every wall, awaiting departure. Heeding her doctors' advice, Queen Marie is sending basic *materia medica* for wounds, fever and diarrhea, as well as a few cases of nerve tonic. Her ladies-in-waiting are busy sorting clothes into hampers marked *For men*, *For women*, *For children*. Some are in charge of making *charpies* for surgical dressings. They have commanded their maids to help, and these are sitting in a circle, tearing strips of linen. New linen, Queen Marie has insisted, for the royal surgeon is adamant that such *charpies* are much better at absorbing discharge from wounds.

Eight days have already passed in this manner, each hour accounted for, measured in packages, bundles, crates bound with braids of straw lined up, ready for transport to Lisbon. The queen's arms hurt from lifting; her feet are swollen from standing far too long. But this is nothing compared with the deep satisfaction born from being of use, anticipating the relief these gifts will bring. This is how she pictures life in convents. The echoing murmur of prayers, the common purpose, the deep sense of being a cog in the vast machine of God's work on this earth.

It is barely four o'clock now, and the room is half dark already. Candles, just lit, flicker. "Get some here," the duchesse de Luynes orders one of the maids, pointing at the table beside her. She is charged with reading the Lisbon dispatches aloud to remind them why they are gathered here. "The young never understand the need for more light," she grumbles, adjusting her spectacles. "But they will!"

The duchess, Bibi, still as tireless at seventy-one as on the day she welcomed her queen to Versailles, is not only Marie's favorite lady-in-waiting but also a dear friend. "All in the Lord's service, Your Majesty," she likes to say, beaming. Only when they find themselves alone does Bibi admit to the indignities of growing old. False teeth that won't stay in place. Skin paper-thin, easy to bruise or tear. A finger that curls and refuses to open by itself. Bunions that make each step a torture. "What kind of Christian soldier does God have in me, Your Majesty?" Bibi asks. "The best," Marie always answers.

"Mothers are digging into the rubble with bare hands, in search of their children," Bibi reads now in her strong, steady voice. "Orphans are told to pray for the souls of the dead, snatched by death without a chance to repent and receive absolution. Pigeons are coming back to their roosting grounds, even as they are consumed by flames, circling over them, until some get their wings singed or, overcome by the fumes, fall into the flames. When rain comes, it rains ashes."

As soon as Bibi stops, chatter takes over the room. Sighs at first and words of compassion, but soon the conversations move to less weighty topics. The comtesse de Polignac gushes over the Chinese screens and lacquered chests she has seen in a Paris salon. Her companion describes someone "uncommonly rich in diamonds." The marquise de Viellard has had plants stolen from her garden, the second year in a row. Tulip bulbs were dug out one night, then her best hyacinths. Someone's servant was bitten by a mad dog. Someone's bed curtains will have to be fumigated, for no amount of scouring and washing can rid them of bedbugs.

To blot out this babbling, the queen is concentrating on the linen she is folding. Each item simple and serviceable. Shifts, shirts, pantaloons, all freshly laundered and pressed. They take little space if rolled tightly so she exerts herself to do just that. As Bibi has said, "They don't need French air in Lisbon."

When the door opens, the queen expects another visitor. Today alone she has already received five merchants, two doctors wishing to travel to Lisbon with the nearest medical shipment and stay there as long as they are needed, and a man claiming to have invented a means of measuring the strength of earthquakes. His invention, which she rather liked, involved a vessel with water in it, dusted all over on the inside with a barber's puff so that the tremors will move the water and leave a mark.

"La marquise de Pompadour, Your Majesty," the footman announces. Clearly her husband's mistress cannot bear the thought of anything happening at Versailles without her presence.

A ripple goes through the room, a reminder of all the vicious talk the queen is trying so hard to banish from her heart. These girls la marquise fetches for Louis now, younger than the youngest of his daughters. In and out of them, her own son has said.

Bibi gives her a sharp, assessing gaze, meant to judge how she is holding up. "My exercise in humiliation," Marie will refer to this visit when they are alone.

A pause, a flutter, a rustle of silks and the marquise de Pompadour—Maman Whore as her son calls her now—makes her grand entrance. All elegance, perfectly adorned. Never too much rouge, or powder, though the nauseous smell of ceruse is not entirely masked by perfume.

Out of the corner of her eye the queen notes that Bibi has left her spot, ready to intervene if necessary. A mark of a true friend, such vigilance.

"My humble offerings, Your Majesty . . . a thousand louis d'or and baskets of necessities," Pompadour chirps before making a dramatic pause, timed so her footmen can enter carrying her gifts. "Undergarments mostly, for I assume that clean linen must be particularly scarce."

"If only everyone were so humble," Queen Marie says.

Pompadour bows even lower.

What next after this awkward moment of silence? What other grand gesture will come now? A recitation, perhaps? Or a thespian show of tears? But Maman Whore merely deposits the rolls of gold coins on the table, among the other donations. There is no opening of baskets, displaying what's inside. Hopefully now she will orchestrate a swift retreat. *See*, Marie can almost hear Bibi's soothing voice. *Not such a trying exercise after all.*

Maman Whore never retreats, though. Another perfect curtsy is followed by a request to be allotted a task. "It's your formidable efforts, Your Majesty, that the whole of Paris is talking about. Your Majesty's tireless work on behalf of the victims."

To stop these gushing praises, the queen places a finger on her lips, but the damage is already done. Whatever she decides, whether she asks Pompadour to read the prayers aloud or puts her into the farthest corner to sort and fold clothes, the purity and the joy of this communal effort have been stained.

"You might help us make lists," she tells Pompadour. What is in which coffer, box, basket before it departs. Kinds of items, quantities. So that whoever opens them can check the usefulness of the contents without having to upset the arrangements.

"I'll do that, Your Majesty."

Maman Whore is lingering, still hoping to prolong this exchange, but Bibi is already taking over, instructing the marquise on the format of the lists. Folded page, items on the left, sorted into categories, quantities. Sizes where appropriate. The destinations: hospitals, orphanages, outdoor kitchens where the survivors can get a meal. "Let's start with the one you brought, Madame," she says, opening a basket and retrieving what's inside. Undergarments, all one size, for a young girl. Petticoats, vests, stays, shifts, nightgowns, pantaloons. All from soft batiste, all freshly ironed.

It must be the air, dense from so many breaths, from the piled-up clothes, yet unsorted, or the need to draw attention to herself at all cost. Whatever it is, it makes Pompadour swoon and only the strong arms of her own waiting maid stop her from falling to the ground. "Madame, Madame," the maid croons. In her hands a flask of smelling salts releases the sharp stink of hartshorn.

All the ladies-in-waiting cluster round, offering help, asking to have the window open. Perhaps Madame la marquise should take a turn around the room. Sitting is not good for circulation.

Pompadour, her face pale, lips trembling, wicks up all this attention. She accepts a glass of wine diluted with water, takes another sniff at the smelling salts, apologizes for her weakness, begs to be allowed to leave.

Good riddance!

How easy to pass judgment. How hard to notice beyond what we think we know. These are the queen's thoughts when, la marquise gone, Bibi says, "It's all my fault, Your Majesty. I should've guessed the undergarments belonged to Alexandrine. This must've been the first time the marquise has seen them since her daughter's death."

Every day after Francine's dismissal, I awaited news about her, but it was as if she had never been at Deer Park at all. Her things were all gone. No one mentioned her name. One morning when I recalled how Francine liked brioche at breakfast, Mademoiselle Dupin gave me a cutting look. Knowing what to say and what to be silent about, she announced, was an achievement every *élève*, without exception, would be judged by.

When I bribed Lisette with more chocolate pastilles, she said that Francine was dismissed because she acted before thinking. She couldn't tell me anything more, other than to remind me of Francine's quick tongue and her paying no heed to Mademoiselle Dupin's lessons. When I bribed Lisette with my best lace handkerchief, she merely added that Francine was well provided for. Not as well as she could've been had she been smarter but still better off than when she came here. The count was a very generous man. He didn't wish anyone's harm.

"Best not to think about her, Miss," Lisette said.

I tried, but too much reminded me of Francine. The empty alcove where her bed once stood, the cuts on the soles of my feet. Even though they were healing well, they still hurt when I walked, and at the end of the day, the inside of my shoes were stained with blood.

"Best mind your own affairs, Miss," Lisette also said. I sensed a new air of importance around her these days. Madame Bertrand often took her to the market, declaring that Lisette's smart bearing and quick thinking helped her assure excellent bargains. Madame also trusted Lisette with bringing her wine from the cellar, a task only Rose had been allowed until then.

When the new girl, Amélie, arrived, I couldn't stop myself from lurking on the landing when Rose and Lisette took her to the scullery for her bath. But as soon as I caught a glimpse of a slight figure in a hooded travel coat, Mademoiselle Dupin called me to the drawing room, chastised me for my most unbecoming curiosity and gave me an embroidery sampler to work on. The following day when Amélie came down to the breakfast table, I saw how unlike Francine she was. Not only because she was even prettier, with her high forehead and full lips, but because she spoke little and paid more attention to Claire than me.

How lonely I felt! I woke up dreading the hours ahead; I went to bed with a heavy heart. One evening I took out a sheet of the fancy paper Mademoiselle gave us for copying maxims and began writing a letter to Francine. *I hope you miss me as much as I miss you*, I began. I told her about Amélie, who would never be my friend. I wrote about Papa, Adèle and the printing house on rue des Jardins. I asked Francine if she knew how far Lisbon was, and if she, too, wondered how it felt to have the earth open up under one's feet or be buried alive under the rubble.

I knew Francine would never read my letter. When I finished, I folded it carefully and hid it in the green trunk, inside the *Fables* of La Fontaine.

My own summons came a week later. "This is your chance to show gratitude," Mademoiselle Dupin said as she ordered me to go upstairs after breakfast. "Make sure you do not spoil it."

I did not quite trust myself to speak, so I nodded.

In my room a new dress was lying on my bed. The cut was simple, but the dress was made of beautiful cream satin. There was a new pair of shoes to match it. Heeled mules I could slip on or off without having to ask for anyone's help.

"What's with this sour look?" Rose said. "Don't you know how to smile?"

"Be smarter than you-know-who," Lisette said, handing me a wet washcloth.

Rose whitened my cheeks with a smudge of ceruse, reddened my lips with just a tiny spot of crimson. Lisette laced my stays far tighter than I was accustomed to.

The cream satin shimmered. Lisette said she had ironed it herself, which wasn't easy, for satin was fiddly to work with, ruined when pressed too hard.

Laced into the new dress, with my curls tamed and neatly pinned up, I looked older and a bit awkward, not sure what to do with my hands.

"How will I know where to go?" I asked.

I was not to worry, Rose said, Michel and Saint-Jean knew where to take me.

"What will I have to do there?" I asked.

Rose shrugged her shoulders. "How would I know?" she said. The sharpness in her voice warned me not to ask any more questions.

As we were waiting for the sedan chair, Lisette and Rose talked about the lackeys. How all they had to do was to look good and be around in case they were needed, and still were paid twice as much as maids. To which Lisette said, "Ah, that's justice for you, all right."

I only half listened, anxious as I was. I knew I had to please His Lordship, but what would this involve? Singing? Playing the harpsichord? Perhaps, but then what? For there was something else, something unimaginable, something that made Francine sob.

A trial Francine had failed.

"Don't get sent back in disgrace," Maman had said.

A sedan chair, I found out, was far less comfortable than a carriage. The swaying side to side made my stomach churn. At one of the hardest swerves my elbow smashed against the window. Mercifully the ride was short, and when I got out, wobbly on my feet, Monsieur Durand was waiting. "What took you two clowns so long?" he snapped at the lackeys, dismissing their excuses with a swat of his hand.

Was this the palace of Versailles? I had expected a grand entranceway, filled with courtiers and flanked by Swiss Guards, but the courtyard I was brought to was small and deserted. The buildings around it, made of a yellowish stone, were quite plain, some even stained at the base, their only adornment the sculptured heads of stags with antlers, displayed like trophies from a hunt. But then I decided that a Polish count, even if a relation of the queen, could not compare himself to the king of France. Was it any wonder his apartment was not in the best part of the palace?

"Were you told what is expected of you?" Monsieur Durand asked me, quite sharply, which did not surprise me. I had seen him a few times at Deer Park, but he had not spoken to me there. I still believed he didn't like me much. I also believed he didn't like anyone much at all.

"To show my gratitude for the generosity I've received," I repeated Mademoiselle Dupin's words.

My answer must have satisfied him well enough, for he nodded and ordered me to follow him. I lifted the sides of the satin skirt and hurried as fast as my new shoes would let me.

On our way we passed many doors but only a few were open. One room was filled with sedan chairs, another with chamber pots nested among sawdust. There were no courtiers in the corridors we walked through, but I saw a boot boy arranging hunting boots in a straight line, heels touching, and a maid watching a small lapdog pee on the marble floor.

We climbed a narrow staircase to the second landing, where Monsieur

Durand retrieved a key from his pocket and opened one of the doors there, to let me inside.

"You'll wait here," he said, pointing at a dark green sofa with gilded armrests that stood against the wall. "Until you are wanted."

I sat at the edge of the sofa, careful to arrange the folds of my dress, mindful of Maman's old warnings that satin didn't take kindly to being creased. The skin of my hands, smeared with goose fat each night on Madame Bertrand's orders, was no longer covered with chilblains, though their faint outlines were still there. The elbow I smashed against the window of the sedan chair hurt but did not bruise. Monsieur Durand gave me one last look, sniffed the air around me, and left the room, just as a clock on the mantel struck noon.

I sat and waited.

For a while the room commanded my whole attention. It was rather small, with a low ceiling, but it was beautifully decorated. I noted the pattern of yellow flowers embroidered on green silk that covered the walls, a paler version of the one on the curtains. A china vase on the side table, its edges trimmed with gold, was filled with pink roses, which gave off a strong sweet scent. Beside it, arranged in a group, stood porcelain figurines. A shepherdess in a blue dress blowing a kiss. A little girl playing with her dog. A milkmaid carrying buckets with milk. A barefoot girl tending sheep. I so much wanted to pick them up, one by one, just to feel their lightness in my hand, but then decided not to. What if the count walked in? What if he got angry with me for touching what was his?

The count, I reminded myself, was my benefactor. Alas, there were no portraits of him anywhere, an absence I pondered for some time. Did he not wish to be painted? Was it because he was old and ugly, perhaps?

Listening for the sound of the count's footsteps, I kept glancing at the clock. The longer I waited, the more uneasy I grew. What if he didn't come at all? What should I do then? Stay here? Wait for Monsieur Durand? And what if he didn't come, either? Should I try to find my way back to Deer Park by myself?

That last thought made me stand up and look through the window. I expected to see the courtyard where I arrived but discovered that the room overlooked the palace park, the far end of which blended with the distant line of the horizon. Closer to me, a row of statues on pillars flashed white against a wall of green. The wide path beside them was filled with courtiers. One group caught my eye, four girls bunched around a stout-looking lady in a gray mantle. Could it be the queen with Mesdames? I wondered, the Daughters of France? Lisette told me once that the queen always wore a strange old-fashioned cap that looked like a small pillowcase tied under her chin. I strained my eyes to see if I could spot it, but the lady in the gray mantle was too far away. She could not be the queen, I decided. If she were, courtiers would have stopped in front of her to curtsy, wouldn't they?

Muted music and voices from somewhere below reached me. Above me, I could hear hens cackling, scratching, a rooster warning them with a sharp crow. Hens in the palace? The thought was so absurd that I laughed. Then a painting on the wall caught my attention. It showed a ship tossed, besieged by waves. I liked the way the sea was separated from the skies with a thin edge of sunlight that broke through the clouds. Next to the painting was a large mirror in a gilded frame in which I examined my reflection, pleased with the flow of the cream satin, the delicate pattern of the lace trim, the becoming way Rose had pinned up my hair, letting a few curls fall loosely over my neck.

The clock on the mantel chimed two. Two hours had passed since Monsieur Durand brought me into this room. By then both my fears and my curiosity had vanished, replaced by boredom, which Mademoiselle Dupin said was a sign of a deficient mind. To distract myself I practiced my dance steps in front of the mirror—forward, sideways, a turn and a curtsy—until my injured feet began to hurt. Assuming a grand pose Mademoiselle taught us, I recited a poem about the glory of France, my face mimicking Mademoiselle's exalted expressions until I began to giggle. I pretended to be Madame Bertrand and gave myself a stern lecture on the importance of obedience and gratitude while taking sips from an imaginary bottle of her heart tonic.

By then I was beginning to feel hungry and thirsty. I tried to open the door leading to the corridor outside, but it was locked and so was the other door in the room. When I peeked through the keyholes, I found them blocked, so I returned to the sofa, slipped off my shoes and lay down. Before drifting into a shallow sleep, I thought I heard noises coming from behind the wall, but they were so faint that I dismissed them as an illusion.

When Monsieur Durand shook me awake, it was already dark. My shoulder hurt, my hair was all tousled. I expected him to chastise me, but he didn't look displeased. "The sedan chair is downstairs, so hurry up!" he said, handing me my shoes. "They are waiting for you at Deer Park with supper."

~❧~

Lebel's repeater watch confirms it is five minutes past ten. The king is already with Madame de Pompadour and will be at her apartment for at least another hour, which should give Lebel time to attend to the Deer Park business.

Should, that is, if he could expect some peace. Instead, from his study he can hear his postillion complain about those dreadful ruts on the road to Paris. He had to replace another wheel, that's two in the past three days. Something heavy is scraping the floor, then comes the sound of logs dropped on the holder. Where is his valet when he is needed?

The court should have moved to Fontainebleau for the winter by now, but the queen has postponed her departure again, determined to continue her relief work for the Lisbon victims. This decision, however noble in motive, has caused a lot of disruptions in the palace schedules. The annual change of curtains and silk draperies in all royal apartments has been postponed, beds have not been scalded yet, mattresses have not been fumigated. Besides, the king is obliged to hold *grandes levées*, which he would not be at Fontainebleau, and consequently is in a bad mood every morning.

A rattling thought, the king's displeasure.

The fiasco with that hussy Francine has not helped. First the stupid girl got drunk, then when His Majesty touched her she wailed as if she were being skinned alive. "Lebel is getting careless," Pompadour has been heard telling the king.

He is not getting careless.

This is why he has taken precautions with that Véronique girl. He watched her in the green salon through the see-through mirror. She did not touch the china figures. She did not rifle through drawers or poke at the fire. "Obedient and will not cause trouble," the governess assured him. Though this in itself doesn't guarantee that Louis will find her to his liking.

The sound of the door opening followed by a scrambling is a sign that Gaspard, his valet, has finally arrived. Admonished to keep quiet for master is at work, the lackeys stop whatever they have been doing. Silence at last.

Lebel opens the ledger, reaches for his pen, dips it in the inkwell. He savors how the nib gets weighted with just the right amount of ink. The royal kingdom of pleasure requires diligent accounting.

"Royal bastards" is an ever-expanding item. No matter how carefully Lebel tries to prevent their arrival, they keep coming, and he must arrange for their upkeep. For the first three years of their lives, he places them with wet nurses in one of the villages around Versailles, where the peasants have learned the value of discretion. If a bastard dies, Lebel pays for the funeral. If a bastard lives beyond the age of six, Lebel makes further arrangements. Boys he first sends to boarding school. Then, depending on their progress, they go into the army or into some other suitable profession. Girls he places with foster parents, which is not an onerous task, given how many Versailles servants welcome the compensation. Most of these girls will stay with their guardians until they are ready to be married off. Any who are religiously inclined Lebel will send to a convent school where he'll instruct the nuns to nurture their vocation with scrupulous care.

Right now, out of the five bastards under his supervision, the oldest girl is only eight. Entrusted to a Versailles cabinetmaker and his wife, she is learning her catechism. Well cared for, too, though one of his spies has reported that *the guardians show her excessive indulgence and draw attention to themselves by lending money at interest, encouraging speculation about the girl's parentage.*

Welcome, such vigilance, deserving a prompt reward.

Tomorrow, the cabinetmaker will receive an unexpected visit and a few words of caution. His first stern warning.

The documents Lebel turns to next offer a pleasing conclusion to old business. The merchant in New France is confirming the arrival of his bride. The bride, one of the Versailles chambermaids the king took a liking to, had caused Lebel no end of troubles. First on account of her loose tongue, then on account of her confinement, which lasted forty hours, tore her inside and ended with a stillbirth. "She almost died?" the king had asked, misty-eyed. "For me?"

The bride arrived in Montréal with her dowry and trousseau. The receipt for four thousand livres is signed: *Étienne Marchand. On this twenty-eighth day of June 1755.*

That was five months ago already, but it takes time to cross the ocean. The New World offers untold opportunities, Lebel hears. Beaver pelts are in great demand in France. The trade in otter skins is even more profitable, if the skins are taken to China and exchanged for tea, which is then sold in England. A thousand percent profit, Lebel has been told, or even more. Fortunes are being made as he sits here, in his room, at his desk.

Enough of idle thoughts. The world may be vast, ever expanding in possibilities, but he commands only a patch of it. A patch he must make run as smoothly as he can, closing his eyes to what lies beyond. Concentrate on what is possible right this moment, he orders himself. On what can be added or subtracted, measured, assessed.

Holding the page down flat, Lebel examines the row of figures he has entered. Eight hundred livres per year for each royal bastard, to cover living expenses. A lump sum of six thousand livres for a boy and four thousand for a girl when the time comes to set them up. Generous and fair. Especially since every time death intervenes, as has happened five times already, the remaining children inherit the vacant share.

"No need to worry, Miss." Lisette quieted my unease. "No one is talking of sending you home."

Lisette was right. At the beginning of December, Monsieur Durand escorted me to the same Versailles salon where I had waited in vain two weeks before. This time the summons had come in the evening and the salon was lit with the soft flickering light of candles, too many for me to count. The fireplace crackled with birch logs, sending waves of warmth welcome in the winter chill.

I was wearing the same cream satin robe as on my first visit, which Rose had since trimmed with lace. Lisette had called it most becoming, for the lace set off the line of my throat. As soon as Monsieur Durand left, I checked my reflection in the big mirror. She was right.

"Bonsoir, Mademoiselle!"

Angered at myself for missing the door opening, I turned around, barely managing an awkward curtsy, catching the sight of an imposing figure in a cinnamon-colored velvet coat. His Lordship, the Polish count. I lowered my eyes but not before snatching another look. Head held high; wig dressed, curled and powdered; a white cravat loosely tied around his neck. There was something familiar about him, too, in the oval of his face with its slightly pointed chin, the thick eyebrows over dark blue eyes, a feeling I dismissed as fanciful.

The count extended his hand. I bent over it, brushed his skin with my lips, the way Mademoiselle Dupin had taught us. Not too hard, briefly, with grace.

He continued watching me in silence, and I found his gaze both compelling and unsettling. No one had ever looked at me with such intensity, and no one else's judgment had ever mattered so much.

My own thoughts were a torrent of uncertainty. Was I to address him without being asked to? Was that what he was waiting for? Was he expecting to be thanked for his generosity? Should I sing the "Ode to Gratitude" my music teacher made me practice? My mind gave a little leap at that thought and I even opened my mouth, but then doubt appeared and the words got tangled in my throat.

I raised my fingers to cover my lips.

"Are you hungry?" the count asked.

A simple-enough question but not without its dangers. If I said I was hungry, would he assume Madame Bertrand was not feeding the *élèves* properly? Or that I was a glutton unable to control myself?

But I was hungry, and Mademoiselle Dupin said that if in doubt, always tell the truth.

"Yes, Your Highness," I said, swallowing to steady my voice.

To my relief, the count was not displeased with my answer. He rang the servant bell and, five heartbeats later, the door opened, and a footman wheeled in a small table piled with dishes. Before leaving, he picked up two chairs that were standing against the wall and placed them by the table.

"Let's see what they've sent us," the count said, lifting silver domes one by one. "Pheasant pâté . . . wild boar . . . pork roast, stuffed with prunes, if I'm not mistaken."

He didn't ask my name. Perhaps he knew it already, I thought. But then he hadn't called me Véronique, had he?

"Sit down, Mademoiselle." He interrupted my thoughts, pointing at one of the chairs, and I obeyed.

My unease faded somewhat. Here he was, Count Casimir Boski, who furnished the rooms we lived in, who paid for the dresses we wore, who would assure our future. "Don't you girls ever forget it," Mademoiselle Dupin's voice chimed in my head.

"Eat," the count urged me, the movements of his hands slow and precise as he filled a plate with whatever tempted him and handed it to me. "I won't have you starve."

I ate just the way our governess had taught us. A few morsels, a few sips of the wine the count poured for me from a crystal carafe. Hunger was vulgar. So was impatience, or curiosity recklessly revealed.

"Is everything to your taste?" the count asked after I had swallowed a spoonful of what turned out to be puréed celery.

"Delicious, Your Highness," I said. The gold thread woven into the trim of his jacket shimmered in the candlelight.

He smiled. How white his teeth are, I thought, how beautifully even.

"Then eat some more," he said. "Don't be shy."

I picked up a piece of roasted turkey. The meat was infused with an earthy, garlicky taste.

"Truffles," he told me. "Have you had them before?"

I was still chewing, so I merely shook my head.

"Dogs can be trained to sniff them out," he said. "Or pigs."

Strands of meat had lodged themselves between my front teeth. I sucked at them, but only one gave in.

The count was watching me through all this with an amused smile, fingers drumming on the tabletop. Then he reached for a bowl of cherries from which the pit and the skin had been removed, dipped one in finely powdered sugar and put it in his mouth. When juice began dribbling down his chin, he wiped it with a handkerchief he had retrieved from his breast pocket. I watched as he licked a speck of powdered sugar off his fingers, a gesture that—should I have tried it—would make Mademoiselle Dupin gasp with horror.

The thought made me chuckle.

"What's so amusing, my dear girl?" the count asked.

I shook my head. I couldn't possibly tell him. I was too embarrassed.

"But you must," he said, leaning toward me. "I insist."

I made him insist a bit longer before yielding. To my delight he, too, found the image of our governess gasping in horror at the sight of a licked finger amusing. "Would she slap my hand, do you think?" he mused. "With a rod?"

"Yes, Your Highness," I said. "Mademoiselle is very strict." Then, making sure he was not offended by my words, I added, "She tries to teach us good manners."

"Is she succeeding?"

"Not always."

"Which may be for the better."

There was a pleasing lightness to our conversation now. The count asked me questions, and I answered them with growing confidence. My father was a printer. He died.

"Of what?"

I described the constant coughing, the flushed cheeks, the parched lips, the longing for sleep. How just before Papa died, he asked why someone put such a heavy stone on his chest. How he asked Maman to open the curtains and let in more light.

"Were these his last words?" the count asked.

I nodded. It still hurt me that Papa said nothing just to me. That he didn't have the time to bless us like other fathers did before dying.

"Let in more light," the count repeated, nodding his head. "I'll remember it."

When I mentioned that Maman started selling used clothing after Papa died, the count wanted to know how much a dress could cost. I was just about to explain how it depended on the quality of the dress, who owned it before and how damaged it was, when I remembered Mademoiselle Dupin's warning. There was a difference between knowing and showing off that you know it. No one liked a woman too sure of herself.

"Anything from a few sous to a few louis d'ors," I said cautiously.

"A dress like the one you are wearing, then," the count said. "How much would I get for it?"

"A hundred livres," I said. "I guess," I added to soften the certainty in my voice.

"Oh," he said, pleased, pouring more wine into my glass, then into his own. "This is what I thought, too."

The wine was sweet, heavy. It quickly went to my head, melting the last of my uneasiness away. The walls wavered, and I closed my eyes to stop the whole room from whirling. I would have liked to drink some water, but there was none on the table.

The count stood up, took off his coat and hung it on the back of his chair. His vest of the same cinnamon color had the same embroidered trim, an intricate tracery of flowers and leaves. The stains of sweat on the underarms of his undershirt looked like deep shadows. Sitting himself on the green sofa, wineglass in hand, he asked, "What have they told you about me?"

I recounted the little I knew. His Lordship Count Casimir Boski who came to France from Poland with the queen. Her cousin.

"Second cousin," he said and took another sip of wine. "What else did they tell you?"

I repeated Mademoiselle Dupin's words: generous, kind, our benefactor.

He patted the spot next to him. I lifted myself up, slowly, for my legs felt weak, shaky.

"I'm glad you are here," he said as I sat next to him.

I dropped my eyes.

He called me a crafty little mouse. He sat me on his lap and bounced me up and down, like one did to amuse a baby. His breath smelled sour. Not that much, I told myself, just a bit.

"Kiss me," he said.

Quickly, I brushed my lips on his chin. Prickly, like my father's.

"You call that a kiss?" he asked, quite sharply. His eyes narrowed; a line appeared on his forehead. The words still burned in the air when I muttered some apology. I didn't mean to offend. I was sorry. Tears welled up in my eyes. Tears I tried to stop but failed.

He squeezed my hand and whispered in my ear, "Forgive me, little mouse. I didn't mean to frighten you."

His voice was playful now, kind, and I was awash with gratitude and relief that I hadn't displeased him after all.

"Come," he said then, and I followed him to the adjacent room where a large bed was covered with a deep blue throw.

"Sit down."

I lowered myself to the edge of the bed.

"Take off your shoes."

I slipped my feet out of the red satin mules. Wiggled my toes, already healed but still tender underneath from the shards of china I had so foolishly stepped on.

"Wait here," he said and disappeared behind a silk screen on which two embroidered peacocks stared at each other. I sat on the bed, fighting the growing sense that it was not just the ceiling or the walls but the whole world that was turning around me. From behind the screen came the sound of peeing, a pause, then the last little rush. Something heavy fell to the floor.

I closed my eyes. My throat burned, my heart thumped, my cheeks felt hot. Something momentous was going to happen to me. Could I still run out of this room, down the stairs? Hide?

"You are not afraid of me, are you?" the count asked, as if he could hear my thoughts. He was standing beside me, a white cambric shift opened on his chest. Without a wig his head looked smaller, less imposing, his hair shorn short, gray and thin.

"I won't hurt you," he murmured as his fingers pressed into my back, unhooking my dress, removing the bodice, the skirt. When I was out of my underskirt, he leaned me back, my body flat and exposed. I wanted to curl up and face away but didn't dare.

"Did Mademoiselle Dupin tell you that you were pretty?"

I shook my head.

"She wouldn't, would she?"

A doll he called me then. Sweet. With such silky-smooth skin. How dainty my little fingers were. How lush my eyelashes. Like a puppy's. "You are not afraid of me now, are you?" he asked again, but it was not a real question so I kept silent.

He lay on top of me. The bristle on his face scratched my skin. His tongue tasted of ash.

I closed my eyes.

How can one be present and absent at the same time? Removed from oneself, and pinned down? Suffocating and torn open with each breath?

I recall it happening all at once. His weight on me, crushing my breasts. His hands holding me down, something hard pushing itself between my legs, tearing me inside. I yelped with pain, bracing for more. I held my breath. I prayed for it to end until, after a few more thrusts, he wheezed and puffed and then stiffened. When it was all over and he rolled off me, I lay still, wet from his exertions, my heart pounding. The tear inside me burned.

Beside me the count began to snore.

The pain stopped after a while, and I touched the spot from which the wetness oozed, raised my fingers up to smell them, catching a whiff of blood. I felt numbed, hollowed out, unable to find words for what had happened. Worthless, a piece of flotsam drifting away, taken by the river current, sure I had brought it all upon myself.

But how? I ran through everything I did that evening. Had I been greedy and eaten too much? Or did I speak too freely? Out of turn? Was it my account of Papa's last words? The admission that my father did not bless me before dying?

Whatever I did, it was terribly wrong, and I would be punished for it, just like Francine had been. This is why she didn't want to talk to me, I thought. Out of shame, not spite. I imagined Madame Bertrand and the lackeys bursting into my room at night, dragging me to the carriage in disgrace, and Maman's horrified face when she learned what I had done.

The count was lying on his back, his mouth open, the lump in his throat just like my father's. His Adam's apple. I recalled the priest's words: a bite of the forbidden fruit stuck in the throats of all men, a reminder of Eve's sin, of the lost Paradise. I looked down along his body. The raised nightshirt revealed a mound of dark curls, a flabby piece of flesh, and two sacks of wrinkled skin under it. A tube-shaped piece of blue fabric embroidered with fleurs-de-lys was lying between us, filled with something and smeared with blood.

I sat up. The burning pain inside me returned.

That flaccid flap of skin could not have hurt me, I thought. I looked around me for the object that must have caused the pain, but there was nothing there. Sitting up, I searched for my shift and found it beside the bed, on the floor. The room was no longer spinning, and the dizziness brought by the wine had turned into a ring of pain around my forehead.

The thought that Monsieur Durand might arrive at any moment to take me back to Deer Park terrified me. I couldn't let him see me in the state I was in. At least I must wash my face, wipe the bloody slime from between my legs.

Snatching a burning candle from the night table I got out of bed as noiselessly as I could. Behind the screen I found a chamber pot, an empty porcelain basin and a water jug lying on the side. The carpet was wet. The count's clothes were a crumpled heap. Remembering the handkerchief in his breast pocket, I lifted his coat up. The handkerchief was still there, stained with cherry juice. I spit into it and wiped first my face and then the spot between my legs. The handkerchief was too small though and was soon covered with bloody slime. Then I remembered the dinner. Perhaps there was still some wine left, and I could use it to clean myself?

On tiptoes, holding my breath, I went next door to the salon, only to find that everything had been cleared. Wine, serviettes, the table itself. But then my eyes rested on the window curtain and, quickly, before I could lose my courage, I peed on the floor, dipped the corner of the curtain in my pee and wiped myself with it.

Before returning to bed I went to the window. The moon was shining through a thin layer of clouds. There were gray shadows on it, shaped like distant mountains on some unknown land. Down in the palace gardens, a night watchman was walking briskly, a lantern swinging at his side. It was so quiet that I could hear his boots crunch the gravel.

When I woke up in the morning, my head throbbed with pain, my stomach was curled into a sour ball, my eyes smarted as if sprinkled with sand. The count was gone. Monsieur Durand was standing over me, weighing the blue sack in his hand as if to assure himself I didn't steal anything from there. Then he placed the sack in a small lacquered box and put it in his pocket.

I wondered if he had already found out about the soiled curtain.

"Get up, girl," he said. "Get dressed. Quick, quick. I don't have all day."

He handed me my dress and after I put it on as well as I could on my own, he fastened a few hooks on the back, just enough for it not to slide off when I walked. Instead of the accusations I was still expecting, he simply led me downstairs, to the courtyard, where Michel and Saint-Jean were waiting with the sedan chair, staring at me.

At Deer Park, I ran upstairs in tears. A few moments later Madame Bertrand came in and told me not to be such a fool. Nothing that terrible had happened to me, had it? Lisette would help me clean myself up, she said, and I could stay in my room afterward, but not more than one day, for she did not condone idleness.

"Don't cry, Miss," Lisette said. "It'll all turn for the better, you'll see."

As soon as Lisette had closed the shutters and left, I fell into a drowsy sleep. In the dreams that came, Papa frowned and shook his head. Maman said that I had brought it all upon myself. Adèle turned away from me, saying she wouldn't be back. I asked her why, but she just shook her head and said she was not allowed to tell.

When I woke up, a silver tray with sweetmeats sat on the table, along with a pot of frothy chocolate, still hot to the touch, and a wooden box, its lid carved with fern leaves encircling a lion's head.

I opened it.

Inside, on a black velvet cushion, rested a small gold brooch on which red rubies were set in the shape of a heart.

In the days that followed, my thoughts were a seesaw of elation and shame, confidence and guilt. In the good moments I took the gold brooch from its box and examined the way the rubies were set, each encased in its own golden clasp. In the bad ones I dwelled on my awkwardness, the soiled curtain, the memory of the pain inside me. Remembering Francine's fate, I feared the night's stillness the most, the creaking floors, the steps in the corridor. But when yet another dawn came undisturbed and my lessons resumed, my heart lightened, and I was able to pretend that nothing had changed.

A week later I was summoned again. A dreary evening it was, with wind tearing twigs off the trees, snow settling on the roof of the sedan chair. I almost slipped on the icy cobblestones as I hurried across the courtyard to the entrance where Monsieur Durand was already waiting.

"You've taken your time," he said.

I followed him as fast as I could, upstairs to the green salon, my shoes soaked through, the hem of my new dress saved from getting muddy only because I had hitched it high up. The dress, of golden yellow brocade, had arrived from the palace just that morning. Lisette declared it far superior in quality and cut to the cream satin. It was buttoned in the front, she said, which was very much à la mode at court.

This time there was no supper and no questions. As soon as the count walked in, he caught my hand, squeezed my fingers, put them into his mouth one by one, sucking on their tips. Thinking it a game I played along, pulling my hand, resisting his grip. He bit the tip of my index finger. I flinched, for the bite was stronger than I had anticipated, breaking the skin.

In the bedroom, he kissed me on the mouth and neck before his lips slid down and closed around my right nipple. He sucked on it so hard that I squirmed. Then he pushed himself inside me, thrashed and wheezed, although this time it didn't hurt that much. Again, he fell asleep right away. I lay awake for some time listening to him snore and grind his teeth. I wondered if counts got worms, too. I wondered what the queen was like. And this Poland where the count had his estates. How far away was it? How many days would I have to travel to get there?

In the morning when I woke up, I was not surprised that the count was already gone, and that Monsieur Durand came to take me back to Deer Park.

⚜

How agitated he is today, Madame de Pompadour thinks when Louis arrives for his daily visit. It cannot be the girl, can it? He must have been pleased with her to call her again.

It is not the girl, it's his ministers. His council. His attendants. His court. Inept. Useless. "Nimble fools. Thinking of nothing but themselves."

His eyes flash, his voice tenses. Already in anger or still only in frustration? Both begin in the same place.

Madame de Pompadour waits. The king of France dislikes being asked to explain what he means. The dogs wait, too, heads cocked, tails wagging. Mimi trembles as if she were cold, which she isn't. Dogs can smell what's still hidden, Louis believes, sniff a malady before it begins.

No, he doesn't want claret. Or water. "Our troops are dying," he says. "In Canada and India, Minorca and Senegal, the Mississippi basin and the Caribbean. The English are beating us everywhere."

Crippled veterans who return to France from the colonies poison his subjects with their tales of defeat. Call it "one stinking, bloody shame," Berryer reports. Getting free drinks in every tavern for their trouble.

Louis walks toward his armchair, changes his mind, turns toward the window. Mimi and Inez trot after him out of a dog's sacred duty, which makes no allowances for comfort. No man is that loyal, that worthy of trust; this, too, Louis holds true.

Madame de Pompadour waits.

There is only one solution, Louis continues. To avert the humiliation of defeat, he needs more payers of taxes, more soldiers, more settlers for the lands that have been claimed but are still lying fallow, inviting poachers to take what is not theirs. Impossible, Sire, say his ministers—each one more useless than the next. The population of France, they all tell him, is plummeting. Army units report shortages of able-bodied recruits. Ships leave for New France half empty.

Why, he asks, and they rattle off reasons like wound-up automata. Protestants are still fleeing the kingdom, Sire. Catholic priests are celibate. Convents are full of women who should've married and borne children. Servants are not allowed to marry while in service. French noblewomen have been spoiled by luxury, forgetting that it is their sacred duty to produce and raise royal subjects.

"Why do I even let them speak, Jeanne? You are a clever woman. Tell me!"

A nod of her head is all Louis requires, a soft murmur of agreement.

And—if more is needed—a few well-tried words: Because you have always been far too modest. Too ready to let lesser minds command attention. Too fair-minded. Too careful not to hurt.

"You know what else they say, Jeanne?" Louis asks.

Madame de Pompadour shakes her head.

"Sire, too many infants die."

A flagrant waste, they say, an abomination. When he asks what can be done about it, they stutter, twitch, wriggle like insects pinned onto a corkboard. It is God's will, or the laws of nature, or the abominable morals of the lower classes that destroy the fabric of the nation. He wouldn't be surprised if they told him Paris deserved an earthquake greater than the one in Lisbon. To teach France a lesson that cannot be easily forgotten.

Louis sinks into his armchair now, unbuttons his jacket. How well warm cinnamon brown becomes him. Especially with the golden trim. And the cordon bleu across his chest. But why this flinch when he stretches his right leg? At the last hunt, he had turned it too much and too quickly. Is it still swollen? It must be, though not bad enough to limp.

The bottle of claret is still waiting on a side table, beside two crystal glasses. She pours, more for him, less for her.

Louis takes the glass from her hands. Holds it to the light, admires the ruby red of it.

"Such are my council meetings, Jeanne. Such is all the advice I get."

This may sound like a complaint, but it is more than that. Louis wants her to help him put his ministers in place, prove them wrong. Which she will help him do. Just as she always does.

A sweet moment, such a request, best cherished in silence. She knows how it irks him when Lebel assumes to know his thoughts. Is the king of France that transparent? Louis has asked many a time. That predictable?

This is why she won't tell him what she will do.

"Be charitable, dearest," she whispers in his ear. "Take pity on us, mere mortals. We can never be like you, can we? All we can do is try."

⋯⋞⋗⋯

Evening after evening the word came to get ready, the lackeys carried me to the palace, I climbed the steep steps to the apartment and waited for the count. The messy part of my visit, which was how I thought of it then, no longer hurt and when it was over the count did not leave.

I could delight him, I discovered, with the most ordinary stories. Madame Bertrand teaching Lisette how to wash lace: "No rubbing, girl, no rubbing. What's so hard to remember about that?" And I would roll my eyes or pout like a fish out of water, just as Lisette did. Or I would rise from the bed to show him the new dance steps Maestro had begun teaching us, the way little Claire tripped over her own feet, making Amélie giggle.

I told him how well-dressed ladies would feign interest in Maman's dresses for sale, only to steal a fichu or a handkerchief. Or that growing chicory indoors turned its leaves white and delicate, and doubled its price. Or how a locksmith advertised his wares by offering a reward to anyone who could pick his master lock.

"Has anyone succeeded?"

"Once."

"How?"

"With a skeleton key."

"How much would I have to pay for one of his locks?"

"Twenty sous, at the most. But I could haggle for you and it wouldn't cost more than twelve."

"Would you?"

How light his laughter, I thought, how gleeful the flicker in his eyes!

He told me stories, too.

When he was younger, he had sometimes been taken out into Paris for a night in the taverns, or a boat ride down the Seine. There were mishaps. Once, he lost money on a wager that gooseberries had perfectly smooth skins. How could he have known that the ones served at the palace had been shaved?

"You would've known that, wouldn't you?" he asked, wistfully, and pinched my cheek.

One evening he told me how he preferred animals to people on account of their absolute, uncalculated loyalty. He had a rooster once who, as soon as it spotted him, would run up to him and give him a look of utter devotion.

A magnificent bird, with black and yellow feathers and a red crown. That rooster died of old age right here, in this room, he said, pointing at a spot near the bed. Until the last breath it searched for the sight of its master's face.

Outside, the wind howled and ice pellets clattered on the windowpanes. I sought his hand and slipped mine underneath. He squeezed it.

"You please me, little mouse," he said. He liked how quiet I was. How unassuming. So unlike others. "Promise me not to change."

My heart melted with gratitude.

"I promise."

He closed his eyes, and I curled beside him and followed him into sleep.

The dozen or so courtiers are in attendance, by private invitation only, a selection made easier for the queen and the royal daughters have already moved to Fontainebleau for the winter.

Like a circus magician's trick, Madame de Pompadour thinks, though the midwife has little magic flair to her. The whispers around her confirm this judgment. The courtiers have already taken a scrupulous tally of the flat shoes, the mud-brown dress, well padded and finished with simple trim. Not unlike the queen with her flummeries, which should've annoyed Louis. Though it hasn't, for he is leaning forward with excitement, an eager boy awaiting a promised treat.

"Most grateful, Your Majesty . . . the chance to demonstrate what I intend . . . not all sovereigns are this enlightened . . . so passionate and knowledgeable about the medical arts."

Du Coudray should move on, for Louis gets impatient with expressions of gratitude. The words are all too similar, too fleeting, threadbare. Though he might like being called "knowledgeable about the medical arts." And the murmur of approval that travels through the audience.

The midwife bows, awaiting permission to start.

Louis nods.

"I'm not a courtier, Your Majesty," du Coudray begins. "So please forgive me if I sound too forthright. A midwife has little time for niceties. We witness too many misfortunes."

She moves about swiftly, laying out the instruments and jars on a tray, explaining each of them in turn. The hollow tube is for relieving incontinence, opening the neck of the bladder. The jars contain ointments for every occasion. To stimulate or soothe, to lubricate her hands when she has to put them inside the birth canal. When difficulties arise. When the baby has to be turned or pulled down.

Behind Madame de Pompadour, the marquise de Guerigny giggles at something the duc de Richelieu is whispering in her ear. She arrived at the last possible moment, breathless, flushed, glowing, so that everyone would know what she had been doing. Who with is another question. Lebel will provide the answer soon enough, if Louis shows the slightest interest.

De Guerigny is a pretty woman. Cheerful, warm, uncomplicated. The dusty pink that Madame de Pompadour has favored for some time and that is now the rage at Versailles brightens her complexion. Whoever is bedding her these days is a lucky man. Those are Louis's words, making de Pompadour imagine the cheerful marquise's fingers unbuttoning Louis's vest, sliding into his breeches, the rustle of her silks dropping to the floor.

Danger or only another passing distraction?

From the corner of her eye she spots Lebel by the door, ramrod straight, observing the room. Cutting a fine if bony figure in his purple suit. Her waiting maid has found out that the red fish for his garden pond cost two hundred louis d'ors. Perhaps she should accept his offering of a pair.

"And now, Your Majesty, we are ready for *la malade*." Du Coudray's voice is confident, even forceful as she lifts the sheet and steps back, pointing not at the mannequin of a woman in labor that everyone expected but at a truncated, bloated belly and legs chopped off at mid-thigh. The whole thing pink and a bit bulky, like an overstuffed pillow.

Louis leans backward, the sheen of disappointment on his face visible to everyone.

"Clever, don't you think?" Madame de Pompadour whispers, brushing the top of his gloved hand. "To concentrate on what is of the essence? Isn't that what you always remind us to do?"

Louis lifts his hands. His applause may be muted, but it is loud enough to make the courtiers take note. There is a murmur of approval. A woman gasps.

"A midwife in training," Madame du Coudray says in a voice accustomed to lecturing, "has to spend months at my side before I can trust her beyond the preliminary examination. With this Machine-Mother, I can let her practice delivery right away. Make her mistakes and learn from them."

It's all a question of time, she explains. Time that, she has been given to understand, France doesn't have. For even now, at this very moment, in the provinces, unskilled midwives wreak their damage. Mothers die. Or they live in constant pain as their mishandled insides lapse and loosen.

Infants, mangled during labor, also die. Or end up with withered limbs, a burden to their families. Infants who could have grown to be productive farmers or able-bodied soldiers. Or happy mothers of His Majesty's many more subjects.

"They say I have a mission, Sire, and I do. I want healthy babies, delivered by expert hands. Not just in Paris where competent midwives abound, but in small towns and in remote villages. I want well-trained midwives in every corner of France. I want them to know how to foresee trouble. How to prevent it if they can. And enough to call a surgeon if they cannot.

"These midwives-to-be do not live in Paris. And most of them cannot come to Paris to become an apprentice or get their instruction at the Hôtel-Dieu. They have families they cannot leave, parents, husbands, children under their care. This is why I want to go to them with my Machine, Sire. Teach them how to deliver healthy babies. Train them during the little time they can spare."

Louis listens, his eyes glued to the bloated belly of the truncated Machine. Oblivious to the marquise de Guerigny, who has pushed her way to the front to be in his field of vision, her smooth face uplifted, eyes wide, tongue lingering over her lower lip.

Her Machine, du Coudray explains further, withstands all mistakes of craft and errors of judgment. It teaches without killing or maiming, and it teaches fast. What takes an apprentice midwife three years can be learned in three months. How? This is what she intends to demonstrate right now.

Louis cranes his neck to see better.

The midwife rolls up her sleeves and is just about to sit on a low stool beside the Machine when—Madame de Pompadour will never know if the gesture was planned and thus brilliantly contrived or if it was utterly spontaneous and therefore just brilliant—she instead turns to the king of France and asks, "Would Your Majesty grant me the honor of delivering this baby himself?"

Madame de Pompadour registers this moment in all its details, for Louis will want to talk about it for a long time. The dead silence at first. The gasps of disapproval at such audacity, including Marquise de Guerigny's. The midwife boldly moving to the side, making room for her king to take over. Waiting.

Louis stands up, steps toward the Machine before some eager fool can point out the inappropriateness of it. Or tries to forbid it on some ridiculous grounds: Surely, Sire . . . a breach of etiquette, Sire.

Du Coudray smiles, a teacher prompting her star pupil. "Here, Your Majesty. Please, take a seat on this stool," she says. "Remove your gloves, please. Follow my example."

Louis peels off his gloves, hands them to a page. Makes a tight fist and then stretches his fingers wide, just like the midwife is demonstrating. A good habit, she assures him, to make hands more responsive. More alert.

The Machine, du Coudray continues, is accurate to the smallest anatomical detail. The pelvis, the womb, its opening, its ligaments, the conduit called the vagina, the bladder and rectum intestine. The placenta with its membranes and the waters that they contain. The umbilical cord composed of its two arteries and of the vein. She demonstrates how by leaving one half of the cord withered up and the other inflated, she can imitate two conditions: the cord of a dead child and that of a live one.

But for now, Sire, labor is still far away.

Du Coudray opens one of her jars and instructs her royal apprentice to grease his hands. This is in case he has to slide them inside the birth canal without causing damage.

"Does Your Majesty need help?"

Louis shakes his head. He can grease his own hands.

First His Majesty must feel the cloth belly, press it with his palms, assess the position of the child. Amazing, our palms and fingers. So much can be known by touch alone.

Placing his hands on the cloth belly, Louis tries to determine the shape inside, but—as he will confess afterward—it is all one bumpy mass.

"Feel for the bones, Sire, the roundness of the skull," the midwife prompts. "And press harder."

He does press harder, and the cloth belly must suddenly relent, for Louis smiles. "I can feel it," he says. "A long bone. Then a bend. Elbow or knee? The skull?"

A moment later he is sure. This baby's head is down, its legs are up.

"Is it thus?" he asks, and when Madame du Coudray confirms he beams. "This is good," he says. "This is how it should be. The baby is not breech." Out of all his children, only Louise was breech. Came feet first, the surgeon said, and almost killed her mother.

"Excellent, Your Majesty. Not many would've known it."

A murmur of approval circles the room.

"Let's speed the passage of time," du Coudray continues. "We have spent hours at *la malade*'s bedside, observing the contractions, measuring the time between them. This is what happens next."

As the midwife busies herself with tubes, the Machine's birth passage widens. A squirting of watery fluid follows, turns red. Then something emerges from inside, the cloth baby's head.

"Is Your Majesty ready?"

As he nods, the midwife bends forward to press some invisible lever. For a moment nothing happens, but then, in one big swish, the baby comes out and Louis catches it in his hands.

"His Majesty the King of France," du Coudray announces, "has just delivered a healthy girl!"

The courtiers are pushing closer. The cloth child grins at them with open mouth. Ugly, but then most newborns are. What matters, the midwife continues, is very basic: ten fingers, ten toes, two eyes, a nose, all in place. Nothing damaged. A child who has every chance to grow up.

Heeding the midwife's prodding, Louis cuts the cord and hands the cloth baby back to her. Then he pulls the cord's end to relieve the Machine-Mother of the placenta inside.

The cloth baby is swathed in a warm towel and put aside. Du Coudray gives Louis another towel to wipe his hands.

A long, thunderous round of applause erupts. When it ends, the courtiers are outdoing each other with praise. "What talent, Sire . . . What poise . . . extraordinary . . . Only the feeble-minded deny that progress is possible."

"How splendid you were, dearest," Madame de Pompadour says. "How precise every gesture you made. How timely."

Du Coudray has joined in the applause. His Majesty's natural ability, she says, is God's gift that France should give thanks for. The court ladies throng about the Machine. Ask to touch the cloth baby, move its joints into different positions, tickle its slightly pointed ears. Does du Coudray have good remedies for the morning sickness? they ask. Where can they send for her salves? Does she take patients? No? Would she recommend a good midwife in Paris? Someone she would trust with her own daughter?

Louis regrets that the demonstration is over so soon. Later he will tell Madame de Pompadour how he would have liked to be trusted with a more complex delivery. Twins, for instance. Like his first-born daughters. It would satisfy him to find out what the surgeon did when Marie was in labor with them. Get answers to the questions his wife always dismissed with "What God has intended."

He will also say that this du Coudray woman, well into her midlife, is smarter than the philosophes or those literary people she, Jeanne, pushes on him all the time. Men who drown him with their fancy words, muddle every simple thought with their objections. Let them, he will tell her, come up with anything more useful and good than the Machine.

How right you are, she will tell him, declaring him in possession of a third eye, in the middle of his forehead, invisible but always at work. Allowing him to see more than others.

Before departing from Versailles, Madame du Coudray presents her most humble request to His Majesty Louis XV, the king of France and Navarre.

Encouraged by her modest success in the provinces, she is asking for royal patronage. Patronage that would allow her to travel all over France with her

Machine, teaching the course she has designed herself, making capable village girls into skilled midwives, expunging superstition and ignorance. *Having practiced all possible emergencies on the Machine*, she has written, *they will be capable of either averting mischief themselves or seeking assistance if they encounter problems beyond their skills. No Frenchwoman should be maimed by childbirth. No French baby should die because of a midwife's ignorance.*

What would it take to make this happen? Louis wonders. An official letter naming Madame du Coudray the king's midwife? A pension? How much should I grant her?

"What do you think, Jeanne?"

What Louis really wants to know is who is saying what at court. What clusters of opposition are already forming. "Beware a mission that sounds too simple, Sire," the duc de Richelieu has already whispered in his ear.

Richelieu fears a backlash from the provincial intendents and master surgeons on whom du Coudray—with her royal backing—will be unleashed. People far less well disposed to innovations than the king of France is, far more invested in their own prestige.

"A mission is not a sin," Madame de Pompadour asks. "Is it?"

"No. You are right."

A few days later, just before leaving for Fontainebleau, the king of France announces his decision. He wishes the council to work out the royal brevet of patronage and protection for *La Demoiselle du Coudray sage-femme*. In recognition of her fine practice of midwifery, her Machine, her tireless and exemplary work. In support of her nationwide teaching mission. He wants an army of midwives working for him and France, delivering healthy babies.

What is he prepared to offer?

Eight thousand livres per year.

They will all grumble, won't they, he tells Madame de Pompadour with visible delight. Consider themselves slighted. A midwife paid as much as a general?

Generals spill blood, he will tell them. This woman and her pupils make sure we have healthy soldiers when France needs them.

Isn't that a mission worthy of royal support?

1756

THE ALMANAC for the Year of Our Lord Christ 1756 is open to a warning: *Blood and humors being now in motion, we must be careful to avoid eating salt, strong or stale meats. Whey is very good for hot stomachs, as wormwood wine is for cold. Fat and phlegmatic people should avoid excess of liquors of any kind.*

"Did you put this here, Nicole?" Madame de Pompadour asks her maid.

Madame de Pompadour considers almanacs to be written by those who cannot write for those who cannot read, a phrase that always makes Louis smile. Her maid, however, being permanently immune to reason, is a great believer in predictions of all sorts. Asked how the weather can be forecasted for every day of the year ahead, including quakes, floods, and droughts, Nicole replies, "How does this differ from predicting an eclipse, Madame?" Making Louis snort: "Have you not heard of the rotations of the moon and the sun, woman? The celestial sphere?"

"I'm only concerned about Madame's health," du Hausset defends herself now. "Dr. Quesnay will surely know if Madame's stomach is cold or hot."

She is always concerned, her maid, about everything. She even crosses herself before the shortest of carriage rides, pretending she is only adjusting her frills. Forehead, chest, right arm, left arm.

She means well, though, unlike so many.

Servants, courtiers! Sycophants all, but if they ever see a chance they will turn around and bite you, Louis warned her when he brought her to Versailles. When she, still only Madame d'Étiolles née Jeanne Poisson, her heart overflowing with love, believed she could conquer all malice. Eleven years ago now, but she has not forgotten a word of what he told her then.

Listen to them, dearest: Your Majesty is generous, benevolent. We beseech

Your Majesty. We beg you to consider . . . grant . . . bestow. Look at this twisted, malicious smile, note that indignation. Read what they write about me: *The king is a coward, a man without heart or brains, a man of evil nature, inflicting suffering when he sees the chance.*

Hypocrites all, Louis had told her, delighting in stripping him of any scrap of joy. You may look but only through this window; walk but only along these paths; eat but only of these dishes. They might as well have chained him to the wall. How does the king of France differ from a prisoner at the Bastille, Jeanne? he asked. Tell me, how!

Nicole flutters around the marquise, covering her legs with a woolen throw, adjusting the cushion under her feet. Obvious signs that her maid has something unpleasant to impart.

"Speak, Nicole. Is it the girl? Does she not like the dress I sent?"

The dress of golden yellow brocade is a bit too stiff at the waist, but the girl would not know it, would she?

"Madame has been exceedingly generous. Far too generous, if I may be permitted to say."

In addition to the dress, she has also sent silk underclothes and her own hairdresser with instructions to hold those unruly locks in place. "Luxuriant but not rampant" is the desired effect. More pomade, perhaps?

"Summoned again, Madame, fourth time this week alone," Nicole interrupts these thoughts. "Eleven in December. Bragging about the earrings His Majesty gave her. Demanding to be waited upon hand and foot. Too tired in the morning to come down for breakfast! Also, she is getting curious."

According to Madame Bertrand the girl is asking about His Lordship's estates in Poland far too often. How big are they? How many days does it take to reach them? Could Mademoiselle Dupin show her on a map where Poland is?

"Is that all?"

"She asked if the queen ever visited him there."

"What did they tell her?"

"That the queen cannot just pack up and go wherever she wants. That she has duties in France."

"And what did the girl say to that?"

"She was quite relieved. Bertrand thinks she may be making rather grand plans, though."

"Bertrand also thinks heaps of silk braid make her look distinguished."

"That is true, Madame," Nicole says, retreating to her nook. Defeated or vindicated, it is hard to say.

The girl is harmless, Lebel has said. Light-headed with the attention she is getting, true, but what "little bird" wouldn't be in her place?

Lebel is also convinced that the girl will keep believing the story of the Polish count, though he is not complacent about it. For when a girl is summoned that often, Deer Park servants begin making their own calculations. Whisper in her ear or not? "This is why," Lebel says, "I always keep an eye on the servants, Madame."

Lebel says what he wishes or needs to say, but Madame de Pompadour knows that *harmless*, in the king's bedroom, can be a powerful weapon by itself.

The following day Madame de Pompadour orders the Deer Park governess to announce an addition to the *élèves'* daily roster. Two hours, daily, devoted to embroidery and needlepoint. Not just samplers but proper patterns. She will send embroidery hoops and thread. Silent time, it will be, all conversations forbidden. No fidgeting, no breaks, for the *élèves* need to learn the virtue of patience and forbearance. "All *élèves*, no exceptions," she stresses, expecting the girl will ask to be excused.

And no excessive praise, either, even if they do well.

No *élève* needs to have her head turned even more.

I was no longer just one of the *élèves*. I, too, could have whims and wishes.

Madame Bertrand said I could stay in my room whenever I wanted. Mademoiselle Dupin praised me at the slightest pretext, Claire and Amélie gushed over the gifts I had received. Claire said that the gold bracelet with diamonds clustered like rosebuds made my wrist look even more dainty. Amélie, whose father had once worked for a jeweler, asked if I knew how much the pair of ruby earrings the count had just sent me was worth. When I said I didn't, she assured me it was at least two hundred livres or maybe even more.

Lisette made a big fuss over the silk underclothes that had arrived wrapped in tulle and the fact that a palace hairdresser was now dressing my hair. She required no bribes to keep me company. She made hot chocolate for me to drink, mixing it with eggs and sprinkling it with ground cinnamon and cloves. She told me that Claire had asked to have her hair pinned up just like mine and Amélie was a spoiled brat who deserved a good spanking. Nothing was to her taste, she said. Eggs were too runny. Bread not fresh enough. There was never enough sugar in the sugar bowl.

"Not like you, Miss," she said. "You have the makings of a real lady. Everyone says so."

Shameless flattery it was, but oh, how welcome!

Madame Bertrand came by every morning when I was being dressed. She mostly talked about her gout or scolded the maids for the smallest negligence—Rose unable to find my new garters, Lisette tightening my corset too tight—but she never took her eyes off me.

"Let me see," she said one such morning when I flinched at Lisette's touch. Reluctantly, I bared my right breast. It was sore to the touch, the nipple reddened, oozing with pus.

Madame sent Lisette for her soothing cream. It was on her dresser, she said, in a jar with a silver lid.

When the door shut behind Lisette, Madame Bertrand turned to me. She had to confess, she said, that her early misgivings about me had been wrong. I had proven to be smarter than she thought. I minded her warnings. I got my reward. "Just don't let it go to your head," she said.

How old and ugly she is, I remember thinking, wrinkles gathering around her mouth, the black mole on her chin. How could I have ever thought her scary?

From the folds of her dress Madame Bertrand fished out a dark brown bottle with *Nerve Tonic* written on the label. Best for soothing all aches, she said, taking a long sip and then offering it to me.

"Go on, girl," she said. "I won't ask twice."

The tonic was wormwood bitter and made me cough, but I swallowed a mouthful. It filled my stomach with lovely warmth.

I didn't quite understand what Madame Bertrand meant by me being smarter than she thought, but her words brought a ripple of pleasure, a heady confirmation of my own importance. So heady that I didn't mind being reminded not to speak about the count to anyone. Too many gossipers around with their ears to the walls, Madame said. The queen would be scandalized if she ever heard about her cousin's liking for a simple girl like me. She would send him back to Poland, and I would never see him again.

"Second cousin," I said.

"Second cousin," she agreed.

"I could never do anything to harm His Lordship," I said.

Madame Bertrand looked pleased at these words. Clearly, I was someone she could confide in. About the servants, for instance. The unreasonable expectations they had. Take Lisette, Madame continued, after another sip of her tonic. Used to be so hardworking, so diligent, but look at her now. Leaving ashes unswept by the grate three times in a row. Misplacing shifts, scorching a bonnet with too hot an iron. "Wouldn't you think that forty livres is a good wage for a maid-of-all-work?"

I nodded, too eagerly, too fast. I leaned forward to hear better.

"Did Lisette ever tell you why she had to leave Buc? No? There was that smithy boy who took liberties and then laughed in her face. I'm not saying it was solely her fault but still. Thinking ahead is not the poor girl's greatest asset."

She offered me another sip of tonic. It seemed much less bitter now, and even more soothing.

I might not know it yet, Madame Bertrand continued in a low voice, but running a house was like commanding a battlefield. One day, though, I would find out. Sooner maybe than I thought.

She paused, as if worried she had gone too far, said too much. Or as if she was waiting for me to ask whose house it would be. The count's? Who would I be there? A servant or a mistress?

I didn't ask. I didn't want to think about the future then. It was easier to let myself dream.

"What took you so long?" Madame Bertrand asked when Lisette entered, a jar of cream in hand.

Lisette's jaw tightened. Not much, but enough for me to see. "I was as fast as I could be, Madame," she said. "It was not on the dresser. I had to—"

"Never mind now. Give it to me."

Madame Bertrand opened the jar. The cream with which she smothered my nipple gave off a sweet smell of beeswax. Then she covered my nipple with a folded piece of gauze.

"There," Madame Bertrand said, turning her face to me. "It'll heal before you know it."

Madame de Pompadour enters the Deer Park salon, a black mask covering the upper half of her face. Du Hausset walks just behind her, or rather waddles, for her maid is getting stouter. Too many cream puffs, though the woman will never admit it. Curious how blind we can be to our own shortcomings.

The governess, face flushed, rises abruptly and curtsies, motioning to the *élèves* to follow her example, which they do, all three of them, gracefully enough. One of the maids, clearly quicker on her feet than the others, moves an armchair closer to the blazing fireplace. Without being told to, the tiniest of miracles, but still.

Most welcome, these waves of soothing warmth, for the carriage ride to Deer Park has left a chill in her bones, in spite of quilted petticoats, furs and a foot warmer. No, I'm not ailing, she told Nicole, who insisted on touching her lips with carmine to hide the purple tint. It's this vicious cold. Thank the Lord Almighty, January is almost over.

"Madame la marquise wishes you to continue with what you are doing," Nicole announces, just as she has been instructed. "Pretend that Madame la marquise is not here."

Véronique Roux, Nicole's eyes signal, is the one on the right.

The *élèves* pick up their embroidery hoops.

The Roux girl pushes the needle through canvas, tugging at the green thread of the stem she is working on. Not as pretty as the other two, Madame de Pompadour decides, her nose too narrow, cheeks a tad too full. Claire, whom Madame de Pompadour has seen once before, strikes her as prettier, especially with that lovely fuzz over her upper lip. The new girl, too, looks quite fetching, with what Lebel calls "that gypsy flair His Majesty sometimes favors."

The governess hovers nervously over her charges, admonishing them to sit straighter, hold the hoops precisely the way she has taught them. "I've been working so hard on deportment, Madame," she says. "But how does one undo years of neglect?"

Three heads bend lower over the hoops, three necks quiver. The flowers of France are the patterns they are working on. Claire on a daisy, Amélie with that gypsy flair on a forget-me-not, the Roux girl on an iris. With each movement of the needle, the stem on the hoop thickens, takes on flesh.

"Stand up, Mademoiselle Roux," Madame de Pompadour orders, interrupting this display of concentration. "I want to take a look at you."

Claire and Amélie stiffen. The Roux girl lifts herself from her chair, puts her hoop down.

"Take a few steps to your right . . . now to your left."

The girl does as she is told. No hesitation in her movements, but the glide in her steps is still not smooth enough. She is not the first one to discover how hard it is to give an illusion of floating.

"Do you have sisters, Mademoiselle Roux?"

"I had a sister. She died."

"How old was she?"

"Almost ten."

"What was her name?"

The girl hesitates, as if asked to reveal a precious secret. His Majesty sometimes confides in her, Lebel said. The other day he told her about that rooster he used to keep.

"Answer Madame la marquise, Véronique," the governess admonishes her. "No need to be bashful."

"Adèle," the girl says, fixing her eyes on the hem of her dress, pale blue, trimmed with lace. One more generous gift, Mademoiselle Dupin could have reminded her, from Madame la marquise.

Never mind Adèle Roux. Never mind the dress.

"Do you do your utmost to fulfill your governess's expectations?"

"I try to."

"Which of the lessons do you find most agreeable?"

"Music and recitations."

"Recite something for me, then."

The girl takes a deep breath and begins.

> *Beware how you deride*
> *The exiles from life's sunny side:*
> *To you is little known*
> *How soon their case may be your own.*

Her voice is smooth, strong, with a natural flow. She is a very good dancer, Lebel has said. The music teacher praises her harp playing, too.

The girl curtsies and bows her head. Expecting applause?

One look in Nicole's direction suffices.

"Madame la marquise is leaving . . . No, Madame la marquise won't take refreshments with the *élèves* this time. No, reading, too, must be postponed to the next time."

"But of course, Madame," the flustered governess stammers, as if anyone has asked her permission. She wants nothing else but to ensure Madame la marquise that she is doing her best. That the *élèves* are worthy of Madame's continuing goodwill. Her generous protection.

As Mademoiselle Dupin's voice rings in the air, Madame de Pompadour glides out of the room in a perfect rendition of the steps the *élèves* are still learning to master.

He began to take me out into other rooms of the palace with him. First to a rather small kitchen where he made an omelet and brewed coffee for us, pleased when I said this was the best supper I'd ever had. Then he took me to a room where he kept his most cherished treasures: a shiny brass instrument he said could always tell him where he was at sea, a giant clock that tracked not just hours but days of the week and phases of the moon.

One evening the count called for a sedan chair and took me to what resembled a little château somewhere deep in the Versailles gardens. As it had just begun to snow, palace lackeys shielded us with umbrellas as we got in and out of the chair and walked toward the door, which opened as if by itself to let us inside.

"Just look at them," the count said, pointing at the row of big iron cages where eagles, buzzards, goshawks screeched and flapped their wings. A raven bigger than the ones I had seen in the fields groomed its shiny black feathers.

The attendants trotted toward us, silent and attentive. One carried a thick leather glove, another a bucket covered with a lid. Hawks and falcons, the count told me, were far better hunters than dogs. They had eyes capable of spotting the slightest rustle on the ground.

Putting the leather glove on his left hand, he opened one of the cages and retrieved a falcon with bells tied to its feet, bells that clunked and pealed with every move.

The falcon, Scratcher, perched on the glove, awaiting its treat.

"Watch," the count said.

The bucket was filled with mice scrambling over one another. The attendant picked them up by their tails and threw them into the air. The mice squealed and thrashed for a brief moment before Scratcher caught them and tore them to bloodied shreds.

My stomach rose, a sour taste filled my throat. I was glad the count did not look at me.

"Now, to my favorite," he said, offering another bird, a hawk, his gloved hand as if it were a lady he was asking to a dance.

It was a lady. Her name was Merline. Snakelike, I thought, the way she flicked her head from side to side.

"Isn't she beautiful?" the count asked, pointing out Merline's long tail shaped for sharp turns through the woods and the spotted feathers that would keep her invisible to her prey until it was too late.

"Yes," I said.

"I'm not a falconer, but I'm a hunter," he said. "I appreciate a clean kill."

I didn't quite know what he meant, but I nodded.

"Here," he said, handing me a smaller leather glove. "Put this on."

When I did, he sat the bird on my hand. Merline tightened her grip. If it weren't for the protection of the leather, the talons would have pierced my skin and rounded themselves around my bloodied bones. Every time a mouse squeaked with fear, the feet contracted and the force of them was crushing, even through the leather.

The killing grip, the count called it. A response to any cry of weakness or pain.

It frightened me, the world shaped according to a simple pattern. The weak and hurt were there to be hunted down and killed.

I steeled myself for another round of mice tossed into the air, but the count waved the attendant away. Mice were skin, bones and fur, he said. Merline preferred something far more substantial.

One more flick of his fingers and another attendant approached with slices of meat arranged on a tray. Picking them up one by one the count let Merline tear at her treat with her beak. The meal finished, she fluffed up her feathers and then shook them back into place.

"It's a sign of pleasure," the count said, answering the question in my eyes.

The wind has been howling all night, breaking tree branches and blowing snow. The morning is cold, with gray clouds scudding across the sky. Outside, in the palace courtyard, horses tread and nicker. A man shouts something, another answers with a sharp whistle.

This is what Lebel thinks about as he hovers over his master, handing him a warmed dressing gown, guiding his feet into his silk slippers.

Trouble in paradise begins with a stumble. One brings forth another, none significant by itself. What truly matters are the questions these mistakes provoke. The questions of why. Take Adam, Eve and the apple. Why did Eve eat the forbidden fruit? Just because it pleased her? Or did she really want to possess the knowledge of good and evil? Or did she do it out of sheer defiance? Or out of a foolish belief that she could not do anything wrong? Or because someone put her up to it? Someone who was playing another game altogether? Someone who knows what the real stakes have been all along?

"A perfect morning for a hunt," his royal master says, interrupting these thoughts. Louis thinks of deer spooked by the wind, hungry, heading for the feeding stands, offering the best shots. He has never forgotten the first big buck he ever killed, on just such a winter morning.

Louis has always been a creature of habit, an actor who doesn't alter his lines, so Lebel braces himself for the old, familiar shapes of the story he knows will follow. The snow-covered ground muffling the hunter's steps, the grove of trees dusted with white, the ten-pointer raising its head. The thickness of winter fur. The perfect shot. The hounds licking at blood-soaked slush.

"Alas, Lebel, today duties call."

Is this annoyance or just a passing regret? With Louis, nothing is ever certain.

"Perhaps tomorrow, Sire."

"Perhaps."

Lebel pounces on some invisible speck on the royal shoulders, adjusts the curls of the royal wig. "About the girl, Sire," he says in almost a whisper.

The king gives him a warning look that means "I don't want to hear it, Lebel," but then, at the same time, he does. He always does.

"It's the girl's mother, Sire," Lebel continues. A few months ago, the woman couldn't get rid of her daughter fast enough. Counting up her money, only to recall yet another pressing debt, just as he has settled the previous one. With a butcher, candlemaker, fishmonger.

The king's lips narrow into a grimace of impatience. Not a welcome sign.

"Now, I'm hearing, she is already borrowing money against what she has called her daughter's vastly improved prospects. Eight hundred livres, Sire. Only the other day . . . from a tobacconist . . . at four percent."

"Stop this slithering, Lebel. To the point."

"Greed runs in the blood, Sire. These ruby earrings you told me to give the girl, Sire. She has been heard asking how much she could get for them."

The royal lips curl. The royal hand pulls at the cuffed lace of the royal sleeve.

"I know what you are thinking, Sire. That Lebel is always suspicious, always sniffing for deceit. But I'm forced to mention this, Sire, since you only see goodness and innocence around you. While others, far less generous and kindhearted, perceive nothing but their own gain."

It was Madame Bertrand who noticed the bloodstain on my shift.

"Didn't you feel anything, Véronique?" she asked, drawing air through her teeth.

I shook my head. I had felt cramps at the bottom of my belly when I awoke, but I thought it was because I drank two full cups of chocolate the day before. Only now I recalled Maman's bloodied rags soaking in a bucket, the woman's curse.

"Natural purge," Madame Bertrand said, called me a little fool and sent Lisette for fresh linen and *charpies*. Then she showed me how to secure the padding between my legs with a belt, helped me change my soiled shift and get back into bed. I was to stay away from chocolate and coffee. Lisette would bring me flaxseed tea to drink and a hot-water compress to ease the pain.

I heard them in the hall afterward, Madame Bertrand angry, calling Lisette blind. "How could you not see it coming? What if she showed up at the palace like that?" Lisette apologized profusely and vowed to be more vigilant in the future.

I stayed in bed all day. Outside, the wind played with the bare branches of the tree. Birds huddled on them, sparrows, small and gray. The night watchman put a tray there with seeds that they pecked at during the day, and a piece of lard for the tits.

That evening I heard Madame Bertrand call Michel to get the sedan chair ready. Did the count send for me in spite of my "natural purge" after all? The thought that I was not ready, that I would keep the count waiting for me, made me jump out of bed. I would have to dress in a hurry. There would be no time to have my hair done.

Expecting Lisette to come running, I sat at the dressing table and picked up a comb. I heard her steps, passing by my door. I called for her, but she didn't answer. A moment later I heard her enter Amélie's room.

How hard the memory of this moment, how heavy still, tinged with injustice, how stinging the pain.

I staggered back to bed, trembling with hurt and anger as I contemplated Madame Bertrand's betrayal. For it was all her doing, I thought, deriding myself for believing she had taken me into her confidence because she cared about me while all she really wanted was to get me out of Deer Park. Francine had been right to think her a viper and a schemer.

I cried until I had no more tears left. Then I imagined that the count would send Amélie back and that Madame Bertrand would be taught her lesson. The courtyard, however, remained empty and silent. Only a stray cat came by, scratched its paws against the bark of the tree and meowed until Rose opened the window and screamed at it to go away.

But hope is hard to kill. When it became clear that Amélie would not be sent back, I recalled how, when Monsieur Durand took me to the palace for the first time, the count never came to see me at all. The thought of Amélie sitting on the green sofa in the count's salon, alone, was a soothing one, and with it I finally drifted into sleep.

In the morning Lisette told me I was expected to come down as usual. From Amélie's room came the sound of carefree laughter. I didn't anticipate the force of self-pity that came over me. As if the floor were shaking underneath my feet, the walls collapsing.

That whole day was punctuated with humiliations big and small. Rose rushing upstairs with a bed warmer and her sewing kit. Hearing the hairdresser who had arrived from the palace calling for fresh paper to test his curling iron. That evening Amélie was summoned again and I was again terrified by the force of my hurt. I cursed the blood seeping out of me, the cramps, the stink of the *charpies* Lisette threw into a bucket of cold water before taking them away.

On the third night no one was summoned.

Amélie did not join us at breakfast. Lisette, sent to her room with a tray, came back to say that young Miss told her to go away.

"Shall we ever see the end of these theatrics?" Mademoiselle Dupin asked and screwed her eyes in the direction of the Heavens.

In the evening a carriage arrived. I opened the window and leaned out of it, oblivious to the cold wind. I saw Madame Bertrand holding a lantern, leading Amélie to the carriage. Michel and Saint-Jean carried her trunk. The carriage driver helped them fasten it to the back with thick straps.

Look at me, I willed her in my thoughts. But Amélie got in without turning back, and all I saw was her gloved hand adjusting her gray traveling hood, just before the carriage took off.

⚜

"Mamusia," Louis-Ferdinand greets the queen, in the Polish way. "How is today?" For a moment he leans on her as if he were still a little boy, all elbows and feet, and she wants to hang on to this feeling.

"The day the Lord has made," she says, watching a smile hover on his lips.

At twenty-eight, her son, her only living son and the heir to the French throne, is getting plump. Just well padded, her own father insists, for Louis-Ferdinand has always been his favorite grandchild, a recipient of swords, sables and muskets from the day he was breeched, waving them about in a manner that made her heart stop from fright.

"How did you like the oysters we sent you, Mamusia?"

She loved the oysters. Ate too many in the end. Her stomach is still queasy, a reminder that gluttony is a sin.

"They're the best. From Brittany."

"Is Maria-Josepha feeling any better?" she inquires about her daughter-in-law, who is pregnant again. Much too early, with Louis-Stanislav only four months old! Her son should've shown more restraint, though this wouldn't be a wise thing for a mother to say.

"Weak in the mornings. Needs to lie down during the day, keep her feet up. Her ankles are swollen."

She suggests compresses. Water with vinegar. One tablespoon per a good-sized jug.

"Yes, Mamusia."

A compress should be kept in place for at least one hour.

"Yes, Mamusia."

And then repeated after an hour or so.

Louis-Ferdinand, bless him, comes to see her every day. Not just out of love—best to be truthful—but so that his mother can bear witness to his dark forebodings. Versailles is turning into a brothel, court women into whores. All? No, Mamusia, he answers, peeved. Of course not all. But how far has virtue taken you in this cesspool?

Touché.

"Did I tell you what I intend to do?" she asks him now, to take his mind off such talk. Despair, the worst of them all, too, is a sin.

She has found yet another use for her printing press in the Green Gallery, so useful for printing invitations and prayers. She will print an alphabet book for her grandchildren. *A* is for audacious ant. *B* is for brave badger. *C* is for crafty cat. The drawings, which she has begun already, are quite intricate. Louis-Joseph, five already, has outgrown such simple entertainment, but Louis-Auguste, who is only two, will love it. Such a sturdy, quiet boy, with beautiful eyes and so very clever. "Who is Babcia's little darling?" she asks him, and he points at himself, beaming with joy.

Her son takes her hand and kisses it, a kiss interrupted by a dry cough.

"Is it the smoke?" the queen asks, her eyes passing over the burning logs, for the smoke does seep into the room from time to time. Even after she has ordered the chimney cleaned.

But Louis-Ferdinand will not talk about his sons or a smoking chimney.

"Must we witness another Easter without confession?" he asks. "Without communion? In sin?"

Her son means the king, who has not taken communion since that time in Metz when he fell so terribly ill.

"That was eleven years ago, Mamusia. The priest had to force him to send his whore away. And how long did repentance last? Three months? Four?"

The dauphin of France is raising his voice.

This is the picture he paints for her. From Ash Wednesday on, for forty days, in every church, priests will thunder: Look at Our Savior on the cross. Contemplate His sacrifice for you. The blood that drips from His pierced side. The crown of sharp thorns on His forehead. Admit your mortal sins, renounce adultery and fornication. Remember that no one is exempt from God's commandments. Not even kings.

"I pray that this year be different," she says.

Her son frowns. "And what signs point to such a change? Has my father's pimp started packing, perchance? Have the whores been sent away from that house of depravity?"

Her son's questions hit like sharp stones.

Louis-Ferdinand stands up, his hands raised. This is his father's grand delusion: Louis of France can sin as much as he wants, convinced that no sudden and unexpected death awaits him. The King of Heavens would never allow the descendant of St. Louis to die without confession. The King of Heavens has already made room for him at his side.

Louis-Ferdinand is right in his indignation, of course he is, and yet Queen Marie would like to see more mercy in his eyes, and also—this is much harder to admit—more shrewdness. Knowing what to say and when to say it is important, as is finding a way to turn people to your side. This is the skill she may not possess, either, but one all kings need in abundance.

"The king is not just putting his own soul in danger. The lowest of his subjects who takes communion this Easter can claim that in the eyes of God he is superior to his sovereign. Must we be silent about this, too?"

What can she tell her son? That the king will not listen to her? That her remonstrations will only make things worse? Or should she speak of the future, point to what might one day be possible? When you are king, you will repair what is broken. You who are not like your father.

But will such words not make Louis-Ferdinand even more angry?

"I'll pray for the king, every day of Lent. With your sisters," she finally says. "Will you join us?"

"Where have you been, Véronique?" the count asked when I was brought to the palace again. "How many days has it been since I had the pleasure of seeing you?"

"Twelve," I said, my cheeks hot.

He edged toward me, wiped his mouth on the back of his hand. The scent around him was of ambergris.

"Have you missed me, little mouse?"

"Yes," I said.

"Did you cry when I didn't send for you?"

"Yes."

"Were you afraid I would never send for you again?"

"Yes."

This pleased him so much that he took off a ring from his finger and put it on mine. It was too big, though. "I'll have it resized," he said, taking it back. "And if I forget, you will remind me, won't you?"

I nodded, my eyes tearing up with joy.

He took me by the arms and pulled me toward him. His kiss came next, insisting, scratchy, his hand squeezing my breast, sliding down to my hips. His groans were of pleasure, not impatience.

The room spun around me, a magic lantern show. What will appear out of shadows: sun, moon and the seven stars? The baker pulling the devil by the tail?

Now that he wanted me again, everything became possible. I clung to him with all my might.

That night, after he rolled off me, he took a hairbrush from the side table drawer and began to brush my hair, patiently untangling my curls. He told me how he loathed the fashionable court ladies with their stiff hairdos. False tresses, puffs that couldn't be touched lest they fall off. Why do women insist on such adornments? Have they forgotten the charm of natural looks, soft hair, the smell of it?

He said many things. That he liked the way I twitched my nose, like a rabbit. That next time he would take me to the stables to see a new horse he had bought, a gray mare that was very skittish. Would you like to go riding with me? he asked.

I nodded.

There was no "messy part" to my visits anymore. I had words for it now, his own words. It was our little secret, one that no one else would ever understand.

A secret meant he trusted me. That thought alone could make me as dizzy as hope did.

⚜

Nicole du Hausset keeps an apartment in Paris, but at Versailles she has a windowless room in the entresol above Madame's quarters, barely big enough for a bed, a chest of drawers, a side table and a single chair. She considers herself well housed, nevertheless. Many courtiers in her position have to be satisfied with rooms above the stables or the royal kennels. Besides, she spends most of her time in a small nook off Madame's bedroom, awaiting her mistress's orders. At night, if her mistress doesn't feel well, du Hausset rolls out a folding bed in Madame's room and sleeps there, attuned to her slightest stir.

The Paris apartment is on her mind now. The pleasure of being her own mistress, of holding her own possessions. A collection of porcelain worth twenty louis d'ors, a new addition to which the king presents her every New Year's Day. A cross worth at least sixty-five, the jeweler has assured her, which was a gift from that strange Count St. Germaine who claims to have lived at the time of Julius Caesar, a gift Madame allowed her to accept.

"My good woman." Madame laughs. "You are dreaming. That is a hairbrush you are holding in your hand, not a baton."

Nicole du Hausset snaps to attention. Madame's hair is getting thinner and more brittle. If she is not careful, handfuls will come out in her hand and Madame will get frightened again. "You will have time to prepare," the fortuneteller assured her mistress once, but refused to tell her the manner of her death. Not easy to get her to think of lighter matters now. With Lent approaching, the mood of Father Aubin's homilies has changed. Last Sunday he spoke about Judas Iscariot. Called him the greatest of sinners, for he had kissed the cheek of Jesus and then betrayed him.

"You've been at the market, Nicole. What do people say?"

"Nothing but complaints, Madame. As always."

Madame waves her hand impatiently. "What do they say of the king?"

The Well-Beloved, they used to call him. The Hunter is what du Hausset hears now, and it is not meant kindly. Or the Fisherman, on account of Madame's maiden name, bleeding France dry. Merchant women blabber about royal dishes thrown to the dogs or fed to the pigs. It is squander they cannot bear, these women who take note of everything that passes through their hands.

"They say that His Majesty has magnificent posture. That his eyes are sad and thoughtful. So unlike those of the dauphin, which show nothing but zeal to see all sins punished."

"Is that everything?"

"No, but I hesitate to repeat it."

"Out with it!"

"But, Madame . . ."

"Out with it, I said."

"They say that the king—unlike his great-grandfather—lacks confidence in himself. This is why he allows others, far less learned and with much less sense, to rule."

"They may be right there."

"Please, Madame. Don't move now."

Madame's hair has thinned so badly that nothing can be done without false tresses, pearls woven in. Du Hausset requires her full concentration.

"Hurry up, Nicole."

"Fast as I can be."

"No, you are not. You like tormenting me."

"Madame is jesting."

The morning light is soft, merciful. Powder and rouge blend in such light, rendering Madame's skin smooth and porcelainlike. There is a whiff of perfume in the air, the rustle of silk as Madame—her impatience victorious—stands up without a warning and walks swiftly to the window.

The garden is longing for spring, for the hyacinths that will bloom first, then lilacs, then roses. It's possible to know which month it is just by smelling the air. The chief gardener is already talking of improvements. New plants are arriving from America. But Madame is not looking at the garden. She is awaiting the king, who should be here any moment.

Madame sighs and turns her back on the window. Last night she woke up startled, teeth chattering. She had dreamed of Alexandrine again, screaming in fear. Madame tried to run toward her daughter, but her legs were leaden, too heavy to move. Do you think she blames me for not going to see her? she had asked. No, Madame, she—Nicole—answered firmly. Alexandrine was wise beyond her years and she loved her mother more than anyone in the world.

How do you please Madame these days? With words, always with soothing words. More and more of them. The ones she longs to hear. How a pretty face and youth are never enough. How His Majesty craves the presence of a true friend who loves him above everything and everyone else.

Madame's portrait hangs above the bed. In it, she is wearing a robe of shimmering silk. Her smile is restrained, mouth slightly opened, to remind everyone of her beautiful teeth and her ease with speech. Nicole du Hausset had loved watching it being painted. First the sketches, which curiously began with the plump cushion, the book resting on the side table, before Madame's figure appeared. Then the big canvas on which the jewels on Madame's neck shone more and more with each highlight, as did the glitter of rings on her fingers. Only when it was nearly finished had the painter begun working on Madame's face. As if he could not render Madame's essence on its own.

Inez and Mimi are whimpering by the door. The dogs, too, are awaiting the king.

She clears the dressing table. False hair goes into the side drawer, so do pins and wires. The negligee is folded and tucked away. As soon as the jewelry Madame won't wear is locked in a jewelry box, du Hausset will call a chambermaid and tell her to wipe the film of powder from the floor.

The room must be aired and tidied up, and space cleared on the table for Madame's surprise, plans for redecorating the rooms at Trianon. They are now hidden in the cabinet next door, but she will bring them as soon as Madame gives her a sign. She will also bring a basket with swaths of fabric, samples of wood, marble, and checkered tiles that Madame will spread on the table. Harmony is not just looks, Madame will tell the king. It's the effect an arrangement of shapes and colors has on the soul.

Surprises depend on clever deceptions. The king must arrive to a scene of ordinary tranquility. Madame reclining on her daybed, reading a book. Nicole du Hausset in her nook, focused on her embroidery, as if she were not there at all.

~∗~

The air was getting warmer, the sun brighter. In the middle of March, when Mademoiselle Dupin took us to church on Sunday, the crucifix on the high altar and the figures of saints were all veiled in purple shrouds. The Jesuit priest invited by Father Aubin to speak of the coming Easter stressed the importance of humility and deprivations. Queen Marie and the Daughters of France were to be our shining example. At the sight of a priest carrying the Holy Sacrament in the street, they not only stopped their carriage but got out and knelt in the mud.

Back at Deer Park no one spoke of humility or deprivations. Lent, which I remembered from home as a time of black bread and chestnuts, here merely meant that meat was replaced by fish and water birds while eggs, cheese and butter were as plentiful as ever. Madame Bertrand said that Jesus Christ, Our Lord, never specifically forbade omelets to his apostles. Mademoiselle Dupin said everyone at Deer Park had been granted an "episcopal dispensation."

Lisette was always in a hurry then, for Madame Bertrand had just commanded a big spring cleaning. All carpets and cushions had to be taken to the yard, thrashed until the last motes of dust were beaten out. Windows had to be washed, floors scrubbed and waxed, curtains taken down and shaken.

When she did steal a moment to come to my room, Lisette complained bitterly. Marianne had given notice and now went about her chores with absentminded neglect, making Lisette work twice as hard and still fall short in Madame Bertrand's eyes. Claire had begun wearing her hair pinned up and now demanded to have her ribbons ironed just so. The new *élève*, Manon, who had arrived right after Amélie's departure, was messy like a monkey in a menagerie. Lisette has found a half-eaten pie under the pillow, torn stockings under the bed. Ashes dragged all over the carpet. "They are not like you, Miss," Lisette said. "Everyone says so."

I smiled with pleasure.

My visits to the palace continued.
All was well.

─⫘⫘─

"Hurry up, Lebel."

Louis is back in the state bedroom. The morning Mass has just ended, and the scents of the royal chapel still trail him. The whiff of nutmeg is the dauphin's, the jasmine with a hint of myrrh belongs to Queen Marie and the royal daughters. What did they pray for today? Lebel wonders, deftly taking off the king's charcoal-gray jacket, motioning to a page to hand him the mauve one. The king's change of heart? His return from the realm of sin? That realm where he, Lebel, devil incarnate, has locked him, as if a servant could ever command his royal master or refuse him.

So predictable, the righteous of this world. Believing that they can fix what's wrong with it.

"Don't you fuss, Lebel. I have had enough of fussing for the whole day."

Mindful of the heavy rings, meant to awe, not adorn, Lebel guides the royal hands inside the sleeves. The operation is not entirely successful. A snag at the lace trim of Louis's cuff may be small but noticeable enough to trigger an old royal grudge. "I wanted to learn how to make lace, Lebel, but when I said that to my tutor he gasped with horror. As if I had asked to eat crow for supper."

Lebel offers a deep sigh, a sign of solicitude from a faithful servant to his beloved master. The mauve jacket is a splendid one, its sleeves embroidered with gold thread. Diamond-studded buttons glitter in the morning light. Examining his reflection in the bedroom mirror, Louis nods approvingly. Enough of a consolation, perhaps? If not, there is Madame la marquise's suggestion of a quick escape to Choisy. The improvements to the bathing pavilion at the Petit Château there need his approval.

"They talk of their devotion, Lebel, but if I died tomorrow, they would all rejoice. My son's heart—"

"Is filled with respect and love for you, Sire."

"I don't need more lies, Lebel." The royal lips draw in, tighten.

"The dauphin is still young and the young need guidance, Sire, as Madame la marquise has so often remarked."

The dauphin with his talk of sulfur and eternal damnation is annoying, but not as important as he believes himself to be. More worrisome are Berryer's reports on the Parisian rabble throwing stones at the carriage windows of courtiers, yelling, "Go back to Versailles." Or the tavern pundits declaring that England and Austria are leading the king of France by the nose while he amuses himself with his whores.

"My son smells sin everywhere."

"Suspicion imagines what it cannot prove, Your Majesty. Some at court can still recall what they used to whisper of the Sun King. Drowned in vanity, indifferent to anyone but himself."

"Is that what they say about me, too, Lebel?"

"May I be allowed to quote Madame de Pompadour again, Sire? Does a lion mind the bite of a mosquito? Or: What do carriages do when dogs bark? Move on!"

"She is right, Lebel. A remarkable woman."

"Indeed, Sire."

A faint smile hovers on royal lips, but we are not yet out of the woods. In the chill of the state bedroom Lebel can see the mist of his master's breath. He waves to the page who is holding the king's overcoat and places it over his shoulders.

So close to Easter, even an ordinary royal cold would get the tongues wagging about God's judgment. Feeble minds, Lebel, Berryer has said, can be led astray with less. A powder keg needs but a spark to ignite.

"Get dressed," the count said the following evening. He was taking me for a walk. Good for digestion, he said.

I dressed the best I could without Lisette's help. The shift, stockings and garters were easy, so was buckling the shoes and putting on my petticoats and skirts, but I left behind my stays for I couldn't fasten them by myself. Then the count rang a servant bell and when a page appeared, he ordered him to bring a pelisse to put over my shoulders. Nights were still chilly, he said.

Wrapped up in fur, I followed him up a flight of steep stairs, then another, to a landing where he opened a narrow door leading to the palace roof.

"Mind that you don't slip, little mouse," he said.

The roof was lit by a full moon. Rain puddles glittered at my feet, and I bent to gather some water in my hands. Enough for a splash, just like my brothers delighted in.

"Is that meant for me?" he asked.

Was it the laughter in his voice? Or the speed with which he bent down to gather water into his own hands that did it? But soon we were both splashing rainwater at each other.

"Peace?" he finally asked, panting, wet.

"Peace," I said and raised my hands to show they were empty.

This is when he pointed out different parts of the palace to me, the queen's wing, the king's, the outlines of the old hunting lodge that had stood there long before anything else. The dark misty luster I saw in the distance was the Grand Canal. In the garden grove three men walked with lanterns in hand, swinging them in the dark. "I wonder what they are up to, there," the count said. "Whoever they are."

The roof was paved, and the stone parapet made it into a long, vast terrace. I had never been anywhere that high.

"What is there?" I asked, pointing at a patch of darkness beyond the Grand Canal.

"Forests."

"Is it where you hunt? With the king?"

He chuckled. "Yes," he said. "But I have to tell you that the king is much less imposing when you meet him."

"You mustn't say that."

"Mustn't I? And why is that, little mouse? What if I tell you I don't like the king that much. Will you slap me?"

"I might."

"Just might? You are not defending His Majesty with much zeal."

"The king doesn't need my defense."

"Should I tell him that when I see him?"

"If you wish," I said.

An owl hooted in the distance. The pelisse over my shoulders was deliciously light and warm, but both my hands and feet were turning numb with cold.

"When I was younger," he said, pointing out a gallery underneath, "I'd slide down to the balcony there. This was my friend's room. I knocked on the window, trying to frighten him."

"Was he frightened?"

"No. He knew it was me."

I tried to imagine him as a young man, arriving at Versailles with the Polish queen. Standing on this roof, looking out into this new world before him. "I assist my cousin in her official functions," he told me once, when I asked what he did at the palace. He received the queen's guests, took them hunting. At first the queen wanted him to be her secretary, but his penmanship was atrocious. "A hen scratching the ground is better at it than I am," he said. When I asked if this was what the queen had said, he laughed and said that she wouldn't dare.

Encouraged by his laughter, I didn't stop my questions. Had he ever been to the king's *grande levée*? Had he seen His Majesty eat breakfast? Had the king ever taken him hunting? Fooled by the obvious pleasure these questions brought him, I blindly followed its scent.

"And the princesses, the king's daughters? What are they like? Much prettier than me?"

That is when it all went so very wrong. First came silence, awkward, chilling. It tightened my heart. It made my stomach shrink.

"Don't be such a chatterbox," he finally said. "Ever again."

I said I was sorry. I begged him to forgive me.

He turned away from me.

Tears were flowing down my cheeks as I followed him back to the door and down the stairs to the bedroom.

He said that he had matters to attend to, that his valet would come for me and take me to Deer Park. "Wait here," he said.

I clutched at these words long after he had left, repeating them to myself, weighing them.

Back at Deer Park that night I slept poorly, in fearful fits. I woke often, thinking of Francine, listening for steps in the corridor, the door to my room opening wide. But then it began to grow light, and Lisette came to help me dress, just as she always did. "Good morning, Miss," she greeted me cheerfully, and I became hopeful again. What had happened on the roof was just an awkward moment, I thought, a flare of impatience I had fully deserved. I would never again allow myself to be too free, too foolish. All would again be well.

I was in the music room with Manon and Claire, practicing the motets for the concert spirituel we were to sing on Easter Sunday, when I heard Monsieur Durand's voice in the hall. Then I heard his steps climbing up the stairs to Madame Bertrand's room, and the door closing.

Try as I might, I could not concentrate on the music. Not with Monsieur Durand leaving, Madame calling on Mademoiselle Dupin to have a word with her, the lackeys dragging something heavy from the attic. "Pay attention, Véronique," our music master chastised me, for I fumbled on my solo part, making Claire and Manon giggle.

The practice was almost over when Madame Bertrand came into the music room and ordered everyone to leave.

"Not you," she said to me when I rose with the others.

My heart began to thump.

"Best not to draw this out, Véronique," she began. Her eyes seemed larger than usual. I recalled Lisette saying that Madame put belladonna in them. To please the wine merchant, she said, who couldn't care a fig.

"Best to have it over with."

I felt a surge of something sour in my throat, my legs softened, buckled and a dark mist descended over me like a veil.

When a sharp acrid stink brought me back, I was in my room, lying in bed. Lisette was holding a bottle of reviving salts under my nose. She had taken off my outer dress and loosened my stays. The palace doctor had been sent for, she said, but I shouldn't worry. It couldn't be smallpox, for I didn't have a fever. My skin was clear, too.

I had never fainted in my life, and in spite of Lisette's assurances, I was terrified. I knew how swift death could be, how unpredictable.

My stomach was still churning, demanding relief. Lisette held the chamber pot when I retched. Madame Bertrand came by with her nerve tonic and made me drink a few throat-burning gulps, which made me cough. I did feel better enough to lie down and close my eyes.

"When did she bleed last?" I heard Madame Bertrand ask Lisette.

Lisette muttered something I didn't catch.

"And you are only telling me now, you stupid, stupid girl?" Madame exclaimed.

"How is it my fault?" Lisette defended herself. "What would it change?"

Madame Bertrand had lowered her voice by then, but I could still hear enough. "The devil's mischief . . . just when everything has been settled . . . we cannot . . . not until the confinement."

The Deer Park servants are talking.

As you sow, thus you shall reap. What else to expect? Nature takes its course. Where wood is chopped, splinters fly. Not the first little bird to have left with a bit more than she counted on and will not be the last. Though not such a bad ending for her, is it? No sending her back to her mother now. They will find her a husband. Lisette has heard Madame Bertrand mention a grain merchant in Brest. So, what if the merchant will have to wait until January. Not for nothing. Four thousand livres dowry. Maybe even more now, to sweeten the bargain.

A new girl has already been sent for. Always an inconvenience at first. Until they settle.

Rose predicts they will see the last of Véronique by tomorrow. She knows the house where she will go, a few streets away from Deer Park, on avenue de Saint-Cloud. She wonders who will be chosen to go with Véronique. She would like to. Especially since, at Deer Park, one maid less—here she looks in Marianne's direction—always means more work for the other two.

Simple, this one, the cook calls Véronique. Won't invent gunpowder. Others have been smarter.

That in itself is not a sin, is it, Lisette thinks. Simple souls should be protected, not thrown to the lions. They are Christian souls after all.

Lisette has been thinking hard. She should be the one to go with Véronique to that house on avenue de Saint-Cloud, not Rose. Véronique likes her better. Also, Lisette is smarter, and works harder than Rose.

Lisette is ready to admit she is looking far beyond Véronique's confinement. If Véronique takes her along to this Brest, Lisette could become her lady's maid. She can do hair and wash lace already. She'd have to learn to read and write, yes, but she recognizes most of the letters just fine. She can follow the prayers she knows in the missal. Not always, but with shorter words she can.

This is why, when Madame Bertrand's bell rings, Lisette jumps up. "I'll go," she says.

Madame is in a foul mood. "Easy for Pompadour to make demands," she grumbles as Lisette helps her undress. "Fetch the doctor, Bertrand. Hire a nurse, Bertrand. Get her a chambermaid, Bertrand. Who am I to run her errands? One house is enough trouble."

"A glass of wine? To calm the nerves?" Lisette asks.

"Just a drop," Madame Bertrand agrees. "Far too much . . . ," she protests as Lisette pours, but Lisette knows better than to pay heed.

The wine lifts Madame's spirit. She is a cheerful drunk, just like Lisette's father. A few sips guarantee that not all is as bad as it seems. A few more suggest a solution. When the bottom of the glass reveals itself, so does a conviction that the world is not such a stinking cesspool after all.

Lisette refills the empty glass.

"You know what they say about *her*, Madame?" she says, folding Madame Bertrand's skirt and petticoats. "Once a Fish, always a Fish. Stingy too, our Madame la marquise, the servants say. Gives you a dress but makes sure all the gold thread is removed first. Cannot quite manage to become the grand lady she wishes to be."

Madame Bertrand giggles. Blood, she agrees, does not lie. It's all there. Revealed when it is least expected.

And that du Hausset woman, Lisette continues, who calls herself a childless widow of noble birth! Not a servant, mind you. Companion and confidante.

It comes in handy, the rapid Buc speech Lisette has known since childhood. The ear for all falsehood, the quick wit of those who call a spade a spade. Wiping a smile from her lips, she imitates du Hausset's countenance and her drawn-out vowels: "Countess D— pays me such attention. So does the Baschi family. On account of a little service I was able to provide for them once."

Madame Bertrand nods with pleasure.

"The Baschi family, my ass," Lisette continues. "Nicole Colleson is her name. Her father was a tanner. A lady's maid *is* a servant. How they laugh at her at the palace. Too many teeth even for such a big mouth."

"Someone scribbled *Du Hausset is hungry again* on her door, beside a drawing of her fat face, gobbling a giant puff pastry. And what does the grand lady's maid say? It's because of my proximity to His Majesty and Madame, this malice."

In the nightshift that envelops her like a shroud, Madame Bertrand is holding her belly. Tears of merriment gather in the corners of her eyes. She hasn't had such a good laugh for a long time. Bless such moments of light, she says. Too rare in this vale of tears.

"Another drop?" Lisette asks, pointing at the wineglass, empty again. "I could bring another bottle."

"No, no, my dear girl." Madame Bertrand lets herself be helped to the bed, which squeaks underneath her. In her bonnet, she looks like a monstrous baby. Two of her teeth are blackened with rot, but her eyes are wide. She is still putting belladonna in them. To please that wine merchant who still doesn't care a rotten fig and never will.

"I want you to go with Véronique, Lisette," Madame Bertrand says and then, lowering her voice, she adds, "We cannot let that du Hausset puff herself up even more."

Two days later Madame la marquise arrived in my room in a flutter of agitation. Her black half-mask was trimmed with gold, making me think of an angry wasp. This time, though, it was Madame Bertrand who followed in her footsteps, not her maid.

I was resting in bed, in my negligee, my feet on a cushion. The palace doctor had visited me twice by then. On his first visit he questioned me for a long time. Did I feel more pleasure than usual in my last congress with the count? Did I feel a coldness or chill or shiver right afterward? The slowing of my heart?

Dissatisfied with my answers, he examined my breasts with a magnifying glass, their coloring, the shape of the nipples. Then he pulled down my lower eyelids to inspect the veins there. In the end he asked me to pee into a glass vial, which he closed with a stopper and took with him for what he called a nettle test.

The following day, after the test confirmed that I was with child, the doctor gave me a long list of warnings. I was to abstain from violent motions, from lifting my arms above my shoulders. I was to avoid sadness, anger and all other perturbations of the mind. I was to keep my bowels loose with prunes and stewed rhubarb. There would be no bloodletting until the child quickened.

The count's child, I thought, clinging to these words as if they guaranteed a reward, the link between us no one could sever. His bastard, a hiss in my head sneered, but I closed myself to its harshness, banished it from my mind.

"I've come to see for myself," Madame la marquise said to no one in particular.

"Stand up, Véronique," Madame Bertrand said, her voice surprisingly kind. "Lift up your shift."

I stood up slowly and did what I was told. My belly was smooth and flat. It seemed impossible a baby could fit inside. I'd seen my brothers right after they were born. I'd seen the loose folds of skin on my mother's stomach.

"Cover her," Madame la marquise said, barely looking at me. She was tugging at her gloved fingers, as if making sure they were still attached to her hand.

Madame Bertrand pulled my shift down and told me to sit. I perched on the edge of the bed. I made circles on the rug with my bare foot, tracing the pattern of pale brown leaves.

They spoke fast, above my head, as if I were not there, as if nothing they said concerned me in the least. You know how the word slips out with servants . . . They must have guessed already . . . Are you convinced we can trust every one of them? . . . Better safe than sorry.

No one mentioned the count. Or Monsieur Durand.

Madame la marquise spun around the room as she spoke. Pausing by my dressing table, she finally took off her gloves and examined the jars the doctor had sent. Oil of roses and violets to massage into the skin of my belly. Goose fat for my privy parts. Almond milk for my face and hands.

"Are you well treated?" she asked, finally turning to me. She had beautiful lips, I thought, heart-shaped and full.

"Yes."

"Do you have any requests?" Hurry up, girl, her eyes warned. Don't try my patience for too long.

Inch by inch I gathered myself, put my thoughts in order. "Does the count know?" I asked the loudest question rattling in my mind.

Madame la marquise cleared her throat and nodded. The count was an honorable man. My future was secured. I was not to concern myself unduly. Words that faded in my ears, none an answer to my question.

"When will I see him?" I asked.

"The count has left for Poland," she said. "He has entrusted you to my care."

"When will he be back?"

Madame Bertrand gave me a warning look. I was getting too bold. Too insistent. Not a wise position to take now.

The count's plans, Madame la marquise said, should be of no concern to anyone in this room, including me. Especially me. Especially in the condition I was in.

Her voice echoed off the ceiling and the walls, as if she spoke into a well into which, like in some fairy tale, an evil sorcerer had cast me. The tone of her voice meant far more than the words themselves: Why would he care for someone such as you?

I heard the hiss of Madame Bertrand's indrawn breath. The smell of something rotting wafted by.

The contents of my stomach rose up to my throat and retreated, leaving the taste of the coffee and omelet I had for breakfast. It was a good thing I was still sitting down.

"You will be taken to another house. It is only proper, in your condition," Madame la marquise continued. "My maid will make sure you lack for nothing."

Madame Bertrand rolled her eyes.

I cried for a long time after they left. Dark thoughts hovered. The woman's lot, Eve's punishment for disobedience, for wishing to know what was not hers to know. In pain you shall give birth, the priests always said.

Lisette brought me a cup of tisane, hot and bitter-tasting. "No use crying, Miss," she said as I sipped it slowly. "It may all turn out for the best."

Hope restored itself slowly, but it did. When Lisette left, I recalled the softness of the count's voice when he called me his little mouse. Or when he said I pleased him and promised to take me to the palace orangery, to a room where butterflies flew all year round. Some as big as birds, he had said.

What if Madame la marquise had lied to me? What if he hadn't left for Poland? What if he didn't know I was carrying his child?

What if she kept me away from him?

If only I could escape Madame Bertrand's vigilance, run to the palace, climb the stairs I knew so well, open the door to the green salon.

The tisane had made me drowsy. I closed my eyes and sank into my bed. Before I fell asleep, I imagined the count's joy at the sight of me and his anger at all those who dared to keep us apart.

~≈~

On Easter Sunday, Nicole du Hausset awakes in her cramped nook to the sound of a bell from Madame la marquise's bedroom. The air is stuffy and smells of stale dust. Just the other day she saw a mouse sniffing under the table. Quite brazen, too. Not even trying to hide. She should get a cat. Not a common one, though. A white angora, perhaps.

The bell rings again, and du Hausset stumbles to her feet, rubbing the remnants of sleep from her eyes. Something in her dream reminds her of a distant cousin who is pestering her for a favor. Cannot understand why she refuses to ask for Madame's help. Never asked himself what a web of dependencies such a request would create, what obligations of gratitude. Besides, what has he ever done for her?

To her surprise, Madame is not alone. The king is pacing around the room, diamonds sparkling in the trim of his jacket, the curls of his wig swaying as he walks. There is a sheepish grin on his face, as if he were a boy caught dipping his wet finger in the sugar bowl.

This is far too early for his daily visit. The king is a man of set habits, usually annoyed when he has to alter or give up even the slightest one.

Madame, a dressing gown over her nightshift, is standing by the mantel, her lips narrowed into a thin smile, as if a toothache bothered her. Has there been a quarrel? Impossible. Other people's actions can cause Madame to rage or weep, but never the king's. This is why he always returns to her, while other mistresses are pushed away. As soon, Madame points out, as they become jealous or start making demands.

"You must go to the house on avenue de Saint-Cloud right away, Nicole," Madame says. "With a young lady in a delicate condition. I've already sent for a midwife. She will visit as often as she sees fit and she will deliver the child. You will visit the young lady every day and then move in with her right before the *accouchement*."

So this is what it is all about, another royal bastard. Not the first, not the last, so what has upset Madame this time? Hasn't she always said that the king doesn't care about his children, for he has too many of them? It must be that Deer Park girl again. Perhaps he still cares about her? Wants her back afterward? Just as it happened with that O'Murphy strumpet?

"I'm making you responsible for that house, Nicole," Madame continues. "Make sure everything that happens there does so in utter secrecy. When the child is born, you will take it to be baptized."

"May I inquire about the child's father?" Du Hausset asks the question she already knows the answer to. But it is important to signal that she is not indulging in presumptions.

The king stifles a chuckle, a naughty boy who knows he has already been forgiven. "The father is a very honest man," he says.

"Beloved by everyone, and adored by those who know him," Madame adds.

Du Hausset curtsies with as much grace as her bulky frame permits. Wobbly too, for she has dressed in haste and misses the solid support of the whalebones against her skin. Dr. Quesnay, who is wiser than any man she has ever met, showed her a drawing of a whale once. A giant beast, and yet its teeth look like a fine sieve.

Madame opens a little cupboard and retrieves a small head comb studded with diamonds. She calls it an *aigrette*, even though it has no feathers. "You will present it to the young lady but not now. Keep it for after she gives birth."

The *aigrette* is not worth more than twenty louis, a gift one would give to a servant. The diamonds are small, and most likely flawed. Madame has many such items—her jeweler's castoffs, ordered by the dozens.

"How kind and thoughtful you are," the king says.

Madame walks up to him and puts her hand to his heart. "This is what I wish to secure."

Nicole du Hausset understands the meaning of this awkward little drama, performed for her benefit. The king's dalliances are of scant importance.

The king takes hold of Madame's hand and kisses the tips of her fingers. Nicole du Hausset lowers her eyes, which means: I have taken note, yet I do not wish to appear nosy.

"Lebel will assist you in all you might need," the king says, turning to her this time, which is both unusual and unexpected. "You will find the godparents."

"Yes, Sire."

"There must be someone in the street. Some servant, perhaps."

"Yes, Sire."

"A man and a woman."

"Yes, Sire."

"Give each twelve francs only, so that they won't think much of it."

"Not a louis?" Madame asks.

"Remember the coachman I once wanted to give a louis to?"

Nicole du Hausset has heard the king tell this story many times. It begins with his ardent desire to visit Madame at her mother's house, without being recognized. There is the hackney coach the duc d'Ayen summoned for him. There is the ride through Parisian streets, as if he were an ordinary man, broken by the delightful rudeness of some merchant's wife who yelled at them for splashing her with mud. The king wished to give the driver a whole louis at the end of the ride, but the duc d'Ayen said, "If you give him more than he has the right to expect, the police will hear of it. And the spies will make inquiries. Soon everyone will know it was you, Sire."

The king loves this story and he loves repeating it. A monarch almost betrayed by his generosity, stopped at the last moment by a watchful friend. At any other time, Madame would have happily listened to it again, but now she allows herself the luxury of cutting him short. "You were too generous, as always, dearest, too good. But the confinement is still months away, so we shall leave these arrangements for later."

"This is the truth," the king says, clearly peeved at being deprived of a treat he was looking forward to. A moment later he mutters to himself, "The police would hear of it. The spies will make inquiries . . ." Then he stops and turns his dark blue eyes toward her. Bewildered, as if he were wondering who she was. It is not the first time Nicole du Hausset has had the distinct feeling the king thinks his servants are changelings. Shadows from some other menacing world, put in his path to bewilder or torment him.

"When the child is baptized, Lebel will give presents to the priest and the midwife," the king continues. "But it is only fair that you should get yours now."

It is a roll of fifty gold louis. A hundred livres.

Nicole du Hausset takes the roll and kisses the king's hand. The scent of Hungary water hangs around His Majesty. Has the king begun drinking it? Restorative elixir, Dr. Quesnay calls it. Rub it on the weak limbs, daily, and behold the results.

It is a pleasant smell. The strongest notes are those of rosemary, lavender and lemon blossoms.

The two-story house Madame du Hausset took me to was a short carriage ride from Deer Park, which meant that I was still in the town of Versailles. A sign—I decided—that the count wanted me near him. In addition to Lisette, there was a cook, a maid-of-all-work and two lackeys. My bedroom was on the first floor, so that—as Madame du Hausset stressed—I would be spared climbing stairs in my condition. The bed was wide and soft, the wardrobe well stocked with shifts and loose robes. All fine cambric, she said, each worth twenty livres at least. Next to the bedroom was a small boudoir where I could rest or occupy myself with embroidery.

"You need to eat well," Madame du Hausset continued. The cook would make bouillon for me to drink. Every morning Lisette would bring me a glass of red wine mixed with water, to thicken my blood.

The door slammed when she left.

From the days that followed I remember the edgy pain of waiting. In the evenings every clatter of horses' hooves or the jingle of spurs would send me to the window, sure the count had summoned me at last. "Did you really think I would abandon you?" he would say. "Is that why you are crying, little mouse?" Sometimes these visions were so vivid that I felt the brush of his hand on my cheek.

When days passed and he didn't send for me, another thought came. Now that I was expecting his child, was he, perhaps, testing me? Gauging my obedience, my loyalty, my trust in his benevolence? Was I being watched? Was every word I said reported to him? This, I decided, was a good thought. It urged me to stand straighter, move with more grace, summon cheerfulness into my voice.

But as days turned into a week, then two, hope was proving a fickle guest, easily frightened away. I thought back to that terrible evening on the palace roof when I annoyed the count with my silly prattle about the princesses. Did he think I thought myself prettier than the king's daughters? Better than them? Could he really think me that vain?

Other memories came to haunt me, too. That impatient look when I threw my arms around his neck and pressed my cheek to his chest. The time when he asked me to play cards with him and I cheated so that he could win only to anger him with what he called my presumptuousness. "Can't you be still for one moment?" he had once asked.

Every time hope gave way to grief, words vanished in my throat before I could pronounce them. Soon I found it harder and harder to get out of bed in the morning, to answer Lisette's cheerful questions, or pay heed to her gossip. Why would I care that du Hausset bossed Lisette around, or criticized everything she did? Or that the cook was stealing fat drippings and selling them to the candlemaker? Or that the maid-of-all-work did not know the first thing about dusting, doing it after she had aired the rooms?

Even the distant sounds of the street were hard to bear. People laughing, calling to each other, someone bursting into a song. Sadness weighed heavy, as heavy as the child growing inside me, the cause of my banishment. I tried to coax the shadows of Adèle and Francine from the murkiness of this time, but they refused to come and offer comfort. And the count, the reason of my dejection, became harder and harder to summon. The moments of tenderness I used to be able to recall at will were growing fainter. Even my own face in the mirror looked blurry, as if I watched myself from some ghostly world far away, as if my real life had never happened at all.

I finally decided to write him a letter. I thanked him for his care of me, asked if he knew that I was with child, and when I would see him again. Not knowing how I should end the letter, I wished him health, inquired about the falcon that had once perched on my gloved hand, and signed it *Your little mouse*. I begged Lisette to take it to him, and she promised, though she would not swear. Not on the Virgin. Not on St. Elizabeth, her patron saint. "If I can, Miss," was all I could get out of her.

To tame the long, empty hours I requested paper and charcoal. The drawings I made at first were simple. A flower in a vase, a view from my window, into the small back garden, the tangled vines climbing the wall. But soon other images replaced them. Maimed creatures appeared, half human, half beast with menacing stares. Eyes, some shaped like buttons, some like saucers, emerging from darkness.

Faced with one such drawing, Madame du Hausset screamed with horror.

"Do you wish to turn the child inside you into a monster?" she asked. And when I didn't answer, she tore the drawing to pieces and burned it.

That day the midwife from Paris arrived, a big woman, heavy-boned, brisk in her manner, with eyes of steel. Mistress Leblanc, Madame du Hausset called her.

La malade, the midwife referred to me, the sick one. When she addressed me, she called me girl, or child. As if I didn't have a name. Old, I thought her then, bossy and harsh. I didn't like her clothes, either, a simple brown woolen dress, a white apron starched stiff, a starched bonnet. The whiff of camphor about her made me nauseous.

"Lie down, child," she said. "Lift your skirts up."

When I did, she felt my belly for a long time, pressing it with her hands. Warm and dry, I noted with relief.

Mistress Leblanc did not hide her annoyance. She was not satisfied with the way I was cared for. Seeing the reddened imprints where the stays had pressed on my ribs, she demanded an explanation as to why I was allowed to wear tight clothes. The skin needed to breathe. Blood needed to flow without obstruction. Was this so hard to figure out? And why was the air in the room so stale? Why did I not have a footstool to rest my feet on?

Du Hausset hovered nearby, hands flapping. I could see her jaw tense every time she stopped herself from speaking. I felt sorry for Lisette, who would soon bear the brunt of her growing fury.

I was still lying down, my stays now undone, when the midwife turned to me. Fixing me with her eyes set in a web of tiny wrinkles, she asked if I relieved myself regularly. Was my stool loose or hard? How many times did I wake up at night to pee?

Nosy, I kept thinking, impertinent.

"No need to blush, child," she said. "Nothing to be ashamed about."

After I answered her questions, she declared me to be in a poor state. My spirits were low. The vital force was receding. Melancholy was bad for a mother-to-be. It lowered the body's defenses, weakened the child inside.

Du Hausset took another deep breath but kept her silence. Lisette would later tell me that the midwife had been Madame la marquise's choice. This is why du Hausset had to clench her teeth and bear it. Which served the gray mare right, didn't it?

Before leaving, the midwife replaced the doctor's ointments with her own pomades. The caul of a baby goat, she said, would soften my skin, prevent me from tearing when the time comes. She ordered weekly bleedings from the arm to keep my humors balanced, enemas to keep the bowels moving and brisk walks in the garden to keep the sinews strong and resilient. She insisted I be served plain, simple food. No more ragouts, sauces or fatty meats, no *aliments de fantaisie*.

"You are young," the midwife said. "You are healthy. If my orders are followed, all will end well."

If it weren't for Lisette, would Véronique have managed to live the rest of her days believing the story of a Polish count, a second cousin to the queen? Prevented from seeing her by his servants, jealous of his fondness for her? Or, which seems to Lisette even worse, sent away because of some terrible transgression for which Véronique thought herself to blame?

Perhaps, but Lisette knows that some beliefs are like boils on the skin. They fester and grow and poison the whole body, and only a sharp cut can heal them. Besides, she has her own interest in mind. If she doesn't look after herself, who will?

It is the evening after the midwife's visit. Having warmed her hands over the fire, Lisette begins to undress Véronique, who is standing with her back to her so that Lisette can undo her hooks.

"Please, will you take me with you, Miss?" Lisette asks when the last hook is undone. "To Brest."

Véronique turns to face her, bewildered. "Why would I go to Brest?"

Lisette gives her mistress a hesitant look, but something in her has already pushed too far and would not be turned back. "To get married, Miss."

"What are you talking about?"

"Everyone knows that, Miss. It's only right you should, too."

This is how Véronique learns that she is going to marry a grain merchant in Brest, live in a big house, with a garden and a brick wall around it. And that she, Lisette, wants to be her proper waiting maid. She is not ungrateful, far from it. Madame Bertrand has been good to her. But she wants to better herself. Like Véronique is about to.

"I'll be faithful, Miss," Lisette says. "You won't regret taking me with you. Ever."

"Madame Bertrand told you all this?" Véronique asks.

Not quite, Lisette admits. She has overheard Mademoiselle Dupin and Madame Bertrand talking. How it is all settled. How the merchant already signed something and even took some of the dowry. How everybody at Deer Park thinks Véronique did very well for herself.

"It can never be," Véronique says. Her voice is firm and far too loud. Her hands are clasped together, so tight that the knuckles whiten.

"Why, Miss?"

Because His Lordship would never allow it. He doesn't know she is with child, but as soon as he gets her letter, he will forgive her all her trespasses and will come to get her. It is all in the letter Lisette has promised to deliver as soon as she sees a chance.

Lisette waves her hand, swatting down these foolish words like annoying flies.

"You promised to give him the letter, Lisette."

This is what does it. The last straw, the final push.

"There is no Polish count, Miss," Lisette says, blunt, unsparing. "It is all a sham." Everyone is in on it, she explains. Madame Bertrand, the Deer Park servants, Madame la marquise who is none other but Madame de Pompadour herself. There is no Monsieur Durand, either. His name is Lebel and he is the king's *valet de chambre*. They would all have sent Véronique back home right before Easter if it weren't for her belly. Why, they even asked Lisette to pack Véronique's trunk!

"Yes, Miss," Lisette says, answering the question that flashes in Véronique's eyes. "The king of France is the father of your child."

Véronique lowers herself to the edge of the bed. Lisette keeps talking, adding up all of Véronique's good fortune that she so stubbornly refuses to see. A merchant in Brest, that big house by the sea, two stories, a balcony and a good-sized attic. Dresses and jewels Véronique can keep. And a dining-room set from the palace thrown in. Véronique was poor, now she is rich.

But Véronique shakes her head.

Some boils fester even when lanced, Lisette thinks. Some people can be shown the truth and still refuse to believe it. No matter how hard it is for Lisette to understand, this is how it is.

Then another thought comes, followed by a shiver of dread. What if Véronique has her own schemes? Keeps her own secrets? For why else would she refuse the good fortune of running a house in which Lisette saw herself rise?

"Please, Miss," Lisette asks, suddenly frightened by what she has done. "Don't let anyone know I've told you, Miss."

But Véronique doesn't look at her at all.

The days that followed after Lisette's confession I recall brokenly, through a fog. I paced the room in agitation, I pushed plates away after taking just a few bites. At night I slept in fits, waking up at the lightest noise.

Du Hausset eyed me with suspicion. Had anything happened? Had anyone bothered me?

I said no. I was worried about my confinement, that's all. When she insisted, I confessed to some bad dream, which, to my relief, always made her tell me one of hers. About a land in which all money had been replaced by a magic powder. About a glorious Versailles ball during which a masked man gave her a bloodied handkerchief with a name on it she couldn't, for the life of her, recall.

If Lisette had hoped the truth would shake me free of delusions, she was wrong.

It fueled my hope.

I had not displeased him. He was not angry with me. He was the king of France. No wonder he never came here to see me. Kings cannot always do what they want. The queen was not his second cousin but his wife. I was his mistress. I was carrying his love child. Even though he had to stay away from me, the signs of his care were all around. In this house, in this very room, where flowers were changed daily, where I had all the comforts imaginable.

This thought made me smile.

Mistress Leblanc arrived every week to examine me. Any misgivings I had about her at first evaporated. She felt the position of the child, bled me if necessary, gave me an enema, massaged my arms and legs. Nothing escaped her attention: not a dry patch of skin, a throbbing vein, not my swollen ankles, for which she prescribed a cold compress and a cushion under my feet when I slept.

Her touch was firm but never painful.

You will cry, she said. All pregnant women cry.

You will be afraid, she said. Giving birth is always scary.

It will hurt, she said, for it always hurts, but I'll be with you all the way.

One day, when I was already eight months gone, Mistress Leblanc asked, "Does your mother know where you are? Has anyone told her of your condition?"

I shook my head.

"Do you wish to see her?" she asked.

I hesitated. But then I said yes.

Mistress Leblanc shouldn't have meddled, Nicole du Hausset thinks, but she did and now Danielle Roux has arrived at avenue de Saint-Cloud, wearing what must be her best velvet and buttoned-up shoes. The Widow Roux of pasty complexion and a few traces of her old beauty, a mere echo of her daughter's, but stubbornly there in the fine line of her nose, the almond shape of her eyes.

"When is my daughter due?" she asks du Hausset, who has insisted on the two of them having a word before the visit. Lebel has assured her that for "Maman" he is still Monsieur Durand, the valet of a Polish count who has done the honorable thing and that she is fully reconciled with the arithmetic of fate.

"The midwife expects it will be toward the end of December."

"And the wedding?"

"As soon as the midwife declares her ready. But she hasn't been told yet, so don't mention it."

Danielle Roux nods.

"Follow me then," Nicole du Hausset says. "See for yourself she hasn't come to any harm."

Véronique, big with child, is standing awkwardly beside a gilded armchair. In a dress of fine gauze worth at least one hundred livres, in a room with thick carpets, satin-covered walls, an ormolu clock on the marble mantel, a mahogany table where Lisette has placed refreshments: sugarplums, fruit tarts, candied almonds, a pot of hot chocolate. All arranged on a silver tray, freshly polished. Does Danielle Roux see it all? Oh, yes, she does.

There are a few words of greeting and an embrace, awkward because of Véronique's belly.

"Are you well?"

"Yes. And you, Maman?"

"As well as I can expect at my age."

Nicole du Hausset removes herself to a distant corner and picks up her embroidery hoop. A sign to remind Danielle Roux that she is here to make sure nothing gets said that shouldn't be said.

Danielle Roux's voice is light, chatty. She tells her daughter that her new shop is right beside the tobacconist. New and altered clothes she sells now. The clientele is not of the highest order yet, but far better than the Quinze-Vingts market bargain hunters. She has moved to a second-floor apartment and keeps a maid-of-all-work.

"Your brothers are at school," she tells Véronique. "If they do well, Eugene might become a lawyer one day. Marcel and Gaston might be better off in the army."

"Do they know all about me?"

"No need, is there?"

"No."

Nothing of concern in these words, Nicole du Hausset thinks. Though she still considers the midwife reckless for insisting on this visit. Stirring up useless memories, if nothing else.

"How are you taking the winter, Véronique?"

"I'm warm here."

"Eating well?"

"Yes."

"Sleeping?"

"Yes."

Danielle Roux takes a sugarplum and eats it with delight. "Do you want one?" she asks her daughter, who shakes her head. "You must have them all the time, do you?" the mother says wistfully. And then, without waiting for an answer, her voice cheerful, she offers accounts of her own pregnancies, all easy enough. Her labor with Véronique took five hours, she slipped out of her without tearing her up. So did Adèle. The boys were harder, but not as hard as other women had it. "You are like me," she says, looking at Véronique with insistence. "You will deliver fast."

"How is your health, Maman?" Véronique asks, as if she hasn't already asked.

This time around Danielle Roux carefully lists her ailments. Gout, muscle spasms, indigestion. She lists remedies she has tried or intends to try. Oils, infusions, purges. In all this a hint: Your mother is growing old, Véronique. You might be required to care for her sooner than you think.

Véronique plays with the hem of her handkerchief, rolling it up then smoothing it out again.

Beads of an abacus moving from side to side, such talk. It is time to stop it. Nicole du Hausset stands up and puts her embroidery away.

"A most peculiar picture, Madame," she tells Madame de Pompadour later that day, as her mistress uncurls newly delivered plans for the Trianon gardens and weighs the edges with the rocks His Majesty had given her. The Widow Roux stuffing herself with sugarplums, Véronique barely, just barely, showing interest in her own flesh and blood.

"And then, Madame, just as she was leaving the mother asked me, 'What if my daughter dies in childbirth? Before marriage?' To which I replied with the only words such a woman can understand. Rest assured. No one will expect you to take the bastard in."

⚓

"The time has come," Mistress Leblanc told me. The birth room has been aired, well-worn soft linen and towels were piled up on a side table.

I lay in bed covered with loose sheets, terrified of what was to come. I gasped and shuddered. "Will it hurt very much?" I asked.

"We shall see."

I clung to her cheerful voice. It meant: I've seen many women go through it. I'll see you through, too. It'll hurt, but I'm here, with two strong hands to catch your baby.

"When?"

"When the time comes."

She laid her hands on my belly. "Everything is the way it should be," she told me. She opened a vein in my arm. "To ease your breathing," she said as my blood seeped into a bowl. "And to soften your insides."

"How long will it take?"

"As long as it needs to. No point rushing nature."

I turned my eyes toward the door.

"Don't worry. I won't let that du Hausset woman come in."

She slipped out of me, my child, my daughter. So quick I feared the midwife did not catch her. This is why she is screaming, I thought.

"Here she is," Mistress Leblanc said, holding her for me to see, swathed in a warm towel, her eyes opened wide. "A curious little mite. Most of them just fall asleep, but not this one."

I extended my hands.

I remember the warm softness of my daughter's skin as the midwife put her in my arms. I remember every fold around her eyes, dark, dark blue, like her father's. I remember the narrow fingers, clutching around mine, a funny tuft of hair.

Auburn, just like mine.

Such a soft sound, my baby's whimper.

"Perfect," Mistress Leblanc said, and I knew that if anyone would be punished it would not be her.

There was a scuffle at the door. Lisette was standing with her back against it, her feet planted on the floor. Madame du Hausset was demanding to be let in. "Who do you think you are?" she seethed.

The midwife sighed and motioned to Lisette to open the door.

I wailed, I begged, I sobbed. I sank my teeth into my lips, drawing blood. "Don't let them carry her away," I pleaded. "Not yet."

Useless words, impotent, futile.

"Where will they take her?"

"There is a wet nurse waiting."

A kind, clean woman, Mistress Leblanc called her, her own child just weaned. Not a blemish on her skin.

"It's for the best, Miss," Lisette whispered in my ear.

Marguerite Leblanc has seen it before, the little drama enacted in front of her and the wet nurse. The godparents supposedly on their way, failing to arrive. Replaced by some strangers who had to be recruited from the street, paid enough to please them but not enough to make them suspect that the father might be someone important. Four sous each, a good day's work earned in an hour. The whispers she is meant to overhear. A Polish count, who has left for his estates, but not before providing for the mother and child. "Ah, the consequences of sweet passion. Oh, the recklessness of the young," Madame du Hausset exclaimed, holding her hand over her heart.

Véronique was asleep when Marguerite Leblanc left, her afterbirth safely extracted, her limbs and belly massaged with oils and salves. There have been no signs of lethargy, convulsions or more forceful bleeding than usual. "She'll be crying a lot in the next few days," she told Lisette. "The body has to come back from where it has been."

The baptism is a sad affair. The parish church of the town of Versailles is freezing cold. The priest is in a hurry, the altar boy who holds the tray with the holy oil sniffles and stomps his feet. The godparents are curious and solicitous by turns, and Marguerite Leblanc cannot decide who irritates her more: the red-haired godmother who giggles as if someone pinched her buttocks or the beefy godfather with gin on his breath?

The thought that the two will be gone as soon as the ceremony ends is a relief.

At the baptismal font, the priest clutches the hem of his stole embroidered with golden crosses. In spite of the heavy coat under his chasuble, his cheeks are reddened, and each breath forms a little white cloud.

"The baby I'm holding in my arms," Marguerite Leblanc testifies, "is a girl, and I, the midwife, have witnessed the birth."

Washed in wine and smeared with butter, the tiny thing quieted down. The wet nurse, bless her, has swaddled her but left her legs free to kick, so that she won't be bandy-legged.

Filius nullius. A child of nobody.

The godmother stifles a hiccup. The priest frowns. Marguerite Leblanc hands the baby to the godmother. The godfather lays his hand on the girl's head.

The priest intones a prayer.

Marie-Louise, who desires to obtain eternal life in the church of God through faith in Jesus Christ, quietly renounces the devil, and all his works, and all his pomps. Only when the priest pours a stream of holy water over her forehead does she wail in her second protest. As robust and as loud as her first.

The name to inscribe in the parish book?

Du Hausset has the name already, all written out on a slip of crumpled paper she extracts from her pocket: Marie-Louise Bosque.

Marguerite Leblanc believes in the wisdom of counting your blessings. Marie-Louise Bosque sounds much better than Marie-Louise Blanc, which is what the foundling hospital would've named her and where she would have been lucky to survive even a few days.

"A gift from the count." Madame du Hausset handed me a small wooden box tied with a silver ribbon.

I turned it in my hands.

"No need to open it now," she said. "It's yours to do with as you please."

I was in bed, shivering in spite of the blazing fire. Madame sat beside me, cleared her throat. Her face was flushed, and she pulled on her fichu, exposing her neck. Wrinkled like a turkey's throat, I thought.

It was time to talk of my future, she said.

She spread it out in front of me, as if it were a dress in my mother's stall, showing only its best side. A good marriage, a merchant with prospects . . . willing . . . ready to take me. A respectable life . . . of comfort . . .

"There will be other children," she also said, to clinch her bargain.

My fingers searched the hem of my sleeve, the lace I once admired so much.

"I don't desire marriage," I said.

"Don't be foolish, girl," she said. A deep sigh followed these words, a twitch of her nostrils. I could imagine her whispering into la marquise's ear. Bemoaning my theatrics, the delusions of those unwisely encouraged to think themselves important.

I pulled at the lace. Then I pulled again.

"Unless you have a vocation to take the veil," Madame du Hausset continued. "That, too, has been arranged before. The Sisters of Charity will take you with open arms."

Since I still did not answer, Madame du Hausset said, she had no other recourse but to make herself plain and straightforward. It was a mystery to her what I was counting on or what others may have told me. The truth is that she has had to take care of many other girls like me before. In the same predicament.

One more pull at the sleeve and I dislodged a thread. I pinched it with my fingers and the lace gave in.

"What are you doing, stupid girl!" du Hausset screamed, slapping my hand. "You'll ruin it."

The slap made me raise my eyes. Something in them must have frightened her for her voice softened. "Nothing needs to be decided today," she said.

Not in the state I was in, sensitive, prone to hysteria and flights of fancy.

When she left, I opened the box and found an *aigrette* studded with small diamonds. No letter accompanied the gift, and I wondered if the king of France knew that he had another daughter. And if he would be with me now if I had given birth to a son.

~⚬~

Take good care of your mistress, the midwife said.

To prevent milk fever Lisette must serve her mistress bouillon every three hours; never from veal, which causes diarrhea. Then some broth-soaked white bread, cut thin and small, easy to digest. To drink, lukewarm water with a little wine, or syrup of maidenhair fern. Lisette must also check the sheets for blood clots, keep her mistress's breasts covered and warm. Rub them with olive oil with flax and honey in it.

And then comes the warning. Don't leave her alone, she might do something foolish.

Véronique has been saying a lot of foolish things. Like asking if they took her baby away to punish her for her sins. Or swearing that she can hear the baby crying in the other room and asking Lisette to check on it. Not just once but again and again. Even though Lisette has told her the wet nurse took the baby to the country where she would be under good care.

Véronique does not sleep well, either. Night after night she wakes up sobbing that something has happened to the baby. The wet nurse has dropped her or left her all by herself to cry.

"How would you know that, Miss?" Lisette asks.

Véronique might not wish to think of Brest and her new life, but Lisette is already making her calculations. She will ask for eighty livres at first, which is what the Deer Park maids have been getting. But as soon as Véronique realizes how much she needs her, Lisette will demand a raise. Every family has its secrets. Every house has its share of scheming.

You need a trusted soul to know what is what.

~⚬~

"What name did they give her?" I asked Lisette. I knew my daughter was no longer in the house as I had not heard her cry for a whole day.

"Marie-Louise," she said, and I turned the name in my mouth, rolled it on my tongue. Nothing of me in it, I thought bitterly. As if I never existed. As if nothing of me mattered.

Mistress Leblanc came back. She wrapped me in sheets dipped in some smelly lotion, to stop me from bleeding. Showed me how to squeeze the unwanted milk from my breasts. Held me when I cried, coaxing me out of despair, chasing away my fears. My daughter was with a wet nurse, she said, a kind, honest woman, from a village just outside Paris. "I know her well," the midwife said. "She has plenty of milk. With her your baby will lack for nothing."

When I wouldn't stop crying, she told me of babies left at the church door, sent to a foundling home. Babies fed pap from oats and sour wine, dying by the dozen. She made me picture tiny bodies bundled in old rags, buried in a mass grave. Tossed a prayer if they were in luck.

Your child has a name, Véronique, she said. Your child has a future.

Her words are still in my ears, the lapping of sea waves, their promise.

"You, too, have a future, Véronique. You are only fourteen, your life is still before you. Your real life."

MADAME VICTOIRE IS holding her throat. "Just a bit sore, Papa," she tells the king, who is sitting at the edge of her bed. "I'm afraid you've come all the way from Fontainebleau for nothing."

Lebel is inclined to think so as well. Nothing really has warranted this rushed escapade to Versailles that the queen has provoked with her alarming note. Yes, Madame Victoire has a fever, but there are no signs of pustules or rash. The doctor who examined her found the source of mischief in the throat. She has been bled and purged, given salvia rinses and caramelized onions for the coughing. The lingering smell in the room is that of burned gunpowder, which has cleared it from contagion. If there was any in the first place.

"Maman says I was foolish," Madame Victoire continues. "I took a walk in the garden without my pelisse. But the day seemed so mild."

"Mild for January," the king says. "Not really mild."

"Yes, Papa."

"Madame is eating exceptionally well," adds the doctor, who has been standing a few steps away ready to answer the king's questions. She and her royal mother, who has so dutifully remained by her daughter's side, will be able to join the court at Fontainebleau in a week.

"Coche, is it true? Are you stuffing yourself like a goose before Christmas?" Louis asks, and Victoire smiles back at him with girlish mischief.

That the doctor has allowed the king inside the room is another indication that this is a mere indisposition, not an illness. When Madame Henrietta was dying, the king was not allowed beyond the threshold of her bedroom. Now he is permitted to feel Madame Victoire's forehead, administer his favorite wormwood infusion. "Five drops," Louis says, putting his spectacles on to read the labels of the bottles he has brought from Fontainebleau.

Victoire is dressed in a frilly nightgown and a lace-trimmed bonnet. Neither too becoming. *Looking more like a stout merchant's wife than my child,* the king once said of her, and Lebel remembers it well. The kind of statement that means: *Such are the manifestations of my children's Polish blood, their temper* polonaise. The queen's undeniable fault.

"Yes, Papa . . . Thank you, Papa . . . Oh, it's disgusting, Papa."

They talk of how the winter darkness descends so early now, but the days will get longer soon. Louis praises the advantages of Fontainebleau over Versailles. Fewer duties, no need for *grandes levées* or eating in public. Only the most trusted servants around. "You'll join us soon, Coche," he says. "But I forbid all garden walks in winter. Even with a pelisse."

Since Madame Victoire is in no real danger, the royal entourage will return to Fontainebleau this very evening. The carriages are already waiting. The dauphin will ride in His Majesty's carriage, which makes Lebel uneasy. The king's conversations with Louis-Ferdinand have been particularly strained recently. The dauphin persists with his thinly veiled admonitions, which leave the king testy for hours afterward. *Our sacred duty to keep the monarchy pure, Sire . . . to provide an example for the populace.* Someone must have told him of the latest bastard, Lebel thinks. Could it be that he has a spy at Deer Park? Or has found an eager soul clamoring for a reward? It might be prudent to offer that Lisette a small raise, just in case she is tempted.

"You must leave now, Papa. It's getting late," Madame Victoire says, quite sensibly, for the ride to Fontainebleau will take a good few hours. Her cheeks are flushed only because, on the queen's orders, the bedroom is overheated. But how does one argue with an anxious mother? Even if she *is* unreasonable.

It is already six o'clock when the king, wrapped in his fur-lined cloak, descends the rear staircase, crosses the guardroom and walks out into the Marble Court. Torchbearers precede him, lighting the way. Behind him the dauphin and the duc de Richelieu, side by side. The duc d'Ayen follows. It's a pity d'Ayen cannot replace the dauphin in the royal carriage. The conversations about botany would make the king much better disposed.

The evening is bitterly cold, with a full moon showing between the scudding clouds and the flames of the torches. The king's soldiers are drawn up in two lines, leading from the palace door to the coach. Lebel, who walks a few steps behind d'Ayen, notes the usual idlers hanging around, gawking. "As if I were a circus monster," the king has said on many occasions. "What do they think I am, Lebel? A bearded woman or a two-headed cow?"

The indistinct figure that springs forward seems to come from nowhere. A force spun out of darkness, a whirl of energy that has no solid shape, shoving two of the soldiers aside. A ghost, Lebel remembers thinking, before he sees the assassin's striking hand.

The man, having delivered his blow, darts back into darkness.

"Someone has just punched me!" the king says to the duc d'Ayen, sliding his hand underneath the cloak where the blow has landed. When he draws it back again, his hand is covered with blood.

There are shouts and screams everywhere. "The one with the hat! Catch him! Quick!"

An equerry, a footman and some of the soldiers fling themselves on the man, pin him down. D'Ayen, shaken, repeats the same dumb question: "What's happening? What's happening?" The dauphin is crossing himself. Richelieu waves his hands as if he were about to fly away. From where the ghostly man struggles with his captors, the sound of thumping is followed by moans.

Lebel has pushed himself past them all. In the torchlight the royal face looks shadowy, grim. "Are you wounded, Sire? Does it hurt?" he asks, but the king looks right through him. "Bewildered and lost," Lebel will describe the king's countenance to Madame de Pompadour. But not for long, he will assure her.

The duc d'Ayen and the others gather to carry the king upstairs, but Louis waves them aside. He can manage on his own. It is just a scratch. He doesn't feel weak in the least.

Seeing that His Majesty is heading toward the state bedroom, Lebel races there through the service stairs only to find the room in utter disarray. The bed has been stripped of all linen, the curtains and the carpet removed for cleaning. The room is cold, too. It will take time to warm up, panicky servants wail, even if they start the fire right now. A sorry lot, all of them, Lebel thinks. The regular staff is at Fontainebleau. So is the royal linen. And the royal surgeon.

"Get any surgeon then," Lebel snaps at a sniveling page who crouches as if threatened with a beating. "Just be quick about it." Two other pages, disheveled as if caught drinking or whoring behind service stairs, are staring at him with wide, blinking eyes. Neither has ever been trusted with serving the king before.

The door opens, the king enters leaning on his son's arm. The dauphin leads his father toward the bare bed and helps him to lie down. Richelieu takes off Louis's cloak, loosens his jacket, revealing its underside stained with blood. To Lebel's eyes the wound doesn't look deep, but he is not close enough to see properly, standing as he is behind d'Ayen. A line has been drawn in this room, a line he cannot dispute. They are royal friends, he is a royal servant, barred from his master until the king calls him.

Richelieu and d'Ayen exchange tense whispers. Lebel hears the word *poison*. The king must have heard it, too, for suddenly his face breaks out in sweat. The dauphin leaves his father's side and darts out of the room.

If Lebel could strike these two on their thick heads, he would. Is it of no consequence to them that they are alarming Louis at a moment so fraught already? Panic, Lebel knows, is like a tidal wave, crushing all resistance. Louis is already picturing this poison coursing through his veins. Imagines the pain, the convulsions, his body opened, viscera all dissolved, flowing through the doctor's hands as he tries to hold them. How long does he have? One hour? Two? Three, perhaps?

"Lebel, get my confessor," he hears.

But, of course, the royal confessor is at Fontainebleau as well.

"Get any priest then," Lebel barks in the direction of the pages. "Quick."

By then the sniveling page has fetched a surgeon from the guards' quarters. Another one from God knows where follows, so the word must have spread. The two surgeons inspect the wound together, terrified of their responsibility. The result is predictable. "Press makeshift bandages to stop the bleeding," says one. "No, keep the wound open. It has to breathe," says the other.

My king needs reassurance, Lebel thinks, and all these fools can do is bicker.

Outside the bedroom, more commotion. Footsteps, shouts, doors banging. Servants trip over themselves, bungle even the simplest of tasks. Assassin . . . Lebel hears . . . a madman . . . The king mortally wounded . . . The queen is on her way.

Among all this the king, covered only with his Versailles dressing gown, for the clean sheets have not yet arrived, shuts his eyes.

A moment later Lebel hears the queen's tearful voice followed by the dauphin's: "Let us inside, in God's name." As if they were divine messengers.

In a moment they will be shoving their pity down the king's throat, brimming with didn't-I-warn-you? Adding a few tears for good measure. They did it to Louis before, in Metz, when he was on his deathbed. Renounce your sins, banish those you have sinned with. Put on sackcloth, smear your head with ashes.

Look at us, praying for your soul so that it will be saved from eternal damnation. Look at us, offering forgiveness.

How bitter, the mercy of saints!

By midnight the king has confessed three times. First quickly, to a garrison priest. Then to the queen's confessor, and finally to the royal chaplain, summoned from Fontainebleau, who also administered Extreme Unction. The sins of thought and deed have been cleansed. All of them, from lying and evoking the Lord's name in vain to fornication and failing to receive communion at Easter. The way to eternal salvation is now clear.

The confession and absolution over, the king's personal surgeon and Lebel's good friend, La Martinière, who arrived from Fontainebleau with the chaplain, begins his examination. After giving his hands a vigorous rub to warm them up, he probes the wound, declaring it shallow and superficial. "No organs touched, Sire, no signs of sepsis or poison. Scarcely more than a scratch."

"The wound is deeper than you think," the king answers grimly. "It has gone right to my heart."

I might have let myself be swayed by the midwife's words if it weren't for the news from the palace. The freezing night, the torch-lit courtyard, the crazed man lunging forward out of darkness. It was Lisette who told me that the king had been wounded. Though I could see she was shaken, she relished the details. Damiens, she said, was the assassin's name. A former servant armed with a knife. A penknife, two-sided, three and a half inches long. If it weren't for His Majesty's winter coat, the thick furs . . .

She didn't finish. I was glad she didn't.

"Oh, Miss." She sighed. "Raising your hand to the king! What's this world coming to?"

My heart lurched, fluttered.

He is safe now, Lisette said, but I knew the corridors of the palace. How easy it was to sneak through them. All it took was a determined step, a purposeful look. What if an assassin was lurking in the service corridors right now? Or hiding in the small apartment I knew so well?

Thoughts like that could make me snap like a dry twig.

I recall the four days that followed as a long stretch of frenzy, endless circling of the room, my nails bitten to the quick. Lisette, angry with herself for telling me the news, smeared the tips of my fingers with wormwood infusion, hoping its bitterness would stop me.

It didn't.

She watched me like a hawk. Slept in my room, on a folding cot, refused to leave me alone. "So that you don't do anything foolish, Miss," she said.

"What can I possibly do?" I asked, shrugging my shoulders, watching the frown on her forehead fade.

Lying was becoming so much easier.

On the fifth day, I saw my chance. Madame Bertrand had summoned Lisette to Deer Park that morning; and even though she left reluctantly, I suspected she wouldn't come back before noon. I didn't need much time anyway. Wrapped in my traveling coat, I sneaked out of the house and headed for the Notre-Dame market. There, as soon as the public coach from Paris arrived, I mixed with the crowd on the way to the palace.

They were mostly women. Merchant wives, in their Sunday clothes, upper servants wearing their elegant hand-me-downs, children clutching their mothers' hands. They were all eager to see the king with their own eyes. To make sure His Majesty was on the mend, they said. If they were lucky, they would catch a glimpse of him on a palace balcony or on the gallery leading from the state bedroom to the offices of the council.

They talked about Damiens, too. A madman, I heard. The English set him up for it. No, not the English. Some crazy monk he listened to. Talking of children kidnapped, taken to Versailles, to their ruin. Just the talk a madman might heed. He wanted the king to repent and change his sinful ways for good.

There were speculations on his punishment. A wheel, his body torn by horses. Whatever it is, it will be for everyone to see.

I walked fast, head down. The conversations turned to the members of the royal family who had come from Fontainebleau to be with the king. If His Majesty didn't show himself, one could watch them at breakfast. The good queen was always so obliging, and so were the Daughters of France. Although Madame Adelaide was too skinny. Not like Madame Victoire, who was so nicely plump. One of the women beside me wanted to see if the Hall of Mirrors was truly as beautiful and full of light as she has heard. She was carrying a baby bundled up in a thick woolen shawl. I was not aware of staring at her, but I must have, for she whispered something to her companion and quickened her pace. I felt the tingling of tears under my eyelids.

The wind was worse than the cold, finding its way inside the folds of my coat. The ground was dusted with snow. Flocks of sparrows descended on the trees along the way, only to fly away a few tense moments later.

As soon as we crossed the threshold of Versailles, I slipped through the nearest door to the service corridor, and no one stopped me. On my way I passed servants, rushing to and fro, carrying linen, towels, jugs of water. Two footmen were carting wooden crates into storage. A maid rushed by with a basket of flowers, all white.

Don't stare, I reminded myself. Slow down.

It was not hard to take me for a lady's maid on an errand. I knew the right step, the right pace, the right hint of a knowing smile. I knew whom to ignore and whom to defer to, stepping out of their way. My voice when I exchanged casual pleasantries had the right inflection, the right ring of certainty. "Good day . . . Still mild, thank the Lord."

I knew where I was going.

At Deer Park the big clock in the hall downstairs has struck eleven. Lisette is getting anxious; she has been in Madame Bertrand's room long enough. Madame has already told her how the snow has loosened the roof tiles and how she predicts a leak as soon as the thaw comes. She has also complained about the new *élèves*. One thought she was in Poland; another tried to run away at night, as if they had no watchman. Manon, it turns out, is long gone, but Claire is still at Deer Park, still being summoned to the palace, though likely not for long. "Hard to tell for sure," Madame says, "but there have been quite a few hints."

Madame Bertrand likes talking, which cannot be helped, can it? Best not to show impatience. Best just to nod and smile.

"Now, Lisette. Tell me about Véronique. You haven't said a word about her."

"Ailing."

"What's wrong with her now?"

Lisette hesitates, what to say and what to keep to herself? So far no one knows she has told Véronique the truth about the count, and she intends to keep it that way. Not a word about Véronique's despondent moods or her foolish hopes then; nothing to make Madame Bertrand wonder.

Véronique's breasts are still swollen, Lisette says, her nipples reddened, releasing milk mixed with pus. The dressings have to be changed daily. The midwife has been obliged to come one more time to check on her.

Madame Bertrand sighs, impatient already. She has never believed in mollycoddling anyone. If it were up to her, Véronique would've been in Brest already. Married. Settling down.

Lisette, who doesn't want to continue talking about Véronique, puts her trust in avenue de Saint-Cloud gossip. Du Hausset hasn't forgiven Mistress Leblanc for keeping her away from the birth room.

"I wish I had been there to see it," Madame Bertrand says.

Lisette describes the scene the best she can: du Hausset banging on the door Lisette is holding, shouting, threatening them with pestilence.

"Pestilence." Madame Bertrand chuckles. "That's something. As if it would spare her, if it came."

In the corridor outside Rose is chastising someone. "Watch what you are doing, stupid girl!" A new maid-of-all-work, it turns out. The second one since Marianne left. It's not easy to find good servants nowadays.

Madame Bertrand will not be diverted any longer. "You are coming back, Lisette, aren't you?" she asks. "You are not thinking of taking off with her?"

"Why would I?" Lisette says. And then, knowing that a lie works best when it confirms what is already suspected, she adds, "Monsieur Lebel has already promised me a raise."

⁂

I heard his voice first. "Is this the truth?" he asked someone.

A girl's voice replied, "The whole truth!"

"Good!"

The service door had been well oiled and it opened silently. They were sitting on the green sofa, side by side, Claire in a lovely muslin dress, the king in a thick dressing gown.

He did not notice me until I let the words flow out of me, all at once, tumbling, blurred, awkward.

I know who you are.

You are the king of France, but you are also the king of my heart.

I was so afraid.

I just wanted to know you were safe. In good health.

I've prayed for you every single day.

I was mad from grief.

Claire giggled, as if it were all a good joke, but I paid her no heed.

He stood up, his face softened with a smile. A tender smile, I thought it, concerned. His eyes were red at the rim, bloodshot. Could he not sleep? Was he in pain? I felt a tug of such tenderness inside me that my knees weakened, and I sank to the floor.

"Shh, little mouse," he said, raising me up. "I'm in good health. The wound has almost healed already."

I clung to him, sobbing out the pain of my confinement, my fear of the future.

They kept me away from you.

They took our baby away. A little girl. Marie-Louise.

I've been waiting. Every day. Every hour.

What did I think would happen? That he would take me back? Let me keep my child? Let me live with her somewhere in this palace?

"You must go home and rest now," he said. "I will come to see you tonight. Will you wait for me?"

"Where?"

"At the house."

"Do you know where I am?"

"Yes. Will you wait?"

"Yes."

"Do you promise?"

"Yes."

"Lebel will take you home. Right now."

When did he ring the bell? I still wonder. For before I could do anything else, strong arms grabbed mine. Two lackeys I did not know took me out of the room. The last sight I had of the king was of his smiling face, his hand touching his lips, blowing a kiss in my direction.

Who are you?

Véronique Roux.

Who is the father of your child?

The king of France.

~❧~

I remember a snow-covered lane, a stone arch, a man dressed in black drawing iron gates closed behind us, the coach stopping with a jerk in front of a house in which all the windows were barred.

Lebel himself took me to Charenton. To make sure I didn't escape again. He didn't trust anyone anymore, he said. "Until you see reason," he said before the door opened and he gave me away. "Until you calm down."

"Where am I?" I asked, my voice boiling with hurt and anger. "Don't you know His Majesty is waiting for me?"

"I never presume to know His Majesty's mind," he said in a voice that made me grow slack inside. "And you shouldn't, either."

His eyes were hard and stone cold. He had brought me here to be cured, he said. Cured of a delusion that the king of France had been my lover.

I heard but didn't listen. "I'm not staying here," I said.

When the carriage door opened, two attendants grabbed me by the arms and dragged me out. I screamed. I cursed Lebel and the lackeys. "The king will hear of it," I cried. "You will all be sorry."

~❧~

During the next two days Lisette sits by her mistress's bedside in a room stinking of vomit and urine. A room with grubby gray walls, a crucifix hanging high enough so no one could reach it; a hard, narrow bed; a blanket, gray, threadbare; the musty mattress stuffed with hay, stiff and prickly.

At first the sleeping draft keeps Véronique calm and sluggish. The nun who checks on her is a kind one, Sister Bernadette, who has placed an orange studded with cloves and cinnamon shards beside Véronique's bed, on account of the smells.

Her dreams must be bad, though, for Véronique thrashes about. "Out, out, right now," she screams, her voice hoarse. "Get out. Fast."

Lisette does what she can. Wakes Véronique from nightmares, throws another blanket over her shoulders when Véronique shivers.

Every morning the same questions are followed by the same answers:

Who are you?

Véronique Roux.

Who is the father of your child?

The king of France.

❧

I was bled. Purged. Doused with water until I thought I was drowning, gasping for air. I was angry with my body for wanting to live. The world shrank to the slap of bare feet on the floor, the taste of blood on my tongue. My voice sounded like a yelp of a dog. Rough hands pulling my arms, seizing my waist. Grips tightened with every move. Blows knocked me out of my head.

When I came to, I was strapped to a bed, a piece of wood lodged between my teeth. From other beds I heard howls and shrieks and fervent pleas: "Take me out of here . . . I am hungry . . . Mother, please . . . I'll kill you and I'll kill her . . . stupid, stupid, stupid."

A woman with long, disheveled hair came up to me, stared into my eyes as if she knew me and spat in my face. "Traitor," she said, and I closed my eyes not to see the frenzy of her twitching face. Another one lifted her skirts, squatted, a stream of piss flowing from underneath her. "My waters just broke," she shrieked, her voice thick with urgency. "Fetch a midwife. Quick."

❧

"Why are you so stubborn, Miss?" Lisette asks, two days later, when she is finally allowed to see Véronique. "Just tell them what they want to hear."

But the day ends, and another begins.

Who are you?

Véronique Roux.

Who is the father of your child?

The king of France.

One moment frightens Lisette more than the others. In the garden where she is allowed to take her mistress, pigeons are pecking at the breadcrumbs scattered on the melting snow. Véronique watches the birds intently. "They don't care about me, do they?" she asks Lisette. "They would peck at the crumbs even if I fell dead."

Véronique bends, picks up a few crumbs, places them on the palm of her hand and waits for a bird to land on it. One does and she grabs its leg. The bird, terrified, begins to bat its wings. It is only when Lisette screams at her that Véronique lets it go.

She also says horrible things. How she will poke her own eyes out or stab herself. How it is the devil putting these thoughts in her head. How when the earth is baked dry with the sun, nothing will grow on it for it's still burning inside.

⤚✸⤙

Someone fetched Maman. "What are you hoping for, Véronique?" she asked me.

She took out her sewing bag, threaded her needle and began mending my clothes, darning the torn lace, reinforcing the seams of my robes. "To make them last," she said.

I bit my lips.

"You don't have to stay here, Véronique," she said.

Monsieur Durand had begged her to end this "unnecessary ordeal." His master wished me no harm. The grain merchant was still ready to accept his new bride.

"His name is Lebel," I said. "Not Durand."

Maman frowned.

"The king is the father of my child," I said.

Maman put her finger on my lips. "It won't get us anywhere, such talk."

"It's the truth."

"Truth won't get us anywhere."

She packed all her conviction into her voice. Marriage is a woman's duty. It won't be easy, but, unlike her, I would have the means to soften the disappointments. Think of the comfort of not having to worry where the next meal was coming from, she said, a husband who—by all accounts—was a good man.

"Whose accounts?" I asked. "You haven't even seen him."

I didn't know my voice could sound so harsh, so unforgiving. "A good man, Maman, doesn't have to buy himself a wife."

"What do you want, Véronique?"

"I want my child back."

"Your daughter is better off without you," Maman said. "No man wants to raise a bastard. There will be other children."

"I wish for no other children."

Who are you?

Véronique Roux.

Who is the father of your child?

The king of France.

It took four more days, four long dark days before I answered:

"A Polish count, a cousin to the queen."

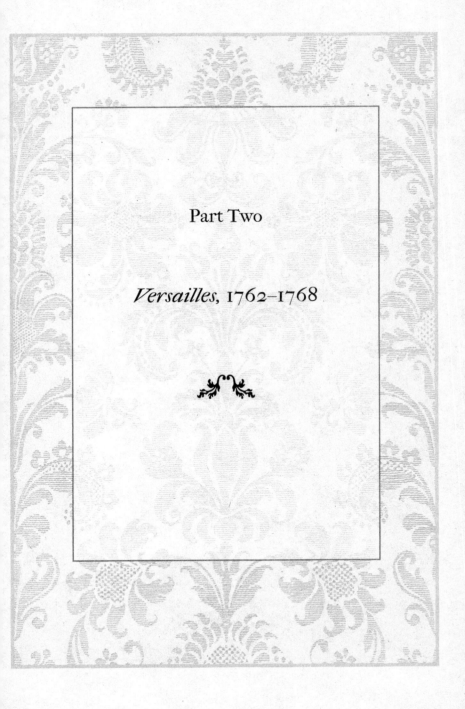

Part Two

Versailles, 1762–1768

1762

IN THE TIME BEFORE VERSAILLES, Marie-Louise lived in the country, with her nurse.

There was a dense thicket there she called her hiding place. A jumble of bushes and brambles, branches smacking her face as she made her way into its center, where the air was moist, minty, tinged with the undertone of mold. There she pulled clover out of the ground, the roots white and sweet. Sometimes she found little bones, or torn feathers, or the crushed shells of small eggs. Snakes slithered past. Once, she surprised a bone-thin, mangy cat that limped away at the sight of her, even though she begged it to come back. She loved staying there, watching the shadow of a tree lengthen, until in the twilight she could no longer see her own hands, until she did not know where she began or ended.

She has other memories of that time. The smithy where her nurse sometimes took her and where Marie-Louise stood in awe of the giant man with blackened cheeks bending over a ball of fire. As the gust of heat scorched her face, her eyes registered the bright sparks, her nostrils the smell of soot and ashes, her feet the grittiness of the floor under the soles of her shoes. Everything fascinated her: the bellows making the fire blaze up, the red-hot piece of metal the blacksmith held with long tongs, the relentless beat of the hammer molding the fiery mass into what increasingly looked like a big nail, the furious hiss of the water in the bucket where the blacksmith dipped the nail to harden it.

"When will my mother send for me?" she remembers asking her nurse.

"I don't know."

"Are you her sister?"

"No."

"My father's then?"

"No."

"Then whose?"

"No one's."

In the summer of the year Marie-Louise would turn six, a monsieur from the palace arrived in a black carriage to take her away. Convinced that her mother had finally sent for her, just as it had happened to other children living with their nurses in the village, she became giddy with joy. This is why when the nurse hugged her and asked if she would miss her, Marie-Louise said no.

"Not even a little?" the nurse asked and made a very sad face.

"Perhaps a little," Marie-Louise conceded, for she didn't want her nurse to stay sad.

Her smocks, aprons and handkerchiefs were all neatly folded and placed in a wicker basket with a lid. So were her toys: Poupette, the doll her nurse had made for her from two kinds of cloth, cotton for the body and silk for the face; a spin top that twirled into continuous stripes of red and yellow, colors Marie-Louise thought were the most beautiful in the world.

The palace monsieur said he didn't have all day. He drummed his fingers on the tabletop. He looked at the ceiling first and then at Marie-Louise. The horses neighed outside. That was when the nurse traced the sign of the cross over Marie-Louise's forehead and gave her a soft pincushion embroidered with a red rose. Marie-Louise began to cry, and her nose got all snotty.

"There, there," the nurse said and wiped the snot away.

In the town of Versailles the houses were big, golden and glittering; the long lanes leading to them were filled with carriages and people rushing about. Bells rang. Someone yelled, "Make way! Make way!" She saw a boy carrying a caged bird, its feathers green, bright red and blue. A man on a gray horse passed them by. A pack of dogs followed the carriage, barking in excitement.

Before Marie-Louise had the time to worry about how her mother could possibly find her now that she was not with her nurse, the carriage pulled into a small courtyard where a different monsieur, tall and thin, in a purple jacket with shiny gold buttons, waited for her. Marie-Louise thought him odd-looking, a bit like the scarecrows that guarded the fields near her nurse's house. His wrinkled face had pinkish smudges on it, and his lips were pursed in a grimace, which made Marie-Louise decide that he didn't like her much and therefore could not be her father.

"I'm Marie-Louise," she said in case the scarecrow monsieur didn't know her name and took her to a wrong mother.

"Are you, really?"

"Yes."

He asked her if she had caused trouble on the way, had been a nuisance, perhaps.

"No," she said. Although she had been, demanding her doll be taken from the wicker basket because she wanted to hold it. Making the first monsieur call her an incorrigible brat. She was still holding Poupette now, upside down, for this is how Poupette liked it best, her button eyes intent on seeing everything Marie-Louise might miss.

"Come along then."

She followed him along a path lined with trees growing in giant pots, as if they were flowers. She wondered what her mother would say first when she saw her. How much she had grown? Would she ask if she had been a good girl when she lived with her nurse? Which she was, mostly, wasn't she?

"Be grateful for being taken care of," the palace monsieur told her as she climbed the stairs after him in a strange-looking house with many doors that was neither golden nor glittering. "Always obey your guardians. Learn what they have to teach you."

Guardians, Marie-Louise told herself, must be another word for parents.

"Give them no reason for anger, ever."

A rooster's crow, his voice, telling her to avoid the sins of bluntness, caprice and contradiction, as if she knew what it meant. *Indolence* was also bad, but this word was easier to guess, especially when Monsieur added, "Idle hands tempt the devil."

This is what adults did. Appeared from nowhere, spoke in riddles and then disappeared. It was pointless to ask them questions; watching them closely worked better. Monsieur in the purple jacket had to be an important man, for the people he took her to welcomed him with a deep bow and a curtsy. "You won't regret your decision, Monsieur Lebel. Neither will Madame de

Pompadour," the woman he addressed as Madame Gourlon said. "With us, the child will lack for nothing."

Marie-Louise felt a tinge of pleasure at these words.

The short, wiry man with a reddened nose who stood beside Madame Gourlon was Monsieur Gourlon. He was holding his hands behind his back the way Marie-Louise's nurse did when she had a surprise for her. Would he give her a horn she could blow and make dogs bark? Or a new doll, perhaps? But when he dropped his hands, they were both empty, which made Marie-Louise sad and a little bit angry, but not Poupette, who was very jealous and wouldn't like a new doll at all.

At first Marie-Louise listened carefully to what was said. How Madame de Pompadour's wishes had to be obeyed. How the child was not to be indulged. "Instructed according to her abilities," the scarecrow monsieur said. "Offered guidance." But since no one addressed Marie-Louise, she let Poupette take a good look around the room they were in. They both loved a picture of a stag in a forest meadow hanging on one of the walls, its head up, lit by the silver moon and a shiny candelabra with six candles that stood in the middle of a table. "Fancy," Marie-Louise's nurse would have called it.

Finally, the palace monsieur announced that his business was done, and he had no more time to waste. As soon as he left, Marie-Louise turned to Madame Gourlon and asked:

"Are you my mother?"

Madame opened her eyes wide and then frowned. "Whatever gave you that idea, child?" she asked.

"Are you?"

"No."

"Take me to her then."

"Listen to this brat, wife." Monsieur Gourlon scoffed. "Barely inches off the ground and giving us orders already."

Guardians, it turned out, were not parents. They were strangers who agreed to take her in out of the goodness of their hearts, to do their Christian duty.

When Marie-Louise threw herself on the floor and began to wail, Madame

Gourlon asked, "Is this how you show your gratitude? Is this the kind of behavior your mother would like to see?" This made Marie-Louise cry even harder. She didn't calm down even when Madame Gourlon, who told her to call her Gardienne, opened her hand and put some sugar shavings on it. Or showed Marie-Louise the nook where she would sleep and keep her lovely new dresses. Or greeted Poupette with great ceremony and asked her name. "She won't tell you," Marie-Louise said, but Gardienne guessed it anyway.

The Gourlons were Madame de Pompadour's servants. Madame de Pompadour was a very important lady, a dear friend of the king himself. Gardienne was Madame's waiting maid, Monsieur Gourlon, whom everyone called Old Gourlon, was her coachman, and this is why he wore livery with purple facings. They lived in two entresol rooms on the first floor of the Grand Commons, the bigger one with the windowless nook where, every evening, Marie-Louise unfolded her bed only to fold it up neatly again each morning.

"Our ward," Gardienne said when anyone asked. Willful, but settling down, thanks be to merciful God and all the saints. "My own little ones are with the angels in Heaven," Gardienne also said. "Too good for this earth."

Sometimes, if more questions followed, Gardienne would whisper in the other person's ear. The words Marie-Louise heard, "a Polish bastard" or "one of those Deer Park girls," were always spoken with a frown. Whatever they meant, they always caused knowing nods and curious looks in her direction. As if there was something peculiar about her, something for which no ordinary words were good enough.

Gardienne said that Marie-Louise had wasted enough time already with "that nurse of hers" and that was why she had duties now. She had to learn to be useful so that one day, like her Gardienne, she, too, could become a waiting maid to a grand lady, maybe even to Madame de Pompadour herself. But before this could happen Marie-Louise had to learn how to sew, darn and embroider so that she could watch over her mistress's wardrobe. And she would also have to learn good manners so that her presence would bring her future mistress nothing but solace and joy.

"Pay attention, Marie-Louise," Gardienne would say every morning, making Marie-Louise practice different stitches until they looked perfectly even and did not pull at the fabric and make it pucker. Or embroider a sampler particularly appropriate for young girls in her circumstances. The lessons went well unless Marie-Louise turned careless and forgot her manners. Her nail-biting was a case in point. For in spite of the wormwood infusion smeared on her fingertips twice daily, Marie-Louise's nails were always chewed halfway down, revealing the pink flesh underneath. That was why Poupette the doll had enough of Marie-Louise and fell apart. Her silk and cotton parts both thinned and tore, revealing the stuffing inside, which turned out to be nothing but old rags and balls of crushed hay.

Gardienne always did something with her lips when she said things like that. Pursed them, or blew air through them, following with a toss of her head, up first then aside. There was no fighting a bad seed, she said. Marie-Louise was a cross to bear. A nail in her guardians' coffin. A scourge.

When her lessons were over, Marie-Louise was allowed to play outside.

In His Majesty's stables the red-haired groom with tiny mud-colored freckles taught her how to calm a jittery horse. In the royal dairy, the milkmaid with eyes that crinkled around the corners with every smile showed her how to squeeze the cow's tits and gave her fresh, foamy milk to drink, still warm from the udder.

"My real mother," Marie-Louise told them, "is a countess who had to hide me from her evil family. My real father is coming to take me with him any time now. But this is a secret, so don't tell anyone."

"If it is thus," they said, "you are a lucky girl."

Marie-Louise nodded and skipped away. Or rewarded them with a cartwheel she had learned to execute perfectly. Or with her imitation of Old Gourlon shaving, which involved holding her nose and scraping her throat with an imaginary razor she sharpened on an imaginary belt.

She was quite a mimic, they said. She could earn her keep in the circus.

Was she a lucky girl, though?

If she was, why was she getting into scrapes all the time? Coming back home wet, dirty, with torn clothes, smeared with tar? Making Gardienne cut tangled strands of her hair, despair over her ruined clothes, ask why on earth couldn't she stay away from trouble?

"Because," Marie-Louise finally admitted, "I was searching for my mother."

"'Searching for my mother'!" Gardienne repeated in a mocking voice, her hands raised up to the Heavens. "And why, pray tell me, would your mother care for such a brat?"

Hurtful words, more hurtful than any slap. They meant that her mother abandoned her because Marie-Louise wasn't good enough, obedient enough, careful enough.

Her mother didn't want such a bundle of trouble, such a wayward child.

Her mother had left her for a reason.

~✦~

Visitors who dropped by the Grand Commons were mostly Madame de Pompadour's maids and footmen. Marie-Louise liked them for the stories they told. A fat-headed royal princess walked down the palace corridor leaving a trail of her piss for them to clean. A Versailles officer killed his valet with a blow of his sword. The king had private rooms on the roof, above the Salon of War: one full of maps and strange rocks, another a workshop where His Majesty was turning lead into gold.

One visitor caused a small commotion every time she appeared. Gardienne called her Nicole, but Marie-Louise was to refer to her as Madame du Hausset. "How can you possibly manage it every day, Diane?" Nicole always asked, gasping for breath after having climbed to the entresol rooms. "First this long walk, then these hellish stairs." To which Gardienne always answered that the walk took a mere ten minutes and the stairs were not that steep. Besides, she knew not to poke a gift horse in the mouth.

"To each his own," Nicole might say to that, or "If such is your pleasure, indeed." Or some other puzzling words that always made Gardienne declare in a solemn tone that she had always been grateful for Madame de Pompadour's generosity.

"Does anyone say you are not, Diane?" Nicole asked with that funny-sounding huff of hers. To which Gardienne replied that she hoped no one would. And if they did, Madame would never pay heed to such words, would she?

Nicole, Madame du Hausset, called herself Madame de Pompadour's companion and confidante. "Madame trusts me in every matter," she would say. "And so does His Majesty, who has given me many proofs of his absolute confidence." Neither the king nor Madame de Pompadour would ever agree to her being away from them even for a day, which was why she lived at the big palace, in a room next to Madame's apartment. Those who envied her this privilege forgot that she was expected to be at her mistress's side mere moments after she had been summoned. Day or night, for poor Madame slept badly, on account of the king, who didn't think of himself enough and let others take advantage of his good heart. This was why Madame de Pompadour was waking up at night in a cold sweat, gasping for breath.

Poor Madame, indeed, Gardienne agreed. Though how fortunate to have someone like Nicole at her side.

For Marie-Louise, Madame du Hausset always had the same questions. Was Marie-Louise a good child? Not inclined to frivolity like some girls she did not wish to mention? Was she grateful to her guardians for taking care of her? How much progress had she made in her lessons? Did she already know how to darn silk stockings? Has she started learning her catechism?

Marie-Louise answered these questions carefully, mindful of Gardienne's hovering presence. Her guardians were kind to her. She was making progress but not as much as Gardienne would have liked, which was her own fault. No, she had not yet started to learn her catechism, but Gardienne said she would, in the new year.

Madame du Hausset believed in speaking her mind, which mostly meant listing Marie-Louise's faults. Her unruly mop of hair, her chewed-up nails, her "puzzling but absolute" lack of grace that testified to the undeniable fact that some apples do fall far from the apple tree. The fact that she and Gardienne both considered curious and quite unexpected and that caused some intense whisperings about "these Deer Park girls." How some things could've been predicted. How some things only proved that blood never lied.

"I do not envy you, Diane. Oh no, I don't."

Gardienne was not always pleased with Madame du Hausset's visit. "Would you listen to her," she might say, after her friend had left. Or "As if I asked for her envy!" Or "As if she were made of a different clay." Or "Sometimes I wonder what she is telling Madame about us behind our back."

"Piss and fart, sound at heart," Old Gourlon would always say to that, which truly made no sense at all.

Marie-Louise still believed that her mother was searching for her, though now that Marie-Louise was no longer living with her nurse how would she know where to find her? That is why she began leaving signs, a trail for her mother to follow. Broken twigs shaped into an arrow pointing in the direction of the entresol rooms or a small pyramid of pebbles with a scrap of paper inside it on which she had drawn the Grand Commons.

But her mother did not come.

1763

THE COURTYARD PAVING STONES were slippery from the snow. Marie-Louise was trailing behind Gardienne on the way to Madame de Pompadour's wardrobe to collect Madame's clothes for mending, for she was old enough to help now. She was minding her steps, just as Gardienne told her to, when she was yanked by her shoulder and told to curtsy.

Only then did Marie-Louise see a lady with a kind, smiling face, a bit like her nurse's. But unlike her nurse she wore a splendid silvery-gray cloak and a black bonnet tied under her chin. Funny-looking, Marie-Louise thought, like a small cushion with frills. A step behind her, court ladies followed, all dressed in pearly blue, their hands hidden in thick muffs. Could it be that the lady was Madame de Pompadour herself?

A curtsy must be flawless. No wavering, no wobbling, eyes down. Gardienne had taught Marie-Louise that.

"What a beautiful face this child has!" the lady in the black bonnet exclaimed. "Like an angel!" Her companions were flanking her now, murmuring their agreement. Look at this copper tint in her hair! The dark blue of her eyes! And how graceful she is! Ah, the perfect innocence of a child!

Gardienne gave Marie-Louise a look of warning, though what she was being warned against was a mystery.

The kind lady bent over her. A gloved finger lifted her chin up, carrying a sweet lemony scent of perfume.

"What is your name?"

"Marie-Louise."

"And how old are you, Marie-Louise?"

"Almost seven," she said, presenting five fingers on her left hand and then adding two from her right.

"And where is your Maman taking you?"

Marie-Louise blushed crimson.

"She is my ward, Your Majesty," Gardienne said and curtsied. Then, turning to Marie-Louise, speaking in what Marie-Louise by then thought of as her *outside* voice, soft and cheerful, Gardienne said, "Thank Her Royal Majesty, the Queen of France, for her immense kindness!"

"Are you a real queen?" Marie-Louise asked, gasping, for the queen had to be even more important than Madame de Pompadour.

The lady smiled. One of her companions giggled.

"Yes, I am."

"Where is your crown then?" Marie-Louise asked with grave seriousness, which made the queen's entourage even more merry.

"I keep it locked in a safe place. I wouldn't like to lose it or, God forbid, have it stolen. Am I right to do that?"

"Yes."

"Shall I tell you what I loved doing most of all when I was your age?" The queen's face was wrinkled around the eyes and her lips. One of her front teeth was darker than the others, but not that much.

"Yes, please."

"Playing my harpsichord. Do you play an instrument?"

"No."

The queen shook her head in disbelief. How could any child be denied such a simple, universal pleasure? It was like blowing soap bubbles.

"I don't know how to blow bubbles," Marie-Louise said.

All her grandchildren loved blowing bubbles, the queen assured her. Even Louis-Auguste, who was deadly serious in all other matters. And who was not that much older than Marie-Louise was, for he would soon turn nine.

It was Gardienne who was being addressed now. God wanted little children to play. Adults could not forget this important truth.

"Yes, Your Majesty. I'll remember that, Your Majesty."

"I have to go now," the queen said, turning to Marie-Louise, her voice again soft. "But before I go, I want to know if you pray every morning and evening?"

"I do."

"Who do you pray for?"

"First for my mother and father, then for my guardians, then for the king and queen and the glory of France."

"So, you pray for me, too," the queen said, sliding her hand in between the folds of her dress and retrieving a small picture. "Then this is for you."

Later, when Gardienne was telling Old Gourlon about the royal encounter—Bubbles, of all things! As if we had soap to spare!—Marie-Louise took out the queen's gift. The picture was of Mary, Mother of God, cradling her son in her arms. Baby Jesus, plump and pink, was smiling at his mother, who had turned her face toward him and was smiling back.

When Marie-Louise sniffed at it, it still smelled faintly of lemons.

Thinking it the most beautiful picture in the whole, whole world, Marie-Louise put it into the wooden trunk where she kept her treasures: the pincushion her nurse had given her; the torn pieces of Poupette; the twirling top, which had lost its tip and wouldn't spin; and her white baby dress, the one in which—her nurse once told her—she had been baptized.

The one Marie-Louise believed her mother had chosen herself.

Turning seven meant that some of the ordinary things Marie-Louise did became very wicked. Like sitting up in her bed, her knees up, rocking herself back and forth. Or sucking on the top of her arms until red marks appeared. Or putting her hand between her legs where it itched.

To stop herself from doing these wicked things Marie-Louise would curl under her coverlet, leaving a tunnel for the air to reach her, and give herself up to stories of her own making.

In one such story her father had just dismounted a shiny black horse with easy grace when he caught sight of her mother. A spark of light crossed the space that separated them. "One look is all it takes," Madame Gourlon liked to say.

The day was beautiful, sunny, not a cloud in the sky. Her parents looked at each other for a long time, exchanged words Marie-Louise would hear in her thoughts for a long time: "Please don't leave just yet. What is your name? How can I find you? Where?"

With time, the words her parents exchanged got bolder.

"I won't leave you."

"Can I trust you?"

"Yes."

"Why are you crying then?"

They called each other by their first names, but since they whispered these names, Marie-Louise could never quite hear them.

Maman, Papa, she murmured, piecing together their looks, borrowing features from those she liked. The warm blue eyes of the chambermaid who let her sniff the flowers she arranged in porcelain vases in Madame la marquise's salon, the raven-black hair of the carpenter who, seeing her play with wooden blocks, gave her a whole basket of them.

To dress her parents, Marie-Louise spied on the royal courtiers. For her mother, this velvet robe embroidered with silver, that muslin fichu, these ostrich feathers. For her father, these white silk stockings, shiny leather boots, spurs and those polished silver clasps.

Black pearls. The scent of ambergris.

Longing, she had learned, could feed the sweetest of dreams.

<hr>

"We shall start with your letters, child," Sister Seraphina, who was to teach Marie-Louise her catechism, said. This is why, every Sunday, in the chapel schoolroom, Marie-Louise copied the letters of the alphabet in the Italian hand until she got all the shapes right and managed not to stain the page with ink.

"A dreamer," Sister Seraphina called her some days. There was caution in this word. Dreamers were led astray by their visions. Not everyone was a saint, trusted by God and endowed with His grace. The devil had his dirty fingers in the affairs of this world. Stirring the hapless souls, seeding them with the fancy of false expectations.

Sister Seraphina had gray eyes, and long fingers with beautiful nails, round and smooth, free from ink stains. Her breath smelled of mint and something sweet.

"Could it be that a mother forgets her child?" Marie-Louise asked.

Some things we may never know, Sister Seraphina said. Nevertheless, this was not a reason to give up hope, or forget gratitude for what we had received.

Nevertheless was an awkward word. *Notwithstanding* was another.

"Why may we never know?"

Sister Seraphina sighed and told Marie-Louise that there were things in this world a child would never understand.

"Why?"

Because this was how God had wanted it. And before Marie-Louise could ask why again, she said, "You will know what I mean when you grow up."

All adult answers always ended with these same words, which really was not fair at all.

Only a few months before, Marie-Louise would've raged against such injustice. Now she buried her disappointment under a beaming smile, for Sister Seraphina was her friend and she didn't want to upset her. Or break the solemn promise to God she made in Sister Seraphina's presence. *I shall not add to the side of Evil in the world but always magnify the side of the Good.*

Being seven also meant that Marie-Louise was growing. The hems of her dresses had to be let down again. Just a bit, but still. During her Sunday lessons with Sister Seraphina, Marie-Louise wrote down whole sentences now that she would later learn by heart: *If all mankind lived in mutual love, this world would much resemble that above.*

"Time flies," Gardienne said, but it didn't. Time chimed like the palace clocks. Or trickled from one bulb of an hourglass to another. The hourglass time, which Marie-Louise preferred, was made of tiny white grains of sand. Once the bulb was empty, the hourglass had to be turned upside down. But even if it were not turned, time wouldn't stop.

"Such a clever mite, aren't you," Old Gourlon said, winking at her.

Sometimes a wink was accompanied by the mussing up of her hair or a pinch on her shoulder. Sometimes it came with a tickle under her chin. "Our little game," he called it, but refused to explain what kind of game it was.

"Beauty," Sister Seraphina said, "is Nature's most dubious gift. Pernicious and often fatal."

Pernicious meant dangerous.

Why?

It was very seldom that a perfectly beautiful woman was in other respects amiable. Such a woman thought Nature had done everything for her. She thought that to enchant all she had to do was to make herself seen, that no other qualities were half so important.

Amiable meant pleasant.

"I'm not a woman," Marie-Louise said, puzzled at what it all meant. "I'm a girl."

"I had a long conversation with a noblewoman of distinction who took note of you," Sister Seraphina said as if she did not hear her. Sensible and agreeable, Sister Seraphina called her, concerned for Marie-Louise's well-being.

Marie-Louise straightened herself up, folded her hands on her lap, one over the other, which covered half of her chewed-up nails.

"That noblewoman," Sister Seraphina continued, "confided in me her astonishment at the compliments you receive on your appearance. 'Mademoiselle Marie-Louise is not a beautiful child,' she said. 'Her look is pleasing but commonplace. They who present her with these exaggerated compliments must suppose her very vain and very silly not only to believe them but to be delighted with them.'"

Marie-Louise felt herself blush. Sister Seraphina kept looking at her. It hurt to hold her gaze, but Marie-Louise did just that, thanking Sister Seraphina for passing on the noblewoman's words. "If anyone calls me beautiful," she said, "I will say that I'd much rather be called sensible."

Sister Seraphina smiled with pleasure, embraced Marie-Louise and pressed her to her heart.

Afterward they put the catechism aside and Sister Seraphina told her a beautiful story about camels. In the deserts of Arabia where they lived, camels could go without water for weeks. Their feet were perfectly formed for walking on the sand.

"Arabia," Marie-Louise mouthed the word first, then muttered it to herself.

The desert was hot, like coals in the fire. This is why camels had such long legs, to keep their bellies away from the desert heat. Their humps, Sister Seraphina told her, stored water, and so did some of their many stomachs.

Camels were trained for hard work. Right after they were born, great loads were put on their backs so that they would be used to them and not expect freedom of movement. They were given little food, for in the desert, where there was nothing but sand, they would not eat much. This was why their knees were so deformed, their bodies so emaciated. But this was also why they would persevere where a horse would have died, where a man alone would have perished.

"How do you know this?" Marie-Louise asked, and Sister Seraphina picked up a thick book from her shelf and showed her a picture of a camel. It had a hump and long legs with knobby knees, just as Sister Seraphina told her. The book, Sister Seraphina then said, had many other beautiful stories. If Marie-Louise worked hard on her letters, she could soon read them by herself.

"I will work harder than hard," Marie-Louise said.

Afterward they put the book and catechism aside and went together to the kitchen garden. Sister Seraphina showed Marie-Louise a small plot where she and other sisters were growing herbs. Chicory for a calming drink. Mint for settling the stomach. St. John's wort to make despondent thoughts go away.

"I'll pray for you at matins," Sister Seraphina also said. "My special prayer."

"Thank you," Marie-Louise said, happy to have proved she was neither vain nor silly. So why, that very same night, did she cry herself to sleep with the thought that her mother abandoned her because she was not beautiful?

Gardienne didn't give two hoots about camels.

Marie-Louise was truly wicked, Gardienne, in her *inside* voice, declared.

For why else would she tell the dairymaid that she lived in a house with no windows? That her guardians had twenty-five cats who lived like kings? That she heard voices telling her: You will die. Everyone you see will die.

"These terrible lies must stop," Gardienne continued. "I will not suffer a dissimulator under my roof. If you persist in your wicked ways, we will send you away."

Dissimulator meant a liar.

Marie-Louise stared at the clouds outside the window, white puffs on bright blue sky. In one of the garden groves she particularly liked, there was a sculpture of happy children playing in the water. She liked to pretend they were her brothers and sisters. If she shut her eyes, she might even see herself among them, splashing water, giggling or pretending they were porpoises, which Sister Seraphina had also told her about. Porpoises were said to cry like babies when sailors caught them and hauled them on board.

Had Marie-Louise really nothing to say? Well then. These were the rules. No more talking of imaginary things as if they really happened. There was no tabby cat who walked through the servants' hall on two feet, wearing a hat. No camel lived at the market, either.

Was that understood?

When she instructed Marie-Louise in her sewing, Gardienne complained that Marie-Louise talked too much and did not pay attention to what was expected of her. But she did. She just wanted to know why, if a dissimulator meant a liar, were there two words for the same thing? Why some words, like *bastard*, sounded vile and mysterious at the same time, and why such words were always whispered or mouthed? "What is a Polish bastard?" she had asked Gardienne once, only to get her mouth washed out with soap and to promise on the Holy Mother of God never to utter such foul words again.

Marie-Louise didn't mind dusting or folding linen, for Gardienne left her alone then and she could spin her own stories, which flowed in absorbing ways. Her mother may have given up searching for her, but not her father. He was a nobleman of distinction, and he wore a perfumed wig that he let her try on if she wanted to. His clothes were impeccably cut, an expression Marie-Louise had often heard and particularly liked. His hands were soft and warm, but very strong, his nails filed into half-moons.

As Marie-Louise told her father about the camels, he nodded and asked questions that were not too hard to answer. How often do they have to drink? Will a camel be strong enough to carry me?

She made her answers short—they drank once, before the journey; they could carry both of them together—for she didn't want to bore her father, make him fidget, or God forbid swoon and fade, as he was doing now.

"Are you ill?" she asked, and she quickly made the sign of the cross, which immediately brought him back to life. The smile lingering on his lips was a knowing one, for her father possessed secrets no one else knew. Even if he didn't want to tell them to her just yet.

"Are all stories lies? Will I go to Hell for telling them?" she asked. He gave her a long, hesitant look and cleared his throat, but just then Gardienne called from the other room.

"Marie-Louise! I need you here. Right now."

Gardienne was altering a pair of what she called harem pants, for Madame de Pompadour. The pants were made of loose, soft folds of silk. The waist needed to be taken in, for Madame la marquise had recently lost weight, which worried Gardienne greatly. Especially since Madame du Hausset reported that with the night chills came long bouts of coughing, harder and harder to soothe.

"Thread the needle for me, child." Gardienne's eyes were no longer as good as they used to be, not even with spectacles.

Threading the needle was easy. The thread, wetted with saliva, stayed stiff and straight as it slid through the eye of the needle. But this didn't mean that Marie-Louise was allowed to leave. It was high time she began learning stitches finer than the simple ones she had done so far.

As they sat together sewing, Gardienne told Marie-Louise how Madame de Pompadour trusted her and valued her above all her other waiting maids because Gardienne was not commonplace. There were many signs of that special trust, but Gardienne's favorite was how, when Madame still gave theatricals for the king every week, Diane Gourlon was always chosen to act in them. Her best role was that of a nymph disguised as a simple village girl. Singing a song she would remember to her dying day:

How pleasant a sailor's life passes
How happy a state does the miller possess
The honest heart whose thoughts are clear . . .

This was a tale of triumph and bliss.

"'Diane,' Madame, bless her kind heart, said, 'I couldn't have done it without you.' And the king stood up and applauded and cried, 'Brava, Brava!' And then he gave me five louis d'ors and a beautiful *aigrette*. Sparkling with diamonds!"

An *aigrette* was a headdress Madame de Pompadour herself favored, for it was very precious.

By then Marie-Louise only half listened, for she had heard this account before. She wondered why adults repeated some stories over and over again. Would she be like that, too, when she grew up? For some time now she had been compiling a list of things she promised herself never to do. Repeating the same stories was one of them. Pinching children's cheeks was another. And tripping them when they passed by. And laughing when they fell.

Her needle went in and out, the cross-stitch Marie-Louise was learning a bit less crooked every time. "Pity those who never saw Madame when she first came to live in the palace," Gardienne continued. "Those smooth cheeks with just a smudge of pink, those pearly teeth, that figure. The king could not take his eyes off her."

The stories of Madame de Pompadour did not interest Marie-Louise much. By then she had seen Madame a few times when Gardienne took her to the palace on one of her errands. Madame was always reading or staring out the window or writing something at her escritoire and paid no attention to them at all. Once she saw Madame and the king walking toward the palace, Madame leaning on His Majesty's arm. The king whispered something in her ear, and Madame laughed, as if he tickled her.

Madame's dogs were far more interesting. Marie-Louise knew them well, for Gardienne was often entrusted with their care. Old Mimi, Marie-Louise's favorite, was a Phalène, which sounded elegant and a little bit mysterious.

There used to be two Phalènes, but Inez died after swallowing something rotten in the garden, a poisoned mole, perhaps, and Madame had her buried outside of her window.

Mimi liked to play tug-of-war and had a special dog bed with a roof and curtains. It was lined with scarlet velvet, and Marie-Louise was often asked to clean it, for silly Old Mimi was a hoarder and liked to hide bones in there.

One row of her blind cross-stitch completed, Marie-Louise rethreaded the needle and began the second row, letting her thoughts slide into her own story. Now, after she had blessed her father with the sign of the cross, he was no longer weak or pale. He was not looking at her, though. Had she made him angry with her? Was it because she asked him if she would go to Hell? Was talking about Hell as bad as evoking God's name in vain?

"I'm never angry with you, Marie-Louise," her father answered her thoughts. "Don't you know that?"

"You never said that to me before," she said, but it was not a complaint. Just a statement of how things were.

"To everything there is a season."

Gardienne's incessant chatter fluttered in Marie-Louise's ears. Madame la marquise was kindness itself! And her patience with her late daughter had been that of a saint. Poor Alexandrine, who, had she not died so unexpectedly, would be married already to the duc de Picquigny. No wonder she was her mother's beloved *chou d'amour*.

Alexandrine, Marie-Louise thought, did not have to be pitied. Even if she was dead now, she had her mother's love all her life. Isn't it right, Papa? she asked her father, but he began slipping away from her, and she could not hear his answer. So she thought of the dairymaid she had seen nursing her newborn, a tiny boy, eyes shut tight, mouth on his mother's nipple. Seeing how Marie-Louise stared at the baby, the maid let her come close and watch until he finished suckling. Then she lifted him up, and bubbles of milk foamed at his mouth. "Here, you burp him," she said to Marie-Louise and let her hold him. The baby was so warm, Marie-Louise decided, because he had soaked up his mother's love.

"I'd like to have a baby," she said aloud.

Gardienne slapped her across her cheek, hard enough to leave a red welt behind.

"For your filthy thoughts," she said.

When Marie-Louise lay curled in her folding bed that night, awaiting sleep, she willed her father to appear in the doorway. Taking out a watch from his vest pocket, he told her to hurry up. They were going away.

"Now?" she asked.

"Right now. Best to seize the moment, my *chou d'amour*, don't you agree?"

She did agree, but then, seeing that she was holding her cheek, her father retrieved a magnifying glass from another pocket and bent over her to examine it.

"It's not hurting anymore," she said.

"Yes . . . I see . . . a mere scratch," he declared. "Not worthy of your tears."

"I'm not crying."

"Of course you are," her father said, and Marie-Louise touched her cheek to find it was wet.

"Never mind," he said. "We are going to find your mother."

His horse was waiting outside, its chestnut flanks glossy. An animal her father trusted more than he trusted people.

She rose from her bed and followed him. Soon they were traveling through a jungle; branches sometimes smacked her face, but it didn't hurt much at all. The ground under the horse's hooves was overgrown with grass. The trees they passed were lush with foliage. On one of the branches a monkey was hanging on its leg, but they galloped by too fast for Marie-Louise to take a closer look.

They stopped by a waterfall, white foam bubbling at its base. Her father helped her dismount, his touch light, almost unreal. He stroked her chin, but she could not feel these strokes at all. Then he kissed her on the forehead, but she couldn't feel his lips, either. "Are you dead, Papa?" she asked, but this was a wrong question to ask, for it made her father's lips turn white as if covered by frost.

When they started riding again, the landscape changed. Trees disappeared, grass turned to sand and was strewn with pebbles and rocks. This had to be the desert of Arabia, she thought, and it probably was.

In the morning when Marie-Louise woke up, she remembered the stark beauty of this land. The rocks tinted blue, narrow passages leading deeper into the mountains, sand dunes with their rippled sides, giving in under her feet. The horse, she recalled, had vanished. Which was just as well, her father said, for in the desert one needed a camel, not a horse.

⋯⋇⋯

One day not long afterward Gardienne sent Marie-Louise to fetch a shawl Madame particularly liked that needed mending. Marie-Louise was to be quick about it. There was to be no lingering whatsoever. In and out, Gardienne said, before Madame is back from her daily stroll in the orangery, ordered by her doctor to soothe the nighttime coughing.

It was like a jewel, this small room off Madame's inner parlor, its walls covered in pale green satin set off by carved, gilded molding. Marie-Louise's eyes flickered over a painting of a woman with a mysterious smile, a vase with pink flowers on the mantel, two armchairs by the fireplace, a table on curved golden legs.

She fully intended to pick up the shawl straightaway and leave, but that was before she spotted the porcelain figurines in a small display cabinet by the door. Monkeys all of them, dressed in suits and robes, making music. Playing drums, flute, clavichord, or singing from music sheets. One was plucking at the strings of a guitar; another was playing a tiny violin. She thought their faces ugly but at the same time utterly fascinating. Perhaps because they were all grinning with delight. The cabinet wasn't locked, and Marie-Louise couldn't stop herself from opening it, lifting the figurines up and putting them down again; they were lighter than she expected, empty inside.

The voices behind the door to Madame's parlor took her utterly by surprise.

Marie-Louise should have put the monkey violinist back where it belonged, picked up the shawl and left through the service corridor, the way she had come. But the door was opening already, and there was barely enough time to scurry behind the curtain.

Two people came in, Madame and His Majesty, whom until now Marie-Louise had only seen from afar. They were talking of some gross and ignorant beings, naturally idle. Someone called *intendant* was being particularly difficult and an utter bore. Someone else's tongue was harsh and unforgiving.

"I promised, though," the king said. His voice was hesitant, as if he were not a king at all.

"You promised nothing. You were taken advantage of."

"I said . . ."

"Because you are always too kind, my dearest. You hate to disappoint. You think of others, not yourself."

"There may be some truth in that."

"You know I'm right."

The conversation continued, less and less comprehensible. Some old flatterer wanted the king to praise that new bronze statue of his. The king was not sure if he liked it, but Madame said the statue was beautiful. "You on horseback, surveying the crowds that gather at your feet. In full glory. It will be there, in the center of the square, for future generations," she said. "Not just to admire but give thanks for their beloved sovereign."

Through the gap in the curtain Marie-Louise watched as Madame opened the cabinet by the door, took a glass from it and filled it with wine. "The future is created every day," she said. "With or without our will."

The monkeys, Marie-Louise thought, had not betrayed her.

"Your favorite Burgundy," Madame said to the king, handing him the glass.

The king took a sip, smacked his lips. "Louis-Auguste is in trouble again," he said. "Caught turning on a fountain. Just when old d'Ayen was walking by. Drenched the man. His tutor made the poor boy copy *If princes but knew all that God requires of them, they would tremble every day of their lives.* A hundred times! His mother ordered a high Mass in his intention. I do not know what's worse. He is still a child."

"Wouldn't you like to drench d'Ayen, sometimes?" Madame chuckled. "He is your grandson, through and through."

"He begs me to take him hunting with me."

"Take him then."

"Not until he turns thirteen."

"How right you are."

It was Mimi who betrayed Marie-Louise's presence, let in when a maid brought a tray with refreshments. Old Mimi, who waddled toward Marie-Louise with a friendly squeal of joy, her bushy tail wagging.

Madame pulled the curtain aside. "Yet another little spy," she said, as if she found children behind her curtains all the time. Her cheeks were flushed, lips twisted, as if she were in pain. "Not too good at concealment, this one."

Yanked out of her hiding place, Marie-Louise considered dashing to the service door, but Madame had already grabbed her by the shoulder, her fingers a vise pinching the skin. "A thief, too, this one," she exclaimed, retrieving the monkey violinist from Marie-Louise's clenched fist, examining it for damage.

"I'm not a thief."

"Are you not? Then why are you here?"

"My Gardienne sent me. To fetch Madame's shawl for mending."

Madame de Pompadour shook her head as if she didn't believe a word of what Marie-Louise was saying. But then she turned to the maid and said, "Take the girl to Diane Gourlon. And tell her to be more vigilant."

The maid pulled on Marie-Louise's hand.

"Wait!" the king said, rising from the armchair, handing Madame his empty glass.

"Wait," Madame de Pompadour repeated as if the maid couldn't hear the king's words for herself.

Freed from the maid's grasp, Marie-Louise turned toward the king. Old Mimi stood on her hind legs, licking her fingers, her rough dog's tongue warm, insistent.

"What's your name, child?" the king asked.

"Marie-Louise."

"How old are you?"

"Seven."

"Where do you live?"

"At the Grand Commons."

The king nodded as if he knew where it was. Marie-Louise fixed her eyes on him, the way she had been taught not to, but now that she was going to get it from Gardienne anyway, why would she care? The king's wig was neatly curled, his chin showed a shadow of prickly stubble. His eyes were dark, dark blue, and Marie-Louise liked the way the king narrowed them, like a big cat. She liked his voice, too, calm and playful. She had already decided that—if it weren't for Madame de Pompadour, who was staring at her from behind the king's back—he would have let her run off unpunished.

"Did you steal the monkey, Marie-Louise?"

"No."

"So how did it get into your hand?"

"I meant to put it back."

"Why did you take it, though? Knowing it wasn't yours."

"I just wanted to hold it for a moment. I like animals."

"Do you like horses, too?"

"Yes."

"Do you know how to brush them properly?"

"Yes."

"You seem to have an answer to every question. Let's try this one then: Can you cook an omelet?"

"No."

"Aha!" the king said, pleased as if someone gave him a honeycomb to suck. "When I was her age"—he turned to Madame gleefully—"I knew how to cook soup and make an omelet."

"Not everyone is as brilliant as you," Madame said.

Old Mimi abandoned Marie-Louise's fingers and slowly walked toward her dog bed, returning a moment later with a headless doll, its body all chewed up. She dropped the toy in front of Marie-Louise and crouched, ready for a tug-of-war.

"Enough, Mimi," Madame snapped. "Back to your bed."

The king yawned and walked toward the window. Something there must have caught his attention, for he chuckled and muttered something. But what it was Marie-Louise would never know, as the servants' door opened just then and Gardienne hurried in.

"Please forgive me for my carelessness," she said to Madame, catching her breath. "I sent the child to fetch the blue shawl. I didn't mean any harm. I won't let her out of my sight again."

"Never mind, Diane," Madame said in a tired voice. "Off with you both now. The king and I have far more pressing matters to discuss."

Gardienne bit her lower lip, which Marie-Louise knew to be a sign of fury postponed, grabbed Marie-Louise's hand and turned to leave.

"Not so fast!"

Abandoning whatever it was outside the window, the king came toward Marie-Louise. "Promise me you would not take anything that isn't yours again," he said.

That was an easy promise to make.

"Good," the king said. "Which hand?" he asked her then, presenting both, clenched into fists. "This one," Marie-Louise said, pointing at the right fist, and the king opened it, revealing a shining coin.

"This is yours then," he said. She was about to ask what was in his other hand, but Gardienne's look made her stop.

Gardienne rattled on as they walked toward the Grand Commons, the chatelaine around her waist clinking, scissors, a thimble, a magnifying glass, a small pouch with reviving salts bouncing off each other. "To have been humiliated like that! In front of His Majesty! I never!"

Marie-Louise followed as fast as she could without slipping on the snowy patches, weighing up the severity of the upcoming punishment. A beating? No supper tonight? No leaving their rooms for a week? Not even for her lessons?

"Mary, Mother of God," Gardienne prayed loudly. "Grant me patience to suffer this child's wickedness without rage."

The coin the king had given her was snug in Marie-Louise's hand. It had his profile on it, the smooth curve of his nose, the wreath on his head. She had already decided she would not spend it, ever. It would be her very own treasure.

"Do you have no shame, child?" Gardienne asked, a question that was best left unanswered.

Shame would be merely part of the storm raging over Marie-Louise for the rest of that day, joined as it was by Fear of God Almighty and her Ingratitude. Giant forces beside which she was a speck, a tiny pebble. Getting tighter and harder was her only defense.

Gardienne vowed never to let Marie-Louise anywhere near Madame de Pompadour's apartments again. No, not even to clean Mimi's bed. Marie-Louise had only herself to blame for it. Luckily, there was enough for her to do at the Grand Commons. The entresol rooms had to be swept, beds made, laundry taken to the washerwoman. There were errands to run, sewing brought in and carried out. A child had to be of use. One way or another.

"You are too tough on her, Diane," Old Gourlon muttered. "She didn't mean any harm."

This, Marie-Louise had not expected, for he had never defended her before. A good child, was she? Just too curious for her own good?

Gardienne, too, was surprised. Enough to recount the story of Marie-Louise's disgrace once again, drag out all the proofs of her carelessness and some more. Not just the monkey violinist taken without permission, but utter disregard for those who raised her. Her ingratitude. Her stubbornness. The airs she put on.

Marie-Louise was a rotten seed. She, Diane Gourlon, regretted the moment she agreed to take her in, a burden she did not deserve. "I've made a rod for my own back," she seethed, her fists all white-knuckled. "I'm raising a viper."

Words Old Gourlon dismissed with a wave of his hand and a wink. It meant: Don't pay attention to her, Marie-Louise.

It meant: You were wrong about me. I like you. I am your friend.

1764

AFTER THE NEW YEAR the trickle of visitors dropping by the Gourlons' rooms thickened. They were all de Pompadour's creatures: maids, under-maids, attendants, lackeys. There was no denying it anymore: Madame de Pompadour was wasting away.

Madame refused to appear at her Parisian residence, Marie-Louise heard, blaming her long bouts of coughing on the foul city air, always so much worse in winter. There would be no more intimate soirées at Choisy, either, for Madame was finding even the shortest of trips away from Versailles too tax-ing. At court she would not show herself but in candlelight, dressed in glitter-ing costumes. Queen of Golconda, all diamonds and veils and bracelets. A Turkish odalisque with her tambour.

By March, Madame was spending her days resting on her chaise longue, receiving no one but the king. The coughing lasted most of the night now; there were the fainting spells, too, heart beating wildly. Dr. Quesnay assured Madame that she was gaining strength, but they had two good eyes to see beyond such consolations. Besides, what can a doctor do when your time comes?

Tears were shed, reminiscences offered. How Madame never truly recov-ered from Alexandrine's death, for a grieving mother never does, does she? How she loved flowers, how she once delighted in her theatricals. The reminiscences always ended with speculation about the legacies her servants could expect. Enough not to have to go into service again? With a dowry of eight hundred livres, Marie-Louise heard, a maid could marry a constable. Or a shopkeeper. Especially if she had collected some good *hardes*: a mattress, a set of linen, a few pieces of silver perhaps. Madame's dresses would have to go somewhere, too. She wouldn't take them to her grave.

With a thousand livres a lackey could open a small shop. Or go back home and set himself up on a farm.

Wine was poured. Glasses clinked. Old Gourlon wiped his mouth with the back of his hand and winked at Marie-Louise. He did it quite often now. As if the two of them knew something no one else did.

Marie-Louise turned her eyes to the floor, which always demanded her vigilance. Boots treaded in muck and sawdust, elbows knocked glasses off the table, spilling the wine. Something always needed to be swept from under the table: a broken saucer, a half-chewed apple core, a squashed sugarplum.

When Nicole du Hausset herself came to the entresol rooms, she no longer complained about her tiring walk from Madame's apartment or steep stairs. Nor did she pay any attention to Marie-Louise. Settling into Gardienne's widest armchair, she would merely ask her dear Diane for a glass of cordial. To replenish her strength in this time of grief.

Over Gardienne's best cordial and sponge cake, the two of them would sink into whispers.

Poor Madame was fast losing her spirits. There had been another night of weeping. There had been another long night of pain.

The lines around Madame's once so lovely mouth deepened, the result of all these sleepless nights. Of Madame insisting on being up every morning, in her court dress, to await the king, even though she could barely keep her eyes open.

"You shall have time to prepare yourself for death," the fortune-teller had told her, which was Madame's great consolation. As was the fortune-teller's vision: "I see a very great man beside you who supports you in his arms until your dying day."

How true it had proved to be! How prescient! With His Majesty coming by every day. Never turning his face away. Not when Madame choked with coughing, not when the handkerchief with which she covered her mouth was stained red with blood.

"Oh, Diane, I tell you. What we have to go through in this world."

Marie-Louise, who heard it all, did not feel too sorry for Madame de Pompadour. She still could not forget Madame's harshness on that day when she caught her holding the porcelain monkey. When Sister Seraphina reminded her of the need to forgive our trespassers, Marie-Louise asked, "Why do I always have to do all the forgiving?"

"Because you are a sinner," Sister Seraphina reminded her. "Like every one of us."

By mid-March Nicole du Hausset's visits to the Grand Commons became shorter. "Just dashing by for a gasp of air," she would say, refusing refreshments, declining to sit down, for Madame could not manage without her for too long.

Marie-Louise, bending over the sampler page that Sister Seraphina assigned for her to copy, listened. How malice never slept. How greed raised its ugly head. How, with death around the corner, the gilding was rubbing off the woodwork, people were revealing their true colors.

This talk of Madame poisoned, Diane? By the Jesuits? Or Madame dying because she did not wish to outlive her beauty?

Or that Monsieur Colin, Madame's steward, Diane. Believing no one but himself cared for Madame. "Do I need instructions on how to tend to her? Do I have to be ordered to bring her chicory water? I was not born yesterday. I know when I'm being pushed aside."

Diane Gourlon should not be so sure of her own position, either.

Weren't her duty shifts with Madame getting shorter and less frequent? Was she not always sent *chez elle* to do the mending? Since then had she become a mere seamstress?

The desire for God is written in the human heart, Marie-Louise copied from the sampler page. Her letters were quite a bit too large and very crooked, but she couldn't just cross the sentence out, could she? Not without Sister Seraphina noticing and getting angry with her.

"Out of sight, out of mind, Diane. Mark my words," Nicole du Hausset continued, to Gardienne's murmurs of agreement. Besides, where was Monsieur Colin when everyone could see that things around Madame began to vanish? "A whole length of new lace nowhere to be found, Diane, another pair of Madame's harem pants missing. So are her batiste handkerchiefs. Though what good can they be to anyone, embroidered as they are with Madame's monogram?"

"Thieves all of them," Old Gourlon said as soon as Nicole du Hausset left. "Mark my words, Diane. We'll end up with scraps, like so many before us."

"And who is saying this, pray?" Gardienne snapped. "Your card table companions?"

"You will see who is right."

Not wishing to be caught in the crossfire, Marie-Louise bent even lower over her notebook. Only when Gardienne retired to her bedroom, swearing pox and damnation on those who tried to put a wedge between her and Madame, did she think it safe to stand up and gather her things.

She didn't pay attention to Old Gourlon.

It was when she was reaching out for her inkwell and quills that he caught her wrist. His hands were big, leathery. Marie-Louise struggled to free herself, but his grip tightened with each of her pulls. "Don't you like me anymore?" he whispered under his breath. "What have I done?"

Nothing, she had to admit.

"Are you putting on airs? Like she says?"

She referred to Gardienne, which was odd and unexpected. It had always been Madame Gourlon before.

Marie-Louise shook her head.

"I cannot find my ivory thimble. Have you taken it, Antoine?" Gardienne called from the bedroom.

"What would I do with your thimble?" Old Gourlon asked, loosening his grip. Enough for Marie-Louise to quickly pull out her hand and head for her nook.

In the first days of April Madame de Pompadour took another turn for the worse. Nicole du Hausset reported on plates of food leaving Madame's bedroom untouched. All Madame managed to swallow were a few spoonfuls of consommé and that only when the king insisted on feeding her himself.

Night after night Alexandrine appeared in her mother's dreams. Floating over the palace gardens in her white dress. Flitting among the trees, laughing. Coming back from the other world as a bird. Pecking at the windowpanes, asking to be let inside.

"Put some rouge on my cheeks, Nicole. Some crimson on my lips," Madame asked every morning before His Majesty came by, and insisted on sitting up, propped with pillows. "Draw the curtains. Light is too cruel." When the king left, she slumped back in her bed and lay motionless for a long time.

The pain was getting worse, and so was the coughing. "Give her something, for God's sake," Nicole du Hausset heard the king tell Dr. Quesnay, but whatever the doctor did helped for a few moments only. Madame was getting too weak to lift herself, even on her elbows, too tired to speak. Her lips were scarred by biting, her nails left deep marks on her palms as she clenched her fists. "I don't know how much longer I can do it, Nicole," she said after every bout of coughing. "You are my witness, that I try."

At the Hôtel des Réservoirs, Madame's residence right outside the palace grounds, the servants kept all the rooms warm and well aired for Madame's arrival. Expected any moment now, for only those of royal blood were allowed to die at Versailles.

"Let me go now, please," Madame asked, but His Majesty refused. "No, dear heart," he said. "You will stay where you are."

Nicole du Hausset, from her nook, saw Madame raise her hand and try to grasp at something no one else could perceive.

On Palm Sunday, the marquise de Pompadour breathed her last in her Versailles bedroom. Two lackeys put her body on the stretcher and carried it to the Hôtel des Réservoirs, where a mourning room was hung in black, lit by a sea of candles. The coffin was already waiting. They put the body in.

Two priests stood at either side of the coffin, praying aloud day and night until, two days later, the royal mistress was taken to Paris, to the convent of the Capuchins. Laid to rest, Marie-Louise heard, beside her mother and her beloved daughter. Her *chou d'amour*.

At the Gourlons the laying-out and the funeral were discussed in great detail. The evening Mass at the Church of Notre-Dame de Versailles, the hearse traveling along avenue de Paris through the night, all the way to Paris. The compelling significance of numbers. Death coming for Madame not quite ten years after Alexandrine's. As if Madame didn't want to live through another anniversary.

Such cruel rain on that day, too. Rattling the windowpanes. What a day to leave this earth.

Maids, under-maids, lackeys and other servants crossed themselves, slurped wine, rubbed their hands for warmth in these chilly April days. The table was littered with breadcrumbs and chicken bones, meat all chewed off. Marie-Louise rushed to and fro, making sure they all had been offered refreshments, relieved of empty plates. She had burned her fingers trimming candles. Scraped her heels raw with all that running about, for she had again outgrown her shoes. Was she really going to be so tall? Very unbecoming in a woman, Gardienne had said.

Pulled by twelve horses, the hearse, Marie-Louise heard. The best horses in His Majesty's stables. Arabs of pure blood. In black and silver silk. A hundred priests in the cortège, twenty-four children with candles. Seventy-two beggars provided with good clothes and hats, which they were supposed to return but of course wouldn't.

Twenty livres at least if they sold them.

Such cold days, this April. Chilling right to the marrow. What is the world coming to?

Nods were followed by sighs. Versailles will not be the same without Madame. The king, bless His Majesty's heart, will not be the same, either.

A baby began to wail. "Won't you rock him, love?" the mother asked Marie-Louise. Madame's washerwoman of ten years. "You are so good with children."

The boy squirmed when Marie-Louise held him to her chest, though, whimpering. It was only when she gave him a sucking cloth dipped in sweet wine that he quieted down and could be handed back to his mother.

One of His Majesty's pages, a boy not older than Marie-Louise, had been brought over and greatly feted, for he was the one who had delivered the news of Madame's death to His Majesty. The king was in the palace chapel, on the balcony, kneeling, with hands clasped tight. His face went stiff and white like a sheet when he heard the news. The vein in his forehead throbbed.

"I saw it with my own eyes," the page said, and Old Gourlon patted his shoulder.

Marie-Louise caught sight of the boy's hands. Chewed-off nails, just like hers.

"Have you seen His Majesty since?" someone asked.

The page shook his head. The king's valet told him never to come back. His Majesty would never wish to see his face again. It would remind him of Madame's death.

"Have another drink then."

"Don't mind if I do."

Voices rose and fell, interrupted by coughing fits, loud belches or stifled laughter. In the corner, beside the washstand, two girls in gray smocks were playing with pebbles, throwing them up into the air and catching them in their palms. Until one of Madame's under-maids told them to stop. They were dragging misfortune to themselves. "You don't want your life to be hard as a rock, do you?" she asked.

Madame's rooms at the palace, Marie-Louise heard, were all deserted. At the Hôtel des Réservoirs Mimi was wailing all night, as if she saw something.

A soul always took its time to leave.

On the day Madame's will was opened, Marie-Louise returned to the entresol rooms with a stack of clean linen to find her guardians alone. Old Gourlon was holding up a bottle of wine, still in its basket, as if it were a trophy. "That's gratitude for you," he announced.

To Marie-Louise's relief he was not looking at her but at his wife, who was nodding her head.

"I never thought."

"Well, you should've."

"Don't tell me *you* expected it."

"I've heard rumors, but I wouldn't believe them."

"Tells you something, doesn't it?"

Words, sighs, sounds of glasses filled up, emptied, filled up again. Slowly the news seeped through, the injustice of it, the coldness. The highest pension of six thousand livres went to Monsieur Colin, Madame's steward; the second highest, of four thousand, to Dr. Quesnay. All servant pensions would be calculated according to Madame's general instructions. Ten percent of wages for each year served. Diane Gourlon would get five hundred livres per year, Antoine Gourlon a measly two hundred and forty.

"Considering all I did for her," Diane Gourlon said, pulling at a dry fleck of skin on her lip. "The sleepless nights. The effort."

And why did she get two of Madame's dresses only, she continued, while other chambermaids got three and silk petticoats as well? And a shift of very fine cambric.

"I guess Madame didn't think us that worthy after all."

Bitterness would spill out for days and weeks afterward. Old Gourlon took issue with how his length of service was calculated. Diane Gourlon grew more and more bitter over the fact that there had been no special legacy for her in Madame's will. There had been no special legacy for Nicole du Hausset, either, which gave you even more food for thought, didn't it? No wonder she had left Versailles in such haste.

Greed and malice trumped love and sacrifice. The rich of this world never spared much thought for those below them.

Three months after Madame's funeral, a visitor was announced at the entresol rooms: Monsieur Lebel, His Majesty's *valet de chambre*, the scarecrow monsieur who had brought Marie-Louise to the Gourlons two years before but paid her no heed since.

Important, judging by her guardians' nervous entreaties to please come in, take the best seat for comfort. "Such a rare honor, such a distinction."

Monsieur Lebel had his own reasons for this visit, and comfort was not one of them. He wished to discuss the current provisions, in view of the recent changes.

Marie-Louise was sent away to her nook while the three of them talked.

"The girl is growing so fast . . . the hem has been let three times already . . . new shoes are needed again . . . we are doing the best we can . . . where the goat is tied it must graze."

"I can make other arrangements, if you cannot manage," Monsieur Lebel said.

"Who said we cannot manage? Is someone spreading vile lies about us? Madame du Hausset, perhaps, causing mischief before she left? She who never had children herself."

Crouched in the corner of her nook, hands tight around her knees, Marie-Louise held her breath. What arrangements did Monsieur Lebel have in mind? Could it be that her parents sent him? That they agreed to take her back after all, for she had not been as wicked or ugly as some said? Sister Seraphina would have told her eavesdropping is a sin, the first step on the slippery path to Hell. But Marie-Louise could hardly stop herself from hearing, could she?

"People see what they want to see . . . they imagine raising a child is easy. Where would we live? What would become of us? Now that our beloved Madame is gone."

Whispers followed, more urgent, more pleading, until finally she heard: "Come here, Marie-Louise. Monsieur Lebel wishes to hear of your accomplishments."

Accomplishments consisted of the hoop with the embroidered fleur-de-lys to which Marie-Louise merely added the finishing stitches.

"Is that all?"

There was also the sampler pages that Sister Seraphina was giving her to copy and that she had learned by heart, though her handwriting still failed to improve.

The desire for God is written in the human heart because man is created by God and for God, she stammered, pointing at each word. *All creatures bear a certain resemblance to God, most especially man, created in the image and likeness of God.*

"Is that all you have learned?" Monsieur Lebel asked, stopping her mid-word. "I was hoping you would be less of a disappointment."

Her cheeks were hot now, and her pulse raced. Luckily, he was done with her. It was the Gourlons who needed to listen closely now.

Marie-Louise was not their scullery maid. Responsibilities and obligations had to be fulfilled with diligence, not dismissed or attended to willy-nilly. Such was his philosophy. Was that understood?

Yes.

Learning catechism once a week was not enough. There would be daily lessons from now on.

Yes.

Monsieur Lebel stood and picked up his cane, which was quite splendid with a glittering jewel embedded in its handle. The floorboards squeaked as he walked out of the entresol rooms, the heels of his shiny black shoes making a clickety sound.

The Gourlons exchanged glances of relief.

From now on, every morning, Marie-Louise, hands scrubbed clean, clothes brushed, hair plaited and pinned up under a freshly ironed bonnet, presented herself at the chapel schoolroom. She followed Sister Seraphina's instructions the best she could, firmly resolved not to add to the side of Evil in this world but to magnify the side of the Good.

Sister Seraphina's white wimple was as impeccably starched as it had always been, her smile as welcoming. But there was something new about her, too, something puzzling. Marie-Louise was not to sit beside her, as she used to during her catechism lessons, but at her own table, like a proper day pupil.

"I take my obligations seriously," Sister Seraphina said. "Unlike others we shall not speak about. Charity is a Christian virtue. So is forgiveness for those who trespassed against us."

"Even if they were wrong?"

"Especially then."

Marie-Louise thought about it. "It is not just," she said. "But I believe it is right."

Sister Seraphina smiled, and Marie-Louise wondered if it was very hard to become a nun. She rather liked the starched white wimple. It made Sister Seraphina's face look round and plump. Rosy too, with tiny blue veins on top of her cheeks, like a spider's web. She wondered if it would be fine to ask Sister Seraphina about it now. Or if, perhaps, she should wait.

"No more idle talk." Sister Seraphina's words answered her question. "Let's begin."

Modest girls should always strive to acquire a reputation for Virtue and Usefulness.

In the weeks and months that followed, Marie-Louise would copy many such maxims and passages and learn them by heart. Even if Sister Seraphina were to wake her up in the middle of the night, she would be able to recite:

To overburden people with attention, to insist upon obligations that they do not desire, is not only to render yourself disagreeable, but contemptible.

She did ask why.

It was the issue of decorum, Sister Seraphina replied, which meant behaving properly in all circumstances. For example, it was not proper to stand too close to people or grasp their hands that hard. Or stare at them like a hungry wolf.

Why?

Why was neither a useful nor a proper question. Sister Seraphina was giving Marie-Louise passages to read, copy and contemplate, not to argue with like some lawyer.

For her own good.

One day, when Marie-Louise asked Sister Seraphina if her mother would ever come to take her back, Sister Seraphina reached into her pocket and took out a small cross on a silver chain. Putting it around Marie-Louise's neck, she told her to always remember that she was a beloved child of God.

Marie-Louise thanked her, and then wondered if this gift was an obligation. One that Sister Seraphina did not desire at all.

GROWING UP MEANT THAT Marie-Louise no longer needed to hurry back to the Grand Commons once her morning lessons with Sister Seraphina were over. Ever since Monsieur Lebel's visit, Gardienne had been giving her fewer chores to do and didn't give a hoot what Marie-Louise did with herself when she was away.

Loneliness, Marie-Louise was learning with each day, could be pushed deeper inside, made to dim amid the vibrancy of the palace colors, the glitter of crystal, the shine of the polished floors. Loneliness would melt away in the palace crowds, among the servants busy with their errands, gawking visitors strolling along the corridors, courtiers rushing by on their important ways.

When Madame de Pompadour died, her apartments had been closed off for renovations, which, everyone agreed by now, were taking far too long. The king, Marie-Louise heard as she flitted in and out of palace rooms or roamed through the service corridors, could not make up his mind what he wanted done. Workmen had knocked down one of the inside walls, only to replace it. A closet next to Madame's bedroom had been turned into a small cabinet, then into a closet again.

The dust, girl!

The mice!

You should see the holes, girl!

They liked her well enough at the palace. The maids said she had such a fetching smile. And she was willing, wasn't she? Never refusing to run an errand or lend a helping hand. In the royal kitchen, a cook's assistant always saved a thick slice of bread for her, smeared with butter. Or a broken piece of pâté or a less-than-perfect slice of pie. In His Majesty's stables, the red-haired groom let her brush her favorite horse, feed it chunks of apple from her hands, feel the silky touch of its eager lips.

Horses did not mind that she overburdened them with attention, did they?

As the days began to warm up, there were the palace grounds to explore. There were gardens with fountains spewing bursts of cool water, and never-ending mazes of gravel paths from which, when some officious courtier chased her away, she could dive behind the wooden fence and roam in the thicket of wild trees and underbrush. There were icehouses, where a friendly guard let her suck on chunks of ice. There were aviaries, where birds fluttered and squawked and from where falconers sometimes brought out hooded hawks, bouncing on their thick gloves until, released, they hovered over the palace to scare off pigeons.

And then she discovered the palace roof.

Marie-Louise found her way there by chance, having climbed a ladder that builders had left unattended. The roof was vast, flat and tiled, a kingdom in itself. She could skip on the tiles, she could walk from one end of the palace to the other, watch chimneysweeps or tilers at work. Above the Salon of War where the king's attic rooms were, she could sit in one of the nooks, reading from a book Sister Seraphina had assigned or just watching the courtyard below.

That was where she first spotted the cats.

Skittish, they had to be tempted with food she salvaged from the scrap pile in the kitchen: chunks of fish, pieces of liver, which she placed closer and closer to where she sat. The bravest ones approached her first, allowing a gentle touch, then a pat on their heads and finally a belly rub.

She fell in love with the softness of their fur, the rubbing around her ankles, the insistent meows with which they greeted her. She gave them names. Mighty was the biggest, with hard muscles and a kink in his tail. Spotty was white with brown patches on his paws and ears. Queenie, whose stretched belly almost touched the ground when she walked.

They were her best friends. Soon they would rush to demand their treats and caresses as soon as she appeared. Purring in answer to her mutterings. "Ah, Mighty, where have you been? Has the cat got your tongue?" They led her to their hiding places, nests where they raised their litters, blind kittens with sharp claws and funny faces. She didn't mind their scratches, how they tested the sharpness of their teeth on the tips of her fingers. She was there when they opened their eyes, chased dry leaves or each other's tails, her heart tightening if any went missing and did not return.

⚘

There were no cats in sight when Marie-Louise climbed onto the palace roof on that warm spring day. By the king's rooms, she discovered the reason: an awkward-looking boy, his long blond hair tied with a black ribbon, his brown frockcoat wrinkled and stained. He must have been running, for his chubby cheeks were reddened and sweaty. He had certainly been up to no good because he was clutching a stone in his hand. Another one, bigger, was lying by his feet.

Knowing her cats would stay hidden, she was just about to turn back and leave when she spotted a white palace cat, a big, pampered angora too slow or dim-witted to realize it might be in danger.

The boy hurled the stone. The cat yelped in pain.

"What are you doing?" Marie-Louise screamed. "Stop it!"

The boy paid her no heed. He stomped his foot, but the silly cat still lingered so he picked up the other stone.

"Are you deaf?"

He did stop then. "No," he said, turning toward her. He was where he wanted to be, did what he wanted to do. Besides, he hated being interrupted. And he was certainly not deaf.

If she had not been reeling with fury, Marie-Louise would've recognized him right then and perhaps held her tongue. "What has that creature done to you?" she asked instead, picking the white angora up, feeling the bones in its legs. The cat meowed in fear.

"The stupid cat has pissed on my window six times," the boy said, still angry but letting his fist open, the stone fall to the ground.

Forgiveness is a Christian virtue, Sister Seraphina's voice reminded Marie-

Louise. Adding: Now that you are eight, God expects even more of you, and so do I.

The angora, its leg bones mercifully intact, limped away as soon as Marie-Louise put it on the ground.

"I've seen you three times already," the boy said. "You are the Cat Mama."

"What's wrong with being a Cat Mama?"

"You may call me Auguste," he said, ignoring her question. "What's your name?"

She recognized him then. Louis-Auguste. The duc de Berry, the dauphin's son. She should call him His Royal Highness, shouldn't she? Even if he didn't behave like one.

"Marie-Louise."

"Want me to show you something?"

"What?"

"Clean your hands first."

She spit on her palms and wiped them on her skirt.

A leather case propped against the stone ledge, which Auguste opened with great eagerness, contained a spyglass. The lens, he said, needed a good polishing with the soft cloth he had brought with him. He showed her how to do it, carefully, without touching the lens with his fingers, for they would leave greasy smudges. She expected he would let her hold it then, but he lifted it to his own eye instead. Turning it in the direction of the stables, he looked through it, chuckling to himself.

"Let me see, too," she asked, annoyed by then, ready to leave again if he but hesitated.

He handed it to her right away, though.

At first she only saw a blurry grayish cloud, but Auguste told her to shut her left eye, hold the spyglass lower and turn it to the right. "Can you see her now?" he asked, and Marie-Louise gasped in amazement for there was a milkmaid there, as clear as if she were close by. Red-faced, a white bonnet tied under her chin, a pail of milk in her hand, not knowing Marie-Louise was watching her.

The maid tripped and waddled, spilling some of the milk on the ground.

"My turn now," Auguste said. "You had it for three minutes and a half."

Marie-Louise handed the spyglass back. Without it the milkmaid was but a tiny figurine in the distance, walking toward them.

The following day when Marie-Louise climbed up to the roof, Auguste was already waiting for her. This time he had brought two spyglasses and handed her one, without even insisting she wipe her hands first. They watched people getting lost in the garden maze, stupidly taking the wrong turns when they were so close to getting it right. There was a boat on the Grand Canal, too, a man in it reading a book.

"Why read when you can sail?" Auguste asked, scoffing.

"Maybe he likes reading more."

"Maybe he is reading about sailing?"

Auguste was very pleased with himself for making her laugh. No one else laughed at his jokes, he complained.

By then Marie-Louise had forgiven him the stone throwing, mostly because he knew many things no one had told her about before. The red slabs of marble the builders lugged across the courtyard below came from Languedoc, the green from Campan, but the most expensive were the white ones from Carrara. Which was in Italy. Which was a country he knew how to find on a map.

"How do you know all this?"

"People tell you things if you ask. You just have to know who to ask."

He had talked to bricklayers, builders, carpenters. Asked them to show him how they join two pieces of stone together with metal pins. How to make sure the wall was even. How to make it withstand winter frosts and spring floods. How to lay lime mortar over bricks and stones, tuck-point the facades. Which kind of Parisian limestone was good for foundations and which one for walls.

"Once they even let me stir boiling tar," he said, his eyes checking if she was as impressed as he thought she should be. And she was.

"I don't tell people much anymore. Do you?"

She shook her head, thinking how many things she had kept first from the Gourlons, and now from Sister Seraphina. Thinking how nice it was to know that someone else did the same.

He also told her about his brothers. The eldest died. So did the youngest. From the two younger brothers who lived, one liked to run like a mad dog, screaming, "Out of my way!" The other preferred tripping anyone who passed him or stood in the doorways yelling, "You are in my way." There was a sister, too, but she was just a baby and couldn't speak at all.

"You don't like them?" she asked, thinking how she would have loved having a brother or a sister. He thought about it a bit and then said that sometimes he liked being by himself best. With which she could not quarrel, could she?

He had brought a basket of food with him that day. Fried chicken cut into pieces, pheasant pâté, rolls with butter. He offered her a share of what he had brought but ended up eating most of it himself. Just because she was slow, not because he begrudged her any of it. In fact, he urged her to eat what he considered the best morsels. The pâté, especially.

"My grandfather prefers hunting deer, but at the last hunt he bagged thirty-three pheasants," he said. "He promised to take me hunting when I turn thirteen." He paused, then added, "Which will be in two years and two months."

Marie-Louise began looking forward to their encounters. She had never considered making plans for the future, but Auguste had mapped out one for himself already. Once, he wanted to be a builder, but now he changed his mind and would be an explorer. He would sail to America like Samuel de Champlain, who had never found the Northern Sea though he had surveyed so much of the New France.

"Is this really how New France looks?" she asked one day after Auguste had brought one of his maps to show her. The thought that a whole country could be shrunk to fit on one piece of parchment thrilled her.

"It might," Auguste said, "or it might not." Maps, he told her, could deceive. An island she was tracing with her finger might not exist at all. Or it might be an inlet, not in fact offering the passage sailors had counted upon. Why? Because not everyone was like de Champlain. His tutor told him that many maps merely showed what people believed the land looked like. Or wanted to believe. For maps to be true, surveyors had to get out there, measure the land from one end to another.

She pictured these surveyors, traversing distant shores with measuring sticks, like tailors. What did they do when they came across steep rocks or dense forests?

"There are ways," Auguste said. "It's done by calculations."

She pointed at the white empty space on the map where the letters formed two words: *Parts unknown.*

"This means that no one has been there yet," Auguste said.

"Why not?" she asked, thinking of the puff-cheeked sea monsters she had seen on palace paintings, blowing plumes of water at sailing ships. Or a giant snake swallowing explorers, but Auguste was adamant that these unknown lands were waiting for him. He had a plan, too. As soon as he turned fifteen, he would run away from the palace and get on a ship. He had already charted the route on a map he had colored himself, to make different elevations visible.

"I'll be an explorer, too," Marie-Louise said, but he shook his head. Did she, perchance, know anything about sextants? Astrolabes? Calculating her position at sea? Could she determine the right amount of ballast? And how to place it on board so that the ship does not list? Does she perhaps know how to cure scurvy and treat fevers? Or set broken bones? Besides, women brought bad luck on a ship, so nobody wanted them there.

"How do you know?"

"From a book."

"Let it be then," she said, standing up, pushing the map away. "Go on your stupid ship alone."

She managed a few steps before he called after her.

"Come back."

She kept walking.

"Please. Don't be angry with me."

She turned back.

"Nobody else likes me," he said, his voice shrill and tense. "Even my older brother used to call me names."

"What names?"

"Just names. Bad names. Mean."

Marie-Louise rolled her eyes. "Why do you care?"

He bit his lower lip and frowned.

The Gourlons, she continued, called her names all the time. It used to be Gardienne only, but it was both of them now. So she just closed her ears. Thought of something else. The horse she would brush later, for instance. How it neighed at her sight and shook its head.

This impressed him quite a bit. "Who are these Gourlons?" he asked.

"Nobody. Just the Gourlons. So, can I get on this ship?"

"They are not your parents?"

"No. My parents live far away but one day they will come and take me with them. Will you help me get on the ship, then?"

"Yes."

"How will we get to the sea?"

"On horseback."

The plans expanded from day to day and needed to be written down, in a thick notebook Auguste began bringing with him. Marie-Louise would dress up as a boy and one of her cats would go with them, Mighty, the best rat catcher, for rats were a big problem for sailors. They will first go to Brest. In Brest they will sneak onto a ship, revealing themselves only when they have passed the rocks of Gibraltar and are too far away from land for the captain to turn back.

At first the captain will be furious with them, but Auguste knew what he will do. He will wait until they have to change course or, even better, when they lose their way in a really bad storm. Then he will impress the captain with his knowledge of how to calculate their position. Only when the captain assures him that he can stay will Auguste disclose who he is. And then he will point to Marie-Louise, still in disguise, and call her "my helper and friend."

They delighted in this scene, acting it out twice. The surprise, the admiration, the awe of the sailors. "Your Highness, I beg you to forgive me," the captain would say. "How could I have known!"

Through the whole summer, every time they met, they worked on the details of their planned escapade. Marie-Louise was especially excited about the list of questions for which they would seek answers during their journey: Are people the same size everywhere? What kinds of food do they eat that we do not? How do they hunt? What kinds of vessels do they have for sailing? How many children do they usually have? Do they keep cats?

"Do they ever leave their children behind, with strangers?" Marie-Louise also added, watching Auguste as he wrote it. His handwriting was small and crowded, even less easy to read than hers.

⁂

That autumn day began so much better than others. Marie-Louise woke up early, did all her morning chores with time to spare. Old Gourlon didn't stare at her, did not ask her his stupid questions, did not tell her she was trying to be too clever for her own good. Sister Seraphina was pleased with her recitations. Pleased, too, that Marie-Louise made only one error in her dictation, which was a great improvement in her diligence and concentration. Sister Seraphina said so herself.

Her lessons over, Marie-Louise strapped her books together and headed for the door. Auguste might be waiting for her already. Since the list of questions for their expedition was almost finished, he now promised to teach her about sextants. Can we measure the distance between two palace gates? she asked. At first he said no because this was not what sextants were for. But then he said they could try.

She was outside, heading for the scaffolding she used to climb to the roof, when Gardienne appeared as if she were waiting for her, saying, "I'll put a stop to this wandering once and for all."

She didn't even ask where Marie-Louise was going.

It was quite a sight. Marie-Louise fighting in vain to pull her hand out of Gardienne's grip. Dragging her feet as she was marched through the yard, back to the Grand Commons, for everyone to see. Such shame. Such abomination. Just you wait until I get you inside, Gardienne muttered under her breath. No one will tell me I'm not doing my duty. Letting you go where the likes of you are not welcome. No one, can you hear?

A thump on her back sent Marie-Louise inside the entresol rooms, the key turned in the door and disappeared into the folds of Gardienne's skirt. What could Marie-Louise do? She pounded her fists on the locked door, skinning her knuckles. She screamed. She sobbed. "What have I done?"

"You have the nerve to ask?"

Reckless, Marie-Louise had been called before. Willful. Ungrateful, too. But never *scheming . . . greedy . . . imposing herself on your betters*. Curses like the bayings of some furious beast.

Words that can break your bones, if you let them.

"Reaching for what is not yours. How you disgust me . . . I curse the day I took you in."

Later, when the Gourlons were finally asleep, Marie-Louise lay in her bed thinking of Auguste. Did he wait for her very long? What did he think happened to her? She imagined him, sextant in hand, peering down the scaffolding. Telling himself she was on her way. Sending his servant perhaps, to make inquiries. He knew she lived at the Grand Commons. He had heard her mention the Gourlons. How hard would it be to track her down, free her from this prison? It made her feel good to imagine Gardienne cringing in front of Auguste, begging His Highness's pardon. Old Gourlon swearing he meant no harm when he called Marie-Louise sneaky and a shameless tease. "What shall I do with them?" Auguste will ask, and Marie-Louise will say, "Throw them both into the Bastille. I have no wish to see them ever again."

But then another thought came. What if Auguste thought she didn't come back to the roof because she no longer wished to? That she was just like his brothers, thinking him boring, laughing behind his back, betraying him at the first chance she had?

The thought she dismissed at first, then argued with, then watched growing.

From that day on either Gardienne or Old Gourlon walked her to her lessons and brought her home, and the door to the entresol rooms remained locked. Marie-Louise could do her chores; she could do her lessons. If she still had time on her hands, there was always more sewing to do. Or embroidery.

When Marie-Louise complained to Sister Seraphina of her unjust detention, the nun said that obedience was a Christian virtue. "Surely God would want me to know why I was being punished," Marie-Louise said. "Stop putting words in God's mouth," Sister Seraphina replied. And then she added, quite tersely, "I was warned you might think yourself above others, child. I never wanted to believe it, but now I'm no longer sure."

A few days later, when Marie-Louise was working on a botanical drawing

Sister Seraphina had assigned her, a lily of the valley with its thin roots sprouting in all directions, she heard the neighing of horses and carriages being pulled out of the Versailles stables, a sign that, like every year in October, the court was moving to Fontainebleau for the winter. By the time she was done with her lessons, pages were running about relaying orders, lackeys were loading up furniture and bedding, strapping large baskets to carriage trunks.

"Are they gone already?" she asked Old Gourlon, who had come to escort her back to the Grand Commons.

His Majesty had left already, and so the best horses were gone, too. All Marie-Louise would see now were the Percherons.

"Auguste?" she asked.

Old Gourlon's bloodshot eyes pinned her to the ground. "What might *you* want with the duc de Berry?" he asked.

By the time the court returned from Fontainebleau, Auguste's father was dead, and Auguste had become the dauphin, heir to the throne of France. Fawning courtiers surrounded him at all times, the occasional visitors to the entresol rooms reported. Satin ensembles had replaced the plain brown frockcoat, but he still looked tense and awkward, as if stuffed into the wrong skin. "Still learning the ropes," they said. "Getting the knack of it." Ruling was a hard job. It had to be practiced, like everything else.

Step up, slide back.

No one called him Auguste anymore. He was Louis now, the future king of France and Navarre. Marie-Louise caught sight of him, from time to time, wearing black in mourning first for his father, then for his mother who died fifteen months later, of the coughing sickness. He had become stouter by then and his face flushed easily.

Once, Marie-Louise saw him riding by the king's side, returning from a deer hunt, tired, spent, reins slack. Trailed by courtiers, grooms, barking hounds; tufts of fur, carcasses of slain deer piled high on a cart, dripping blood. The king looked at his grandson with obvious pride.

If the dauphin of France saw Marie-Louise, his eyes slid over her as if she were made of air.

1768

DEATH, MARIE-LOUISE HAD HEARD, arrived uninvited and spared no one, leveling all that had been uneven.

Queen Marie, who once gave Marie-Louise a holy picture and said she looked like an angel, died in June, on the feast of Saint John the Baptist, and was buried in the cathedral of Saint Denis. Even though a month had passed since the funeral, the grand apartments at Versailles were still hung with black and the king still went there every day and prayed for his wife's soul. Courtiers made sure they were heard repeating his words: "She never caused me any grief, apart from dying." By the palace gate, merchants still sold fringes from the cloth that had covered the royal coffin, and dried petals plucked from the floral arrangements after the Good Queen's funeral.

"It is Lebel's turn now," Marie-Louise heard. "Not much longer on this earth." Released from his duties, the king's *valet de chambre* had moved to a house in town, on avenue de Saint-Cloud. A royal servant was not allowed to die at Versailles.

A rich old man with houses, gardens, furnishings, paintings, the Gourlons said. No wife. No children. Who would inherit it all?

The palace rumors had it that Lebel's favorite nephew could easily count on at least sixty-five thousand livres. Lebel's servants would not go begging, either. Every one of his lackeys would get three thousand livres and a yearly salary. His *valet de chambre* would get six thousand livres, in addition to his master's clothes, canes, hunting guns and knives and the repeater watch made by none other than the horloger du roi. Marie-Louise had also heard that this *valet de chambre* would live at the Louvre Palace in Paris, where

Lebel had bought rooms for him and furnished them with his own furniture. And that one had to wonder what merited such generosity. That last statement had often been followed by a wink or throat clearing, both equally puzzling.

"A lonely man, on the threshold of death, about to face the day of divine judgment," Sister Seraphina said through pursed lips, eyes looking upward. No matter how unpredictable the ways of the Almighty might seem, justice always triumphed in the end. Then, looking sternly at Marie-Louise, she added, "A Christian soul in need of a prayer."

Marie-Louise let these words brush right past her. Why would *she* pray for the man who never looked at her with kindness? She had enough to pray for already.

⁓⁕⁓

Fear, Marie-Louise would learn that summer, was not unlike death. It also arrived uninvited and it didn't spare her.

The days were hot and stuffy, wicking away the last drops of strength from her body. When night finally brought a cooler breeze, she would fall into exhausted, dreamless sleep. Nothing would rouse her, she thought, and yet one such night she woke to see Old Gourlon standing over her bed, candle in hand. "Where is my cane?" he muttered as Marie-Louise burrowed deeper under the coverlet. "Have you hidden it, you little thief?"

She was twelve by then and such threadbare lies didn't fool her. She didn't like the thickening of his voice, head turned sideways, the licking of lips, either, and she knew the value of playing along to buy time.

"It's by the door. Where it always is."

"Is it, now," he half asked, sitting himself on the edge of her bed, breathing rot mixed with sour wine. The candle he was holding in his left hand tilted, and a drop of melted tallow fell onto the floor. In the past months he delighted in plying her with stories of the hairy beast of Gerandon, hunting little girls for their soft meat. Or spooking her by coming up behind and stomping his foot. Or grabbing her shoulders, saying, "I gave you a fright, didn't I?"

"You called me, Marie-Louise," he muttered.

"No, I didn't."

"Don't lie to me. I heard you call me."

His voice took on the tone of righteous insistence; his right hand hovered over her head. "Now, why would you do that, Marie-Louise? Why would you wake a God-fearing man in the middle of the night like that?"

His hand descended, resting on Marie-Louise's shoulder. Heavy and hot. Fear that started low in her spine was now shooting upward, seizing her heart.

"Gardienne could've taken it," she said. "We can ask her. I can hear she is awake."

"No, you can't," he said, but the very mention of his wife brought forth the familiar litany of grievances. Madame Gourlon was a proper bitch with no heart. Nothing but sneers and taunts from her. She hid his wine jug right after dinner. She wouldn't let him near the keys to her medicine cupboard. In His Majesty's stables the grooms laughed behind his back. When he was Pompadour's coachman, they called him Bruiser. Now it was: How is your gout, Grandpa? Or: Still have any teeth to chew with? They only invited him to play cards to cheat him blind. For how could he have lost otherwise, with three aces and two kings? "Tell me, Marie-Louise, how is *that* possible?"

Sticky words, like tar.

Through the open window came the croaking of frogs and the distant chatter of men. A night-soil cart rolled by, under-footmen collecting rot and feces from the garden grounds, taking it all to the dunghill. If the wind changed, the stench would make Marie-Louise gag.

The candle spluttered; more tallow dripped to the floor. Finally, from behind the wall, came Madame Gourlon's groggy voice. "Antoine? Where are you? Come back to bed."

Old Gourlon, Bruiser, sighed and lifted himself up. "Can't a man take a piss anymore," he said, far too loud.

"I'm not a fool, Antoine."

As Old Gourlon walked away, dragging his feet, Marie-Louise allowed relief to melt the tension in her muscles, release the grip on her heart.

In the morning when Marie-Louise woke up, stiff and sweaty, Old Gourlon was already standing shirtless over the washstand, sharpening his razor on a leather belt. "A true coachman can shave anywhere," he boasted. "No need for a mirror."

Eyelids half closed, she watched as he soaped his chin and cheeks, scraped them with his razor blade. Sharp enough to slit a naughty girl's throat, he had said many times. When he was done, he wiped the soap from his face with a washcloth and put on his old faded livery, from which Madame de Pompadour's purple facings had been removed. This meant that he would leave soon enough, in search of company. If Marie-Louise were lucky, she might not see him until the evening.

A moment later, the door opened, and she heard his steps descending the stairs.

Marie-Louise had just enough time to fold her bed and tidy the room before Gardienne got up. She worked fast, mopping up splashed water from the floor, emptying the basin into the slop bucket, picking up the washcloth and rinsing it well before she hung it out to dry, for it was speckled with blood.

Then she scraped the candle spills from the floor. For now, just with her fingernail, to get rid of the outer layer. Later she would remove the rest of the tallow with an iron. Just hot enough to melt it so she could soak it up with a soft rag.

They had new neighbors occupying the rooms next door: the Jalettes, an under-gardener and his wife, Charlotte. Their son, Jacques, was still in leading strings, and there was another baby on the way. "A proof of recklessness," Gardienne had said when they moved in. Old Gourlon just smacked his lips.

"I hope for a daughter," Charlotte told Marie-Louise when they met on the stairs for the first time. She lifted Marie-Louise's hand and placed it on her belly, pressing it down. "Can you feel it?" she asked.

Marie-Louise shook her head.

"Press harder. Don't be afraid."

She did press harder and then she felt it. A flicker of movement, the push of a small something. An elbow, Charlotte suggested, or a heel. Something still hidden but already alive.

"It would've been my fourth," Charlotte said, "but, if the merciful God allows, it will be my second."

God took you if He wanted to punish you or if He wanted to have you at His side, Sister Seraphina would say, if Marie-Louise still cared to ask her.

Little Jacques pulled on his mother's apron. "A determined little fellow, this one," Charlotte said, picking him up. "Want to hold him, Marie-Louise?"

A small round-faced boy with bright gray eyes and a beaming smile. She did want to hold him, feel his plump little fingers clutch hers, his lips planting a wet, warm kiss on her cheek.

There had been many such moments since.

Charlotte liked to talk. Of Buc where she came from, of her father's tavern where she worked like a slave while Papa was drinking away the profits. Of a widowed palace gardener who came to Buc to visit his mother. "Stopped by the tavern. Liked what he saw," she laughed, pointing at herself. "And that was that."

Their rooms were still crammed with baskets and crates, half unpacked. "I don't even know where to put the cradle when the new one arrives," Charlotte said, throwing her arms up. Marie-Louise had already decided that her new friend's eyes, gray like her son's, were far more beautiful than her own dark blue. And that being short and plump was far more appealing than being tall and lanky, as she was turning out to be.

Charlotte didn't like Versailles or the Grand Commons. Far too many people milled about with their noses in the air, she said. Not seeing you as you passed. Never remembering your name but always having something nasty to say behind your back. She would like to go back to Buc, but her husband wouldn't hear of it. This was what happened when you got married. Things got decided in ways you did not predict.

"I don't want to get married," Marie-Louise said.

"Never?"

"Never."

"What will you do then? You are so good with children."

She was good with children. Little Jacques had become addicted to the hand-clapping game Marie-Louise had taught him. Patting a cake, marking it with imaginary letters, pretending to eat it. Fast, fast, fast! When he laughed, spit dripped down his chinny-chin-chin, but he never objected when she wiped it. When she picked him up, he flopped against her shoulder and mur-mured something to himself that sounded like a lullaby.

These Jalettes, Gardienne would exclaim. Noisy, messy. She did not need to see Charlotte Jalette's rooms, ever. She knew a lazy, gossipy woman when she saw one, and Marie-Louise could wipe that smirk off her face right now.

A common woman, too, Gardienne said.

Parading her belly for everyone to see, Old Gourlon added with that sly grin Marie-Louise loathed.

Besides, the Jalettes, both of them, were sticking their noses where they had no business. There had been far too many chance encounters on the stairs. The word *chance* Gardienne pronounced with a hint of menace. Why was Charlotte always at the door when anyone passed by? Always asking ques-tions? Why would her under-gardener husband inquire about Monsieur Gourlon? And why had the Jalettes been given rooms at the Grand Commons at all, and not in one of the houses at the edge of the Grand Canal with other garden staff? Someone put them there, obviously. To spy on the Gourlons, perhaps?

"Keep your voice down, Antoine," she warned Old Gourlon. "These walls are thin. We don't need trouble."

◆

At the beginning of August, Gardienne received a letter from Madame du Hausset inviting her to Paris for a few days. Her dear Nicole wished to consult her on some important matters. "Besides, I have earned a few days of respite, haven't I?" Gardienne asked as she began packing. Marie-Louise would keep the rooms tidy, bring Monsieur Gourlon's meals from the kitchen. She could manage that much on her own, couldn't she?

The first day went well enough. Old Gourlon returned home late, drunk, and fell asleep mumbling dire vengeance on some thug who had snubbed him. In the morning, when Marie-Louise left for her lessons with Sister Seraphina, he was still asleep. He only got out of bed when Marie-Louise brought his dinner. The cook had been generous with goat stew and bread. She thought it would put him in an agreeable mood, but to be sure she had also brought two bottles of wine.

"Burgundy?" Old Gourlon asked as he emptied the first glass. "The cook gave you Burgundy?"

They ate together. Old Gourlon tore pieces of bread and soaked them in the stew. Then he asked Marie-Louise about her lessons, which was odd but not troubling. "I made only two mistakes in the dictation," she said, omitting the fact that Sister Seraphina thought it was two too many.

Good, he murmured and poured himself another glass of wine.

The wine, he said, was surprisingly decent, too. Did she want to try it?

"No."

"Go on, just a taste. I won't tell her," he said, meaning Gardienne.

"No."

He sighed then and repeated his old accusations. The missus had no heart. He could do nothing right. Then, staring at Marie-Louise, he asked, "You are not as bad as she says you are, are you?" His red nose was pearly with sweat. A crumb of bread was stuck on his chin.

Marie-Louise didn't answer. She knew what a bait was.

"Such a small thing you were when we took you in. Cheeky, too," he continued. Teary now, he recalled how awed Marie-Louise had been by the palace then, the giant mirrors, the crystal chandeliers. How curious she was, too, always asking questions. Where does the king go to sleep? How many dogs does he have? If the king rules, what does the queen do?

"A clever little mite, you were."

She was still clever. The cook hadn't given her the Burgundy. When he was taking a rack of hot pastries from the oven, she took the two bottles, still in their straw wrappings, from a crate and hid them at the bottom of her basket.

Old Gourlon took off his jacket and opened the collar of his shirt. There was a yellow stain around it. Gardienne would have made him change it.

Never mind. Head down. Don't catch his eye.

The wine had been a stupid, stupid mistake. It had been enough to make Old Gourlon take a long nap after dinner, but not enough to keep him asleep through the night. Marie-Louise should've blocked his bedroom door. She should've hidden his clothes and his shoes. She should've found a hiding spot somewhere in the service corridors and slept there. Enough of them under palace stairs.

She hadn't and now, in the middle of the night, he was staggering toward her, his breathing ragged, mumbling something she wished not to hear.

"What do you want from me?" she asked in the loudest voice she could summon.

"Shh . . . you will wake up everyone."

He was still a wiry man, but no longer fast, which, she decided, would be her salvation as she made a dash for it.

This was another mistake. All his life Old Gourlon had worked with horses, far more skittish and panicked than her. He knew the power of a steady hand.

Caught, Marie-Louise fought with all the strength she had. Kicking, clawing the flesh of his hands. But at eleven she was still a child, not strong enough.

In the end it was her screams that saved her, loud enough to merit bangs on the ceiling from the footmen who slept in the attic above. Followed by bangs on the wall and Master Jalette's voice at their door, asking if everything was in order.

Next door was where Marie-Louise ended up, choking with rage and tears, her teeth chattering. Charlotte sat her on one of the still-unopened crates in the room strewn with the spoons and pots little Jacques liked to play with, while Master Jalette argued with Old Gourlon, who was demanding Marie-Louise return home.

Charlotte busied herself with a basin of cold water and a washcloth. "Looks like you have lost some of your lovely hair, child," she muttered, dabbing at Marie-Louise's scalp, smearing a layer of salve on her cheeks and arms. Marie-Louise twitched her nostrils, for the salve gave off a bit of a stink, like wet paper dipped in brandy.

"Witch hazel," Charlotte said. "Does it hurt much?"

Marie-Louise felt no pain. In fact, she felt nothing but relief and gratitude.

"It'll be worse tomorrow," Charlotte said. "You'll have bruises all over. And look at your shift, all torn."

It didn't matter, did it?

"Has it happened before?"

Marie-Louise didn't know what to say. It hadn't, really, but it had, too. Just not in the same way.

"He says that he was teaching you a lesson," Master Jalette told Marie-Louise when he returned. "That you've stolen wine from the kitchen. Is this true, child?"

She hesitated.

"Reason enough for your guardian to punish you, if you ask me."

By then Marie-Louise had made up her mind. She would lie about the wine, say the cook gave it to her. If the Jalettes try to send her back, she will dash through the door and run away. They won't find her that easily. She knew her way inside the palace. She could hide there for days.

"She is not going back there," Charlotte said. "I don't care what he says. Look how scared the poor girl is."

Her husband sighed, not quite convinced, but Marie-Louise could see he was not going to argue. For now, she was safe.

They cleared a bit of the floor, spread a layer of fresh straw on the floor-boards, put a blanket over it. Gave her another to cover herself with. After rummaging in one of the wicker baskets Charlotte pulled out a coarse linen shift to replace the torn one.

"A bit too big for you, but never mind."

Marie-Louise removed her shift and slunk in between the blankets. Before leaving, Charlotte patted the top of her head and told her not to worry. Things could be done . . . would be done . . . she promised. As soon as Diane Gourlon came back, she, Charlotte Jalette, would have a word with her. And if that didn't help, she knew where to go next.

Two days later, back in her nook, Marie-Louise listened to Gardienne seething with indignation at having had to endure a talking down by those upstarts, the Jalettes. Was she a prisoner at her own home? Unable to leave even for two days to visit a dear friend who needed her advice on the memoirs she was writing?

It was all Marie-Louise's fault, Old Gourlon said. The shameless way she walked through the room, the looks she gave him. Hadn't she always been wily, untamed? Blood didn't lie, did it? Thicker than water . . . what got around came around.

"We've made a rod for our own backs, Diane," he said. "We've raised a viper."

Gardienne clasped her hands at her chest, hard.

"So we have, Antoine," she said. "So we have."

~·≈·~

The summons came three days later. Monsieur Lebel, too weak to leave his bed, desired to see Marie-Louise and Diane Gourlon in his house on avenue de Saint-Cloud. Just the two of them. No one else.

"No one said anything about a carriage," the page who delivered the summons said haughtily. No one said anything about a sedan chair, either.

Gardienne didn't hide her annoyance. They would have to walk to town. "In this stifling heat," she complained in a voice that indicated this, too, was Marie-Louise's fault.

Marie-Louise didn't mind. The walk was not that long and, besides, she quite liked seeing her guardian flustered and peeved. Not much of a comeuppance, but still. Ever since her return from Paris, Gardienne had been finding fault with everything. The way Marie-Louise carried herself, hair in tangles, fichu out of place. The way she spoke (too loud) or did not speak (which was rude). How she was never around when needed. Underfoot when she was not. And the company she kept! "Clinging to that Jalette woman like a stray dog!"

The two-story house on avenue de Saint-Cloud was decorated with carvings of birds: a falcon, a hawk, an eagle painted in lifelike colors, on a gilded background.

"Fancy, aren't we?" Gardienne muttered. Then she shot a look at Marie-Louise and shook her finger. "Don't you dare repeat that to anyone!"

The anteroom where they were told to wait was crowded. Men in their somber-looking ensembles, women in modest dresses, some with children, were milling about, casting wary eyes on each other, wiping sweat off their faces. All hoping for a legacy, Gardienne had said.

The *valet de chambre* who would live at the Louvre Palace turned out to be a portly man with a gap between his front teeth. "Master wishes to see the girl first," he told Gardienne after they had waited for quite a long time. Gardienne managed to keep her face blank, as if she did not mind it in the least. Turning to Marie-Louise, the valet then instructed her to speak in a clear, loud voice, for master was hard of hearing.

"Go on," he said, opening the bedroom door and pushing her inside in front of him.

The bedroom was far brighter than Marie-Louise expected, its musty stuffiness barely broken with the smells of lavender. The floor was covered with a thick carpet that muffled her steps. Monsieur Lebel was lying in a four-post bed, its curtains open, his head resting on a lace-trimmed pillow. His long, thin body was covered with a quilted coverlet, as if he could no longer feel the August heat.

"Who is it, Gaspard?" he asked. Without his wig, his face looked shriveled, but his voice had not changed. It was as sharp and dry as Marie-Louise remembered it.

"The Gourlons' ward, Master."

"Alone?"

"Yes, Master, just as you requested," the valet replied. "The Gourlon woman is waiting outside."

"Good. Let her wait."

The valet chuckled as if it were a good joke.

"Leave us alone, now, Gaspard," Monsieur Lebel said. He flinched as if a spasm of pain had coursed through him.

As the door closed behind the valet, Marie-Louise felt a tinge of unease. What would she do if Monsieur Lebel died while she was alone with him?

"Come closer, girl, I'm not dead yet," he said, as if he could hear this thought.

She took a step toward him and saw that he was clasping a golden watch in his hand. Was it the repeater his *valet de chambre* would get? And what was a repeater watch anyway?

"I said closer."

Marie-Louise took another step, bracing herself for a sermon on what a heap of disappointment she had become to everyone. Squandering the opportunities she had been given, bringing grief to those who took care of her. The Gourlons. Sister Seraphina.

"Is it true what I'm hearing about you?" he asked. "That you are making a spectacle of yourself?"

She stared at him in silence, at his drawn, bony scarecrow face, his bloodshot eyes, sunken into the skull.

"Speak," he demanded. "Explain yourself."

She felt her jaw set in defiance.

"I cannot hear you. What did you say?"

"Nothing."

"I thought so. Come closer, I said."

She took another step toward the bed, her nostrils catching the whiff of rot.

"Lying. Stealing. Arguing with your guardians like a terrier with badgers."

"It wasn't my fault!"

He closed his eyes, breathing hard. "Whose fault was it then?" he muttered.

"His."

"I've heard otherwise."

"You've heard lies."

"You care for stray cats and other people's children more than you care for your lessons. You forget your duties. You disobey orders. Are these lies, too?"

"Yes!"

"And you expect me to believe it?"

She lifted her eyes to the ceiling, covered with paintings of tangled vines, among which clusters of purple grapes glittered. Outside the room someone coughed, loud enough to remind the dying man that more important matters awaited.

"If you go on like that, you will never amount to anything."

Anger was beginning to boil inside her now. Why couldn't they all leave her alone?

"Foolish," he continued. "Believing yourself so much wiser than anyone else. Flighty, just like your mother. As they say, birds do not fall far from their nests."

She didn't expect that. No one has ever said they knew her mother, let alone that Marie-Louise was just like her. Foolish? Flighty? She gripped the bedpost to steady herself before she could ask what he must have known she would: "You knew my mother?"

He gave her a sharp, impatient look. "Your mother has always been rash, acted before thinking, and let herself be ruled by her whims."

"Where is she now?"

"Doing as she pleases, deaf to anyone's warnings. Not surprising, considering that she never thought of anyone but herself."

Marie-Louise closed her eyes and opened them again. She wouldn't let this horrid old man see her cry.

"It was my duty to see that you would turn out differently," Lebel continued. "A duty I have tried to discharge the best I could." He wanted to say something else, but another bout of pain stopped him. "Go now," he murmured through clenched teeth. "Just go."

Marie-Louise staggered out into the antechamber, thoughts coming at her all at once, making little sense. Her mother was alive? Doing as she pleased? Thinking of no one but herself? Leaning against the wall, she tried to pry these words open, find what they carried inside, but all she could do was let tears flow down her cheeks.

"What did you tell him?" Gardienne managed to ask, sharply, before the *valet de chambre* pointed at the door, ordering her to get in.

When Gardienne emerged from the room, her cheeks were as red as if she had been slapped. She didn't look at Marie-Louise at all. She didn't ask her anything, either.

They took a carriage home. It was a short ride the sullen driver resented, but Gardienne paid him no heed. Mostly she stared out the window at the trees, the people strolling by, the washerwomen with their laundry baskets heading for the lake.

The carriage deposited them at the palace gate. The driver said that he was not allowed past it; they would have to walk the rest of the way.

Gardienne searched her coin purse. Whatever she gave to the driver could not have been enough, for he swore at her and told her to get out. He was not a beggar, and he had just bloody had it with the snotty palace people. They were all the same. Thought they shat flowers.

Hit with the whip, the horse neighed and jerked forward.

Gardienne walked fast toward the Grand Commons, and Marie-Louise followed, repeating in her mind the same few words.

Stubborn. Foolish. Rash. Ruled by her whims.

Is this why her mother left her then? Is this why she never came back to find her?

The Gourlons closed the bedroom door.

Your fault. You old fool . . . what have you done . . . what has she told him . . . where will we live now? Then Gardienne began to sob and Old Gourlon pounded the table with his fist.

When Madame Gourlon emerged, she called Marie-Louise to her. "You will have a new guardian," she said in a stiff, small voice. "May merciful God have her unsuspecting soul in His care."

Part Three

Paris, 1768–1789

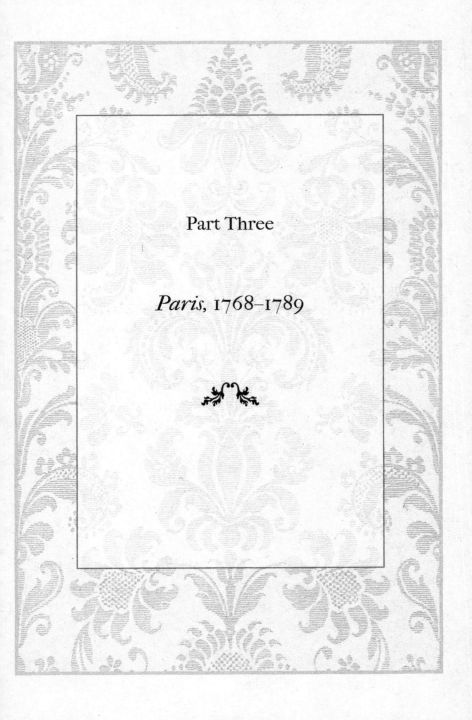

1768–1770

IN MARIE-LOUISE'S LAST MEMORY of Versailles, a stout woman in a plain brown dress, white bonnet tied under her chin, tells the Gourlons in a firm voice: "I'm Marguerite Leblanc. It was Monsieur Lebel's last wish and his order that I care for this child." Unmoved by the display of indignation her words cause, she adds, "Of which I trust you've already been duly informed."

It would always strike Marie-Louise how willingly she went with a stranger. The recklessness of youth, this stubborn conviction that luck was on our side, against all evidence to the contrary. Nature's way to encourage the young, blind them to the dangers ahead.

After the long ride from Versailles to Paris, they arrived at this house on rue du Cygne, with its midwife's sign over the door, a cradle beside a messenger carrying a lantern. She would remember walking through the front door, Hortense gasping at her bony frame: "Didn't they feed you at this grand Versailles, child?" She would remember the dirty water after her bath, lice squashed between Hortense's fingernails. She would remember the warmth of her new bed, the crisply starched nightshift, the bitter taste of the deworming tea, her new guardian patting her shoulder, saying she wished to be called Aunt Margot. In her mind the old questions reeled.

"Whose child am I? Where is my mother now? Where is my father?"

It had not left her, the howling pain at the answer. "That I don't know. But I'll take good care of you."

It was not easy, the time that followed. She was not easy. Anger had sunk into her too deeply, braided too tightly. Anger she could neither explain nor control. She remembers the flower vase carelessly brushed against and made to shatter; soot trodden all over the carpets; her voice raised, boiling, harsh, crackling with fury. "I didn't ask to be brought here!"

"True, you didn't ask. I shall look after you all the same and that's that."

Mistress Margot, Hortense called her. Aunt Margot, Marie-Louise would. Not right away, but she would.

A handful, she was. Oh, yes! A holy terror. The bane of her aunt's life, the trial of her patience, making her hair go gray, as Hortense, hands folded in that way she has, chewing a bay leaf to avert ill luck, would remind Marie-Louise daily.

Imprisoned in this house, she thought herself. Hortense, charged with minding her, proved impossible to fool, her sharp voice stopping Marie-Louise in her tracks. "Jesus, Mary and Joseph, help us now and in the hour of our death. Where to, grand mademoiselle from Versailles? The gutter? Intending to keep company with rats?"

She didn't know. She didn't care.

"Whereas I do."

Locked in the room in which she now keeps her own patients' records, Marie-Louise pounded her fists on the door until her knuckles bled. Hortense the fat dragon, she called her then, spewing fire.

And yet it was with Hortense that Marie-Louise first began losing the sharpest edges of her anger. Hortense, who showed her how to bank the fire in the stove in the evening and how to break it in the morning. Which parts of which herb to crush for infusions, how to render fat and turn it into salves. Amid her complaints about her rheumatism or finicky lodgers, Hortense noticed when Marie-Louise's skirts needed to have the hem let out, when her shoes pinched or when a quilted petticoat for winter was in order.

Still, Marie-Louise did try to run away, ungrateful wretch as she had been then. Crept downstairs one night, her traveling cloak on, only to hear Aunt Margot's voice:

"Where are you heading, child?"

Marie-Louise didn't answer. Where would she have gone, she still wonders sometimes, or—more likely—how far before she turned back?

In the hall, her midwife's bag in hand, Aunt Margot was wrapping herself with a warm shawl. "Hold my bag then," she said. "I can use some help."

A boy with a lantern was waiting outside. They didn't have far to go, just a few streets toward Les Halles. The house in front of which Aunt Margot stopped was a small one. A man stood in front of it, waving, his face drawn with worry.

"Is there enough light up there?" Aunt Margot asked.

The man shook his head and watched sheepishly when Aunt Margot negotiated with the boy until he relinquished his lantern and took off pleased with his bargain.

"Enough water warmed up?"

The man nodded. Did the cat get your tongue, Hortense would have asked.

"Enough soft rags?"

Only after another nod did Aunt Margot follow the man up the creaking stairs to the upper landing. The loud groans that reached them there did not seem quite human. "You stay here," Aunt Margot told the man while motioning to Marie-Louise to follow her.

Inside the room Marie-Louise, who was now holding the lantern, saw a woman lying on a bed, hair disheveled, face covered in sweat. Her enormous belly looked ready to burst, and Marie-Louise truly thought that it might.

"I reckoned you'd never come," the woman said, lifting herself on her elbows.

"Right here. Just as I promised."

Marie-Louise watched as Aunt Margot swiftly moved about, lifting the woman's skirt high around her bare thighs, dipping a rag in a basin of warm water, wiping that big white belly. Each movement so firm and precise, each word so filled with calm. "You are coming along nicely . . . not long now."

"You said that with the other one."

"And wasn't I right?"

The woman stifled a chuckle.

"Hold the lantern closer, Marie-Louise!"

In the yellow light Marie-Louise saw the black hairy patch between the woman's legs and swollen flesh from which something round was emerging. She didn't know it then, but this baby was pushing itself into the world faster than most.

As vivid as if it happened yesterday, the memory of that first birth. The rush of bloody water, the small grayish body slithering out into Aunt Margot's hands. The deft certainty with which Aunt Margot extracted the yellow mucus from the baby's mouth, held the sharp razor with which she cut the cord before tying it into a knot.

Are all midwives like that? Marie-Louise wondered.

Soon the father was on his knees scrubbing the floor clean of afterbirth and blood. "As you say, Mistress Margot . . . Right away, Mistress Margot." The mother was crying and laughing and cooing to the child, as if she had never been in pain.

"Is it always like that?" Marie-Louise asked Aunt Margot as they walked home through the morning mist.

"No. Sometimes everything goes wrong."

"What do you do then?"

"Fetch a surgeon."

"Then what."

"Then you pray."

Once inside the house on rue du Cygne, Marie-Louise tried to dash upstairs, but Aunt Margot grabbed her by the shoulders and made her hold her eyes. Watery blue, Marie-Louise remembers, rimmed with red, blinking after the sleepless night.

"This anger in you, child," she said. "You can keep feeding it or you can start feeding what's best in you."

Only a crack, perhaps, but enough for a chink of light to creep through.

Marie-Louise quieted down not long after. Helped Hortense in the kitchen, lingered in the best room when Aunt Margot's friends came on Sundays. Midwives all, with their talk of fate written into women's bodies. Of lying-ins, slow or fast, in pain or with an ease that had to be marveled at. Of women feasting on red meat in hope for a boy, on fruits if they desired a girl. Of babies pulled out with their strong, skillful hands, babies weak or robust, in need of revival or in possession of iron lungs. Midwives laughing as they recalled a tug-of-war with a new mother begging them to reshape the baby's head. "Be patient, I told her . . . give God a chance!" Or sending shivers down Marie-Louise's spine as they whispered of a girl found half naked on the rampart, frozen to death, clutching her dead baby to her chest, or another giving birth to a daughter without a face.

Midwives, she heard, had to be ready for anything.

What pains Marie-Louise still is the time she wasted chasing phantoms, refusing to see what was staring her in the face.

That she had found a home.

That the past didn't have to stain her.

Mugwort, wormwood and black pepper settled the stomach, promoted rest, strengthened the vital force. Chamomile tea soothed overwrought nerves. The mysterious jars on the windowsill in Aunt Margot's room were there for the nettle trial: Put green nettle in her urine overnight. If she is with child, it will be full of red spots in the morning. If not, it will be blackish.

But in the end it was Aunt Margot's books that broke the last vestiges of Marie-Louise's anger, left opened as if by chance on a side table, on the mantel. A drawing, a passage marked, a trail of temptations. Vesalius, *On the Fabric of the Human Body*: "the temporary lodging and instrument of the immortal soul." The web of muscles and veins under human skin, showing the ways bones attach to each other, organs connect. Madame du Coudray, the *Abrégé de l'Art des Accouchements*: "presenting the womb in its position, its opening, its dilation by gradation, its contraction and obliquities." Two hands with white cuffs holding a baby's head, pulling it out of a bone basin or turning the baby around, to make birth possible. A midwife's strong hands: nimble, supple and all-powerful.

Esteemed Madame Angélique du Coudray, Marie-Louise knew, had been Aunt Margot's beloved teacher, with whom Aunt Margot had apprenticed for three blessed years. Who taught Aunt Margot everything she knew. "A teacher I miss every single day," Aunt Margot would add, as by then Madame du Coudray had no time for Paris, traveling as she did all over France, training country girls in the art of midwifery. Here Aunt Margot might show Marie-Louise a drawing of the Machine that Madame du Coudray had invented, the cloth mannequin with its big belly on which would-be midwives could practice their skills without endangering anyone. Or tell her the story of Madame taking this wondrous machine to Versailles, where His Majesty himself delivered a cloth baby girl himself, with great pride, to the thunderous applause of the court.

Breadcrumbs leading Marie-Louise on.

"I can begin teaching you . . . if you truly wish it . . . if you prove you can apply yourself."

How do you prove that? By keeping your eyes on the lodgers.

"My girls," Aunt Margot called them. Some brought by relatives, others showing up on their own, in tears and in fear. Fleur, who resembled the Madonna in the print Hortense kept by her bed, swore pox on her deceitful lover. Pascaline, who asked Marie-Louise every morning, "So what's happening in the grand world of the mighty?" Catherine, who, seeing a one-legged beggar, asked, "What bit his leg off? His sweetheart, the devil?"

Begging Aunt Margot for help, all of them, only to complain that a room was too small, Hortense pointed out often enough. Or the soap too harsh, or a cake not sweet enough. As if they paid Mistress a fortune, she would add, taking a dim view of Aunt Margot's accounting. For why could other midwives charge twelve livres a day while Mistress Margot only took ten? Why did Hortense have to threaten to leave before mistress allowed extra charges for laundry?

That, Marie-Louise would say, was not a good question. Why did Aunt Margot listen to Hortense's threats at all was a much better one. For how often did Hortense threaten to leave? Twice daily? Thrice? Which couldn't do much to enhance her position, could it?

"Smart, aren't we, palace girl?" Hortense would snort. "What else did you learn at Versailles?"

"That the best marble comes from Carrara. Which is in Italy."

"Is that all?"

Her Versailles education was not the topic Marie-Louise wished to dwell upon any further. Especially since the memory of Old Gourlon's taunting voice could still chill her blood. *Why would you call for me in the middle of the night, Marie-Louise? An honest, God-fearing man like me?*

For what if she didn't escape that night? What if she had been weaker, slower, less lucky? What if Aunt Margot didn't come to take her away?

To stop these thoughts, she would pinch her arm hard, to remind herself where she was.

You prove you can apply yourself by being useful.

This is why, when Aunt Margot checked on *her girls*, Marie-Louise was always around with a warm towel, the right jar of salve, learning to spot the earliest signs of trouble: bleeding, swollen feet, breath growing foul. To sniff out the despondent thoughts in the silly talk, prayers that took too long, nails bitten to the quick. Learning how Aunt Margot—her voice firm but never unkind—led *her girls* through darkness, through pain. How when she held a newborn in her arms, she whispered, "Poor, innocent mite. I'll make sure you shall not want."

You knew you had proven yourself when Aunt Margot takes you on her rounds. "My apprentice," she says and makes you flush with pride.

1773–1774

IT WAS NOT UNTIL Marie-Louise turned seventeen that Aunt Margot could sign a proper apprenticeship contract with her, in a notary's office on rue des Jardins. A contract that promised three years of training, during which "sworn midwife Madame Marguerite Leblanc pledged to show her apprentice the whole art, without hiding or disguising anything." Not only of childbirth itself, but also of "medicines and remedies, bandages, fomentations and fumigations."

All of it preparation for the qualifying exam at the College of Surgery. At the cost of 169 livres and 26 sous, in front of the first-surgeon to the king, senior members of the college, four sworn midwives from the Châtelet. "And other esteemed judges," Marie-Louise would add quickly, not to terrify herself even more.

They formed her, these apprenticeship years, hardened her, made her who she is. Every day she accompanied Aunt Margot on her patients' rounds. On the first Monday of every month, like all Parisian midwives, they attended Mass at the church of Saint-Côme and then paid charitable visits to poor women in need of a midwife. At the adjacent Saint-Côme College of Surgeons, they attended monthly lectures and observed dissections of women who died in childbirth, each a glimpse into why things went so terribly wrong. *Pelvis too narrow, deformed by rickets . . . baby's head too big*, Marie-Louise would write in her thick, leather-bound notebook. *Bleeding that could not be stopped . . . fever that would not abate.*

Elations and losses filled up many such notebooks. Ninety-seven babies delivered alive in the first year alone. Twelve stillbirths. Seventeen mothers dead in childbirth, two with their babies still inside, the surgeon summoned in time but unable to help. Twenty-one miscarriages, five of which made Aunt

Margot frown and question the patient for a long time. Drawings of pelvic shapes, childbirth positions, descriptions of labor, marked with question marks, exclamation points.

Notebooks Aunt Margot reviewed at the end of each week, pointing out in that voice of hers, half stern, half teasing: "*La malade* doesn't give a damn about your doubts, Marie-Louise, or your feelings. She has a baby to deliver. By the way, the baby doesn't care, either.

"And yes, Marie-Louise, a good midwife does need a strong bladder."

It would all have been harder without Anne and Madeleine, who began their own apprenticeships the same year with two of Aunt Margot's midwife friends. Anne was a little plump, with hazel eyes; Madeleine nearly as tall as Marie-Louise but thinner, with teeth that crowded her mouth.

Soldiers on a battlefield, Marie-Louise would refer to the three of them. Intrepid, charging forward while bullets swished past their ears, still standing as around them others fell. Remember Josée, who fainted at the sight of her first corpse at dissection? Or Jocelyn who mistook the bones a butcher sent for the Saint-Côme guard dog for human ones? Or that fiery girl, what was her name, who came to the dissection drunk and said all she had was a sip of her nerve tonic? And whom no one has seen since?

They saw each other daily, studied together whenever they could. It was not all seriousness. They made paper horns for themselves once, smeared their faces with soot and sneaked into the kitchen, scaring Hortense to inches near death, getting Aunt Margot into a fit.

Weren't they supposed to copy anatomical drawings? What did they have to say in their defense?

Nothing?

Precisely.

"How many inches?" Anne whispered in Marie-Louise's ear, proving that one can choke with laugher. Which fact Madeleine recorded in her own midwifery notebook, next to a drawing of two horns and a clenched fist.

When Marie-Louise completed the first year of her apprenticeship, a painter arrived for a sitting to commemorate the milestone with a suitable portrait.

It was Aunt Margot's idea. A midwife and her apprentice together, a reminder of what each day was for.

The painter wanted to have the two of them seated on the green ottoman, Marie-Louise leaning her head on her aunt's shoulder, looking up to her. Either serious or joyful, the painter suggested. If the former, Aunt Margot should focus her gaze on Marie-Louise, soft light illuminating their faces. If the latter, the joy would find its locus in Marie-Louise's dark blue eyes and her smile.

Aunt Margot would have none of it. The two of them would sit side by side, leaning over Madame du Coudray's manual. The open page, she demanded, must depict the open womb with a baby curled inside.

"As Madame who pays me wishes," the painter said stiffly, forewarned no doubt. Midwives had a reputation. Opinionated, or, to put it more frankly, pigheaded. Unnatural, some said; it wasn't right to allow that much power to be vested in a woman. A midwife's word taken for truth in the court of law? Even against a man's?

After four sittings and two months of waiting for the paint to dry before the unveiling, the portrait stood on an easel in the best room. The painter lifted the veil, not quite in one clean gesture as he intended but gracefully enough. For a moment everything looked as it should, the two figures seated side by side on the green ottoman with its yellow tassels. The book between them was opened to the picture of a pregnant womb.

But take a closer look and then you begin to notice that Aunt Margot's painted hands are a tad too big. Make it two tads. Or three. Her half-opened mouth is gaping; her elbows are too pointed. Marie-Louise's expression is more absentminded than self-assured.

Hortense, asked to speak her mind, declared, "Mistress does not have crooked teeth."

The teeth had been fixed. Hands made a bit smaller, though this only after a round of aspersions and the threat of withholding the last installment of the payment. The portrait still hangs above the ottoman, which Marie-Louise thinks got the best deal as it resembles both itself and its essence.

And what about Marie-Louise, herself?

"Forgive me for being blunt," Madeleine had said. "But you look a perfect goose in it. A mighty pretty one, though . . ."

Which is the whole, unadorned truth.

⁂

Wasted, Marie-Louise thought of her Versailles years. Bitterly, too.

To overburden people with attention, to insist upon obligations that they do not desire, is not only to render yourself disagreeable, but contemptible.

She was never wanted there, was she?

A bastard child taken in for money. Suffered, like a punishment. A duty to fulfill.

Not much was needed to bring such feelings roaring back. A Parisian cat might have the same tint of gray stripes as her rooftop Queenie or a limp like that of the white angora. Someone might whisper behind her back and disappear when she turned around. A man staggering out of a tavern swearing pestilence on all hussies might have something of Old Gourlon in him; a woman with a set jaw arguing with a coffee seller in a shrill voice might resemble Gardienne. Once, Marie-Louise was startled to spot Monsieur Lebel strut through the Palais-Royal, as if he were still alive. Dark suit, silver trim, a cane swinging in his clawlike hand. She quickened her steps and turned the corner, not because she believed in the dead returning to earth as Hortense did, but because—as Aunt Margot liked to say—a moving target was harder to hit.

Who were my parents, she still wondered, although by then she scorned her old childish dreams. Those drawings left under stones! Those deserts of Arabia!

A fruit of sin. The other side of the blanket.

A love child, Aunt Margot insisted. Her father didn't wish to be known, true, but he had made generous arrangements. Every quarter an allowance was paid for her upkeep. There would be a dowry, too. Countless others have it much worse.

"Arrangements" were what Aunt Margot called the flurry of negotiations each time a lodger asked her to find a home for her baby or simply vanished, leaving it behind. She meant the search for adoptive parents, the trading of assurances and demands that followed. Sometimes money changed hands. Sometimes money was put aside, in trust or in an annuity. A mother might have to swear never to search for her child. A midwife might have to arrange the baptism on her own and come up with the child's last name. The street where such a child was born might do, or an object the mother stared at while giving birth. Swan, Candle, Bird. Or sometimes simply Blank—for the empty space where the father's name should have been inscribed.

Mistress Leblanc? Le Blanc?

"One day I'll tell you, Marie-Louise, but not now."

"What about my own name?" she asked. "Is there a street called Bosque? Or a town?"

"That I don't know."

This was what Aunt Margot did know. Marie-Louise's father was a foreigner, a Polish count who came to France with the queen's entourage.

"And my mother?"

"Pretty."

"Did you know her?"

"Being pretty is a misfortune," Aunt Margot said, which was not an answer, but the beginning of a litany that Marie-Louise had heard many times before: Pretty girls don't know their own minds. They are like weathercocks, turning whichever way the wind blows. Too dependent on the constant flow of admiration, addicted to it.

"Is that how my mother was?"

Aunt Margot drew a breath, held it and then let it out. "I swore on the Virgin Mary to hold my tongue," she said. And then, seeing how Marie-Louise blinked to stop tears, she added, "Silence is not such a high price to pay for keeping a child away from the foundling hospital, is it?"

How could Marie-Louise quarrel with that? After all, she, too, would say those very same words, many times.

⁂

Versailles was another country, people said. The king shunned Paris, so Paris shunned the king. "His Majesty is not universally respected," a midwife at a Saint-Côme gathering might remark. After Sunday Mass someone might say that the Great Sinner was still not taking communion, proof he was not in a state of grace. Or refer to the "well-known profession" of the current royal mistress, Madame du Barry. Or simply call her a royal whore. "How much does she cost yearly?" Marie-Louise might hear. "More than all those Deer Park girls?"

It was lucky for France that the dauphin did not take after the old king. No royal mistress in sight, no royal bastards to pay for. A tad too shy, Madeleine thought him, and so awkward. To which Anne said that luckily his Austrian wife, Marie-Antoinette, was pretty and vivacious. A pity she might be barren, though. Five years married and still flat like an ironing board.

Aunt Margot would cut such speculations short. Didn't they know by now it was not always the woman's fault? Didn't Madame du Coudray say midwives were to keep all possibilities in mind? Didn't she remind them that midwives were called "wise women" for a reason?

She did.

It was a well-known and undisputed truth that venerable Mistress du Coudray had a saying for every occasion. And if she didn't, Aunt Margot would invent one on the spot, without as much as a stammer.

Marie-Louise was halfway through her apprenticeship when the old king took ill. It was almost the end of April of 1774, three weeks after Easter. Hortense came home from the market announcing that His Majesty had caught a chill at a deer hunt. So severe, she said, that he had to be carried back to Versailles.

A day later the market women talked of a raging fever and the king's body covered in pustules. The devil's claws, Hortense heard, a proof that sins always leave marks for all to see.

What sins were these?

Children kidnapped. Spilled blood of virgins.

"What else do they say at the market? That the earth is flat?" Marie-Louise asked Hortense. "And you will fall off the edge if you sail to it?"

"No smoke without fire, is there?" Hortense replied, swatting Marie-Louise with a tea towel. Hortense, who had only grown stouter and more solid over the years and was still well able to show a scullery maid how to haul two big buckets of water at one go. No wonder scullery maids did not last long at rue du Cygne, Aunt Margot said.

Hortense kept bringing home more gruesome details of the king's condition. At the beginning of May the pustules erupted. Two days later doctors gave up all hope. A priest heard the royal confession, absolved the royal sins. Lackeys escorted Madame du Barry to her carriage. Madame Whore sobbed her wicked heart out all the way back to Paris.

Our Father who art at Versailles, hallowed be thy name, the market women mocked the daily calls to pray for the king: *Thy reign is played out, and thy will is no more done in earth than it is in Heaven.* Rumors had it that the old mangy lion at the Jardin des Plantes had been pelted with stones. On account of being the king of the beasts.

The king's death, a week later, did not stop the tongues from wagging. The stench was so terrible that no courtier would approach the body, Marie-Louise would hear. Four paupers were brought in and paid to put the royal corpse into a wooden coffin. One of the paupers dropped dead before the coffin was sealed. The wooden coffin had been put into a lead one, which also had been sealed. Then both were put into a third. Still the stench was making people swoon. When the funeral hearse was on its way to the crypt at Saint-Denis, people in the street imitated hunt horns. Howled like hounds closing in on their prey.

Never since the world began had anything like that happened, Hortense declared.

As if she were there when the world began, Marie-Louise told Madeleine, who *did* laugh. Unlike Aunt Margot, who only grimaced when Marie-Louise recounted Hortense's story. Said something about people remembering only the worst of their fellow men and about that being a slippery path. "Besides, unlike some around here, I'm not presuming to know God's mind," she also said.

To be truthful, Marie-Louise did not give the Old Louis that much thought. But she did say a prayer for the boy she had known as Auguste, who once wanted to run away to sea and take her with him. Especially when she heard of the courtiers racing through the corridors of Versailles to be the first to reach him with the news that he was now king.

King Louis XVI of France and Navarre, people said, fell to his knees and begged God's guidance, for he was too young to rule. The new queen, Marie-Antoinette, knelt beside her husband and burst into tears.

"I'VE YET TO MEET A MAN who didn't resent a woman with a mind of her own," Aunt Margot might say.

But then: "Pierre Vernault is spoken of with much respect, I must admit."

Or: "I don't want you to rush into anything."

But then: "I want to see you settled, Marie-Louise, before I close my eyes."

For a while it was merely something to laugh about with Madeleine and Anne. Aunt Margot's reasoning: Could I please eat all of my cake and also have it for later?

Anne got engaged to a very handsome surgeon from Saint-Côme and walked about with a smile Marie-Louise referred to as beatific. Madeleine called it annoying. Anne, they both agreed, had a knack for falling upward, which was a compliment.

Pierre Vernault was a lawyer whom Aunt Margot had consulted over a legal suit she was considering. Overdue payments for lodging, delivery and expenses, amounting to three hundred livres. Monsieur Vernault had been exceedingly helpful. Checked out the family, found them to be in arrears with five tradesmen. Not worth Madame's trouble or precious time, he said. Aunt Margot was much obliged for these efforts, mortified when he refused compensation most adamantly. So, she invited him to rue du Cygne. Since he was from Nancy and had no family in Paris, Hortense decided he deserved her best marzipan cake.

Because of Aunt Margot's words *he is spoken of with much respect,* Marie-Louise had imagined Pierre Vernault to be a stern and grim man, but he was nothing like it. Cheeky, she described him later to Madeleine, but not quite devil-may-care. Cagey then, Madeleine said, which unexpectedly made Marie-Louise quite annoyed.

"Do you prefer being admired or amused?" Pierre had asked when she showed him the way to the best room. "Are those my only choices?" she shot back and saw him smile.

The best room was suddenly quite embarrassing. Too many side tables covered with crocheted doilies. Gifts from grateful patients everywhere: a china figurine of a milkmaid, a wooden plaque with a prayer to Saint Margaret, each letter carved and stained with soot. On the wall that awful portrait of Aunt Margot and Marie-Louise. She did look like a goose in it, she had to concede. Among all this Pierre, handsome in his simple black suit, wig immaculately curled.

A man of well-measured words, Aunt Margot had said of him.

Not quite well measured, Marie-Louise thought, for Pierre talked with much passion between hearty bites of marzipan cake. About the cases he had fought lately, their significance. Squeeze the fiscal vise and suddenly common land is no longer common? Someone has to stand for equal chances in the army, the church. And for free thought and free speech. Why should reading a censored book constitute a crime?

"I bore you, Mademoiselle Bosque, don't I? I should've limited myself to praising the cake."

"Hardly. But I would praise the cake far more, if you wish to be invited again."

"Delicious. The best I've ever had. Marzipan was such a touching choice. My mother's favorite."

"I'll make sure our Hortense hears of it."

She wasn't accustomed to men holding her gaze quite like that.

Stories of the Vernaults, *en famille*, in Nancy, flowed. Pierre's father swatting down wasps on the garden table as if his life depended on eradicating every last one. Calling them vile brigands depriving him of the divine pleasure of fresh fruit. While Pierre's two sisters wailed, and his mother reminded him about mercy for every living creature. "This is how I learned to speak loudly. No other way to be heard."

"For or against wasps?" she asked.

"Against. There were too many of them by far. Have you ever tried to wave your hands and eat your delicious cake at the same time?"

Aunt Margot stirred impatiently in her chair. Did she guess already?

She could've, judging by her questions, which Pierre answered with eager seriousness. His father, a respected lawyer, struck dead by apoplexy two years ago already. His mother followed him three months later. The two sisters, younger, still lived in Nancy. Both married. One childless still, the other with three boys, aged eight, six and two. The eight-year-old wanted to be a lawyer. The six-year-old wanted to be eight. The two-year-old had not yet decided what he wanted.

"I haven't laughed like that for a long time," Aunt Margot said after Pierre left.

Marie-Louise didn't help Hortense clear the table but slipped out into the back garden. She walked slowly, noting the flowers opening up, the old cherry tree extending its branches. A starling landed on the fence, flapped its wings and waited, as if for her. She became aware of the shape of her breasts, the outline of her lips, and wondered how it would feel if Pierre kissed her.

Something in her whispered, What now?

In response a thought flashed that if she married him, she would become Madame Vernault. A bearer of the name carried by his father, grandfather, all of whom were buried in the same cemetery, beside their wives and children. In a family grave. She smiled, for wasn't it odd to find such a thought attractive?

Pierre did everything right, even Aunt Margot had to admit that much. Sat in the dining room, drank coffee, praised Hortense's cakes. Answered more of Aunt Margot's questions.

Prospects?

Good and getting better.

Right now?

He was representing a peasant disputing his seigneur's rights to chase his cows from the commons. A small case, some may say, but he disagreed. There was nothing small about justice for the downtrodden.

Two weeks later, Pierre asked to talk with Aunt Margot in private. The conversation lasted twenty-eight minutes by the mantel clock and thirty-five by the one in the hall. There was the matter of Marie-Louise's unknown parentage, the dowry meant to compensate for it, the midwifery exam she was preparing for. As Aunt Margot put it afterward, "Ifs and buts and everything in between." As if Pierre had not already said that he wanted Marie-Louise the way she was. Love child or not. A midwife-to-be with her patients, medical books, the life interrupted by night calls. The messy, bloody, miraculous business of midwifery.

When they finally emerged from Aunt Margot's room, Pierre flustered, but both smiling, Marie-Louise knew that permission had been granted. "To court, not to marry," Aunt Margot would remind her for months. Which sounded mean, but it wasn't.

Smitten, as Marie-Louise was already, she babbled on and on about him. Pierre was ambitious. Pierre planned to go beyond his current practice. Pierre said, "Mademoiselle Bosque, I admire your resolve even more than your beauty." Seeing a dog chasing a carriage, Pierre said, "As if it believed it would know how to drive it."

"Clever," both Anne and Madeleine agreed, though they were getting tired of hearing about Pierre. Especially Madeleine, who, unlike Anne, had no fiancé to quote.

"Your most esteemed gossips," Pierre called them, but this Marie-Louise kept to herself.

On their many strolls in Luxembourg Gardens, Pierre gave her books, with passages marked.

> *The great become small, the rich become poor, the monarch becomes subject; are the blows of fate so rare that you can count on being exempted from them? We are approaching the state of crisis and the century of revolutions.*

That was from Jean-Jacques Rousseau's *Émile.*
"What crisis?" she asked on one of these strolls.
"Of trust, that what is broken can be mended."
"Why would trust matter? It can either be mended or not."

"You have a point, which proves mine."

"Which is?"

"Beauty is the least of your merits."

"You said that before."

"And I'll keep saying it."

About Rousseau's *Confessions* they had a long, animated discussion. Marie-Louise, who having read *Julie, or the New Heloise* and *Émile* had thought Rousseau sensitive and caring, now found some of these confessions despicable. How could someone who professed there was no greater wisdom than kindness leave all his children in an orphanage?

"I refuse to read any more of this man," she said, quite grandly.

"Now that you pointed it out to me, I do find it odious," Pierre said.

"Did you not find it odious before?"

"At that time, I admired Rousseau's sincerity. His willingness to expose his own sins. Not trying to make himself look good, which is what people do all the time. Obviously, I hadn't thought about it hard enough."

So much for having yet to meet a man who didn't resent a woman with a mind of her own.

"Does it still hurt so very much?" Pierre asked her then. He meant the Versailles years, growing up among strangers. Not quite an orphanage, he said, but close enough.

How it all spilled out of her. The memories of scorn, the slaps, the loneliness. The parents who did not come for her. The whispers behind her back. The odd looks. Being so very much unwanted for so very long, pretending so hard that she did not care.

She had to sit down after saying all that. Right there, on a bench in the Luxembourg Gardens, blinking hard to stop tears. A little boy ran past them, rolling a wooden hoop, leading it with a stick.

"You are wanted now," Pierre said, which was the only thing that mattered. Then he added, "We never need to speak about those horrid years again."

The first time Pierre kissed her it was in the back garden, by the cherry tree, which Marie-Louise agreed with Madeleine was not a particularly strategic location. Well visible from the kitchen window, as evidenced by Hortense grinning in that way of hers, as if she possessed all the wisdom of the world. And by the titter of the latest scullery maid, who did not last any longer than her predecessor.

A long, warm kiss, promising so much. Too much perhaps, for Aunt Margot told Marie-Louise to be cautious.

Meaning what? The running amok of passions? The legacy of bloodlines?

It fades fast, the memory of waiting. First for the midwifery exam, which was hard but not impossible just as Aunt Margot had promised. Then for her swearing-in, after the morning Mass, after taking communion, vowing to care for her patients to her utmost ability, *never to administer an abortive remedy, always to call masters of the art to help in difficult cases and honor the monthly service to poor patients at Saint-Côme.*

First, Marie-Louise became *mistress matron midwife of the city and faubourgs of Paris,* her name inscribed in the register of the Châtelet police court. Underneath Madeleine's and above Anne's. Then came the summer wedding. The fuss of it. The dress of pale blue satin, Alençon lace. Silk stockings. A bouquet of tuberoses, later dried and still hanging from the attic rafter. Hortense's fricassee of rabbit in wine, eel fried in butter with mushrooms and onions, ratafia flavored with angelica to sweeten the palate.

"Time to come clean, I'm afraid," Pierre whispered in Marie-Louise's ear. "Hortense's cooking is the only reason I'm marrying you."

They made such a handsome couple, didn't they? Monsieur and Madame Vernault. Residing at rue du Cygne just as Aunt Margot desired, where— considering how Pierre's newly expanded practice brought in good money— there would be no more need for lodgers.

Is that what *he* decided? Aunt Margot asked. Doesn't *he* think I should've been consulted first?

To which Marie-Louise said the only thing she could. That they both wanted Aunt Margot to rest more. That there were too many patients to care for as it was. That they would soon need a nursery.

Have it your way then, Aunt Margot said.

Which was better than saying *his* way. Even though it was clear that Aunt Margot and Pierre were like two burning logs, spitting fire just because of their proximity.

Sometimes. Not all the time.

MOTHERHOOD CAUGHT Marie-Louise by surprise. Not the stages of labor she knew so well, not Aunt Margot's fussing, but the feelings that descended on her.

Nothing predicted it at first. The pregnancy went well. The baby quickened and turned on time. When her water broke, Aunt Margot ordered the two new maids, Suzette and Cecile, to bring in the towels and sheets she had kept ready. Hortense insisted on releasing all the locks in the house to assure a smooth delivery. And on putting bay leaves under her pillow to ward off ill luck. Just as we did in Saint-Christophe, she said.

Marie-Louise, purged and bled, thought herself ready. Aunt Margot was at her side. Both Madeleine and Anne assisted, for how could either of them be spurned. Pierre was banned from the room. Hortense came and went, reporting on the mood of the house: Master Pierre is pacing up and down the hall again. Jacques, Pierre's manservant, is taking bets. Ten to one that it'll be a boy. The maids are both sure it will be a girl.

When the first wave of fear came, Marie-Louise hid it well. It was the midwife's curse, knowing what might go wrong. After all that studying, all that she had witnessed, no wonder that her mind supplied her with one disastrous possibility after another. A baby stuck in the birth canal. Contractions too weak. The umbilical cord tightening about the baby's neck.

Yes, this all could have happened, but it didn't. It hurt, but not more than she expected. She did not tear. The placenta was all out. The bleeding was moderate and stopped on time. The baby was pink. Cried loud enough to get Pierre running upstairs two steps at a time.

All was well, wasn't it? Marie-Louise was holding her baby son in her arms. Her perfect son, who looked at her, stopped crying and yawned.

You are part of me, she thought, looking into his dark blue eyes, just like hers. Even if, as Aunt Margot reminded her, children's eyes often changed.

No one else is mine in the same way as you are.

When she touched his lips, he sucked on her finger. *You'll always know who your parents are.*

The sobs came first. Then the conviction that something terrible was just about to happen. To him and thus to her, for they were tied together, inseparable. She prayed that God would take her, if it meant that her child would live. That she was ready to die for him. Or suffer in Purgatory. That she would beg for alms for him, grovel at people's feet.

Is this how my mother felt when she held me? she wondered. *And yet she agreed to give me up?*

"Shall we let the father in?" Madeleine's voice pulled her out of this darkness. "He will wear his shoes out if we don't."

Pierre declared his son a genius and a future lawyer. A genius on the firm basis of yawning and sucking on his clenched fist. Yawning at the fuss everyone made about him, especially the women. Clenching his fist at the sorry state of the country he had just been born into. Sucking? Why, the sensible fellow was hungry!

"And why a future lawyer?"

"Just look at him."

"Is that enough?"

"The baby has just been born, what do you expect? That he recite Cicero's orations? Or defend his poor henpecked father?"

Marie-Louise did manage to laugh, even though laughing hurt her insides. But she was relieved when Aunt Margot shooed Pierre out of the bedroom. "Go brag to your lawyer friends," she said, her voice just playful enough. "If they find babies of any interest. Apart from making them, that is."

"You think the worst of men, Aunt Margot, don't you?"

"Just go. She needs to rest."

Marie-Louise did need to rest. But why sob like a fiend? Wail like a beaten dog? Lash out at Aunt Margot, who wanted to put the baby in his crib? Had

Marie-Louise not seen too many infants smothered in bed? Then why did she ask, in such a steely, harsh voice: "You think I'd ever do anything to hurt him? You think I'm that careless?"

Aunt Margot just shook her head.

Marie-Louise cried because she was like every woman who ever gave birth before. A molting bird, shedding what was no longer needed. Earthbound, helpless, exposed, until new feathers grew back.

The baby was baptized Jean-Louis.

Jean, after Pierre's father. Louis an echo of Marie-Louise's own name.

Jean-Louis Vernault.

Vernault and son?

Sons?

Marie-Louise nursed Jean-Louis herself for a few weeks, until her nipples became inflamed. At first she tried to hide it from Aunt Margot, then submitted herself to all possible cures. Finally, after two weeks of pain, she relented and a wet nurse, Joséphine, came to live with them. A nice-enough country woman with a good disposition, as Aunt Margot put it. Clean, young, her own child weaned.

Lots of babies, Marie-Louise had once promised herself, a big family. Anne had her second a year after her first. Boy, then girl, both plump, both with Anne's hazel eyes and the same shape of lips. "If my daughter married your son, we would be in-laws," Anne said once when she brought them over to rue du Cygne. A statement on which Pierre later commented, somewhat unkindly, that Anne couldn't conceive of the world outside her own view of it.

"Meaning that Jean-Louis could do better than a midwife's daughter?" Aunt Margot asked.

"Meaning that we can all do without such silly talk," Pierre said.

The first miscarriage happened well before quickening, so Marie-Louise didn't worry too much. The next one came when she was already showing and thought herself safe. She was sitting downstairs, updating her patients' notes, when she felt a twinge in her belly. A heartbeat later, thick, slippery fluid slid through her. In the bedroom upstairs, breathless, she uncovered a layer of sticky, dark blood all over her shift and thighs.

That is where Aunt Margot found her, on the floor, slumped against the bed frame, pierced with grief. She cleaned her up, held her. "It was a tiny girl," she said. "Nothing wrong with her. Just didn't want to be born."

"To me?" Marie-Louise asked, which was such a foolish, unreasonable thing to say, wasn't it?

She was neither foolish nor unreasonable, Aunt Margot said, holding her even tighter. She was in pain.

But she had Jean-Louis, didn't she?

She did.

"OUR PIERRE HAS EXPENSIVE TASTES," Aunt Margot said when Pierre used the first two installments of Marie-Louise's dowry to establish and then expand his practice. She meant gilded lettering on the sign, leather furniture, good-quality carpets.

Marie-Louise let this pass.

The Vernault Chambers employed five clerks and an ever-changing fleet of young lawyers seeking to make their mark. All from the provinces, where, as Pierre had put it, lawyers were more numerous than rabbits. Business was booming. Merchants were suing customers for unpaid bills, suppliers were suing merchants, neighbors were suing neighbors. France was a bubbling mess, ministers rose and fell, tempers flared, erupted. Everyone harassed everyone else, pecking at those on the lower rank.

In the evenings, with the house asleep, Marie-Louise and Pierre talked about it all. In the best room, from which the offending portrait had been removed after another terse conversation with Aunt Margot that ended with: "Hang it in my bedroom then." Making Pierre say to Marie-Louise: "She never liked it, either. So why such fuss now?" While Aunt Margot said, "Why some people have to be so damn rigid is beyond me."

This is how it would have to be, Marie-Louise thought by then, resigned to their constant struggle over who rules where and at what cost, with her caught in the middle, pulled at by both sides. Which she mostly managed well enough, didn't she?

Pierre thought so. This was only household sniping after all. Annoying at times, yes, but nothing more. The fate of all families, he said, the Vernaults of Nancy included. His own sisters were either the best of friends or swearing never to talk to each other again. He resolved to stop paying attention long ago. There were many far more important matters to consider.

The current state of the country, for one.

France was ruled by a well-meaning—perhaps—but wavering king. His queen, Madame Deficit of the what-can-I-buy-now persuasion, cared about winning at cards more than about her subjects. Versailles was a nest of incompetence and spiteful greed. France belonged to the rich, idle, bored out of their minds, who disdained everyone else.

The church? Don't even ask! Holding France in a chokehold. Caring for its wealth far more than for the Christian souls in need of salvation.

Yes, France *was* a cesspool that had to be drained, cleared of miasmas that harbored disease.

How?

Not by buying government offices like some lawyers Pierre knew. Or pandering to the rich. What Pierre wanted was a constitutional monarchy. Well-defined limits on the king's power.

How he lit up when he spoke!

"Why should only the commoners pay taxes, I ask you? Why not the nobles and the church, too? Why let another inept fool into office only because he has bought it? Shouldn't we choose the best among us for it?"

How his voice rose, deepened, filled out the best room! This is how he must be in court, Marie-Louise thought. Making everyone listen, remember his every word.

But in the end they always talked of Jean-Louis. His wobbly first steps. His first words: Mama . . . Papa . . . Auntie . . . Ortens . . . The clever drawing he made of Papa at work. A giant stick father, hairs spiking out of his head, spectacles crookedly perched on his nose, presiding over tiny stick people.

"My son doesn't believe in wigs?"

"Your son has seen you without one."

"He thinks I'm bald?"

"He thinks you are important."

"And bald?"

Their clever son, tall for his age, lithe, well balanced. Looking good in any garb, a simple pair of breeches and a linen shirt or his best Sunday silk jacket.

"Handsome cavalier," Suzette and Cecile called him. "Taking after his maman."

Marveled at his thick brown curls, God's gift they would've wished for themselves. His dark blue eyes, which did not change as he grew older.

❧

There was yet another miscarriage. Then there was a daughter born before her time. Baptized Angélique at Aunt Margot's request, she lived just five days, her tiny gravestone at the Sainte-Catherine cemetery a reminder of what could have been.

But Jean-Louis was growing up, strong and healthy and beloved by all. "I'm up," he announced every morning upon waking, making the maids giggle and ask him if he were perchance a prince. Cecile pronounced him more handsome than an angel and predicted a throng of girls at their door pining with love. "Soon Mistress will have to hire a Swiss Guard to stop them from kidnapping you," she said, laughing.

Just after his sixth birthday Jean-Louis climbed the cherry tree in the backyard only to climb down right away. "I want to see where the sun sets, Maman," he protested when she caught him heading out the garden gate. "But it hid behind that house. I'm going there now."

She told him about the horizon. The outer edge of what can be seen.

He pondered her words. His shirt was torn at the shoulder, stained with resin that wouldn't wash off. Not as bad as tar, Marie-Louise thought, recalling her own escapades on the Versailles roofs, but saying nothing for fear of putting ideas into his head.

"And if I go there, Maman? To the edge of the horizon?"

"You cannot, my *chou d'amour*. It'll always move farther away."

MARIE-LOUISE HEARD OF George-Jacques Danton long before she met him. One of the Café Procope regulars, Pierre said. A young lawyer from the provinces, in Paris to make his fortune, working at Master Vinot's chambers. "I think he looks up to me, an older colleague," Pierre said. "Perhaps I should steal him from Vinot."

George-Jacques Danton, Marie-Louise also heard, was never at a loss for words. Calling Troyes, where he lived before coming to Paris, "a backwater even mosquitoes stay away from." His family, he liked to say to the Procope crowd, did not merit mentioning, apart from a sister in a convent who was continuously praying for the salvation of his soul. Which made George-Jacques conclude that he could indulge in a few more vices for good measure.

When Pierre finally brought George-Jacques home, Marie-Louise could barely contain a gasp at the sight of him. She had pictured him sleek and suave, but he was big and beefy, and his face was scarred with old gashes that had been sloppily attended to. "The phrase you are looking for is *chewed up*, Madame Vernault," he said, seeing the expression on her face. "But not eaten."

He was witty, she had to give him that. Expansive, too, in a powerful sort of way. A man not to be overlooked.

A hungry man in need of supper. "I'll accept, but only if you assure me I'm not causing an upheaval in your kitchen," he said. "After all, this is not a planned visit but a casual invasion."

"Are you suggesting we do not know how to handle hungry men in this house?" Marie-Louise asked, liking him already.

Hortense liked him, too, for as soon as he finished eating Monsieur Danton demanded a serious word with her about the rabbit pie. "How did you make it so tender and juicy?" he asked and listened in utter absorption when Hortense described her way with the lemon and egg yolk sauce. How it had to be poured inside as soon as the pie was out of the oven, penetrating every nook and cranny before it set from the heat inside.

A few days later, Marie-Louise and Pierre were cordially invited to the Dantons' apartment at Cour du Commerce. With seven big rooms and space on the mezzanine for the servants to sleep, it was a great improvement over where they had lived for the first few months after their wedding. "Rented, not bought, though," George-Jacques said with an exaggerated sigh. "For, like France, I'm in debt up to my chewed-up ears."

Madame Danton, Gabrielle, had a lovely, plump warmth about her and beamed with energy. The dinner invitation had been extended on her insistence, she said, as soon as she heard of her husband's "invasion" at rue du Cygne and Hortense's rabbit pie. She, too, knew a thing or two about unexpected visitors demanding to be fed. "My parents have always had a tavern," she said. "I learned young."

Gabrielle also knew about cooking, for the dinner was a proper feast. Oysters, followed by consommé and roasted capons, were accompanied by excellent Burgundy, a fare from which, Marie-Louise noted right away, Gabrielle largely abstained.

As soon as Pierre and George sank into a long discussion of the sorry state of France, Gabrielle pulled Marie-Louise aside. "Everyone tells me I've married an exceptional man," she said. "A man destined for great things. I presume this means I should be prepared for a rather hard life."

They talked about that. And about Jean-Louis, almost ten already, thinking himself hardworking even if the Latin tutor who was preparing him for his entrance exam for the Collège Louis-le-Grand didn't agree. Collecting rocks now, which was a bit easier on the servants than bringing in frogs or, as had happened twice already, a live mouse. And about Gabrielle's parents, who were selling the tavern where Gabrielle met George and of which she was therefore immensely fond and moving to Sèvres because her mother hated Parisian noise and mud.

They talked about Cour du Commerce, too. So conveniently close to everything. Friends living nearby. The Desmoulins family a few doors away, dropping in at all hours. The Gélys, upstairs, who have a daughter, Louise. Only eleven but extremely wise for her age. "Do girls grow up faster because they have to?" Gabrielle asked.

Voices rose from the center of the room. Pierre and George, well past two bottles of wine each, agreed that "the present circumstances cannot continue." What would come after was not as easy to agree upon, though. For how was the constitutional monarchy Pierre so favored possible with a king who likes to say, "I wish it, therefore it is law"? Once a tyrant, some say, always a tyrant.

"So how far along are you?" Marie-Louise finally asked.

Gabrielle colored slightly. Her brown hair shone, Marie-Louise noted. She was lively, did not tire easily. These were all signs a midwife liked to see, especially since Gabrielle was twenty-four already, rather old to be having her first child.

"The baby is due sometime in early May," Gabrielle said. And then, clutching Marie-Louise's hand in hers, pleaded, "My mother insists on a midwife she likes but I don't. And I've heard so many good things about you, Marie-Louise. Will you, please, take me as your patient?"

<hr />

"The present circumstances" were getting worse. Hortense would come home from the market furious. There was no spring lettuce. Leeks had vanished. Vendors pushed wilted carrots on her and when she protested told her not to be too picky if she wished to be served at all. Her regular cheese merchant tried to charge her almost double what he charged last week so she had to go elsewhere. Bread had gone up in price again. People said it was because of vagrants, though what vagrants could have to do with the disappearance of leeks or the price of bread was a mystery. Try saying that at the market, though. You get spat on. Or pushed into the mud. A young fellow got beaten up because a fishmonger called him a king's spy. No one minded their own business anymore. Everyone had an opinion to defend. The more outrageous the better. People no longer talked but yelled. Where is it all heading? Where will it end?

"The worse the better," Pierre would say, scoffing every time Hortense crossed herself.

Pierre was spending more and more time at Café Procope with those-who-will-be rather than the have-beens. The king was fighting with the *Parlement*. If there was no agreement about taxes, Louis would have to summon the Estates General. In times like these it was essential to choose who to side with. Otherwise, as George Danton put it, you will end in the dustbin of history.

"That Monsieur Danton has a way with words," Aunt Margot said.

For a long while Aunt Margot had managed not to comment on Pierre's ever-lengthening evenings away from home, the new tunes he hummed in the morning when Jacques gave him a shave, the not-so-funny jokes he repeated. Though Marie-Louise did overhear her call "our Pierre" awestruck by "that Monsieur Danton and his friends."

"George Danton has a way with words because he is first and foremost a lawyer, like Pierre," Marie-Louise replied.

Aunt Margot swatted an invisible fly. "This is precisely what I meant. Pierre is first and foremost a lawyer. So why, pray, is he neglecting his practice?"

It could not be denied that Pierre *was* neglecting the Vernault Chambers. Marie-Louise had seen him writing his newspaper polemics long into the night, dulled quills piling up. Once, he fell asleep curled in a chair. When she woke him up, he was still muttering, "We do not want anarchy but limitations to the power of the Crown."

To answer Aunt Margot's question, Marie-Louise said what Pierre would have said himself. That there were better ways of fighting injustice than arguing in the court of law. That one well-written pamphlet could raise hundreds of voices.

It was to Aunt Margot's everlasting credit that she managed not to say anything to that.

Gabrielle's pregnancy was going smoothly. The baby grew at a steady pace, quickening and kicking on schedule. Gabrielle bubbled with plans. She would buy new furniture, new carpets. A baby would of course be an upheaval, though not the kind George and all the other men were talking about.

Gabrielle's confinement went as well as the pregnancy. François was a strong May baby, plump and happy most of the time, screaming only when he had a good reason. "Just like George," Gabrielle said. She nursed the baby herself, without a sign of inflammation or excessive soreness. Her parents came from Sèvres once a week, to help they said, though Gabrielle called them "spying missions, pure and clear." Her mother was hoping for another grandchild right away, preferably a girl. Or—alternatively—for Gabrielle not to have another baby for at least one more year.

Expressing contradictory opinions with firmness, Gabrielle declared, was her mother's specialty. Is that how we will turn out to be, too, Marie-Louise? Which made Marie-Louise laugh and say she hoped not.

Another annoying thing about Gabrielle's mother was that she was forever pressing Gabrielle to come to Sèvres with François, and not just for a few days but for at least a month. "Think of the fresh country air, Gabrielle," she kept saying. "And the quiet."

Quiet if you don't mind the rooster waking you up at dawn, that is.

For Gabrielle was happy just where she lived with George. Cour du Commerce was leafier than other streets. Even if quite a few of the trees had to be cut down after the horrible storms in July. Hail the size of eggs.

Yes, true, many had it far worse. All those orchards around Paris ruined, stripped bare.

On rue du Cygne the cherry tree lost its thickest branch but survived, which made Jean-Louis very happy, for he loved climbing it. Ever since Marie-Louise told him of the comte de Lapérouse's voyage of exploration, he declared the V-shaped spot on top his crow's nest. He could sit there for hours, pretending he was on one of Lapérouse's ships, scanning the ocean for land, just about to discover a new continent. Though lately, alas, he climbed there mostly when he was supposed to work on his Latin declensions. Which annoyed Pierre greatly and meant that Marie-Louise had to spend more time smoothing out family wrinkles.

But Marie-Louise did not tell Gabrielle this. It was not that important, was it?

1789

THE YEAR 1789 WAS not off to a good start. In January the Seine froze solid and barges could not make it to the city, which meant that food went up in price again. Some midwives, Marie-Louise heard, preferred to be paid in kind. Among the vagrants who always drifted into Paris in winter, Marie-Louise began spotting whole families in rags. At night, she heard, they huddled for warmth in back alleys, under bridges and in the cemeteries. At Saint-Côme, a mother, father and a baby froze to death in the nook by the church entrance. On rue du Cygne, gaunt, shivering children knocked on the back door every morning asking for food. By breakfast time Hortense was forced to add water to the pot of soup she always kept on the stove for the hungry.

"The worse it is, the better" now included the burning of straw dummies of this or that minister. In the place Dauphine, royal guards fired into the crowd of protesters. On the pont Neuf, an angry mob overturned the stalls of the orange sellers. There was yet another useless and inept government shuffle for which the king and his Austrian queen were entirely to blame.

Making history was a messy, bloody business. "Like giving birth," Pierre told Marie-Louise. Standing by the window in the best room, in his plain black coat, white cravat tied neatly around his neck.

"There will be elections to the Estates General, Marie-Louise. There will be a constitution. The king will have to give up some of his power. These are monumental changes."

Pierre had taken to holding his hand up as he talked, palm open, whipping air. "Our time has come. For centuries the Third Estate had been nothing. Now it will become everything."

Patrician was a good way to describe him, but not quite appropriate. *A man of purpose and gravitas* was much better. Marie-Louise could not take her eyes off him.

"I'm not neglecting my practice, as some say. We are transforming France!"

Some meant Aunt Margot.

We meant Danton and his ever-expanding circle. Of collaborators? Supporters?

"Friends, Marie-Louise. Our friends."

In April the Dantons' baby, François, fell ill. Perfectly healthy one day, he developed a fever, slight at first, then spiking. Refusing to nurse, he wailed, choking on his saliva. Gabrielle held him, walked with him, rocked him in her arms. Then she put him down and he died.

Gabrielle shut herself in her bedroom.

"Did I kill him?" she asked, her eyes bloodshot, nose red and puffy from crying, when Marie-Louise came to offer what had to pass for comfort.

Before Marie-Louise could answer, Gabrielle continued her questions. Why did God take her son away from her? Was it to save him from future sins? Or to punish her and George for theirs?

Who told you that? Marie-Louise asked.

The priest.

Why?

Because George would not take communion.

The priest had also told Gabrielle that everything looked different from the perspective of the immortal soul. While George told Gabrielle he abhorred such statements, forever used to condone all injustice. And her mother told her to think of the future children she would soon have.

Marie-Louise did not tell Gabrielle anything. When Angélique died, the only words that had made any difference were Aunt Margot's: "Cry as much as you need to but don't forget Jean-Louis. Don't terrify him with your grief."

Gabrielle had no other child, so Marie-Louise simply sat beside her and listened.

No, it was not of much help.

~✥~

Jean-Louis turned eleven in June. He had yet another tutor tasked with preparing him for Louis-le-Grand's exam, for which fluency in Latin was demanded, in addition to an elementary knowledge of the classics and arithmetic. Pierre's questioning the exact meaning of *elementary* had led to the previous tutor's abrupt departure.

Perhaps not the most diligent, but how well liked, her son. Neighbors stopped Marie-Louise to ask about him. Suzette called him her beloved. Cecile still predicted a throng of maidens chasing him, each offering herself as his wife. She would soon have to barricade the front door against them. "But I don't want to marry anyone," Jean-Louis protested. Ah, my dear boy, Hortense joined in, you'll have no peace until you choose one. To Jean-Louis's question "Don't I have the right to freedom?" she would reply, "Not if they have anything to say in the matter."

Getting into Louis-le-Grand meant Jean-Louis would live in a dormitory. How would he fare? Marie-Louise wondered. With no one to nudge him through his duties? To bribe a flagging soul with a treat, a timely promise. "You are far too soft on him," Pierre said.

His own conversations with Jean-Louis were turning into interrogations.

"Are you angry, Father?"

"Yes, I'm angry."

"What about?"

"Treachery. The ill will I see everywhere. Duplicity. Lies. Everybody blaming someone else, never themselves."

"But not at me?"

"Why? Have you done something wrong?"

Something was such a vague word, filling up with circling thoughts, leading to the pools of fear.

"Look me in the eye, son. Speak the truth, no matter how tempting the lie."

~✥~

On the morning of July 14, Marie-Louise was at home, resting after a long night delivering twins, two boys, robust enough after she poured a few drops of wine into their mouths, though smaller than she would've liked. Since Pierre had already left for the office, she was trying to sleep but then gave up and came downstairs.

In the kitchen the maids, Suzette and Cecile, were smashing strawberries with a wooden stomper, the tabletop strewn with hulls. Jean-Louis, lips already stained red, was trying to snatch as many berries as he could. One of the yard cats managed to get inside, and the scullery maid was trying to shoo it out. In the corner by the back door, Jacques was polishing Pierre's best pair of riding boots. One pot of jam was already bubbling over the fire. Hortense was stirring it with a wooden spoon she banged on the pot's edge from time to time, making Aunt Margot—who was adding up tradesmen's bills—cover her ears and declare she was living in a madhouse.

Into this chaos Pierre staggered, disheveled, his wig lost, crying, "The Bastille has been taken. Nothing will be the same anymore." There was a nasty cut on his arm, which he brushed off as a nuisance of no consequence, though it wouldn't heal for weeks. He had seen grown men sobbing like children. Throwing their arms around strangers. France had woken up. France had shed the shackles of tyranny and injustice. France was free.

"Oh, the joy," he said. "First you think the impossible, then you see it happen!"

There was a piece of green ribbon tied to his lapel. Some girl, he said, gave it to him. The color of hope.

Aunt Margot sent Jacques to the cellar to bring up the metal rods she kept there and told him to reinforce both the front and back doors.

I know what I am doing, the flash in her eyes warned Marie-Louise. So don't even try to stop me.

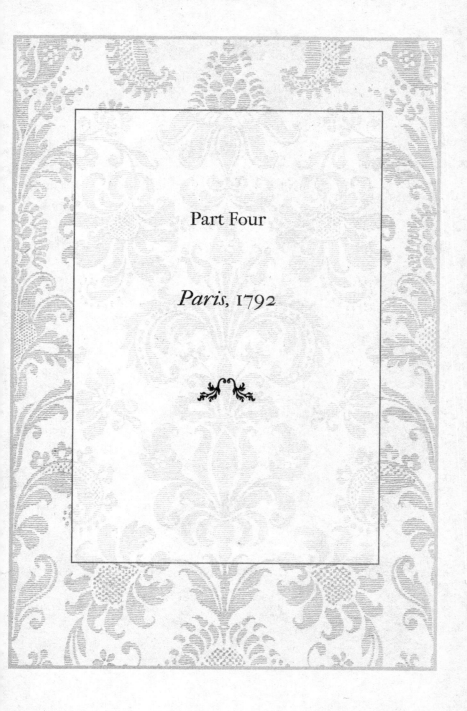

Part Four

Paris, 1792

October

NOW IN ITS THIRD YEAR, the revolution is feverish, unsure of its trajectory; it is the time of marches forward and sudden reversals. The Bastille is still being dismantled for bricks and scrap iron. Slowly, since the job pays twenty sous a day and those lucky to have it want to make it last. In the meantime, its once-secret files are being churned into pamphlets that printers' boys loudly hawk in the streets for a few sous:

> *Behold the cesspool of the monarchy!*
> *Versailles Unveiled ... Police Unveiled ... Clergy Unveiled ...*

Under despotism silence was a virtue, under the rule of Liberty it is a crime.

Riots and demonstrations erupt daily. Against rising prices, speculators hoarding food, counterrevolutionaries hiding among *dependable patriots*. Against émigrés, these vile *mercenary lackeys of tyranny* stabbing France in the back.

The king? Louis XVI? Locked up in the Temple prison with his family.

Louis the Last, they call him in the streets, for France is now a republic, free from kings. Or Louis the False, a source of endless arguments. Is he a traitor to the Motherland or a simple bungler? Can anyone, ever, reign innocently?

How hard to believe he was once Louis-Auguste, Marie-Louise thinks, the awkward boy on the palace roof dreaming of running away to sea.

The women at Les Halles market call Louis a pig of giant appetite. His wife is a harpy who eats France's money in the hope of one day devouring the French themselves, an Austrian slut responsible for all of France's woes.

Answer us, Marie-Antoinette, wall posters demand, *what have you done with your husband's heart? You reigned in his name while he was drunk, making locks and bolts, or hunting.*

"Where is it coming from?" Marie-Louise asks. "Such hatred."

She is mixing up hatred with anger, Pierre says. The powerful anger of the people. Raw and vicious, yet necessary. It is an inescapable result of justice too long denied. Marie-Louise, of all people, should know that no birth ever comes without pain or blood.

More and more refugees throng in from the provinces. Gaunt women in tattered capes, men with long, thick sticks. Children trail after them or run loose, in packs, like feral dogs. In the streets small dirty hands pull on Marie-Louise's skirts, pleading for a piece of bread, for mercy, for alms. Whatever she brings with her is never enough. "I have nothing more" merely makes the hands pull harder, dive inside the folds of her dress.

On the wall of the Palais-Royal someone drew a tree of despotism crawling with vile serpents. The tree is bushy, the serpents have flickering tongues and mean reptile eyes. Underneath the tree a three-colored rooster urges: *Citizens, be vigilant. The enemy is hiding among us.* In the arcade a street troupe is performing a cautionary tale in which the ghost of the old king, "the incestuous Louis XV whose memory is odious," haunts the now-empty chambers of Versailles, muttering that the time of reckoning is near.

"Reckoning for what, you old lecher?"

"For all the whores I brought to Versailles, all the money I squandered. For all my spawn, still bleeding Mother France dry."

~◆~

This October morning Marie-Louise wakes up moist from sweat, Pierre's heavy arm across her chest. Last night's lovemaking is a pleasing memory, in spite of too much wine and her husband's rough impatience. Stockings, shoes, petticoats lie scattered on the floor. His breeches, her fichu. Pierre will be peeved to find his favorite frockcoat crumpled underneath it all. Worsted black wool, silk lining. A calling card, such clothes, not a frill.

Careful not to wake him, Marie-Louise lifts Pierre's arm and swings her legs over the side. The floorboards under her feet are smooth and cool. No bedside carpet for Pierre, not even a woolen rug. Recently her husband also disdains bed curtains, quilted coverlets. Seeking comfort softens the soul, strengthens the legacy of servitude.

Marie-Louise glances into the mirror above the washstand. Freed from the night bonnet, her hair reaches her hips. It isn't quite as curly as it used to be, but it has kept its copper tint, and looks good pinned up without the help of false tresses. Smiling, she recalls the caresses of the night, their silly murmurings: "'They tell me I have an exceedingly pretty wife' . . . 'Who does?' . . . 'You don't want to know' . . . 'What if I do?' . . . 'That's what I'm afraid of' . . ."

Her calico dressing gown is draped over a chair. Before putting it on, Marie-Louise pours some water into the basin, dips the washcloth and carefully wipes her breasts, her belly, her thighs. Her right nipple is swollen and red, in need of a dollop of wax cream. Her husband is a strong, forceful man.

This is a satisfying thought.

The marital bedroom is the most spacious room in the house on rue du Cygne. On the large table by the window Pierre's papers are neatly stacked in piles the maids are strictly forbidden to rearrange when they dust. Ever since Pierre has withdrawn from the everyday running of the Vernault Chambers, these are no longer court briefs but drafts of Convention speeches and articles he writes for the *Gazette nationale* and other revolutionary newspapers. Or pamphlets he has picked up in the street, with passages underlined and marked in different inks. Keeping his ear to the ground, Pierre calls it. Being aware of what people are talking about.

By now Pierre Vernault has become one of the Convention's most popular speakers. Eager young men follow him around, try to catch his eye. His words, his turns of phrase pop up in other delegates' speeches. *Revolution is like a well-tended tree. Its shade gives respite from the harshness of the sun but does not seduce with darkness or secrecy. It won't shelter a plot.*

They mistake rhetorical flourishes for substance, Pierre says, but Marie-Louise knows he is pleased. Proud even. She has heard him instruct Jean-Louis on the skill of recitation. "Make your voice come from deep inside . . . Breathe with your muscles here, right above your stomach . . . Demosthenes practiced by speaking in stormy weather to overcome noise . . . recited verses while running . . . Once again, son, with feeling: *Men are born and remain free and equal in right . . . These rights are liberty, property, security, and resistance to oppression.*"

The house is still quiet in the murky October dawn. If Aunt Margot were alive, she would be downstairs, stirring up the fire Hortense had banked for the night. Or already sitting at the kitchen table, updating household accounts, cursing her garters for making her legs swell. Asking Marie-Louise: "Be an angel of mercy and make me a fresh cup of coffee, will you?"

Aunt Margot died eight months ago, in February, but her grave still doesn't have a headstone. Every time it rains Marie-Louise finds herself thinking of muddy water soaking through the earth, seeping into the coffin. The stonemason says the ground has to settle for a full year before he can start working. Nothing lasting can be built on shaky foundations.

Hortense crosses herself every time she passes Aunt Margot's room. She says that in her dreams Mistress appears in the kitchen as if nothing has happened, demanding bean soup, whitened with fresh cream and sprinkled with finely chopped chives. Or swiping cake batter with her finger to taste it, ignoring Hortense's warning that it will give her a stomachache. Always refusing to tell Hortense how it is in Heaven. Only once she began to speak, but Hortense woke up and could not remember a single word Mistress said. "She is not allowed," Hortense concluded. "Not to us sinners."

The two of them bickered for as long as Marie-Louise can remember, but never as badly as in the last few weeks before Aunt Margot fell ill. "Running about at all hours? At your age? With your swollen feet?" Hortense would ask. Told to mind her own business, she would tense her jaw, bang the pots and refuse to speak to Aunt Margot at all for hours on end. "Tell her she is not immortal," Marie-Louise would be ordered when she tried to intervene. "Tell her that even the Almighty God has no patience with such foolishness."

Hortense still blames herself for not being even more firm. I should've barricaded the door, she says, with grim determination. I should've thrown myself on the floor.

I should've known, shouldn't I?

Which is the very question Marie-Louise still asks herself.

Right after the New Year what Aunt Margot had been dismissing for days as merely a scratchy throat turned into a hollow cough. The fault of the unseasoned logs they were forced to burn, Aunt Margot maintained, filling the house with smoke, making everyone cough. Which was sort of true, or at least plausible.

When the cough persisted, Marie-Louise wanted to call Dr. Simons but Aunt Margot refused. She also refused bleeding. *In January bleed not, except upon necessity*, the almanac warned. All she needed was a good rest and more of Hortense's linden infusion with honey. An orange perhaps, too, if the sellers on the pont Neuf hadn't run out of them, but nothing else. Certainly not all that fuss and flap!

Every time Marie-Louise checked on her aunt, she heard: "Can't you find anything more useful to do?" Jean-Louis fared better. Every day, as soon as his tutor left, he would rush to Aunt Margot's bedroom, and the two would talk for hours. Or rather Aunt Margot listened and Jean-Louis talked. Mostly of Lapérouse and the uncertain fate of his expedition, by now declared lost at sea. Shipwrecked on an uninhabited island, Jean-Louis was quite sure, soon to be rescued by the two ships sent to bring his beloved explorer back to France.

"But I want to hear it," Aunt Margot insisted when Marie-Louise protested that perhaps Auntie does not need to hear of Lapérouse every single day. Jean-Louis must have taken her words to heart though, for the following day she heard him tell a story of how Mark Antony tried to impress Cleopatra with his fishing and ended with a piece of salted herring attached to his fishing rod.

The end of January brought a sudden spike in fever and piercing headaches. Dr. Simons did come then, called Aunt Margot a stubborn old woman who should've known better, and bled her. "Too late," he told Marie-Louise a few days later, when Aunt Margot's fever soared again, flushing her cheeks and making her eyes glassy. "The damage has been done."

From then on, the sickbed vigils turned into a rotating roster of prayers. A priest came to hear Aunt Margot's confession and give her the last rites. A new one, for old Father Daneau had refused to take the loyalty oath to the revolution and left Paris. If Aunt Margot minded, she did not say.

"Take care of what I'm leaving undone, Marie-Louise."

The memory of Aunt Margot's words, and of the faint squeeze that followed from her once-so-strong hand, comes with images. The creased skin around her eyes, puckered, turning purple. On her chin a barely visible smudge of the pea soup Hortense had been trying to feed her. As if eating even a spoonful was a proof that life could still defeat death.

"May the Mother of God bless you in these hard times."

Marie-Louise recalls her aunt's gnarled fingers clasped over the black rosary beads. A breath, longer than usual, followed by a gasp. She recalls Hortense's piercing wail and the heavy slaps of her own thoughts. Death, all-powerful. Life, fleeting. A speck in the vastness of eternity. All its earthly warmth gone in a flash.

She cried, she crossed herself, she prayed for the departed soul and for those left behind. She held her son's quivering hand, said what she hoped would soothe his choking sobs: "Aunt Margot has gone to Heaven. She will be looking after us. Until the day we see her again."

Pierre was the only one with dry eyes. Marie-Louise didn't find it hurtful. Every midwife knows pain finds different ways to surface.

The Commune Section doctor came to examine the body and draw up the act of decease. The maids draped the front door in black. Marie-Louise helped Hortense wash Aunt Margot's body with warm water and dress it for the funeral. They stuffed rosemary and dried rose petals under the clothes. As they turned the body over, the air wheezed out of the lungs, and Marie-Louise almost believed—for that split second—that Aunt Margot would stand up and chastise them for all the fuss. Say with that twinkle in her eyes: "It'll take a lot more than a fever to strike *me* down."

After the funeral, tears mixed with chuckles. What would our Margot make of it? Fuss she wouldn't have wanted, but she would love seeing us all here. Midwives she trained. Children she delivered, now grown up, with children of their own.

Marie-Louise, Pierre and Jean-Louis stood together in the best room receiving condolences in the deep mourning of black wool one wore for a mother or father. Pierre muttering, Yes . . . truly exceptional . . . a pillar . . . Nothing will be the same without her . . . Marie-Louise silent, her heart heavy, each breath an effort. Jean-Louis clutching her hand, as if he were still a small boy, terrified of getting lost.

So many tears, so many whispers, so many memories.

She taught me everything I know.

Without her I would've died.

You were her pride, Marie-Louise. Her joy. Don't ever forget that.

Jean-Louis! How you have grown! Let me look at you, child!

Didn't you want to be a midwife when you were little?

Didn't you scream at the wind once, when it blew off your hat? Stop it, right now, you said. How old were you then? Three?

How well beloved, her son. By all.

In the days immediately following the funeral a bird smashed against the windowpane and dropped lifeless into the snowbank. A door to Aunt Margot's room blew open with such force that it loosened the hinges. A printer arrived with a set of patient ledgers Aunt Margot had ordered. Marie-Louise bent to pick up a darning needle she had dropped and under the armchair, in a crack of the floor, found the silver clasp that Aunt Margot said she wanted her to have and that had gone missing months before.

So much sorting out, after death.

The rue des Jardins notary presented them with her aunt's will. Marie-Louise was her aunt's sole heir, responsible for the payment of the legacies, gifts and endowments for which money had been set aside. The house on rue du Cygne was hers, the notary said, although since it was the husband who paid taxes, it was now registered under Pierre's name and was under his administration.

The legacies were for Jean-Louis, Hortense and the maids, five thousand livres in total not counting the clothes and other gifts. The commitments had all been meticulously listed. Outstanding payments to tradesmen, provisions for three elderly midwives and two former wet nurses *of my acquaintance no longer able to sustain themselves*, a destitute widow now residing with the Sisters of Charity whom Aunt Margot had pledged to support *until the end of her natural life* and a sum to the foundling hospital to be *solely used for the hiring of wet nurses*.

Even six weeks later, when deep mourning allowed for changing from black woolens to silk, letters addressed to Mistress Leblanc kept coming: a former patient joyfully reported the birth of her first grandchild, a midwife from Sèvres asked for a recipe for Margot's *famous* salve. And, from Bordeaux, from the esteemed Madame du Coudray, an urgent request. Could dear Margot intervene with Master Charbonne, that cloth maker in the Marais who still hadn't delivered the new Machine for the Bordeaux clinic? As of now the order was late by six months and ten days. Madame du Coudray was forced to ask for help only because none of her own letters had been answered or even acknowledged. To which Marie-Louise was obliged to respond with the sad news and the account of Aunt Margot's last days.

What are we to rocks and mountains, Marie-Louise?

Aunt Margot's voice is still firm in her memory. So is the touch of her bony fingers.

What will Jean-Louis remember of her when she is gone?

Oh stop it, Marie-Louise. More castles in the air? Have you got nothing more useful to do than fret?

She does.

Marie-Louise buttons up her dressing gown. From the bed, a groan. Pierre turns on his side, muttering something about an ungodly hour and Marie-Louise making a racket that would raise the dead. Dawns are for birds, he says, not humans.

"I'm leaving right now. Go back to sleep," Marie-Louise says, opening the bedroom door. Still squeaky, even though she has already asked Jacques to oil it twice. First time he merely forgot; second time he said he had "more important duties to attend to."

What duties might those be, Hortense wanted to know. Scaring the maids with his constant talk of the guillotine?

The guillotine has been set up in the place du Carrousel, in front of the Tuileries, moved there from the place de Grève. What makes Marie-Louise cringe is that most people call it the *machine*. As if it were Madame du Coudray's birthing mannequin!

Why wouldn't Jacques talk about the guillotine, Pierre said when she complained that his manservant was giving the maids nightmares. Doesn't Marie-Louise remember Damiens's execution? The hand that dared raise itself against Old Louis plunged into boiling pitch and sulfur? Flesh torn with red-hot pincers? Boiling oil poured into the wounds? The body broken on the wheel? Damiens still alive for hours until horses finally pulled him apart? How can she not admit that the guillotine is fast and painless in comparison?

"You don't really know that," Marie-Louise argued.

"You have a point there," Pierre conceded. "I don't know. And not being a forger of assignats or a convicted murderer, I don't anticipate being guillotined. Not even to win an argument with my wife."

"Don't joke."

"Why not? You are not superstitious, are you?"

Marie-Louise doesn't anticipate being guillotined, either. And yet every time she passes the place du Carrousel, she cannot stop herself from touching her neck. How would it feel to wait for the blade to fall? To lie bound, knowing she had just a few more moments of life left? Smelling the air, hearing the noises of the city, feeling her stomach clench with terror?

The house is waking up. Marie-Louise can hear Hortense's shuffling steps, Jacques's voice demanding warm water for shaving so that Master doesn't have to be kept waiting again.

The stairs creak under her feet. Downstairs, in the kitchen, the maids have folded up their cots and are helping Hortense with breakfast. The pot of coffee on the table is still untouched, another glaring sign of Aunt Margot's absence.

Jean-Louis, if he were not at Louis-le-Grand, would be at this very table now, gobbling up his fried eggs and asking Hortense if she saved any leftovers for him from last night's supper.

"To think he is there all on his very own, poor lamb." Hortense sighs as if she heard these thoughts, recalling Jean-Louis eating her rabbit stew, with leeks and parsnips, mopping up the sauce with chunks of bread. "Always hungry, this boy," she says with pleasure. "Always asking for more. I hope they won't starve him there!"

With her peasant wisdom Hortense has always wanted Jean-Louis plump and well rounded. Insurance for the lean days ahead.

"What's that smell, Hortense?" Marie-Louise asks to stop this lamenting over her poor, starving son.

It's the smoke. The chimney needs to be cleaned. The chimneysweep who promised to come yesterday did not arrive. Neither did the rat catcher, whom Jacques later found in the tavern and brought home. The man was half drunk, head bruised from tripping over a milestone. Hortense had to send the wretched creature home with a supply of camphorated castor oil. Even though, as Jacques had said, all he deserved was a good kick in the pants.

Enough of this time wasting. Monarchy or republic, women do not stop getting pregnant and giving birth. Upstairs, packing her midwife's bag for the daily round of visits, Marie-Louise is coaxing Aunt Margot from the shadows, telling her how much she has been spared.

Spared from what, Marie-Louise?

The sight of the royal palace of Tuileries gutted, the Swiss Guards killed, mattresses and pillows all slashed in search for hidden jewels, making the air white with flying feathers. The royal family barely escaping alive, begging the deputies for protection. On the palace gates a card: *House to let.*

The fear of Prussians marching on Paris. Trenches dug along the city walls. The sound of church bells ringing the "tocsin" alarm night after night. Windows on rue du Cygne opening. Neighbors asking, "Has it started already?"

What are you not telling me, Marie-Louise?

Crowds armed with pickaxes are gathering in front of prison gates. The Temple, la Force, the Conciergerie, Salpêtrière, Bicêtre. Prisons are full of traitors . . . We have all been marked for revenge . . . It is better to kill the devil before it kills us.

The pont au Change is littered with torn hats, crushed shoes, broken carriage wheels. What she takes for a flattened bird turns out to be an ostrich feather trampled into reddish mud. A carriage rushes past her, close enough to almost knock her over, its curtains tightly drawn, the driver cracking a whip.

What is it, Marie-Louise?

By the Conciergerie, walls are splattered with rusty stains.

The pike with a head jammed on top stands upright, propped against the narrow window. It is a man's head, its hair dressed, powdered and curled. She registers the bulging eyes, the fistful of hay shoved inside its mouth. The two women who lean on the stone ledge beside it are gaunt and pockmarked, their top skirts hitched up, their gray hair tangled and matted. "What are *you* staring at?" one of them yells. "He would've done the same to us, if he could."

Marie-Louise heads for Cour du Commerce, where the Dantons live, right after looking in on Citizeness Valour, whose newborn girl is sucking vigorously. Sacred, Claire Valour named her, short for Sacred Love of the Native Land. For a boy, she considered Reason or Right of Man. One of Madeleine's patients wished her son had been born with curled fists, ready for a fight with the enemies of France. Mercifully, no one has yet announced a birth of a baby with a tricolor caul.

At the Cour du Commerce the brass knocker has been muffled with a length of white cotton. Gabrielle's headaches must be getting quite severe. This is her fourth pregnancy, the baby due in February. After François, may the poor lamb rest in Heaven, came Antoine, almost two and a half now, then François-George who is eight months old. No complications with any of the pregnancies or confinements, but Marie-Louise knows how quickly things can change.

"Mistress is leaving for Sèvres, with the children," the sour-looking maid, Catherine, announces, after she finally opens the front door. "I've started to pack." From the kitchen comes the sharp smell of burned milk.

The apartment is in disarray. Trunks and baskets half filled with baby toys, linen, woolens are scattered everywhere. Two quilted petticoats await folding. A pile of shoes in the corner needs sorting through. From the basket of baby toys, a clown puppet sticks out its painted, smiling face. From the bedroom a scream: "Stop it, Antoine! Right this minute!"

Marie-Louise draws in her breath and follows the maid in.

Gabrielle is lying on a chaise longue, among more chaos of scattered blankets and quilts. The baby is in his crib, hands stretched toward the teething ring he has thrown to the floor. Antoine is pulling on his mother's sleeves. "Want up up, Maman," he whines, already on the verge of anger.

"Just like his father," the maid says, picking up the teething ring and giving it to the baby. "And you, little rascal, come here," she says to Antoine, scooping the boy up before he realizes this is not what he has set his mind on. By the time she leaves, pretending to be a horse, Antoine is squealing with pleasure.

Gabrielle's long hair is loose under her bonnet, matted, quite a bit thinner than it used to be. She looks bigger than she was with François-George, bloated rather than plump and her hands are swollen, which is a concern. In the past months five of Marie-Louise's patients miscarried and two gave birth at seven months, both to stillborn girls. Madeleine lost three mothers in the past month alone. There have been altogether too many frightened whispers, Marie-Louise thinks, too many sweaty hands gripping hers, a surge against which a midwife can only mutter her brittle assurances: We've been through worse. The future is never certain. It'll be all right. It will be fine.

"Catherine said you are leaving. With the children. That's sudden."

Gabrielle lifts herself onto her elbows. George has to go to Belgium, she says, on a mission he cannot divulge, so there is no point asking how long he will be there. She overheard something about at least two months!

A blink just manages to clear a gathering tear.

"I cannot stand being here on my own."

The baby chews on the ring, a promise of respite from the game of throwing it to the floor. The window is opened a tiny crack, a feeble attempt to get rid of the sour smell. From the room next door, a girlish voice is tempting Antoine with a promise of a sucker. "But only if you eat everything on your plate."

A new nursemaid?

Gabrielle shakes her head. That is the neighbor's daughter, from upstairs. Louise Gély. A child still, at fifteen, but serious, responsible, levelheaded. An angel with the children. "I'm quite lucky she is so close by."

A stab of pain distorts Gabrielle's face, not what a midwife wants to see. Still too pale by far, too, in spite of Marie-Louise's recommendations to eat more liver. Taking Gabrielle's hand in hers, she feels for the pulse. Too fast.

"Has Dr. Souberbielle examined you already?"

Gabrielle nods and then shakes her head. Here it is, the whole amusing story.

Souberbielle did come, to dinner, for which Gabrielle roasted four capons. George put on his red frockcoat, which always spells trouble, and proceeded to eat one bird all by himself. Souberbielle polished off his, too, and both asked for a second helping. Then the great doctor wiped his greasy fingers on Gabrielle's tablecloth and complimented her on her healthy glow. Then he talked about Robespierre's ulcer, which, apparently, is very persistent and requires radical treatments. For Souberbielle, radical means eating lots of oranges, which, luckily, are still plentiful, even if getting expensive.

"I might not be quite fair, of course," Gabrielle concludes with a fetching smile.

"Please, Gabrielle. What did he say? But be serious."

Souberbielle recommended the change of air and plenty of rest. This is why Gabrielle is going to Sèvres. Her parents have bought two properties in the parkland there, one of which Gabrielle suspects "must be ours." Suspects, for if her husband put up the money for it, he has never told her. Which shouldn't surprise her, for George always does what he wants and never tells her anything. Or rather he tells her what he thinks she wants to hear. Which is either callous or considerate. Depends how you look at it.

"You didn't sleep last night, did you?" Marie-Louise interrupts.

"Does it show?"

"A bit."

"Do I look like a ghost?"

"Not quite."

"A fat, bloated ghost then?"

"Just tell me how you slept."

With a deep sigh Gabrielle Danton admits to being sick all night. Retching without any relief. Which, in her fifth month, she shouldn't. The usual remedies, lying down, a compress of lavender water on her temples, a small pillow under her back, have not helped.

"It won't be like that all the time," Marie-Louise says, measuring out a spoonful of a wormwood tonic, its bitterness making Gabrielle grimace even though it is well diluted with water.

"Good, for February is a long way off." Gabrielle half laughs, listing what she calls her Inventory of Grand Misfortunes. Her scalp itches. She has the beginning of a toothache. Her feet swell. She is tired all the time. "Tell me I'm the worst of your patients, Marie-Louise."

"Hardly."

"But getting there?"

Marie-Louise asks Gabrielle to pull up her shift. No odd-looking bumps, no discoloration, no rash. Pressing Gabrielle's belly with both hands, she traces the continuous resistance of the baby's back on the right, the multiple knobby bumps of shifting knees, elbows, heels on the left. The hard mass of the head is right underneath Gabrielle's stomach. A possible reason for the vomiting?

Placing her ear firmly to Gabrielle's belly, she listens for the baby's heartbeat. It is strong enough and regular.

"Kicking a lot?"

"This one prefers somersaults." Gabrielle laughs softly. "George says if it's a boy, we can always send him to earn his keep at Franconi's circus."

"When is it most active? When does it rest?"

"Active in the evening, when I lie down. Most quiet when I walk, exert myself."

"A smart baby."

"Yes. Just like my other ones."

The examination is over, but Gabrielle makes no attempt to stand up. The headaches are the worst, she admits. Like an iron vise, squeezing her head. Must be from not sleeping well. What with all this retching, and George coming home at all hours. Stumbling, waking her up. Saying it is because of the toys scattered everywhere. Cursing the maids.

"You'll have more peace at Sèvres," Marie-Louise says.

"Will I?" Gabrielle answers. There is nowhere to escape or hide, really. People are so vile, so hateful. The things they say about George. As if she were deaf. How he spends too much money. How no one knows where this money comes from. How this or that man's wife "accommodates" him. She hates this word, *accommodates*. Because it means he wants it more than they do.

"Is it because I'm pregnant again, Marie-Louise?" she asks. "Is it because he is thinking of leaving me? Divorce is getting so easy now."

Before Marie-Louise has the time to protest, Gabrielle adds, "George says I always see nothing but the bad in everything."

What can Marie-Louise say to that but offer assurances that country air will lift Gabrielle's spirits? So will being with her mother or having a good night's sleep with no interruptions, or taking brisk walks in fresh air for constitution. She repeats the necessity of eating liver or kidneys every day, of drinking red wine, rather than white, to fortify the blood. Reaching into her bag, she extracts a jar of goose-grease salve she has brought with her and puts it on the side table. Had she known Gabrielle was leaving, she would've brought two.

François-George has had enough of biting on the teething ring and throws it out of the crib again. It rolls for a brief moment and then topples flat.

As Marie-Louise stands to leave, Gabrielle cocks her head. "Why do they hate him so much?" she asks.

"Hate Danton? Who on earth told you that?"

But Gabrielle Danton is no longer speaking of her husband. She means the king now. The prisoner of the Temple. And his poor children. The boy, especially, the dauphin. Still too young to understand what is happening to him. "George says I'm just like all women. Ignorant of historical truth. That I should only speak of what I know. But I know the king is not a criminal. So why put him on trial? Can we not forgive him for whatever he has done? We have won, haven't we?"

"Pierre says they still argue about it at the Convention," Marie-Louise says. "Whether he should be tried at all. I've heard they want to send him to America. To a farm in Virginia."

Gabrielle shakes her head. "There will be a trial," she says grimly. "Then they will kill him. I've heard them say it, right here, in this apartment. Louis must die so that the nation can live." And then she adds, "My husband will vote for his death. And so will yours."

November

EVER SINCE JEAN-LOUIS LEFT for Louis-le-Grand, the door to his room is kept wide open. It looks painfully tidy, Marie-Louise thinks, every time she passes by. Books are lined up from the tallest down, Bezout's grammar followed by *Cours de Latinité*. Next to them a thick notebook in which Jean-Louis recorded everything he could find about Lapérouse's voyage of discovery. The intended trajectory of the two ships, *La Boussole* and *Astrolabe*, which should have brought the expedition back to France in 1789, the reports from captains who encountered them on the way, speculations on their recent whereabouts. She should put a writing table in here for when Jean-Louis comes home in the summer, but maybe not yet.

In the judgment of the principal and four examiners Jean-Louis Vernault has been accepted as an aspirant for one year, the letter from the college said. *After which he will have to submit to another examination.*

An aspirant? Not a full scholar?

It still goads her, the memory of Pierre's harshness that day.

Is this the best my son can do after the expense of all this tutoring? At the very school where Maximilien Robespierre received a special award? I'm talking to you, son. Look me in the eye. What awaits a man who cannot sacrifice a pleasure today for the firm goal of the days ahead? Can you answer this simple question, son? Fully? To my satisfaction?

Jean-Louis shot her a look of such anguish then.

She wonders how he is managing this year of probation? Without a tutor, at the dormitory, beset by temptations? And if he fails the exam?

Pierre's voice weaves into these thoughts: He is fifteen years old, Marie-

Louise, for God's sake. What do you have in mind for him? A nursemaid on call?

Still only fourteen, she insisted.

Turned fourteen in June, Pierre said, so he is fifteen. There is only one way to count.

Marie-Louise recalls Jean-Louis in his Louis-le-Grand boarder's gown, his trunk tightly packed. As the school instructed, she put the quills and the ink bottle in a separate box, away from the books, writing paper and linen.

Anxious, she thought her son.

Serious, Pierre said. Belatedly realizing the gravity of the moment.

Jean-Louis's first letter home was short: *The school is very good. My bed is comfortable. My Latin professor is very good. The food is quite good, though not as good as at home, please tell Hortense.*

"So much for an elegant turn of phrase," Pierre said. "Or erudition."

"Give him time," she said, imagining Jean-Louis in the dark dormitory room at night, listening how around him breaths thicken, turn into coughs, sniffles, grinding of teeth.

In her reply Marie-Louise wrote that everyone was well, and that the house felt empty without him. To lighten the mood, she described household mishaps. Mice got into the pantry and made a nest under the flour sack. Did he remember his old penknife he believed lost? Hortense found it. Someone put it into the tool drawer, in the cellar, but there is no way of knowing who. Jacques blamed Suzette, Suzette blamed Jacques, which is a proof that nothing much changes, does it? Everyone, including neighbors, was sending good wishes, urging him to eat well, wear a scarf and gloves and apply himself to his studies.

Jean-Louis's second letter covered a whole page. He listed all his professors: Masters La Garde, Germain and Le Provost. He was learning the history of insects and political science. La Garde taught Latin and Jean-Louis liked him because he was young and told them excellent stories. The school rules were strict. No talking in the courtyard. No tardiness. No trading of any kind among students. No personal gifts of any kind, no formation of exclusive relationships, which meant he had to talk to everyone whether he liked them or not. Yes, he did pay attention to the law students. They left the college in the morning and returned right before the evening meal.

Answers to Pierre's questions, obviously. Diligent, meant to please.

Marie-Louise has seen Jean-Louis twice since his departure. The first time she went to Louis-le-Grand during their afternoon break knowing she wouldn't be admitted inside without the principal's permission but grateful for the sight, through the railings, of her son strolling through the courtyard, stopping to talk to another boy.

It is called Equality College now, Maman, Jean-Louis would remind her if he could hear her thoughts. Also, it is recreation, not a break.

That day she tried to see him like a stranger might, how tall he was, how beautifully formed. Commanding, she would describe him, if this was a word fit for a first-year *grammarian*, already transformed by this new life that has claimed him.

The second time was a formal visit, granted by the principal, Citizen Champagne.

Since visitors are not allowed inside the dormitory itself, not even mothers, she was brought to wait in a small reception room, empty but for a table and two chairs. The table was stained by melted candle wax, its surface scarred and uneven where someone had meticulously removed carved inscriptions. Prints nailed to the wall showed the planting of a liberty tree and the removal of the royal statue from what is now the place de la Révolution: Louis XV on horseback, tied up with ropes, being pulled down to the ground. On the wall, in big letters: *Be the children of light against the demon of darkness.*

Jean-Louis walked in, still her son but different. His thick curls were cropped quite short and there was a touch of gauntness to his cheeks, dark circles under his eyes. She longed to embrace him, but would he not be embarrassed?

"Are you warm enough?" she asked, her voice hoarse, strangely timid.

"Yes, Maman."

"Is your bed comfortable? Do you have enough linen?"

"Yes."

"How is the food?"

"Good. You really shouldn't worry."

The master who had brought her into the waiting room gave her what must have been a well-worn welcoming speech. He emphasized how the college prepared young men as social beings, for participation in society not as it *used to be* before the revolution but as it *would be* from now on. How it developed the student's character, not just cultivated his talents, helped him to avoid mistakes arising from his own negligence, stressed the formation of work habits. "I teach Latin," the master said. "A medium for the formation of taste, a training ground for expression." And then he warned her against agitating Jean-Louis's memories of home. "Growing up is hard enough," he said.

Marie-Louise thought it excellent advice.

They had only half an hour together. At her request Jean-Louis accounted for his days: Rising at half past five, reading in the study hall before breakfast, classes interrupted by meals and recreation. By nine in the evening he was back at the dormitory. Did he find it difficult? No. Did he have trouble understanding lectures in Latin? Sometimes. But he was studying hard, every day. "We are improved by what we repeatedly do. Excellence, then, is not an act, but a habit." That was Aristotle, he told her with pride. His favorite by far.

"Not Lapérouse?"

"Aristotle is a philosopher, Maman. Lapérouse is an explorer. Each belongs to a different category. You cannot compare them. It would be a fallacy."

She longed to throw her arms around his bony shoulders. Feel his heartbeat. Breathe in the faint smoky scent around him. A ray of sun came through the window, making him squint. She had a vision of him as a boy, in the kitchen watching Hortense gargle with one of her infusions. "Look, Maman, Hortense is calling monsters," he said, giggling. Then on her lap, his body sinking into hers, asking her in his piping childish voice: "Do we *all* have to die, Maman?"

"Why don't you write more often, Jean-Louis?"

"I don't know what to write about."

"Anything, really. What you learn in class. Who your friends are."

"I don't know who they are. It's not that you can ask, Maman. It would be prying. They wouldn't say anyway."

"I don't mean things they would have to tell you. Just what you see."

"Even if it is boring?"

"Not boring to me."

Slowly, he was becoming himself again. Shoulders softening, his dark blue eyes locking with hers. Mindful of the master's warning, she steered the conversation away from home. Last night, he admitted, he didn't sleep well, for the boy next to him had a nightmare and kept screaming. The master came and took him away to the infirmary. Then the boy was fine.

"What's his name?"

"Gaston."

"Gaston who?"

"Gaston Parot."

"From Paris?"

"I'm not sure. But he knows an awful lot about making candles."

By the end of the visit, he let her cover his hand, feel it cup under hers. Cold, in spite of his protests that he was warm enough. Then he confessed to losing his nightcap. Perhaps another boy mistook it for his, though Gaston said it was surely stolen. He would be reprimanded for negligence if he didn't find it. Which would make Papa upset.

"I'll send Suzette with another."

"Today?"

"Yes."

Time measured by an hourglass, grains of sand dripping slowly, forming a mound. When it was time for her to leave, the Latin master walked her back to the gate. Only then she noted his weak left arm, held close to his body. Breech birth gone wrong?

She inquired how Jean-Louis was doing in Latin. Three times already Pierre has mentioned that next year the *concours général* of colleges would be held at the Jacobin club. There will be a big celebration, he said, with parents in the gallery, a delegation of the National Convention present. How he would like to see his son there, among the winners. Erasing the shame of being admitted as an aspirant, not a scholar.

"He needs to work harder on his grammar," the Latin master said after a pause Marie-Louise tried to disregard. His chin was bristly, she noted, spotted with patches of black and gray stubble.

"His father wants him to become a lawyer."

"Then he will."

Her heels made a clickety sound as they crossed the courtyard, not as fast as she would wish, for the master lingered, slowing her down. He pointed out the windows of the dormitory, the library, the classrooms. One wing of the school was cordoned off with thick ropes. "Soldiers' quarters," he said. "Parents ask about it a lot, but we guarantee no disruption for the students."

By the gate he cleared his throat. "One more thing to always keep in mind, Citizeness Vernault," he said. "The college has a duty to all pupils, especially those of lesser abilities, who are all the more in need of our help."

The words sent a chill through her. Was Jean-Louis in danger of failing? Already?

"There is no need to think the worst," the Latin master concluded rather stiffly. "Many boys of slower mind, cultivated by skillful and patient hands, have become valuable men of whom we are all proud now."

At breakfast, Suzette brings in fluffy, buttery omelets, a luxury possible only because Gabrielle Danton has sent butter and sugar, which has nearly vanished from shops. Trouble in the West Indies, Pierre says, but he has no good explanation for why bread is up from nine sous to eighteen.

"Greed," Hortense says. Besides, she has heard bakers add chalk to the dough. She wouldn't put it past them to add nails as well, to make the loaves heavier. She also suspects Cecile of carrying on with a National Guardsman. For what other reason could there be for a pair of laced shoes? Polished every day?

With coffee, Suzette delivers a pile of letters. The one on top is from Pierre's youngest sister, Charlotte. Marie-Louise met her sisters-in-law only once, when they came to Paris for the wedding, and she much preferred the older one, Diane, who laughed in such a natural, winning way and made no fuss over Pierre, like Charlotte did.

"Guess what this is about?" Pierre asks, breaking the seal, his eyes skimming the page. His new spectacles, like Robespierre's, have green lenses, which everyone now claims to be easier on the eyes but which give the skin around them an unhealthy tint. He has abandoned his wigs, and wears his hair cropped short, like a Roman senator. It's the latest fashion, as is always wearing riding boots instead of shoes, and wider cravats that reach up to the chin.

Short hair becomes him. Pierre is a handsome man.

"First your beloved brother becomes a delegate, then his letters get shorter and shorter, and he no longer even replies when you remind him of his promise to visit."

"You promised we would visit?"

"Probably. She does know how to whine quite effectively. Wait . . . there is a post scriptum. *Your visit would, of course, be an indulgence at the time when patriotism commands us to sacrifice.*"

"Uff. Saved."

"Barely."

"Still saved."

Nothing from Jean-Louis today.

Most of the letters end up crumpled on the floor the moment Pierre opens them. Appeals for help or favors. Threats, curses, promises of divine retribution for Pierre Vernault's part in the destruction of the natural order. Backed up by prophecies for the future. Nostradamus. Thomas Moult, whose "cyclical and true" predictions have been reprinted again.

"From the enslaved populace, songs, chants and demands while princes and lords are held captive in prisons. A great nation will govern itself without a prince, nobles or priests." All making Pierre sneer: As if the future were already cast in stone for centuries ahead!

One letter, though, is different. Marie-Louise knows it the moment Pierre's face flushes.

"Who brought it?" he asks Suzette, who has come back to clear the breakfast plates.

"I don't know, Master," Suzette says, fingering the ribbons of what was once Aunt Margot's bonnet.

"Hortense!" Pierre yells, repeating his question when Hortense comes, her apron splattered with grease.

"A boy," she says. "Cheeky one, too. I gave him a slice of bread, for he looked half starved. 'You are feeding a true patriot,' he said."

"Is he still here?"

"No. Gone already."

"And it didn't occur to you to inquire who gave him the letter?"

"Is this what I'm supposed to do now?" Hortense asks, her jaw set. "Interrogate all messengers?"

Hortense, always on guard about her position, puffs herself up, readying for a fight. "This house is almost as bad as the Convention," Pierre has laughed. To which Marie-Louise replied, "It is worse. You don't have to eat what other delegates cook. If you anger Hortense, she will burn your roast."

"It is common sense, not another requirement," Pierre says now, waving Hortense away with scoffing impatience. She leaves with her head held stiffly, letting the door slam behind her. Master's outburst will be discussed in the kitchen in all its minute details, for hours. Picked at like meat off bones. The injustice of it, unreasonable, heartless. Marie-Louise will have to intervene, go through all the tedious rituals of appeasement.

She can see her husband the way he must look to the servants. The chin jutted forward. The steely assurance in his voice. Harsh, they must think him, unyielding. Except Jacques perhaps, whose thoughts are a mystery.

"What is it, Pierre?" she asks.

"I don't know yet," he says, crumpling the letter and throwing it toward her.

She picks it up, smooths the paper flat.

I cannot, Monsieur, stay silent any longer and keep you ignorant of the fact that I am in possession of papers signed by the Secretary of the Comptroller of Finances that detail considerable sums of money you received from Versailles.

Blackmail?

Pierre's voice seethes with indignation. "Royalist scum . . . ever since we put Louis Capet in prison . . . such are their dirty tactics."

Marie-Louise's eyes return to the letter.

I intend to send the documents in my possession to the President of the
National Convention unless you can convince me otherwise.

Unlike countless anonymous letters that end in the fireplace, this one is
signed: *Bertrand Dillaud, residing at 56 rue de la Croix.* There was no need to
scold Hortense after all.

"A lie," Marie-Louise says.

"A royalist lie."

By now Pierre's indignation has turned into anger. Such is the royalist for-
mula: Accuse a loyal citizen of taking bribes. Repeat this accusation enough
times, and plenty are willing to believe it.

"Bertrand Dillaud? Do you know him?"

"I know of him and others like him. They harass deputies. They speak of
the loyalty we all owe to Louis, as if he didn't betray us many times over.
Now, knowing there will be a trial, they scramble for anyone's support."

Pierre gets up from the table, walks to the window and peers outside, as if
Bertrand Dillaud were there, lurking on rue du Cygne. His voice is jittery,
raw. "Mostly they make promises. Used to be we'll make you a baron or a
marquis if you side with us. Now it is we'll make you a minister. This Dillaud
scum obviously prefers blackmail."

"What will you do?" she asks.

"I'll go to him and demand to see the papers. I've seen enough forgeries to
spot one."

"Alone?"

"I'll take Jacques with me. Don't worry."

From the kitchen comes the sound of banging pots. Hortense is declaring
something in a high-pitched, wounded voice. There will be a lot of soothing
to do.

***

A few hours later Hortense, placated, has withdrawn her threats of immediate
departure and turned to ordering the maids about. The kitchen shelves have

been lined with fresh butcher paper, table scraped and scrubbed clean, ashes scattered in the garden.

There will be rabbit pie for supper. It is out of the oven already and Hortense is carefully cutting a hole in the pie crust, for her lemon sauce. Rabbit pie is Pierre's favorite, so perhaps he has been forgiven.

In the best room, Marie-Louise wonders what is keeping her husband so long. She is not overly concerned. There have been far too many libels, denunciations, earth-shattering revelations to mind them all. Every day someone is accused of taking bribes. Danton, most recently, and with great malice, which makes Marie-Louise grateful Gabrielle is leaving for Sèvres.

By the time Marie-Louise hears the fumbling at the front door, the mantel clock is striking six. In the hall, a moment later, Jacques is saying something in a low voice. The door lock must have jammed again.

Not wanting to appear impatient, she waits in the best room. But as soon as Pierre appears, she rushes toward him.

"What was it about?"

He peels off his gloves and drops them on the side table. "Why is it so cold in here?" he asks as if he hasn't heard her question.

It is not cold. The fire has been on since morning. The old cherry tree, which survived the hailstorms of two years before, died in the spring. They have enough firewood, at least for now.

"What happened?" she asks. "What did he say, Pierre?"

"That I took money from Versailles. Eight thousand livres, to be precise. From Louis Yon, Secretary of the Comptroller of Finances."

She reminds him of hacks in the garrets spewing libels, sparing no one. Not even Robespierre, of whom they say he is a relative of that Damiens, who raised his hand on the Old Louis.

"'The worse the better,' isn't that what everyone says?" she asks. "Words are cheap, didn't you say so yourself?"

"The only eight thousand livres I ever received from anyone," Pierre says, "was your dowry."

~❧~

It is like waking the dead.

Aunt Margot's old room is cold and damp; the fire here has not been lit for a while. The portrait on the wall has not improved with time: Marie-Louise looks stiff and awkward on it, Aunt Margot stern and disapproving. Drawers overflow with papers. On every shelf there are bound ledgers with records of patients, apprentices, wet nurses, children placed into care.

Where should they start?

The first batch of letters is tied with a tattered ribbon: *I'm seeking the whereabouts of a boy born in January of 1768 . . . I was one of your lodgers and I gave birth on April of 1767 . . .*

"Keep going," Pierre urges. It is all irrelevant now, including Marie-Louise's own letter to *Dear Aunt Margot*, so carefully crafted on the day Marie-Louise passed her midwife's exams . . . *I owe you everything that is good in me* . . . A dried tuberose from her wedding bouquet. And an outline of Jean-Louis's tiny foot.

Scraps of the past all of it. "Great nesting material," Pierre grumbles, sniffing at the mousy smell inside the pine cabinet where Aunt Margot kept her receipts and tradesmen's bills. "How could she ever manage to find anything in this infernal mess?"

A tug of resentment pulls at Marie-Louise's heart. Surely there is no need for slights. Not that Aunt Margot would have minded. She didn't hold grudges. Not over trifles, at least. And if she did, she knew how to hit back.

And sure enough, infernal mess or not, there it is, tucked among the ledgers, a folder with the initials *M* and *L* on the cover, tied with a ribbon of red silk.

Pierre leans over, pressing on her shoulder as she opens it. The candle splutters on a letter from Diane Gourlon denouncing the vicious cabal of smears that has deprived her of her *beloved* ward, a loss heavier now that she is widowed and penniless due to her late husband's bad investments. Aunt Margot's note underneath records: *three hundred livres sent under the condition that I never hear from her again.*

This is what I've been shielding you from, Marie-Louise, Aunt Margot's voice whispers. *Burdens not of your own making.*

The first batch of receipts signed by *Monsieur Louis Yon, Secretary of the Comptroller of Finances at Versailles*, cover a yearly allowance of five hundred livres for *the living expenses of Marie-Louise Bosque*. Appended to them are Aunt Margot's meticulous lists of payments: calico dresses, flannel petticoats, linen, books, quills, ink. Even pin money is there. And the midwifery exam fee of 169 livres and 26 sous.

All accounted for, Marie-Louise, Aunt Margot's voice insists. *I didn't take a single sou for myself.*

The dowry statement is tucked at the very end: *Eight thousand livres . . . entrusted to Madame Marguerite Leblanc, to be paid to the groom, Pierre Vernault*. Signed by the same Monsieur Yon.

"Clever Mistress Margot," Pierre says, his voice thick, not at all like his own. "I should've known she didn't trust me."

"What do you mean?" Marie-Louise asks.

What Pierre means is that while Aunt Margot received the dowry money all at once, she paid him in four installments. Of which, he recalls, the last was late by three months, causing problems he won't dwell upon now. Unnecessary problems, as it turns out.

Mistress Margot. Cunning . . . playing her own games.

"What games, Pierre?"

He refuses to say anything else. He won't speak ill of the dead.

A dowry is not a bribe, Marie-Louise insists. Or payment for services rendered. That Dillaud has been shooting into a barrel, hoping he will hit someone. He has hit the wrong man.

Pierre should be pleased, but he is not.

The frown on his forehead deepens. His eyes flit from her to the door as if he were expecting someone at any moment.

"Do you really not see the seriousness of it, Marie-Louise? How it can be made to look bad?"

Her dowry came from Versailles. Her dowry paid for the expansion of Pierre's legal practice. Hence, he took royal money. Now monarchists have the temerity to expect his support. On the threat of public infamy. Pierre can already picture his name on the list of traitors to the revolution, or headlines in *Le Père Duchesne*: Vernault rolling in Versailles filth!

He lets out a breath with a hiss. "Can you see it now, Marie-Louise?"

She nods, perplexed, unsure where this admission is taking her. She doesn't know what to say. What he wants her to say. "Are you angry with *me*?" she asks.

Pierre bites his lower lip, just like Jean-Louis when he thinks himself wronged. Then he sits across from her and takes off his spectacles, fixing his eyes on her.

Interrogation is the only word Marie-Louise finds appropriate to describe what comes next.

How long did you live at the palace?

Who with?

Where, exactly, did you live?

She strains her memory, extracts what she can from it, suspicious of what it all might now reveal. The Grand Commons, Gardienne's searing outbursts, the tightening grip of Old Gourlon's bony hand. Monsieur Lebel, Sister Seraphina. The old queen giving her a holy picture, the old king asking her if she knew how to make an omelet, giving her a shiny coin with his profile. Her memory churns out once-overheard whispers:

Be grateful for being taken care of . . .

A Polish bastard . . .

One of those Deer Park girls . . .

The gentleman who has been watching you said . . .

The loneliness, the fear, the hurt of not being wanted.

You are wanted now, Pierre told her once. We never have to speak about it again. Pierre, who is not looking at her now, who is pacing the room, ready to overturn whatever is in his way. A side table wobbles, a chair scrapes the floor.

"These servants who raised you, who were they?"

"A maid to Pompadour and a coachman."

"Did they know who your father was?"

"If they did, they never told me."

"Did Aunt Margot know?"

What can Marie-Louise say that Pierre hasn't heard already? The story of her father, a foreigner, honorable enough to have secured her future. Her mother, one of so many women a midwife attends to. Young, frightened, forced to give her bastard away.

Her love child, Marie-Louise, Aunt Margot's voice insists.

All lies?

"Did you ever meet Old Louis?"

"Once, by chance. He was with Pompadour. Gardienne sent me to fetch Madame's shawl."

"Did he ask you anything?"

"If I knew how to make an omelet."

"An omelet? Are you sure this is what he asked you about?"

"Yes."

"Nothing else?"

She shakes her head, thinking it best not to mention the coin he had given her.

"Louis Capet, have you ever met him?"

"Yes."

When? Where? How many times?

Here she thinks she is on a firmer ground, with the account of the palace roof, the chance encounter, the spying glass, the plans of sailing a ship across the ocean. It was all innocent. They were both children. He called himself Auguste.

"Spying on people? Planning an escape?" Pierre asks. "Already, then?"

Why is he twisting her words, hearing what he wants to hear? She shouldn't have told him about those silly childish plans. And she shouldn't have mentioned the cats. "Citizen Capet hunting cats on the palace roof. Pure gold!" It strikes her as false, lampoonist, the way Pierre slaps his knee and grins. "So how many of these ferocious beasts has our glorious royal master slain with his mighty sword?"

She starts biting at one of her fingers, at the skin underneath her nail. This is how calumnies are born and fed.

"Louis the Cat-Slayer!"

"Do we need to talk about him now?"

"The whole country is talking about him. Why should we be different?"

There is so much anger in her husband's voice that Marie-Louise takes a while to register something else. Fear?

For what if someone put this Dillaud up to these accusations? To flush Pierre out, force him to make some rash move, reveal his position. Someone Pierre might still be taking for an ally or friend whispering in the Convention corridors: If Vernault concealed this from us, what else is he concealing?

If Pierre suspects anyone, he will not tell her. Just as she won't tell him of the old question still rattling in her mind: Whose child am I?

There is a scurrying along the wall, a swift race to the safety of darkness.

"Not a word about any of it," Pierre says. "To anyone."

The Revolution has enemies waiting for just such gutter scraps. Enemies sitting in back rooms, scheming and plotting. They will accuse you of anything they can think of, Danton has warned him. Setting fire to their châteaux or stealing their linen.

On the Convention door someone painted in big red letters: *Hell is empty, and all the devils are in there.*

She nods, glad to be sitting down. The conversation has left her drained, emptied out.

"I won't let them make me into a traitor, Marie-Louise. Do you understand?"

"Yes." Her voice is low, aimed at her own clasped hands. *Them* is such a chameleon of a word. Adept in the art of disguise.

The big clock downstairs strikes twelve as Pierre gathers the dowry statements and all the Versailles papers and puts them in the fireplace.

"Not a word," he repeats, lowering the candle to light them. "To anyone."

The candle splutters. The flame is quick to catch, brightening the room. But paper burns fast. A few moments later there is nothing left but a heap of ash.

Having nudged the ashes with a poker to make sure no scrap has escaped, Pierre stands up and puts the candle back on the writing table. It is a cheap tallow one, giving off a whiff of lard. Rats gnaw at them, Hortense complains. For years, on Marie-Louise's orders, she has been leaving scraps for alley cats. Where are these damn beasts when *we* need them? Not hungry enough?

"I'm going to bed," Pierre says. He is calmer now; his shoulders sink, his breath deepens. There is a soot smudge on his fingers, which he wipes off with his handkerchief. "Are you coming?"

She points at the scattered letters. "I can't leave it like that."

"You could do it tomorrow."

"I wouldn't be able to sleep anyway."

She can hear him in the corridor, saying something to Jacques, who has already unfolded his bed in the nook.

Alone in the silence that follows, Marie-Louise puts old ledgers back on the shelves, folds the scattered letters, ties up the ribbons around them. She should burn the whole lot, really, most of it anyway, but not tonight.

She works fast, filling drawers one by one. It is only when she picks up Madame du Coudray's letters that she lingers: *Miscarriage is most often the result of poor nutrition, which, in your niece's case, cannot be possible . . . Have you felt any thickening of her uterus? . . . I recommend cramp bark and black haw in the usual doses . . .*

You are much too generous with your gratitude . . . If it's a girl I'd be honored if your niece allowed you to name her Angélique . . .

Her daughter would've turned twelve in December. Losing the last of her baby teeth? Wishing to have nothing to do with midwifery?

No, Marie-Louise will not cry. She has a son, healthy and strong. Beloved of so many.

Thinking of Jean-Louis warms her inside. The child he was. Hard at work on the drawings Aunt Margot numbered and dated so carefully: a large head sprouting spidery legs and feet, a bird's nest with three speckled eggs inside, a map he drew of the streets around their house: rue du Cygne, rue Saint-Denis. How clever you are, Jean-Louis, Aunt Margot said, when he showed it to her. For he has always been clever, hasn't he, just not with everything.

Such could have been the end of this day. A warm thought, a good memory to fall asleep with, hold on to for the days to come.

It would have been, if the drawer where Marie-Louise tried to put the last bundle of letters didn't get stuck. If she didn't have to empty it again, put her hand inside. If she didn't feel a small jointed piece of wood under her fingers. Didn't move it, didn't hear a click.

The dead, once wakened, may not stay silent. She should've known that.

A narrow panel opens at the back of the desk, and a little oblong drawer springs out. Inside she finds a letter, written hastily, in an unsteady hand. An ink blot in the corner has been smeared with a finger, its imprint preserved.

> *Madame Berlin, who is unable to help me any longer, has urged me to write this letter and swore to take it to you on my behalf. I don't intend to cause trouble to you or to my daughter, but I have been told you have been receiving money from the palace for her upkeep. I'm destitute, forced to beg for your help.*

Signed *Véronique Clerantin.*

Pinned to the letter are receipts: eight hundred livres, received by *Widow Clerantin on this 4th day of June 1776*; three hundred livres received in December of the same year; four hundred livres in February of 1777.

If you ever wonder what it is about, Hortense's peasant wisdom rings triumphant, it's always about money.

Marie-Louise stares at the yellowed paper, her heart pounding. She doesn't have to be told that Madame Berlin's establishment is a well-known Parisian brothel.

To get to Madame Berlin's, Marie-Louise hires a two-wheel chaise, nimbler and less ostentatious than a carriage but safer than walking now, with the streets patrolled by revolutionary squads. Just the other day Madeleine was threatened with a whipping for not wearing a cockade, even though only men are obliged to do so by law.

The streets of Paris are crowded, tense, stinking of piss and excrement, sweat and rot. By an open cellar two drunk men, bottles in hand, are cursing Marie-Antoinette. A beast. A whore. Insatiable in her orgies. Holds fury in her insides. Does it with men, women, her own son, for God's sake. Morning and night. Lolls in it.

Traitors, both, she and her husband.

You know what happens to traitors.

A blob of saliva lands on the pavement. A hand swipes under a throat.

On rue Saint-Honoré, street criers flaunt today's newssheets. *Is Louis Capet a victim or a tyrant?*

The door of the house where the chaise driver deposits Marie-Louise is splattered with mud. Its portal has been recently stripped of insignia and re-painted, a sight common in Paris. It is prudent not to advertise one's prove-nance.

Marie-Louise lifts the heavy brass knocker and lets it drop.

"Announce me to Madame Berlin," she tells the tense-looking maid who opens the door and takes her calling card. The words *sworn midwife* must've quelled the maid's misgivings, for Marie-Louise is ushered to a spacious room furnished with small alcoves, each with a scarlet sofa and a table. In one of them two young women are deep in conversation. Behind them a keg of beer bears an inscription: *True patriots don't drink until they are really thirsty.*

The women give Marie-Louise a quick look but keep talking. The prettier one is examining her fingernails.

"Do you know where these white spots come from?"

"Not enough milk?"

"You might be right."

"Chantal, Cherie, off with you both," a woman says briskly as she walks into the room, clapping her hands. No longer young but elegant in dove-gray satin, a cockade pinned to her breast. "Still a handsome woman," Aunt Margot would have called her.

Chantal and Cherie leave but not before asking about a harp that has been promised. Will it arrive tomorrow?

"We shall see," Madame Berlin says and asks Marie-Louise to follow her into her boudoir. Big enough for two upholstered armchairs with gilded arms flanking the fireplace and a small table. By the window, a writing desk, with an ink horn and a china doll in a red satin dress. A ginger tomcat is pushing it with his paw.

Marie-Louise has braced herself for what is coming. She feels nothing but desire to get through this as quickly as possible.

"I've come about—"

"Citizeness Vernault, please, sit down," Madame Berlin tells her, pointing at the armchairs by the fire. The flames are small, barely clinging to the remnants of a birch log. "Coffee? I warn you, though, it is made from chicory. This is not a complaint, please note. We all have to make sacrifices. For *la patrie*."

I'm a woman of business, her eyes say. I believe in being cautious.

"I've come—" Marie-Louise repeats, louder this time.

Madame Berlin scoffs. This is not the way to have an important conversation. "Let's go back to the beginning," she says, ringing the servant bell. "Coffee?"

"No, thank you."

"As you wish. I'm going to have some, if you will allow me."

The maid comes in, the chicory coffee is served, to both of them in spite of Marie-Louise's refusal. The cat leaves the doll and jumps on the table, sniffing at the cups. "His name is O," Madame Berlin says, patting the cat's head with one hand, lifting her cup with another. On the cup, the Gallic rooster struts proudly, its head high.

Madame Berlin's gaze is fixed on Marie-Louise. The cat, she says, is vicious with rats, which he decapitates and leaves on the doorstep. With her, O is perfectly content and will follow her like a dog. Hates being picked up, though. Also, forget trying to scratch his belly. "You may ask me now: What does O stand for?"

"What does it stand for?"

"It depends."

In the pause that comes Marie-Louise hears a voice from the room next door: "And then he told me, 'Citizen Jesus never liked the rich.'"

Madame Berlin takes a sip and puts her cup of chicory coffee down on the table. "The weather is so unpredictable these days," she says. "Remember the hailstorms the year before the Bastille fell? Orchards devastated; crops flattened in the fields."

"I've not come here to talk about the weather," Marie-Louise says, anger rising in her. "I am—"

"I know who you are."

"I've come to inquire about Véronique Clerantin. The woman who sent you to my aunt to ask for money." She has barely stopped herself from saying demand: "Is she my mother?"

Madame Berlin never lets her sharp eyes off Marie-Louise. Her frown is a sign of a quick calculation. Give just enough to satisfy, but not an inch more.

"Yes."

"Is she alive?" Marie-Louise asks, hating the way her voice breaks.

"Yes."

"Is she here?"

"No."

"Do you know where she is?" Marie-Louise asks, lowering her eyes to the surface of the table, the shapes of wood grain, long and whorled. The clock chimes the half hour.

"Knowing is my business."

O arches his back and purrs, giving Marie-Louise a look of what she decides is mockery. Would have held his own on the palace roof, this one.

Madame Berlin places her palms together, as if she were about to pray. "You may not like what you hear," she says.

Marie-Louise fixes her gaze on the edge of Madame Berlin's powdered hair where yellowed strands mix with white. "Let me be the judge," she says.

"Lots of judges these days, Citizeness Vernault. Perhaps too many?"

Madame Berlin gives a magnificent show of well-rehearsed sincerity and frankness. Her voice shakes at the right moments, quiets then rises when needed.

Unlike other Parisian madams she won't name, she, Julie Berlin, is not a vulture, lying in wait at the city gates, waiting for runaway girls from the villages to sell their virginity to the highest bidder and then cut them loose. She has always picked her girls carefully. For some talent, like graceful movements and manners, or a lovely singing voice. A talent can be a ticket to a better future. If Julie Berlin's girl does well, they both profit. If she fails, they are both sullied.

Connections are everything in her business. Connections and excellent memory. Girls, clients, other madams, those Julie Berlin pays and those who pay her. You are only as good as those who can help you when you fall.

She has her code of conduct. Number one: Never cross the police. Number two: Keep your records straight. Number three: Never pass up an opportunity to make your girls noticed and enhance your reputation. Number four: Never abandon a girl in trouble.

Served her well, all four.

There are good reasons girls seek her out. Girls without money or connections, with nothing but good looks. Most of them, she must say, in need of a stern reminder that good looks last but a few years only, and that it is prudent to drive hard bargains when it's still possible.

"Your mother came to me," Julie Berlin says. "Of her own will."

A picture slowly forms in Marie-Louise's mind. This very room warmed by the glowing embers. Véronique Clerantin, a young widow with nothing but debts, telling Madame Berlin how her late husband—a grain merchant—gambled away his fortune. How her in-laws turned her out of her house. How she came to Paris, where her mother who helped her for a while had died. How her brothers wished to have nothing to do with her.

Childless, she called herself. Two sons buried in Brest, one lived but a week, another three months.

There had been good intentions. An attempt to work as a *repasseuse* with a hatter, removing fur from beaver pelts, getting ugly sores on her hands and arms from the solutions the furs were soaked in. Then Véronique took some sewing and embroidery home, as she was an excellent seamstress. Foolish attempts, of course. Doomed from the start. When has merit or hard work guaranteed a decent living? When did tears and hand-wringing ever help?

"My dear," Julie Berlin said to Véronique Clerantin. "When the earth shakes, you get the hell out of your house. And if your house falls down, you sift through what is left, pick up what you can still use and move on. You do not sit among the rubble wailing, waiting for God's mercy."

Not if you are that pretty, Julie Berlin thought. With such excellent deportment and manners. Not if you have a beautiful voice, into the bargain. Not if you let me work with that.

"You might as well know this about me, Véronique. I don't believe in beating around the bush," she said.

Julie Berlin began making inquiries. First, about the pretty widow herself. Not that she suspected her of lying, but there is always something hidden under the mattress, isn't there? Rumors, whispers. Anything that could come back to haunt, spoil the arrangements she was trying to weave.

She had her channels. First of all, Inspector Marais, as much as she disliked him. For good reasons, too. His predecessors always paid for the girls they fancied; he didn't. Bad for my business, Monsieur Inspector, she once said, bad for yours. I disagree, Madame, he said, and that was that.

Her girls complained to her afterward, about his stinking breath, the fingermarks on their arms and thighs. Grin and bear it, she told them. There is enough trouble in their line of work without Marais against them. If they needed a sterner reminder, she mentioned past customers who refused to pay, or sent a girl back claiming she had been either too modest or too libertine for their tastes. If Marais were not on her side, then what could Julie Berlin do to defend *them*?

Yes, Marais had his faults, but he needed her as much as she needed him. Like all Parisian madams, she supplied him with reports. Names, dates, time and duration of each visit, predilections of the clients. Anything said to the girl, however trivial. Bastards born, kept or placed. Mercury cures. Having fulfilled her end of the bargain, she could ask for favors in return.

It was all in Marais's files, Véronique Clerantin's whole sordid story. The printer father who lost his business and died, the mother left destitute, the five children. The used clothing trade, the king's scouts reporting on the girl's charms, the offer to take her to Deer Park.

Madame Berlin leans back. A new tone rings in her voice, one of satisfaction well earned.

"You shouldn't have kept it from me, silly girl, I told Véronique. Deer Park girls always attract the highest bidders."

It didn't come cheap, mind you. Dresses of fine embroidered silk, hair pouffed and powdered, new gloves, stockings, shoes. Investment all, not luxury. Having planted a few enticing hints in well-placed ears, Julie Berlin took "her dear friend Véronique" to balls at the Palais-Royal, for leisurely strolls at the Luxembourg Gardens. As she predicted there had been a deluge of sweet notes and grand promises, but only Monsieur Bout offered one thousand livres a month, an excellent apartment on rue Saint-Honoré, plus wages for three servants and the use of a carriage. The welcome gift for Véronique was nothing to sneer at, either. A ruby necklace and some good pieces of furniture, the best of them a carved bed with damask curtains. Worth ten thousand livres at least in all. Hers to keep no matter what.

"They say I drive hard bargains and I do."

Monsieur Bout tried to haggle her down, of course, to which she replied, "I can probably get Véronique to agree to a lower price, for our sweet girl is terribly fond of you. Only this will not stay secret for long, which is not good for your reputation. A mistress is an accoutrement, Monsieur. The more you spend on her, the more you show your worth."

With which he had to agree.

Ah, if only the rest had gone as well.

The first symptoms Véronique kept to herself. A rash that disappeared quickly enough. Tiredness she could explain away. Headaches she treated with cold compresses. But when she began losing her hair by the handfuls, her maid came to Madame Berlin in tears, begging for help. A good girl, that maid, Lisette. Decent and smart. Could do miracles with a bit of rouge and ceruse.

Julie Berlin quotes the doctor's bills: Four rounds of *grand remède* for syphilis treatment, six weeks each. Bleeding, purging, regular application of the ointment, followed by a two-week-long recuperation on a restricted diet. Three hundred livres per round.

An avalanche, the rest of it. Sores on Véronique's lips, refusing to heal. Gray skin, purple circles under her eyes. Black spit and darkened teeth. The patron withdrawing in disgust at the sight of her, as they all do. Eventually.

"I lent her money," Julie Berlin says. "I paid her most pressing debts."

The mercury treatment worked. Véronique did recover. In candlelight, with Lisette's expert help, she could still charm. There were visitors, but no patron. Once people start talking, they never stop, do they?

A dismissive wave of Julie Berlin's hand is enough to summarize the rest of the story. Fewer clients of quality. Smaller and smaller rooms, shabbier dresses, mounting debts. Lisette stuck around as long as she could, but even she left in the end. Who can blame her? We all have to eat.

The room wavers as if a gust of wind swept through it. Marie-Louise clutches the edge of the table. Her mother was one of the Deer Park girls? *The royal whores extending their greedy hands*, as the pamphlets put it. *How much did they cost France?*

As a child, she soothed herself with stories of love and longing. This is what she sees now:

The old king on the prowl, flushing out his prey. A wild chase through the grounds of Versailles. Girls, naked, plied with wine, found unconscious in the bushes, drowning in their own vomit. Dog bites, blackened eyes, bruises on their bodies. Extending their hands for a payoff. Counting up the rewards they have earned. That much for bruises, that much for a virgin's first blood, that much for silence. That much for a bastard left behind. Which one of them gave birth to her?

Why would your mother care for such a brat?

Why would she care for such a mother?

Unanswered questions crowd in her head, clawing their way out.

"Where is she now?" is what she asks.

Back in the mud-splattered street, she walks slowly. The trees are already bare, lower branches all broken off and carted away for firewood. In the confectioner's window, Marie-Louise catches her reflection. Looking startled, she thinks of herself, pained. She pinches her cheeks to bring some color to them, licks her forefinger to smooth her eyebrows, erase the frown between them. She won't give Hortense reasons for asking, in that tone she has, what on earth has happened now.

An ostrich buries its head in the sand and thinks itself invisible. Or this is what we like to imagine. Ever practical, Jean-Louis used to ask, "But, Maman, how can it breathe then?"

December

SHE SHOULD'VE TOLD Pierre everything. Isn't he her husband? The father of her child? She should have said: I'm the old king's bastard. My mother was one of his Deer Park whores.

She should've said: Aunt Margot knew. She paid my mother off. She wanted to spare me from knowing.

Then why does Marie-Louise keep silent?

Lots of judges these days. Perhaps too many?

In the streets these days the criers denounce royal duplicity. Accusations are spurred by the recent discovery of an iron chest cleverly hidden behind false paneling from what used to be the royal palace at Tuileries. The truth is out in all its ugliness. Louis the False never supported the revolution. He called the constitution "absurd and detestable." He was plotting with Prussia and Austria. He was bribing deputies, paying for their secret support.

Bribing whom?

Mirabeau, who is conveniently dead, and others as yet unnamed.

The iron chest, Pierre says, had been opened without proper witnesses from the Convention. There is talk of evidence suppressed or doctored. Robespierre is reeling with rage, demanding the unmasking of hypocrites. No one will dare to oppose the trial of Louis Capet now.

Pierre is coming home later and later, tense, tired, impatient with anything that is not to his liking. An orange, unpeeled to preserve its freshness, must be served with his coffee. Absolute silence must reign in the house when he works. His boots must be freshly blackened and polished, his jacket aired and brushed. Some mornings Marie-Louise wakes up and finds him already gone, only the imprint of his body on the mattress or the clothes he has left behind a proof that he had been home at all.

A Deer Park girl always attracts the highest bidders.

"Dillaud?" Pierre dismisses her question in his new, mocking way, as if she asked of last year's snow. Doesn't she read newspapers? If that Dillaud has ever had his chance, he lost it. What is eight thousand livres for a dowry paid out of the Versailles coffers years ago? Danton has just been accused of "misplacing" a hundred thousand.

Has Pierre always looked so angry? So unapproachable? How long has he had these dark circles under his eyes?

They are in the bedroom. It is past midnight, time to rest. Marie-Louise has just unpinned her hair and is brushing it before she plaits it for the night. Suzette has already laid out her nightgown and her bonnet. Pierre is still at his writing table. His glasses have slid down his nose. The table is strewn with papers, open books, notes, drafts of depositions. Corrections are in the margins, some of them crossed already.

"Talk to me," she pleads, hoping to drown her own guilt.

Pierre takes off his glasses and lifts his hands up, like a priest at the end of Mass, just before the blessing. A rhetorical flourish, she reminds herself, not a mark of surrender. In his voice there is no wavering, no hesitation.

France is in mortal danger.

The impure blood of the tyrant must be shed.

Such are the terrible but necessary truths.

Pierre doesn't look at her when he speaks, at least not directly, for his eyes do glance over her from time to time, checking that she is listening.

She is.

The accusations must be formulated with absolute precision. It is not just Louis who will go on trial but the future of the revolution. No, far more than that: the future of the world, for France is a beacon for all the oppressed, everywhere. With stakes like these no one has the right to put personal comfort ahead of duty, which is what Robespierre repeats every day, demanding perfection of everyone and of himself.

Pierre stands up, pushes the chair back, scraping the floor. The woolen rug that used to lie there is in the attic, rolled up, a feast for moths. She should get the maids to air it. Or give it to Hortense, who is complaining of a draft coming from the cellar.

"This is not the time for dithering, splitting hairs, Marie-Louise."

She thinks: Is that what I am doing? Dithering? Splitting hairs?

Pierre takes a step toward her. He has lost weight, which has added a boyish spring to his movements. Even these dark shadows under his eyes become him. What if she threw her arms around his neck, buried her face in his breast?

"The revolution, Marie-Louise, is in grave danger. Not just from royalists."

It is the many-headed hydra of the old morality Pierre denounces now, old rules, old faith. You slash one head off, another appears. People are weak. They cling to their old beliefs. They want a revolution without a revolution. As if such a thing were at all possible.

Once people start talking, they never stop, do they?

Marie-Louise has finished plaiting her hair and has put on her night bonnet. "Who needs enemies," Pierre says, undressing quickly and getting into bed. "We are tearing each other to bloodied pieces on our own."

The clock in the hall chimes half past twelve. She blows out the candle. Beside her, Pierre is already snoring.

When she, too, falls asleep, her dream takes her into a deserted street. The heads that are staring at her have their mouths gagged with hay.

⁂

The convent of the Sisters of Charity is on the other side of the Seine.

Former convent, Pierre would have reminded her, for the revolution confiscated all church property. *Former* Sisters, who have been liberated from their vows, can now marry or find useful work in hospitals or schools. The Convention favors the latter as it repays some of the expenses the nation incurred on their behalf.

In the place du Carrousel, where the guillotine stands idle today, someone taps Marie-Louise on the shoulder, but she doesn't turn her head, suspecting a pickpocket sizing her up. She knows that is how they create diversion, misdirect your attention.

"Why such a hurry, Citoyenne?"

"Watch out, pretty Citoyenne, or you may stumble!"

There is an art to becoming invisible, to blending with the crowd. Your face has to turn blank, your gaze indifferent, your steps purposeful. It helps to know where you are going and to get there by the shortest route. Past the onion sellers, past the guardsmen in liberty caps, pikes in hand, across the pont Royal.

Sister Geneviève, hands hidden in her loose sleeves, cannot be more than twenty; worry lines have not yet set into her skin.

"Follow me," she says, and Marie-Louise trails her crisp white bonnet and simple black dress down the corridor, wondering if Sister Geneviève has seen the pamphlets. The ones calling nuns sinners consorting with priests, giving birth to bastards, pamphlets providing directions to once-secret cemeteries filled with baby bones.

The sister deftly maneuvers past a pile of trunks ready to be carted away. "Many of our charges are gone but not all," she says, turning to Marie-Louise. "We are grateful for those who, like you, take interest in the unfortunate few still under our care. God will repay you."

"I do not expect repayment."

"Madame Clerantin is a loving soul," Sister Geneviève continues, and then, casting Marie-Louise an uneasy look, corrects herself. "I should've said Citizeness Clerantin. Please forgive me."

"There is nothing to forgive."

Sister Geneviève walks in silence. But then, unable to rein in her curiosity, she asks, "A relative?"

Marie-Louise hesitates. The knowledge is still only half real, its consequences fluid. Still, she has to swallow hard before she can force a lie through her lips.

"A distant relative I've only just learned about."

"Oh, yes," Sister Geneviève says. "We see that a lot." She means the surprise of discovering a hidden family obligation, an unexpected duty, another mouth to feed. She will say a special rosary for Marie-Louise and the Widow Clerantin.

From one of the rooms they pass, an old hunchbacked woman waves, asking them in a pleading voice: "Please bring me more of your willow bark tea, Sister. My feet are still hurting."

"I will, on my way back," Sister Geneviève promises but does not stop.

The thick door at the end of the corridor, unlocked with two turns of a big key, squeaks open, revealing a small darkened room. The stench of an unwashed chamber pot seeps out.

Marie-Louise, whose heart is beating fast, is a rational being. She has never seen her mother and thus she cannot possibly recognize her. And yet, inexplicably, she is hoping for a tug of knowledge.

The woman sitting on a chair, her back bent, is tiny, a doll's body wrapped in the folds of a simple cotton dress. Her face looks all wrong, lopsided, as if someone has cut it up and then rearranged the pieces. The deeply set eyes are emptied out, hollowed, like a troll's. Out of the folds of the dress a foot emerges. It, too, is small, but shapely, shod in a black stocking and a heeled shoe.

The woman lifts her head and Marie-Louise, her eyes now adjusted to the dimness, sees the gaunt cheeks, the smooth forehead, the uncertainty in the smile on her collapsed lips. Her teeth are black, as if she feasted on soot.

Marie-Louise thinks: She cannot be my mother.

The woman stands up with the stiffness of an automaton, but the very moment she raises her eyes toward Marie-Louise her face softens, becomes less lopsided, almost beautiful. And then comes a smile of such joy, a lurch forward, a tight, frantic embrace, as if someone was trying to tear them apart.

"Adèle, you've come back! You are here!"

Marie-Louise frees herself from the grasping hands and steps back. She tastes ashes. Whoever this Adèle is, she is the one remembered, awaited, missed. Not the bastard child left behind.

"I'm not Adèle."

"I knew you would come, Adèle, I knew."

"Hush, my dear," Sister Geneviève intervenes with an apologetic smile, as if it were all her fault. "Madame's name is Marie-Louise Vernault. She has come to pay you a visit."

Widow Clerantin doesn't listen. She is all joy, lurching forward again to hold her visitor, as if they were playing tag.

Marie-Louise's thoughts are a tumbling whirl. The child she had once been still craves her mother's touch, her smile, her admonitions even. The child she had once been longs to bury her face in her mother's skirts, feel her hands smooth her hair, hear her voice that she has so vividly imagined as sweet and soothing. For that child, being in the same room as her mother should be the most wonderful thing imaginable.

Be careful what you wish for, as Aunt Margot would have said.

Widow Clerantin clings to Marie-Louise's hand, fingers like claws digging into her flesh. "Adèle is here. Adèle has come for me," she repeats, beaming. "Where have you been so long, Adèle? At the market? Have you brought me something?"

"No, Madame Clerantin."

A shadow flicks through Véronique's face. "Why are you angry with me, Adèle? What have I done wrong? I'm Véronique!"

A knock on the door is a salvation.

"This is her time to eat," Sister Geneviève says, opening the door to let in a servant girl carrying a wooden tray that she sets on the small table by the window. Marie-Louise slips a coin into her hand. "A small gift," she mutters as the girl colors with pleasure.

Véronique Clerantin takes her seat at the table, hands folded on her lap. Her whole being focuses on the plate in front of her now. The fare is simple: a slice of coarse bread, grated carrot sprinkled with sugar shavings. Though, these days, the last should count as luxury.

"You have to eat, too, Adèle," Véronique insists, pointing at the other chair. "Or you'll start coughing again."

Marie-Louise sits at the table. "I'm not Adèle," she says. "I'm Marie-Louise Vernault. I've come to visit you."

She mentions Madame Berlin. Julie Berlin. "Do you remember her, Madame Clerantin?" she asks.

"I'm Véronique."

"Do you remember Julie Berlin?"

Véronique Clerantin shakes her head.

It is like walking in a stream of treacle, Marie-Louise thinks, peeved with herself for continuing this flighty exchange. Questions she wants answered seem suddenly, cruelly pointless.

"Mistress Leblanc, the midwife from rue du Cygne. Do you remember her?"

Véronique Clerantin is eating with great relish, smacking her lips. "You have such beautiful eyes, and beautiful hair, Adèle," she babbles on. "If you won't eat these carrots, can I have them?"

Marie-Louise nods.

Having swallowed the last of the carrots, Véronique Clerantin grabs Marie-Louise's hand once again. "Look," she says. "La Grise has come back, too."

It is only then that Marie-Louise notices a half-grown gray tabby, peeking from under the bed. Young and curious, but extremely cautious. Diving back where she came from the moment Marie-Louise moves.

The *former* abbess, a tall, thin woman with pursed lips and waxy skin, stops Marie-Louise on her way out. Her stern spiky voice evokes the unwelcome memory of Diane Gourlon's admonitions.

"It's about Widow Clerantin . . ."

The cough that interrupts the abbess is raw. Pulmonary trouble, she says, when she recovers. Temporary, though all is in God's hands.

Now, the business at hand.

Yes, Mistress Leblanc had been generous in her endowment. Yes, the Sisters of Charity pledged to care for the Widow Clerantin until God summoned her. But the light of the church is being extinguished. There is no Sisters of Charity anymore.

Marie-Louise draws herself up as the unsaid rings in the air. Extinguished by the revolution. By men like Robespierre, Danton and those, like Pierre, who trail in their steps.

"Human actions taken against divine wishes," the abbess continues, "set afoot unpredictable consequences."

Beware the self-declared righteous, Pierre would have said. They always believe they own the truth.

"Widow Clerantin is one of God's unfortunates. I'm in no position to judge either her sins or the severity of her punishment for them. However, Widow Clerantin cannot stay here any longer. We have been ordered to vacate the house before the new year. Liberty, as it turns out, is not permitted to everyone. Such is the unadorned truth that you, Citizeness Vernault, cannot in good conscience dispute."

Outside, from a distance, comes a burst of musket fire. It is a sign of the times that neither of them is surprised or startled.

The abbess clasps her hand on her lips, managing to stifle the cough this time.

Marie-Louise has no intention of disputing any truth, adorned or not. The obligations of the dead become the duties of the living. She has promised to take care of what her aunt was leaving undone and she will.

The streets as she walks back home are mostly empty, until she reaches rue Saint-Denis, which is crowded but strangely silent. No criers with the latest news, no pamphlet sellers hawking their latest revelations. People are craning their necks, whispering to each other. Groups of gendarmes are standing at the corners, facing the crowd.

It doesn't take Marie-Louise long to learn what they are all waiting for. The king is being brought from the Temple prison to the Convention to hear the charges against him.

The trial has begun.

When Pierre doesn't make it home at night, which happens more and more often, Jacques comes by in the morning to pick up clean linen. "Plundering the closet," Hortense complains. "Not even bothering to tell me what he takes. Twelve of master's best shirts gone, but what else?"

Jacques frowns when Marie-Louise questions him. No, he doesn't know his master's plans. Citizen Vernault has many duties. It is *his* patriotic duty to shield Citizen Vernault from anything that could interfere with his.

He cannot divulge anything else.

Divulge?

Marie-Louise turns on her heel and walks away.

It's all in the papers, anyway:

> *Louis, the French nation accuses you . . . of having committed a multi-*
> *tude of crimes to establish your tyranny, in destroying her freedom . . .*
> *Louis, you caused the blood of Frenchmen to flow.*
>
> > *And what does Louis say to this? I know nothing . . . Provide a writ-*
> > *ten proof . . . I do not remember . . . My ministers were responsible . . .*
> > *There is not a word true in this charge.*
>
> > *His conscience, he claims, reproaches him with nothing! Back in*
> > *prison he ate six cutlets, a chicken and some eggs, and went straight*
> > *to bed.*

Marie-Louise believes that Danton got the better end of the stick by scooting off to Belgium. What do you mean by "scooting off," Pierre asked, quite
sharply. Danton is investigating complaints against the French army, necessary if France doesn't want a Belgian uprising on her hands.

"Stick to what you know, Marie-Louise. Don't interfere in men's business."

Three days into the king's trial Pierre shuffles into the best room, in his riding
boots, chin darkened by the day's stubble. His frockcoat, opened, reveals a
shirt stained with brown coffee patches, the yellow of egg yolk. His breath
reeks of wine.

The Convention, Madeleine says, is such a perfect excuse for a man.
Unpredictable hours, late-night voting, women in the gallery listening to the
deputies' every word. Applauding if they are pleased, jeering if they disagree,
waiting in the corridors for their favorites when the session ends. "To put it
bluntly, throwing themselves on them. Who can resist?"

This, of course, is nonsense. Pierre is not like George Danton, on the hunt
for women who will accommodate him.

"Cheap wine," Pierre says, interrupting these thoughts, placing the palm of
his left hand on his breast. "I would like it to be noted and recorded, Your
Illustrious Honor, that it was a very cheap wine."

Marie-Louise gets up from the ottoman where she has been darning Jean-

Louis's woolen socks. *In the morning, icicles hang from the windows inside the dormitory*, he has written.

"Are you hungry, Pierre? There is still some roasted capon in the pantry."

"I'm not hungry."

"You look tired. Will you have time to rest?"

"No. I've only come to pick up a few things."

"There will be food at the trial?"

"We get donations. Hot pies, ices for dessert."

"Any good?"

"Not bad. Too salty. The pies, I mean."

Ping . . . ping . . . pong . . . pong off a shuttlecock, this conversation, skimming on the surface, ignoring the turmoil inside. She does blame herself. Her secret is acquiring a life of its own. "Not a relative," she told the clerk at the Commune Section, where she went to report the new tenant. "I need to fulfill the obligation placed on me by my late aunt's will."

"Will you come home later tonight?"

Pierre tugs at his sleeves, brushes off some invisible specks, runs his fingers through his hair. As black as ever, but already thinning in front.

"Is this a complaint?"

"God, no."

"Good."

He pours himself a glass of brandy from the decanter on the side table, spilling some. He is careless, or his hand shook, or both. There will be ugly stains on the surface.

"I was just asking."

"And I am just answering."

Marie-Louise watches her husband fiddle with the already empty glass. Upstairs Jacques is ordering Suzette to get him something for Master's papers. "Think for yourself, woman: a basket, a sack," he demands in the searing, self-assured voice of the military committee member he has just become. Recruiting volunteers for the army, Pierre has told her, with my full support.

She does imagine herself saying: I'm a king's bastard. My mother was a Deer Park girl first, then one of Julie Berlin's whores. But then, what? Will

Pierre with his lawyer's mind start interrogating her the way he did about the Versailles dowry? Who knew what and when? What if he forbids her to bring Véronique here?

Childless, she called herself.

"That widow for whom Aunt Margot left provisions in her will," she says. "The convent has closed. I'll have to take her in."

"One of Margot's midwives?" Pierre asks.

She shakes her head. "A poor widow in her dotage." A household matter best left to women, her voice says.

"Will you manage?"

"We have a spare room and no lodgers."

Upstairs Jacques yells after Suzette: "What were you thinking, you wretch!" The maid is calling on Hortense to be her witness. To what?

"I'd better see what this damn fracas is about," Pierre says, getting up.

Marie-Louise wipes the spot where Pierre spilled his brandy. The mark is already there, but not as bad as she feared. A bit of lemon oil will take care of it.

"It was nothing," Pierre says when he comes back, a few moments later, a thick dossier under his arm. Suzette took some paper for curling her hair. A clean sheet, so no writing has been lost. He must leave now; he'll be gone for a while. Danton is still in Belgium, sending new demands for inquiries in each letter. How many volunteered for the army? How many actually enlisted and left? As if Pierre didn't have enough to do with the trial. Why doesn't Danton ask others? Desmoulins, for instance? Is it because he thinks Desmoulins too important?

There is bitterness buried in these words, a hint of a chasm widening. Unavoidable, he would tell her if she asked. Equality is the trickiest game of all.

She walks Pierre to the hall, where Jacques, a leather sack across his chest, is opening the door locks one by one.

Pierre leans toward her, brushes her cheek with his lips, smelling of brandy. The dossier he has picked up is tied with a black ribbon.

"What will happen to . . ." she says, not wanting to say *the king*.

"The Capets?"

"Yes."

"Would they care what happened to you?"

Is it a tinge of anger she hears in his voice? Or just impatience.

"It would be us, if they won, Marie-Louise," Pierre says as he walks out into the street. "Only a complete fool would forget that!"

"The Widow Clerantin, one of Aunt Margot's protégées," Marie-Louise tells Hortense and the maids the following day. "The convent has closed, and she has nowhere else to go." To which Hortense says, "Mistress always had a soft heart," the tone of her voice leaving no doubt as to the impending sacrifices. What with prices bursting through the roof, bread vanishing from the bakery by late morning.

At the convent, Sister Geneviève deftly empties the contents of the table drawer into a linen sack and places it inside a battered green trunk with rope handles. And then there is the cat. "Will you take her with you?" Sister Geneviève asks. "La Grise has brought Madame Clerantin so much joy. If you don't take her, we'll have to let her loose in the streets."

"Are we going home, Adèle?"

The carriage driver Marie-Louise has hired is obliged to take a roundabout route home on account of the cordoned-off streets. Twice the carriage is stopped at checkpoints, questions are posed. Who? Why? Where? On what business?

Widow Clerantin, or Véronique, for Marie-Louise will not think of her as her mother, listens to these exchanges with a frown, clutching La Grise in her arms. If a voice is too loud, she shudders but mercifully keeps quiet. It is only when they finally stop on rue du Cygne that she exclaims loud enough to make the driver wince: "This is not where I live!"

"You live here now."

"Have we moved, Adèle? Is Papa here now?"

The front door opens, and Hortense appears, eyeing the green trunk with suspicion. "Is that all she has brought with her?" she asks.

Since the driver refuses to carry the trunk inside—he has wasted enough time already—the maids have to be summoned. It's best to hurry. The coffee seller is already outside, wanting to know what is happening. A few days ago, the rue du Cygne tobacconist had been robbed in broad daylight. Two men claiming to be from the Commune, one with a musket and the other with a flour sack, took all his money, pipes and a bag of his best tobacco. When he tried to call for help, they called him a bloody royalist and smashed the window.

Suzette and Cecile lift the trunk easily enough.

"It is mine," Véronique says. "Don't touch it."

"Yours," Hortense agrees. "But you cannot carry it upstairs all by yourself, can you?"

Véronique gives her a sharp look but doesn't argue.

The spare room has been fumigated, the bed frame scalded with hot water. The straw mattress is new, for the old one had to be burned. The mirror, the small table and the walnut armoire—cracked but without any signs of woodworms—come from the attic. So does the carpet, the one Pierre cast out of their bedroom. The armchair and footrest are Aunt Margot's. The footrest is embroidered with hummingbirds hovering over open blooms. When Jean-Louis was little he called them bird-flies.

La Grise, released from Véronique's arms, dives under the bed, turning into another of Hortense's worries. "Are we to keep that cat locked up now? To piss on the carpet?" For her, a peasant's daughter, all cats belonged in the yard, catching vermin, earning their keep.

Cecile knocks on her head.

Perhaps, Marie-Louise thinks, if I keep it all to myself. Perhaps if it is my secret only.

~⁂~

In the pantry a smoked ham dressed with bay leaves is already hanging from the ceiling. So are two rabbits, waiting to be skinned and de-limbed. Hortense has enough fine flour for Christmas baking. They will have homemade bread, madeleines and a sponge cake with sugar glaze and almonds. What luxury, since now even the oatmeal cake has grated carrots or beetroot in it to make it go further.

How much will it all cost?

People remember past kindnesses, Hortense says, shooing Marie-Louise out of the kitchen for being underfoot.

Past kindnesses or not, Marie-Louise had to double Hortense's housekeeping allowance, and then some. The assignats, or paper money as people call them with disdain, are worth less and less. Many merchants refuse to accept them altogether, demanding silver coins. But, as Aunt Margot would say, Christmas only comes once a year.

I'm doing what you've asked of me, Marie-Louise assures Aunt Margot in her thoughts a week later. *I'm fulfilling my duty the best I can. The doctor is coming to see her.*

The upstairs room is kept locked ever since Madame Clerantin gave the maids a fright when they caught her halfway down the stairs, in her night-shift, barefoot, looking for some Lisette. In a sack she was carrying, the maids found a teaspoon, a handful of bone buttons and a wood splinter wrapped with a piece of yellow wool.

The key hangs on a nail outside.

Véronique looks up when Marie-Louise enters. Her loose hair is tangled, her outer skirt stained blue. With ink?

"Adèle! Where have you been?"

"I'm not Adèle."

"Why are you angry, Adèle?"

"I'm not angry."

"But you are."

Downstairs, in the kitchen Hortense is calling Suzette to get moving. "She is always like that, isn't she, the fat one?" Véronique murmurs, cocking her head, mimicking Hortense's pursed lips and folded arms. "I've never liked her."

A handful, the maids say. Suzette was told to go to hell where her devil lover is waiting for her. Cecile, who was only trying to undress her for the night, has teeth marks on her wrist. And that trunk of hers? Reeking of mildew, but Madame Clerantin won't let anyone open it.

Véronique beckons to Marie-Louise to lean closer. "Where am I, Adèle?" she asks in a whisper. "You can tell me. I can keep a secret."

"I'm not Adèle," Marie-Louise repeats, her voice still calm but barely.

The cat is sticking its nose out from behind the trunk, which does smell of mildew. "Come out," Véronique coos. "Adèle won't hurt you. She just wants to play."

La Grise slowly abandons her hiding place and rubs herself against Marie-Louise's leg. A few scratches on her furry neck later, she yawns, revealing her sharp teeth and a pink tongue.

"See how she likes you, Adèle."

We have a cat now, Marie-Louise will write to Jean-Louis. *A bit hard to please, but you will find her amusing. Her name is La Grise and she belongs to a new lodger I was obliged to take in, quite unexpectedly. La Grise is timid but very lively, though still not yet in Hortense's good graces as she has failed to catch a single mouse.*

She needs to prepare her son for the changes that await him when he comes home for his short Christmas break. La Grise and her antics make for a good, innocuous beginning.

❧

Philippe Pinel comes well recommended. A doctor from Toulouse, who before the revolution couldn't get a medical appointment in Paris for lack of patronage, is now one of the very best in the city, particularly for mental disorders. Madeleine said that there is even talk of him heading the Bicêtre hospital.

The doctor arrives at rue du Cygne on foot.

"What a handsome house, Citizeness Vernault," he says when Suzette brings him to the best room. Quite ordinary-looking, short, dressed in black, a cockade pinned to his lapel. His gray hair is tied with a black ribbon.

The house may be handsome, but it is far too close to Les Halles. Just the other day a runaway pig rooted through the back garden, making a mess of it. The smells from the market—if the wind comes their way—can be off-putting, which, as Aunt Margot would say, is the kindest thing one can say about stink. But perhaps the doctor lives in even more modest circumstances.

"Yes," Marie-Louise says. "It belonged to my late aunt."

"Whom I had the honor to meet on a few occasions."

"Paris can be small that way."

"In many ways."

"Very true."

Before he examines Citizeness Clerantin, Dr. Pinel wants to know the patient's likes, aversions, appetite. Any observation, however small, may be of significance in his diagnosis. He trusts a midwife's keen eye. He always has. "He is quite a flatterer, though, so be warned," Madeleine also said.

"She likes her food. Her cat. Her appetite is excellent. Dislikes when the maids undress her, but then forgets about it and thinks they are her friends."

"Her moods?"

"Unpredictable. Anxious, lately. Demanding to be taken places."

"Any particular places?"

"Yesterday she asked me to take her to her mother. She said she was waiting for her and was very sick."

"And what happened when you offered to take her there?"

"I didn't offer. Her mother is long dead."

"Not in her mind."

Marie-Louise wonders if this is a reproach, but there is nothing but attentiveness in the doctor's face. She has heard that his patients get calmer and happier, even if they do not lose their delusions.

"What else does she say?"

Marie-Louise recounts the mutterings she has heard.

Everything disappears. They are stealing everything from me. I have nothing. Nothing. When did my mother die? Why didn't anyone tell me? Where was I at that time? And my father died, too? But when? Everyone I ask about is dead. You know what? Now I'm afraid to ask about anyone.

"And why is she here?"

Marie-Louise is ready with her well-rehearsed answer.

"My aunt paid for her upkeep at the Sisters of Charity. The convent closed."

Philippe Pinel listens, perfectly still, his hands clasped. Not unlike a priest taking confession, a comparison he would find, no doubt, utterly inappropriate.

"How does she treat you?"

"She calls me Adèle. She thinks I'm younger than she is. That we used to play together. Jumping until her mother told us to stop."

"She is quite fond of you then."

"Yesterday she said I was treating her like a servant and will be mighty sorry one day."

The room smells of vinegar, Hortense's remedy for all household mishaps. Véronique rises from the bed, her head cocked, her eyes flicking from the doctor to Marie-Louise.

"Has he sent for me?" she asks. The skirt she is wearing doesn't match the bodice, which she has put back to front and tied up crudely. She is barefoot; her shoes are nowhere to be seen.

"This is precisely what we shall talk about, Madame," Dr. Pinel answers with a deft bow. "Alone, if Citizeness Vernault will kindly allow us."

"Go, go." Véronique dismisses Marie-Louise with an impatient wave of her hand, letting the doctor slip his arm under hers and lead her toward the window.

Downstairs in the kitchen La Grise, allowed to leave Véronique's room for the first time, curls around Marie-Louise's ankles, making her furry figures of eight. Marie-Louise picks up a scrap of cow lung and drops it to the floor. La Grise pounces on it and carries it into the corner, pins it with her paw and gnaws at it.

"As if there were not enough mice in the world," Hortense grumbles, but then sets a steaming cup of real coffee in front of Marie-Louise.

"Guess who it is from?" she asks as Marie-Louise takes a long, slow delightful sip.

"The Valours?"

"Do you remember Pascaline?"

She doesn't. Not until Hortense reminds her of Aunt Margot's lodger from when Marie-Louise first came to live at rue du Cygne.

"Our Haughty One," Hortense continues. Pascaline, who sniffed at a piece of soap and said, I'm used to better, did well for herself. Married an innkeeper. Came by with the coffee for dear Mistress Leblanc. Could not bear thinking dear Mistress Leblanc who is so fond of coffee would have to go without it this

Christmas. How could it be you didn't see the death notice, Hortense asked. Last February! We had mourners come for three days.

"But still, Mistress would've been pleased."

"She would."

"What on earth is going on there?" Hortense asks, pointing at the ceiling. The sounds coming from Véronique's room are indeed odd. Heels tapping on the floor, in circles. Is she dancing? With the doctor? She must have found her shoes, then.

"Are you certain he is a real doctor?" Hortense asks, rolling her eyes.

Lymphatic dementia is the diagnosis.

Back in the best room, Philippe Pinel enumerates the symptoms: thoughtlessness, extreme incorrectness both in behavior and speech. The mind creates a succession of isolated ideas that escape rational explanation or judgment. Passionate feelings surface, only to be forgotten a moment later. There is severe loss of memory regarding what has just occurred, while the patient retains some selective and very vivid memories of the distant past.

Marie-Louise nods.

"The important question, of course, is what are the causes," Dr. Pinel continues. "I believe these could include a sudden severe reversal in life, from success to failure, from a dignified state to disgrace and being forgotten. It is of great help to know the patient's former life. Be aware of what might've triggered an outburst, a crisis. Grief after big loss, unhappy love affair perhaps. Are you aware of any such occurrences?"

If Marie-Louise hesitates, it is for a brief moment only. "She lost her husband, her children. Wouldn't that be enough?"

"Perhaps."

For treatment Philippe Pinel does not recommend opium. Yes, it would diminish Citizeness Clerantin's anxiety but at what price! He has seen asylum patients sitting motionless, lost inside their sedated minds.

"What can we expect?"

"I cannot say. Illness is never constant. There might be more lucid moments, followed by even more muddled ones. Patients have surprised me before."

In the end, in spite of his reluctance to prescribe any *materia medica*, Dr. Pinel does recommend regular bloodletting and laxatives. Preventing nervous excitement is always easier than stopping it. Soon, he assures Marie-Louise, she will discover ways of calming the patient he cannot yet foresee.

In the hallway where Suzette is waiting with the doctor's hat and winter overcoat, Dr. Pinel adds, "Citizeness Clerantin likes to laugh and is a spirited dancer. I consider both to be most effective treatments."

~❦~

A week later, on the morning of December 24, Marie-Louise picks Jean-Louis up at the college gate, and they walk to rue du Cygne together. By the Pantheon they stop to see a man on stilts juggle flaming torches. Children crowd in front of a puppet show in which the Holy Family keeps knocking on the doors of palaces, begging for shelter, only to be chased away.

"I'm not a child, Maman," Jean-Louis says when she asks if he would like to stay a bit and watch.

His voice is light enough but still there is something odd, unsettling about her son, Marie-Louise thinks. He is avoiding her eyes as they walk; he is brushing his nose with his fingers, licking his lips. When, just as they are about to turn the corner to rue du Cygne, she asks him what is wrong, he says he needs more money. He has been very frugal with his allowance, but everything is getting so terribly expensive. The laundrywoman charges double what she used to a month ago. So does the hairdresser. Of course he can have more money, she tells him. She cannot have him in dirty linens, can she?

At home, Hortense and the maids surround their golden boy, marveling at how he has grown since October. Taller than Hortense, that they expected. Taller than Suzette, fine. But now Jean-Louis is taller than his maman, by a whole inch! How handsome he is, too. Cecile declares that young ladies must be lining up by the college gate to steal a glimpse of him. Isn't it so, she asks, and Jean-Louis calls her "silly old Cecile." Not that silly, am I, she shoots back. And not *that* old.

A man, not a child. Suzette calls him "Young Master" and says she wouldn't recognize him if she passed him in the street! Which, of course, is a blatant lie but very pleasing to Jean-Louis.

He repays them with his delight at being home again. Eating everything they put on his plate, telling them outlandish stories about school. They may think it is all toil and drudgery, but it is not. From his dormitory window he can see soldiers practicing formations in the courtyard, or bayoneting straw men. A friend took him to see a perfumer who lives just by the college gate, a man with a wooden leg. How did he lose it? A crocodile attacked him in Africa.

"What was a perfumer doing in Africa?"

"He was not a perfumer in Africa, but a sailor. He has tattoos on his real leg. He has a parrot, too. With a very long tail. It swears when it wants a treat."

"Oh, how I missed you, my dear boy!"

"Maman, tell Hortense I won't come back if she doesn't stop crying!"

Jean-Louis is home for two days only. This is a sore thought, since many college scholars are taking a longer winter break. "Scholars, but not aspirants," Pierre said. "Many, but not all." The principal has assured him that the school will remain open. Masters will hold classes, supervise study hours. Exams are still scheduled for June. How would keeping Jean-Louis at home be better?

From the upstairs room the sound of footsteps. On Dr. Pinel's recommendation this is the time for Véronique's morning walk through the house. Riddled with disappointments, if the maids are to be believed. "The music room is gone, too?" Véronique complains.

"Is it that lodger you wrote to me about, Maman?" Jean-Louis asks. "The widow with the funny cat?"

There will be no wandering through the house today, and the result is predictable.

"Walking in circles like a caged badger," Hortense mutters, rising. "If she doesn't stop, her feet will start bleeding again."

"You stay here," Marie-Louise says. "I'll see if I can get her to sit down."

"Just don't give her any more cake. She'll just hide it under her pillow."

Jean-Louis laughs. "That would be such a waste," he says.

"Not funny," Hortense says, sternly. "Try getting the stains out."

Upstairs Véronique is circling the room with unsteady steps, head bent, muttering. "People are terrible. They steal everything. I have nothing left."

"Steal what?"

Véronique raises her hand to her head.

"A bonnet?"

No, not a bonnet. Something red, something she wants back. "Lisette might know where it is. Tell her to come here right away."

Don't argue with her, Dr. Pinel said. Distract her.

The dress for the evening festivities is hanging on the wardrobe door. Blue, with clusters of white roses and lace-trimmed sleeves. Widow Clerantin, Suzette says, is very particular about her dresses. Fusses with folds and lace. Always reminds her not to press satin too hard when she irons.

"What a beautiful dress!"

"You are not listening, Adèle," Véronique says, stopping in front of Marie-Louise. Too close. "Where is Lisette?"

"I don't know."

The room looks bare now, for Hortense ordered the maids to remove first the carpet, then the curtains. "Let's just say easier to clean like that" was all she would tell Marie-Louise, though the maids were more forthcoming with complaints of urine puddles behind the curtain. The mirror is also gone, for Véronique insisted there was someone in there, spying on her. "I'm not stupid," she said when Hortense tried to convince her it was her own reflection. "I know who you are. I know more than you think."

Thank God for La Grise, Marie-Louise thinks when the cat jumps out from under the bed, making Véronique giggle. A moment later she settles calmly into her armchair, La Grise on her lap.

Downstairs it is even noisier than before: neighbors have left offerings, wine, a basket of apples, a plate of fried giblets. Madeleine and Anne, who have just dropped by to see Jean-Louis, are in the best room. "Don't worry, dear boy, I won't tell you how much you have grown! I promise," Madeleine says as Marie-Louise walks in. Anne demands an account of his school days, which Jean-Louis gives with delight. Master Simons has made them reenact the

Battle of Thermopylae. Master La Garde allows them to ask each other questions in Latin.

No footsteps upstairs. La Grise is earning her keep.

Anne has news: she is leaving Paris. She has only seen her husband five times since he became an army surgeon and with three children, she wants to be close to her parents. Madeleine rages against yet another midwife opening up shop on the street where she lives. A woman no one knows has been sworn with alarming carelessness. The midwifery exam has been simplified, requirements to attend lectures and autopsies dropped. Wasn't the revolution all about making things better?

There will be no midnight Mass this Christmas; the Commune ordered all churches closed. For public safety. Hortense has called the orders godless and crossed herself. Oh, we do believe there is a God, Pierre has said. We also believe that Citizen Jesus would have had nothing to do with the Church. That he would have taken *our* side.

The mantel looks empty without the old manger that Aunt Margot always brought down from the attic on Christmas Eve. If anyone else notices its absence, they don't ask. Just like no one is talking about the king's trial.

Or about Pierre.

The guests are all gone by the time Pierre finally arrives home. Tired, cold from walking, but here, pecking Marie-Louise's cheek, patting Jean-Louis's cropped hair, motioning to Jacques to remove his riding boots and take them to the kitchen to be cleaned.

The depositions against the king have all been made, evidence brought forth. The defense will begin right after Christmas.

From the kitchen comes Cecile's giggle at something Jacques has said, followed by Hortense snapping, "Mind your language on this day out of all days, you heathen."

"Mind yours, you stubborn peasant."

"Better stubborn than deluded."

Véronique is descending the stairs in her blue dress, wobbly in her heeled shoes. Suzette is right beside her, holding her arm, until she is safely down, beside Marie-Louise.

At the sight of Pierre, Véronique stifles a gasp.

"Aunt Margot's protégée?" Pierre asks. "A pleasure to meet you, Citizeness Clerantin."

Véronique gives him a wry smile and mutters to Marie-Louise, "Now he thinks he can say whatever he wants. But where was he all this time?"

If Pierre has heard it, he lets it pass. A widow in her dotage, Marie-Louise did say, did she not?

Jean-Louis greets Citizeness Clerantin with an elaborate bow.

"I've never thought you would come to see me," Véronique says, if a bit stiffly, but with evident pleasure.

"But I did," Jean-Louis says, beaming a smile.

"You did," Véronique agrees. "Who is he?" she then whispers to Marie-Louise.

"He is my son," Marie-Louise answers, hoping not to be called Adèle and make things worse.

"You are too young to have a son," Véronique says, which is vague enough to pass for an ordinary compliment.

Pierre takes Jean-Louis aside, putting his arm over his shoulder. Marie-Louise strains her ears, but she can only hear bits and pieces of their conversation. "Yes, Father" gets repeated quite a few times. Then: "Latin . . . not quite . . . but I truly am . . ."

"I want to eat," Véronique declares, quite grandly. "I am hungry."

It is not the Christmas Réveillon as they used to have in this house, but it is good enough. In the dining room the table is set and decorated with yew branches. There is rabbit pie, rabbit stew, thin slices of smoked ham. Desserts are waiting on a side table: baked apples with honey, gingerbread, a plate of madeleines and a marzipan cake with a layer of quince preserves, Aunt Margot's winter specialty, spooned over it.

The feast begins with the stroke of midnight. Hortense, the maids and Jacques will join them at the table, though for now they are still busy bringing in food, pouring wine and licorice water into glasses. "Ours is a republican household," Pierre has said.

Jean-Louis has taken the seat beside Véronique and is putting food on her plate. "This?" he asks, pointing at the rabbit pie, and she nods. "This, too?" he asks, lifting a slice of the smoked ham, and she gives another nod. Hortense has finally lowered herself into her seat, panting from exertion. Earlier that day Marie-Louise suggested hiring a new kitchen maid to help her. To which Hortense snapped, "I'm not that old, yet."

Pierre's toast is to liberty, equality and brotherhood. "And justice," he adds, "so long awaited and so long delayed." They drink to that, and to Aunt Margot's memory, may she rest in peace, richly deserved. And to Jean-Louis, who has been very much missed in this house.

"What have you learned at school so far, son?" Pierre asks.

"The importance of good conduct and moral behavior."

"Which means?"

"Accepting discipline and authority."

How hard Jean-Louis tries to please his father, answering questions promptly, with clarity and precision. No stammering, no hesitation.

"I will be a lawyer, Father. I've made up my mind."

"Will you? And why is that? Just to please me?"

"I do not see any other way to create a just society."

"You don't see?"

"There is no other way."

Véronique sits bewildered, covering her ears every time a voice is raised. On her plate, a mess. She has managed to dip a piece of cake in rabbit sauce and spits it out with disgust. The tablecloth around her is stained red with wine. "Oh, I'm an awful girl," she says. Hortense, ever watchful, sprinkles the spot with coarse kitchen salt. Sometimes Véronique leans to Marie-Louise to whisper: "He gave me red stockings, you know . . . Look at him now, thinking himself so important . . . Ask him about the money he stole from me . . . They all steal, you know." A good thing Pierre doesn't hear any of that. Or Véronique's complaining: "Why have you brought me here, Adèle? How much longer am I to sit here, waiting? As if I had nothing better to do, for God's sake!"

Marie-Louise has given up on answers. Luckily Jean-Louis, giddy at having pleased his father, has found a way to make Véronique laugh. Nothing much, a few stock gestures. Fingers playing the flute on his nose,

click-clacking with his tongue, slapping his own hand and making a startled face.

"You, young man, are quite a charmer!"

"So, Madame, are you!"

A kind soul, our Jean-Louis, Aunt Margot would have said.

Later in their bedroom, Marie-Louise, hair let loose, sits on her side of the bed
in her nightshift, untying her garters. Pierre is bending over the basin, splashing cold water on his face. He has taken off his shirt, dropped it to the floor.
The towel follows. Will he come to her? Or should she go to him?

Morons, Pierre mutters. Fools. From the slight slurring of words, it is clear
that he has had too much wine.

He doesn't mean the king's defense. He means those who've made him a
target of vitriolic attacks.

What has happened?

The Convention has become a cesspool of jealousy and suspicion. Danton's
enemies are forever harping on about his secret funds. Demanding accounts
as if they had the right.

Why him?

He is Danton's man. A factotum, he has been called to his face often
enough. While the real enemies of the revolution are growing in strength.

Pierre heads for his side of the bed, past her, and throws himself on it with
a grunt. Is it an apology or an excuse?

Marie-Louise leans forward to snuff out the candle, but Pierre stops her.
He no longer wants to talk about the Convention or Danton's enemies but
about Jean-Louis. All these lofty declarations at the table! I'll be a lawyer,
Father! As if one became a lawyer merely by declaring it.

Pierre, it turns out, has met with the principal, only to learn that the only
area Jean-Louis has truly improved at is wasting his time.

What has he done now?

"What has he done?" Pierre repeats Marie-Louise's question in a mocking
voice. "How about skipping lessons? Sneaking into the soldiers' barracks to
play cards? Keeping company with a well-known wastrel by the name of

François Cocarde, the two of them heard muttering *Vive le Vin*, when everyone else shouted *Vive la Nation*?

"Champagne let them get away with it this time, out of respect for me, but he won't next time.

"Your son," Pierre says, "is a disgrace to the Vernault name."

"Our son," she corrects him, making sure her voice is light. For surely Pierre is making too much of schoolboys' pranks. "Were you always a perfect son in your father's eyes?" she asks.

Pierre looks at her as if she made no sense at all.

"What does that have to do with anything I've just told you?"

This is how the quarrel begins, dragging out old accusations. She has always been too lenient; he too strict. A child needs encouragement; a child needs to obey.

It gets worse. She and Aunt Margot have always been making decisions behind his back.

"What decisions, Pierre?"

"That dowry paid in installments, when Margot had all the money in her hands."

"You are still angry at her for that?"

"That lodger of yours, Marie-Louise. Did you even ask if I wanted her here?"

"I've told you why I had to take her in."

"Precisely. You told me. You didn't ask. Just so that some lowlife at the Commune Section could wonder why I didn't register her myself?"

"You are never here."

Pierre is sitting up in bed now, away from her. What is he going to tell her now? That by law, everything a wife inherits belongs to the husband? That if he wished he could turn her out of the house?

"Do you have any idea of the duplicity around me, the blatant lies everywhere?" he asks. "Do I have to endure that at home, too?"

Is it merely wine that has turned anger into self-pity, or is it a gesture of appeasement?

Marie-Louise snuffs out the candle and waits. In the dark, Pierre's voice is disembodied, distant. He lowers himself and then extends his legs but does not move closer to her. A few moments later, she can hear him snoring.

❧

"Mistress says to please come by today. She is just back from Sèvres."

The messenger is Danton's servant boy. Foxy, Marie-Louise thinks of him not without sympathy, focused on what is in front of him, looking for his chance to swoop, grab, run; appear or disappear. A boy against whom her own son wouldn't stand a chance. If it ever came to it, that is.

Even with a two-wheeled chaise, it takes Marie-Louise twice as long as it should have to reach the Dantons' apartment.

"I apologize," Gabrielle says, as if the checkpoints and blockades were her personal failings. She is standing by the mantel, nervously pulling at the torn sleeve of her dressing gown. She has put on more weight; her cheeks are puffed, eyes red-rimmed. "I find it hard to even think of making myself presentable," she adds, as if Marie-Louise has chastised her.

The room is stuffy, baskets of clothes still lined up against the wall. In the corridor the sound of a child's footsteps breaking into a wild run. "Horsey, more horsey!"

Gabrielle's voice quivers. The visit with her parents didn't do her much good. It was nice enough for the children, but her mother can be so fussy, demanding everything be done her way. On top of it her maid openly carried on with her mother's steward, declaring it was her own business and no one else's.

"Servants are so terribly straightforward now," Gabrielle says with a heavy sigh. "I don't really like it. Though I suppose they have the right to be."

"December is always dreary for everyone," Marie-Louise says.

"You mean I'm not that special?" Gabrielle attempts to joke. "Is that to make me feel better?"

"It should."

"All right then."

Big with child, clumsy in her movements, Gabrielle makes a few wobbly moves toward her, the carpet muffling her steps. Why is she wearing heels now? Her ankles are still swollen, covered with red blotches. She is not wearing stays, though, which is good.

"Lie down, Gabrielle. Let me take a proper look at you."

Gabrielle lowers herself to the chaise longue and unties her dressing gown, revealing a stained cambric shift underneath. Her belly is taut, with new stretch marks around her navel. The baby has not yet turned, but this is no reason for concern. There is still plenty of time.

"Does it hurt if I press here?"

"No."

"Here?"

"No."

A midwife's very presence is always a reassurance, though Marie-Louise finds it harder and harder to keep her patients calm. A brewer's wife from the Marais showed her a knife she keeps under her pillow. "For when they come here for me," she said. Austrians? Prussians? The street mob? More and more things are better left unsaid.

"People think the worst of you with such utter ease," Gabrielle says. Vicious rumors are all over Paris, breeding like fruit flies, out of thin air. Used to be just about George, about how Citizen Danton took bribes from anyone who would pay. Or how he kept mistresses. Or got drunk and smashed chairs at some tavern. But now they are also about her.

"They call me a thief," Gabrielle continues. "They say I stole things from the Tuileries when it was ransacked. They say I have a wardrobe filled with royal robes, petticoats, shifts. That I have a silver hairbrush engraved with *A*, for Antoinette. That I have royal butter in my pantry. That I drink royal chocolate. That I put royal cream on my face every night."

All proof that Gabrielle Danton wishes to be the queen of France herself. As if she were an aristocrat, not an innkeeper's daughter!

That is not all, Gabrielle continues, her voice breaking. Yesterday, in the street, a man spat in her face. An old man, too, with a long gray beard and a filthy jacket hopping with fleas. Called her a republican whore who turned her husband against the king. As if she could make George do anything he doesn't want to do.

"When is George coming back?" Marie-Louise asks.

Gabrielle doesn't know. She has received five letters from Belgium so far, each promising something different. In the latest he vowed to kiss her and the children on January 1.

"Four more days, then."

Gabrielle nods. "The scullery maid is gone," she whispers. "She stole my favorite blue shawl and George's red waistcoat. What if she has cursed me? What if this baby kills me?"

Marie-Louise sits with Gabrielle through the sobbing that follows, holding her hand, fighting her own unease. Too many things are out of order with this pregnancy. Pulse too fast. Skin too pale. Breath getting sour. Now these despondent moods.

"Are you warm enough, Gabrielle?"

"No."

Marie-Louise fusses with the blanket, woolen, checkered, woven with green, red and blue, determined to control what can be controlled. Those damn heels, she tells Gabrielle, have to go. Wear slippers; go barefoot. Anything but risk stumbling and falling. Also, don't even think of unpacking these baskets. The maid can manage. What else does she have to do when the boys go to sleep? Dream of the steward at Sèvres?

Is that a snicker I hear, Gabrielle? Or a sniffle? Or both?

Gabrielle blows her nose into her lace-trimmed handkerchief and lifts her head up. She will do as she is told. She has a pair of old slippers that will do nicely. A bit worn out, but wide and comfortable. She is not leaving the house much anyway, and now wishes to leave even less. Besides, February is not that far off, is it?

Marie-Louise steers the conversation to lighter topics. How fast the children grow. How they change, and yet something in them always remains unchanged, doesn't it? The essence, visible from the day they were born. That look of curiosity Jean-Louis always had, that need to climb every tree, every hill. That intensity of despair if thwarted.

It's all there, a seed of the future.

"Or the past," Gabrielle adds. François-George has her own father's absorption in whatever he is doing. Stacking up blocks, riding his rocking horse. Frowning, too, just like his grandpa. Whereas Antoine is more like

George. Whatever he wants must be right now, or he will bang his head on the floor. Or scream until he begins to choke. "We should have named them François and Antoine-George, but who knew."

Gabrielle closes her eyes. Her full cheeks have slowly taken on a rosy hue. Her feet, elevated on a cushion, are warm, the skin clear enough now. Compresses with water mixed with vinegar will do the rest.

The sound of soldiers marching comes through the window. A dog howls. Another answers. When Jean-Louis was small he insisted he knew what dogs talked about. Always simple things it turned out: where to find food, a warm place to sleep, the company of other dogs.

A boy still, though turning into a man. Taking after whom? Not Pierre. This is all Marie-Louise can say. The rest is best left alone.

Thinking Gabrielle asleep, Marie-Louise rises to leave. She is already at the door when Gabrielle asks, "Why does everyone always blame the women?"

Part Five

Paris, 1793

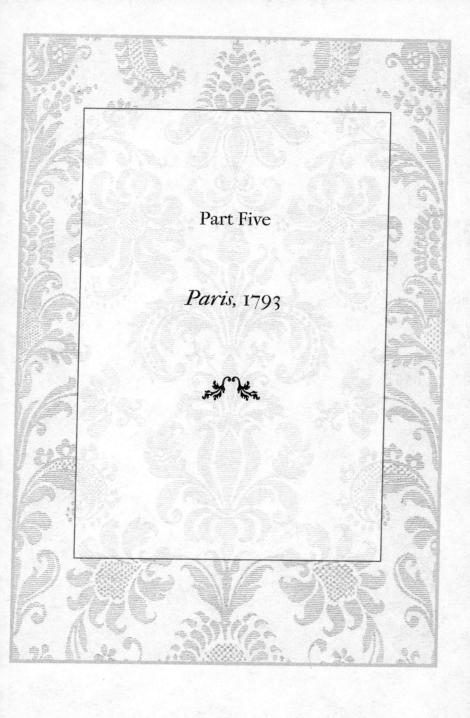

January

"I HAVE SOME unsettling news, Citizeness Vernault."

Marie-Louise registers the pauses in Principal Champagne's speech, the caution with which he chooses his words.

Jean-Louis hasn't been seen at the college for two days. His things are gone, all except his books, that is. The students closest to him have nothing but conjectures. There was the winter break, of course, which might have . . .

She doesn't understand. "For two whole days? And no one took note until now?"

Principal Champagne's lips twist into a disapproving grimace. "As I have been trying to explain," he continues, "we have had a lot of commotion with scholars leaving for the winter break. And with the soldiers coming and going. Your son must have slipped out. Students have gone missing before. Mostly they have gone home. Quite a few have volunteered for the army."

"My son is only fifteen. Too young to enlist."

The principal thinks little of such motherly arguments. "The young have strong patriotic feelings, Citizeness. Many believe in sacrificing for their country."

He pauses, unsure if he should say more before Pierre arrives. They can hear him in the corridor already, announcing that Citizen Champagne is expecting him, demanding to hear what she already knows.

"Are you telling me you have no idea where my son is?"

Citizen Champagne raises his voice to match Pierre's: "I'm telling you that your son left the school grounds without permission. He has betrayed our trust. As you well know, Citizen Vernault, Equality College has standards to uphold."

The two of them are like bulls staring each other down, stomping, huffing, puffing themselves up. Is there nothing more important now than who wins?

"These students closest to him," Marie-Louise interrupts. "What do they say?"

François Cocarde confessed that the two of them talked about running away. Attaching themselves to one of the units, heading for Holland.

"So why is Jean-Louis gone and this François is still here?"

The principal is staring at both of them now, his anger barely contained. "Because it was all fanciful talk. Because there had never been any real plans."

"When did the Cocarde boy notice that Jean-Louis was missing?"

"Last night, at bedtime."

"And he didn't alert anyone?"

"He assumed your son was playing cards at the barracks. Expected him to sneak inside before dawn."

"Has that happened before?"

"Alas, it has."

Citizen Champagne straightens up. He will be blunt. If Jean-Louis indeed ran away with the soldiers, it was not from a surfeit of patriotic feelings. As Citizen Vernault has already been informed, Jean-Louis's academic progress has been dismal. Having been warned—and warned repeatedly—that he was in danger of failing his exam, Jean-Louis did nothing to improve his standing.

They want examples? Asked to provide an example of syllogism, this is what he came up with: *Rocks are hard. Aristotle is hard. Aristotle is a rock.*

No, it was not meant as a joke.

The masters of Equality College are scrupulous in helping students avoid mistakes, even those arising from their own negligence. But they cannot perform miracles. No matter what some parents might expect.

Citizen Champagne rises from behind his desk. There is nothing left to say. In the matter of accounts, his have just been tallied up and found accurate.

They leave the school with nothing but promises of further communication should anything else become known. Jean-Louis may be anywhere. On his way to Holland or back home already. Winter, Champagne said stiffly at their parting, is a pretty harsh and unforgiving teacher. The young can be oblivious to the fact that reality doesn't bend to their wishes, but this never lasts long.

Pierre calls Jean-Louis a coward. Afraid to face his father, afraid to admit his failures. Irresponsible. Flighty.

Marie-Louise walks alongside her husband, half listening, willing Jean-Louis to be at home, waiting for them. Cold, shaken, but safe.

Deserting his duties, Pierre continues, callous, bent on doing only what he wishes. Where is it coming from? Surely not from the Vernault bloodline!

This is not a question. It doesn't need to be answered.

"After all we've done for him!"

"This is your fault, Pierre."

"You blame *me*?"

"Yes."

"How reasonable of you! And what precisely do you blame me for? For wishing him to do well at school? To become a lawyer like his father and grandfather? Is that such a terrible thing, to aim at a worthy goal?"

"You called him a disgrace to the Vernault name. Nothing he did ever pleased you."

It surprises her, the force of her own voice. A passerby, a beefy man in a brown jacket, stares at her, a woman harassing her man. The revolution has made women uppity, the word has it, demanding what is not reasonable, expecting far too much.

It surprises Pierre, too, for he pauses. But not for long.

Hers, he declares, is a woman's way. Wavering, unsure, weighing too many aspects of each thought, too many consequences of each action, coming up with excuses. And how, pray, is that better than being decisive? Knowing what needs to be done and just doing it?

Jean-Louis is not waiting for them at home. A search of his room reveals that his notebook with the accounts of Lapérouse's voyage is missing. Also a blanket, and Pierre's old canvas backpack with leather straps.

"So now my son is also a thief," Pierre says. "What else do I not know?"

"He took what he needed," Marie-Louise says. "This is his home. He is not a thief."

Which only makes things worse.

"I have tried for so long," Pierre says, heading for the door. "I've been thwarted at every step. My son has been mollycoddled, spoiled by everyone in this house. Is this the result you wanted, Marie-Louise?"

The door slams behind him.

In the kitchen, Hortense is smashing boiled carrots into a pulp. Suzette and Cecile are sobbing. From Véronique's room, blissfully, silence.

In the best room, Marie-Louise sinks into the green ottoman. Tears fill her eyes, too quickly to stop them from flowing.

Pierre will be back, she tells herself. He will not leave her alone like this, terrified, imagining the worst. They are both terrified, aren't they? No matter what they said.

They are both hoping Jean-Louis will return. Perhaps he is hiding in the garden? Afraid to face his father? Will he come in now, with Pierre gone?

How she will chastise him then. Make him see how cruel this escapade was, how thoughtless. You've caused us pain and worry, she will say. Then she will clasp him to her heart.

Marie-Louise strains her ears. No sounds from the garden. None from the street.

Every few moments she calculates where Pierre might be now. At the corner of rue Saint-Denis? On rue Saint-Honoré? By the Tuileries already?

The light is fading around her. In the fireplace the last of the cherry logs have almost burned down. What remains is glowing white, scaled with ash.

The day passes, then another. Pierre doesn't come back. In the hastily scribbled notes that Jacques delivers, Marie-Louise pecks at her husband's words. Louis Capet's trial has entered the last stage. To chase after a wayward son at such time is a luxury he cannot allow himself. Revolutionary duty demands a heart that has not been spoiled by egoism. She is not to expect him back before the final vote and the sentencing.

Unbending, she thinks, cruel.

Revolutions, Marie-Louise, Pierre answers her in her thoughts, *are not made out of rose water.*

She puts the word out. People do remember past kindnesses, Hortense reminds her in the days that follow, as news trickles in. On the day Jean-Louis disappeared a contingent of soldiers left for Holland, but the recruiting officer who dispatched them saw no one resembling young Vernault. One of the midwives saw a boy fitting Jean-Louis's description heading toward Les Halles. A cheesemaker there noticed him helping a wine merchant load a cart. The merchant was from out of town, the cheesemaker said. Jean-Louis could've gotten a ride with him.

He could have, but did he?

Alone at the end of the day Marie-Louise still awaits her son's return. Those rapid steps she hears in the street could be his. This cough. This whisper. Hortense has noted signs. A bird pecking at the windowsill. A vision, just as she was emerging from sleep. Jean-Louis, standing in the door, saying he is on his way. "With that cheeky smile of his," she has said.

In the newspapers, accounts of the speeches in the king's defense: Hapless, not cruel. Mistakes not crimes. Think how history will judge your judgment.

In such moments years shrink. Auguste, the awkward boy on the palace roof, lets his fist open, the stone falls to the ground, the white angora limps away. "Look," he says, opening a map to show Marie-Louise the lands yet unknown, lands he wants to survey and measure.

Innocence needs no defender and crime deserves none, Pierre ended his last note. *For the harvest of liberty, the field must be sown with blood.*

❧

On Monday, January 21, all the gates of Paris are locked at dawn. The execution has been scheduled for ten o'clock.

The machine is ready, scaffolding built high, sawdust scattered. Citizen Capet will die in the place de la Révolution next to the empty pedestal where the bronze statue of Louis XV once stood. The old king, for even in her innermost thoughts Marie-Louise refuses to call him her father.

The morning is foggy and bitterly cold.

Murderous scum, someone has scrawled on their front door. It takes Suzette a whole hour to scrub the paint off. "Not a word about it when Master comes back," Marie-Louise has warned.

Hortense thrashes about the kitchen predicting floods, earthquakes, pestilence, famine. You raise your hand at the king, you open the gates for the Angel of Death.

The clock in the hall strikes ten. In Marie-Louise's thoughts Auguste is making plans for their escape. On horseback to the sea, onto a ship. Carrying sextants and astrolabes, for they know that maps can deceive. A leather-bound notebook fills up with questions to explore.

When the mantel clock chimes ten thirty, Marie-Louise crosses herself, muttering a simple prayer for the departing soul. Eternal rest grant unto him, O Lord.

Death can be a release. Every midwife knows that.

At noon when the city gates reopen, flakes of snow twirl in the air. The streets are crowded, noisy. Children run about, screaming. As if a line hasn't been crossed, the order of things not challenged, the course of history not irrevocably altered.

This is what Marie-Louise will add to the list of what Aunt Margot won't have to hear:

That Louis was pensive but not downcast on his way to the scaffold. Or that he merely hid his despair.

That he fought to keep his coat on or relinquished it peacefully. That he was outraged when the executioner tied his hands behind his back, or that he said: "Do as you please, I will drain the chalice to the dregs."

That he stumbled on the scaffold's icy stairs. Or that his steps were firm and steady.

That the priest said: "Courage." Or: "Ascend to Heaven, the son of Saint Louis!"

That his last words declared his innocence. Or that his last words were silenced with the roll of the drums.

That when the blade fell, the people danced with joy. Demanded to see his severed head. Dipped handkerchiefs in his blood. Tasted it and pronounced it well salted. Or that when the blade fell, there was silence.

That the grave was ten feet deep. That his body dissolved in quicklime. That there is nothing to remember, for the world has been reborn.

February

PIERRE HAS RETURNED TO rue du Cygne. Or rather, as Marie-Louise thinks, is dropping in for a day or two before departing again for Lyon or God only knows where. Getting his arse shaken in yet another rickety carriage, he says. Resting his head on some flea-ridden pillow.

Is that all you can tell me? she has asked.

Doesn't she know that the revolution is in danger? The Convention is swamped with reports of corruption. Public funds are being diverted to pay off private debts. Pierre is not the only one putting out fires. Danton is back in Belgium, where the French troops are being accused of daylight robbery. France is at war with England and Holland already. In whose interest is it to make Belgium an enemy?

Resentment simmers, thickens. Grudges stick to it, grow like patches of mold in the cellar. Conversations cut short, as the territory of what is best not to talk about expands.

Louis Capet and the execution. The street posters on the Parthenon wall: *Widow Capet, perverted mother, the people of Paris are watching you. Dogs are waiting to feed on your corpse.*

Jean-Louis, who could be anywhere. Starving, cold, ill.

"Thinking of no one but himself," Pierre has said.

Pierre has had enough of all her wild and baseless speculations. Why listen to rumors of another inconsequential sighting, another vanishing lead? Or pick at the past, which is Marie-Louise's own favorite torture. "Talk to me when you know what my son has to say in *his* defense."

Little, as it turns out.

For a letter finally arrives in the first week of February, addressed to

Mistress Marie-Louise Vernault. The boy who brings it doesn't know much. Some man at the market gave it to him to deliver to the midwife on rue du Cygne. Said he would be well rewarded. No, the man was not young and tall but short and stocky. He had black hair and was missing front teeth.

Dear Maman,

By the time this letter reaches you I'll be aboard a ship, a deckhand most likely, for I know so very little of use to an explorer. I've heard that many men have made a fortune in otter pelts on the North West Coast of America and this is where I want to go.

I beg your forgiveness for leaving in secret, but if I did come for your blessing, you would've stopped me, wouldn't you?

I'm not callous or thoughtless, Maman, and I've never wished to cause you and Father so much grief, but I can no longer pretend I can live the life Father wishes me to live. Please believe me, that if I could do otherwise, I would have.

Do not be angry with me, Maman, I beg of you. Please show this letter to Father if he finds it in his heart to read it.

I shall write again as soon as I know my whereabouts.

Your loving son
Jean-Louis

Underneath the signature a postscript: *Please tell Hortense her rabbit pie is the best in the world.*

The paper the note is written on is stained with oil in two places. The ink of the signature has run. When Marie-Louise lifts it up to her nostrils, she smells woodsmoke and soot.

The messenger has left well rewarded, promising to come back if he ever sees the man who gave him the note. Hortense, clearly softened by the postscript, declares that running away to sea is much better than joining the army. A smart boy like Jean-Louis, willing to be of use, will find his luck. She left home at fourteen and look at her now.

Marie-Louise forces a smile. How many weeks before another letter? Or months?

"Running away like a coward," Pierre says when he returns from Lyon. Just when France needs her young the most, traitors turn around and leave.

He might as well not have had a son at all.

~✦~

Gabrielle's mother arrives from Sèvres well ahead of the confinement. Gabrielle is grateful at first, but then the two of them quarrel bitterly. "Downright cruel," Madame Charpentier has called George's rushed return to Paris, just to vote for the king's death. In her ledger books George's prompt return to Belgium "revealed his true colors." His rambling letters promising to return before the baby arrives are "yet another proof of his callousness."

As if I need to be reminded of it, Gabrielle tells Marie-Louise.

Marie-Louise, worried by her patient's erratic pulse, has asked Dr. Souberbielle to examine Gabrielle twice already. Madame Danton, the doctor said both times, was strong and sturdy. An example for all patriotic mothers. This is what he said to Citizen Robespierre, who fully agreed.

When Gabrielle's waters break, all is as it should be. Marie-Louise arrives to find that the baby has turned, just as she hoped it would. Gabrielle is wearing a loose cambric shift. She has been purged and bled. A white bonnet is keeping the hair away from her face.

Madame Charpentier is all smiles and encouragement. "I hope it's a girl this time, Gabrielle," she has said. "Daughters are such a blessing." The boys have been sent to the neighbors upstairs, where Louise Gély has prepared a lovely toy kingdom. In the bedroom, aired and then warmed up, the curtains have been drawn. Clean towels and sheets are piling up on the armchair, all well worn and soft.

For the next few hours Marie-Louise keeps Gabrielle calm, monitoring the contractions. Coaxes her to change position when necessary, rubs her back to ease the gathering pain. Now and then Madame Charpentier comes in, to inquire about the progress and report on the boys. They've asked for their rocking horse for their toy kingdom. Then for the swirling top. Then they sent Louise for the book with the story about a naughty goat. Finally, Madame Charpentier put an end to this constant running up and down the stairs. Put the boys to sleep, she told Louise, and come back in the morning.

At midnight everything begins to fall apart.

Five hours into labor the contractions have weakened and grown far apart, Marie-Louise writes in her note to Dr. Souberbielle, marking it *Urgent. The pain intensifies; the cervix no longer dilates. In the last hour Madame Danton's pulse has quickened.*

"What is wrong?" Gabrielle asks.

Marie-Louise doesn't believe frightening her patient does any good, but Gabrielle is already frightened.

"You are getting weak. We might have to pull the baby out."

"We?"

"I've just written to Dr. Souberbielle."

Gabrielle nods, but she doesn't ask anything else, which is not a good sign. And she has closed her eyes.

"Don't go to sleep. Talk to me."

A whisper.

"I cannot hear you, Gabrielle."

"He promised he would be back." The bitterness in her voice leaves no doubt that she means George. "What is so important in this stupid Belgium that he cannot keep his promise?"

Marie-Louise adjusts the pillows, moistens Gabrielle's parched lips. It pleases her to see Gabrielle alert again.

"What did George say before leaving?" she asks to keep her talking.

"That I look like a balloon."

"Which is quite accurate," she says, expecting at least a chuckle, but Gabrielle doesn't laugh.

"God has turned away from us," she says.

In Gabrielle's feverish mind, God is angry with her, with George, with France. "Because we have murdered the king. Because we have flouted the divine laws."

"You haven't murdered anyone, Gabrielle. You have a baby to deliver."

Gabrielle's voice is growing stronger, more insistent. "I never wanted any of it, but that does not matter. No one is innocent. God will punish us all. He is punishing us already."

"You cannot know God's mind, Gabrielle."

But Gabrielle is not listening. She has grasped Marie-Louise's arm. "If I die, tell George what I said. Tell him to repent."

In the corridor someone is sobbing loudly. Madame Charpentier? Doesn't she know better?

"Promise me you will tell him, Marie-Louise."

"I will. Now, rest."

Outside the room the maid is praying to Saint Margaret for the alleviation of her mistress's pains, for comfort in her sufferings. Loud knocking on the front door silences her.

A moment later Marie-Louise hears Dr. Souberbielle demanding calm. Madame Danton is strong. She has everything going for her. He has seen women recover from worse.

Marie-Louise leans her back against the wall. The smells of blood and sweat and urine have soaked deep into her clothes. Her fingers are crusted with something brown and rusty.

The newborn, a boy, livid blue, limp, has taken a whole lot of slapping and rubbing before the first whimper. The red marks where the forceps dug into his soft skull are a reminder that the midwife's hands, however strong and nimble, are not always enough. The raw onion smeared under his nose made him grimace, but there has been no robust cry yet.

The doctor is talking to Madame Charpentier in a low, serious voice. Gabrielle has asked to see Louise Gély, who is with her now.

You have done everything you could have done, Marie-Louise, Aunt Margot's voice insists. *All is in God's hands now.*

When Louise emerges from Gabrielle's bedroom, she is shaking her head in disbelief. Gabrielle Danton has asked her to take care of her children.

"Has she lost her mind?" Madame Charpentier gasps. "You are still a child yourself!"

Louise shakes her head. Gabrielle has not lost her mind.

"Why would she even ask you, then? As if she didn't have a mother! Did you tell her?"

"No."

"What did you tell her, then?"

"That I would."

Madame Charpentier pushes Louise aside and walks into the bedroom. Marie-Louise is about to follow, but Dr. Souberbielle puts his hand on her shoulder to stop her.

He is right. The mother and daughter need to be alone.

From the bedroom the sobs come muffled, mixed up, indistinguishable.

Catherine, the maid, is tightening the shawl wrapped around her head and shoulders. Madame Charpentier, she says, has told her to bring a priest.

Gabrielle has been buried for five days by the time George Danton returns. Catherine, who has come for Marie-Louise, says that Master has locked himself in the bedroom. Every time she asks if he needs anything, he tells her to go to hell.

"Light the fire, Catherine, for God's sake," Marie-Louise says when they arrive at the Cour du Commerce apartment. She doesn't remember it ever being so damp and cold. "You don't want the children to get sick when they come back."

Antoine and François-George are upstairs with the Gélys, alone in their toy kingdom. The little brother they had been promised lingered for two days only. As if he knew he had killed his mother. As if life were already too heavy a burden.

Marie-Louise knocks on the bedroom door, presses the handle. To her surprise the door gives in.

The bed in which Gabrielle died is covered with a black bedspread. On the edge of it, George Danton sits. There are red blotches on his scarred cheeks. His eyes are bloodshot; his hands are clasped over the handles of Gabrielle's work basket.

Marie-Louise expects him to tell her to go to hell, too, but he doesn't.

"Shall I tell you what happened?"

He nods.

She tells him of the troubling signs, the doctor's assurances and the forceps with which he got the baby out, quickly enough. She tells him how, for a short while, they hoped it was over, until Gabrielle began to bleed, and nothing would stop it. How she said, "It is not that hard to die." How she fell asleep and then slipped away.

"Did she ask about me?"

"She asked if you had arrived."

"Anything else?"

"She wanted you to repent."

George Danton stares at her like a wounded bull, about to charge at his tormentor.

Marie-Louise can hear her own pulse loud in her ears. "She said that God had turned away from her, from you, from us all, because we have murdered the king."

The work basket smashes against the wall. Balls of yarn fall out, followed by knitting needles stuck through a tiny bootie. Pins scatter.

Thinking of the children, Marie-Louise bends to pick them up.

"Don't you dare touch it!"

She obeys, watching George Danton's massive body sink to the floor, racked with sobs.

"It's all her mother's doing . . . She thinks I killed her. She doesn't dare say it, but that is what she thinks . . . I made her daughter pregnant, so I seeded her death. I was not here when she was dying, so I have to be punished . . . That is why she put these vile thoughts into her head. If anyone needs to repent it is her!"

The following day Marie-Louise will hear how George Danton bullied his way into the Sainte-Catherine cemetery with a sculptor he knew. Together they dug Gabrielle's body out of her grave.

George embraced her and asked her forgiveness.

The sculptor took a death mask from which he will make a life-sized bust.

Then they put Gabrielle back into the ground.

March

RIOTS ARE ERUPTING ALL OVER FRANCE. In the Vendée, peasants arm themselves with scythes and pitchforks, chanting: *Long live the priests, religion and the king.* Inexplicable, Pierre has said, just before leaving again one cold, miserable evening. Give people freedom and they revolt against you. They call *that boy* Louis XVII!

It's so much better when he is gone, Marie-Louise thinks, sitting alone in the best room. From the direction of Les Halles come the sounds of a day winding down. The market animals have all been either sold or carted away. The merchants gone, the gleaners are now searching the stalls for anything still edible or useful.

Watch out, Aunt Margot's voice reminds. *This is how a marriage withers. In silence, in the dark.*

In the morning, when Suzette takes Madame Véronique her breakfast, a commotion upstairs. Madame is gone, and the room looks as if someone plundered it. Dresses are out of the wardrobe, thrown into a pile. The gray overcoat is missing. The green trunk has been left open, its contents rifled. The floor is strewn with papers, some merely crumpled, some torn.

Gone? How is it possible? Who left the door unlocked? Suzette and Cecile redden, look away. Has it happened before? Why didn't you tell me?

When the cat is away the mice play, Marie-Louise, Aunt Margot would've reminded her. A duty shirked.

What else has been going on?

Interrogated, the maids confess that Madame Véronique has been a handful since Christmas. Opening the window, leaning out, screaming, "They've taken everything from me! Thieves. Brigands. Scoundrels."

Suzette has had to explain herself to "that Peon girl." Like a criminal.

That Peon girl is a nosy neighbor. Eavesdropping, accusing Hortense of buying sugar and coffee from "eternal enemies of the people." Or worse.

"What could we have done?" Cecile asks. She means Véronique now. All that sobbing, asking for Adèle. Tell me where she is. Tell me what happened to her.

They search through the house, in vain, unless you count finding La Grise crouching in the root cellar, frozen in fright. Véronique is not on rue du Cygne, either. The neighbors, including the snotty Peon girl, have not seen her.

It is Hortense who notices muddy footprints in the backyard leading toward the gate. Hers? How far could she go? Les Halles?

At the market they ask around. Small, limping, Marie-Louise describes Véronique, gray overcoat. Black teeth. Our lodger. Not quite all there.

The cheesemaker who had once seen Jean-Louis help the wine merchant load his cart quips: "Another one of yours bolting, Mistress Vernault? What's so wrong with rue du Cygne?"

The word spreads. The Widow Clerantin, Mistress Leblanc's protégée . . . on her own . . .

There? By the shack with used clothes, making a ruckus?

It is Véronique. The ruckus is over some gray russet dress she insists is hers. The seller is calling for the wrath of Heaven. She is not a thief. Nor a scoundrel.

As Hortense whispers into the seller's ear, Marie-Louise takes Véronique by the elbow. "We've been looking for you everywhere," she says, perhaps too sharply.

Véronique, her face still distorted with anger, pulls her elbow free. "Who are you?" she asks.

"Don't you remember me? I'm Adèle."

"Don't lie to me," Véronique says, her chin trembling. "You are not Adèle. Adèle is dead."

~❧~

Véronique is safely back in her room, but the escape has taken its toll. She has been listless all week, sleeping most of the day. Or staring out the window when the maids get her out of bed and into the armchair. "Go away," she tells La Grise when the cat tries to get onto her lap. If she is to eat at all, the maids have to feed her. Bite after bite, as if she were a child.

The green trunk filled with what the maids gathered from the floor is now in the scullery. Marie-Louise, sleeves rolled up, opens it to a whiff of mold, which makes her cough. Inside, a jumble. Fichus rolled into tight balls, a pair of sleeves torn from some dress. A soiled linen napkin slipped into an old glove, an empty glass vial, a pinecone. Sheets of writing paper covered with unintelligible scribbles, row after row. Pages from old almanacs, some crumpled and stained, most torn up into pieces.

Fodder for the fireplace.

A book of La Fontaine's *Fables* has been wrapped in a woolen shawl. Underneath it, a roll of papers uncurled testifies to past luxuries. Swatches of fabric pinned beside descriptions of gowns *with lace trimmings and whalebone buttons*, supper seating arrangements with Monsieurs B and L, during which *asparagus, oysters and roasted partridges stuffed with truffles* had been served. There is a bill for *two hats with ostrich plumes and a dozen of silk stockings, red, embroidered on the ankles* and a music sheet entitled *Motets et élévations de M. Expilly.*

In the hall the clock strikes five. The scullery is getting murky. If Marie-Louise doesn't want to waste candles before she sorts it all out, she must work fast.

The silk work bag with faded tassels at the bottom of the trunk holds a few letters and two tattered notebooks. The letters, written in a big clumsy hand, are from Danielle Roux, who wishes to inquire about the five dresses her dear daughter had promised, and which have not yet arrived. Her health has been poor and is not improving. Eugene is still at school, in need of a new set of clothes and linen as he is growing rapidly. Marcel and Gaston have just been apprenticed at considerable cost, Marcel to a Quinze-Vingts butcher, Gaston to a tobacconist. Could dear Véronique attend to the enclosed bills?

Grandmother, uncles by name only, reeking of greed.

The thinner of the notebooks begins with the *Examination of conscience*. Véronique Clerantin *evoked God's name in vain . . . prayed for what has been forbidden . . . gave in to despair*. The ink has turned brown, which is what happens if you buy a cheap one. Pages are dog-eared, stained with black and yellow spots.

> *My husband's sisters say I'm not worth a button and that Yves Clerantin deserved better than some whore . . . Our sons are dead for a reason . . . My husband's words are like sharp stones. "What a sight you are, parading my shame for all to see. My mother warned me against discarded goods, but I didn't listen."*
>
> *Right after the funeral Lisette said that if we took the coach, we would be in Paris in three days . . .*
>
> *Julie was very kind. As she talked, I stared down at my hands. A Deer Park girl always attracts the highest bidders, she said. Think it over. It's the best I can do for you.*

Marie-Louise leafs through the pages, impatient. At the Palais-Royal ball a smitten admirer slips a billet-doux begging *divine Véronique* for the next dance. *Generous Monsieur Bout* becomes *my dear Luc*. In the apartment at 84 rue Saint-Honoré, the carved bed with red velvet curtains and satin sheets has just been fumigated. *Dear Luc* has asked Véronique to make arrangements for a supper, *eight guests, music and dancing, with no thought of expense.*

A page is crossed and smeared with inkblots.

> *Knotted whips are more popular than smooth ones.*

Dear Luc's generosity lasts long enough to pay for the first round of mercury cure. Lisette, the maid, cooks her special broth and forces Véronique to take daily walks to restore her strength.

Two weeks ago, I was only able to make a few steps, but today I walked to the street corner and then back.

I'm shrinking. I totter as I walk. My legs hurt. I catch myself staring at an object in my hands, wondering why I picked it up in the first place. It is as if my head was emptying, filling up with fog. I don't know how to live with nothing.

The woman upstairs gives me hard looks. "It used to be a respectable building," she says when I pass her.

My memory sometimes turns into a dark well into which whole chunks of time disappear. A morning turns into evening. I wake up at night and see people around me. They are talking but they do not pay me any heed. As if I were not there at all. I scream at them, but they do not go away.

Today I caught myself standing by the door, not knowing what I intended to do. I called Lisette, but only when she did not come did I remember that she went back to Buc. Why did she leave me? Then I recalled her, in this room, in her good yellow dress, looking at me with terrified eyes. "What did you do this for?" she asked. She pointed at a bread knife lying on the table.

I didn't hurt her, I know that, for there was no blood. I didn't hurt myself, either. Did I threaten her with it?

The new maid is stealing whatever she can, candles, firewood. My silk stockings are gone, so is my good kerchief, the one with red roses in the center. Her name is Solange. She has a sweetheart who comes here every day, a chimneysweep who acts very polite but knocks at the side of his head when he thinks I'm not looking. They whisper together and stop when I'm close enough to hear them.

Marie-Louise is just about to put the notebook aside when the words *rue du Cygne* stop her.

I couldn't resist going there. My face obscured under a veil, I walked past the house on rue du Cygne with the midwife's sign, a cradle and a messenger with a lantern. A string of onions was hanging on the outside, below the attic window. A servant woman was carrying out a kneading trough. A neighbor stared at me briefly from his window, but no one came out to demand my business. A midwife's neighbors must be used to women coming by, alone, hesitating to enter.

Then I saw her. My daughter was walking toward me, from the direction of rue de la Grande-Truanderie, accompanied by a stout elderly maid. Oh, the loveliness of her, the unruly curls, auburn just like mine, pinned high, the fichu carelessly tied, revealing a bit too much of her neck. She was laughing at something the maid had said. How she reminded me of Adèle, that toss of my sister's head, the bouncy step.

She entered the house and I could no longer see her, but by then a giddy recklessness had seized me and wouldn't let go. I chatted with a woman who was selling coffee in the street. The coffee was thin and bitter, but I feigned pleasure. Do you know anything of the midwife who lives here? I asked.

There were two of them, she said. Aunt and niece. Good neighbors, quiet, always ready to help. Hortense, their housekeeper, knows her herbs like no one else around, grows them in the back garden.

"Are they good midwives?" I asked.

Mistress Leblanc, I heard, was one of the best in Paris. The market women at Les Halles swore by her strong hands, her quick thinking. She knew how to stop a woman from tearing. Turn a child when it was still time.

"And the niece?" I asked.

The niece had only just passed her midwifery exams, but she had been her aunt's apprentice for the past three years. Her wedding is in August, to a lawyer from Nancy, the dress will be of blue satin, with a lace shawl and a muslin veil. The seamstress has already done the third fitting.

Not much, such talk, mere scraps, for which I had to pay with my own confidences. I lied about having just moved to Paris from Buc to be with my daughter who is expecting her firstborn.

I was still talking to the coffee seller when my beautiful daughter leaned out a window. She called out to another young woman in the street, a friend perhaps, for the two of them exchanged a few teasing words.

"You are a perfect goose, Madeleine."

"Look at yourself, Marie-Louise."

"Come up, Hortense has baked madeleines."

"I might, if you swear not to eat all of them."

"Aunt Margot says not to swear."

Nothing really, but I carried these words in my heart for days. The easy flow of their banter, the signs of a family at ease.

I imagined myself knocking the brass knocker on the door, asking admission, making my claims. Tempting, until I take off my veil, my wig, wash the ceruse and rouge from my face and look at the dark blotches, gaunt cheeks and blackened teeth.

Do I really want to scratch the old wounds? Cause her pain? What can I give her in return?

The letters swim before her eyes, blur. Marie-Louise blinks a few times, hard. A woman with a veiled face is standing in front of the house on rue du Cygne. Hesitates. Turns away in shame.

How simple in the end, the words that change everything. She has never been forgotten. She has always had a mother.

Julie Berlin's voice pushes through the story as she reads on. *A daughter's duty is to help her mother. Especially when things are going so well for her. Especially when she lacks for nothing . . . If you don't go there, Véronique, I will.*

Marie-Louise imagines Julie Berlin arriving at rue du Cygne, knocking on the door, asking to speak to Mistress Leblanc. "In confidence," she tells Hortense. "Alone." Julie Berlin sitting on the green ottoman in the best room, telling Aunt Margot that she is here on behalf of a destitute widow who doesn't wish to cause her natural daughter any embarrassment or pain. Offering her a straightforward bargain. Silence for money. Enough to pay for a room at the Sisters of Charity until the end of the Widow Clerantin's natural life. To be confirmed in writing.

When was it?

Before Jean-Louis was born? Not the time to trouble an expectant mother with what cannot be remedied or changed?

My name is Véronique. They call me Madame Clerantin. They call me Widow Clerantin. If I do not write it down, I forget.

The woman with powdered hair who comes here sometimes is Julie Berlin. She expects me to be grateful to her. I do not know why.

I have a daughter. Her name is Marie-Louise.

The nuns are good to me, but I want to go and find my mother. I know how to get to her house, if only they will let me go. They do not listen when I ask them to take me there.

They are called Sisters of Charity, but they are not my sisters.

If they say Véronique, they mean me.

Who is the father of your child? they ask me. I must always say: A Polish count.

She doesn't come here. Why not? I have done something wrong, but I don't know what.

No one will tell me.

The last pages in the tattered notebook are filled with strange drawings of people with lopsided faces, crooked houses without windows, circles getting smaller, entangled, twisting into a snakelike chain.

I cannot see very well.

I cannot ask about Adèle for they get very angry.

I cannot ask about Maman.

The king is the father of my child. The king is dead. Is Francine dead too?

I have nothing.

In the kitchen, pots bang, water sizzles. "What's taking you so long, Marie-Louise?" Hortense calls out, her heavy steps getting closer.

In the scullery Marie-Louise is praying for Hortense to go back to her pots and scoldings, without another question. A prayer answered.

She takes a long, deep breath before reaching for the thicker notebook. Her hand quivers as she opens it.

My mother didn't tell me much, she reads.

Can what has been lost for so long be recovered?

Marie-Louise opens the door to the upstairs room with her elbow, careful not to upset the tray she has brought from the kitchen. On it a small jar of diluted cream, a pot of chicory coffee, a plate with Hortense's latest invention, oatmeal cake sweetened with molasses that Marie-Louise has cut into small chunks. Not as good as proper madeleines, but warm and smelling of dried apple peel. There is also a bowl with the last of the rose-hip jam.

Véronique is sitting up in her bed, holding a strand of her thinning gray hair between her fingertips, staring at it with bewilderment. This is the resemblance between them: the line of the nose, the shape of the cheekbones, their little fingers bent inward just so.

Marie-Louise sits on the edge of the bed, places the breakfast tray beside her. She can feel blood pulse in her temples. It takes a moment to steady her voice, force the words through the throat. "Look what I've brought you," she says, picking up a piece of oatmeal cake. "Maman."

Véronique does not lift her eyes.

"I'm Marie-Louise, Maman. I'm your daughter."

Marie-Louise is not expecting much. How can she? But still she is hoping some words can penetrate the fog in her mother's head, find their way inside. Isn't it how numbness melts? A crust softens, cracks, a layer underneath turns pliant?

Words bounce off, fall, roll away. It is only when Marie-Louise begins to sob that Véronique cocks her head to the side. "Has anyone died?" she asks.

Not an act of reason, but hope, what follows. The story of loneliness and fear, of questions no one would ever answer. The story filled with childhood words, sullied with old pain: "I thought you didn't want me, Maman. I thought you left me. I waited. Year after year I waited."

A story her mother cannot understand.

"Is your mother dead?"

"No."

"She doesn't come here to see you?"

"She doesn't know I'm here."

"Didn't you tell her?"

"I did, but she forgets."

"Oh, I don't know what to say to that."

But something has changed. For her mother is wiggling like an impatient child now, looking up at the ceiling, then back at Marie-Louise. Suddenly, she brightens up.

"Look at me, Adèle! Look! I'm a puppy!"

She has straightened herself up and is bunching her hands up in front of her like paws. "And I'm very hungry."

It is so good to laugh, even through tears.

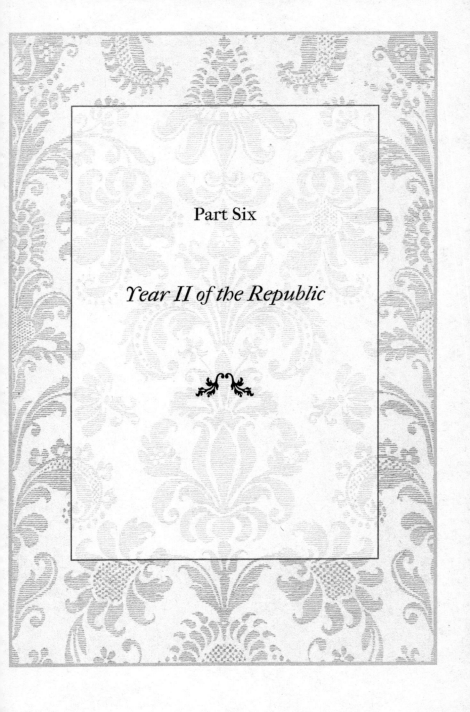

Part Six

Year II of the Republic

Vendémiaire

THE PRINT PIERRE ATTACHED above his writing desk shows two shiny figures in flowing robes, Liberty and Reason, holding hands outside the Temple of the Year. At their feet the toppled saints wallow among the crumpled Church standards while, from the side, a revolutionary crowd watches in awe. The new republican calendar has vanquished the old Gregorian one.

From now on the new year will begin on the autumnal equinox, when the sun enters Libra, the sign of Equality. Twelve republican months, named after the changing seasons, begin with Vendémiaire, the month of the wine harvest. Each month is divided into three *décades*. There are ten hours in a day, of one hundred minutes each. The leftover days—five or sometimes six—will be devoted to festivals of virtue, talent, industry, heroic deeds and ideas.

"They'll banish the sun next," Hortense predicts.

Every time Pierre returns to Paris, he is pensive and terse. Yes, he is tired. No, he cannot rest. There is no time. The enemies have not yet been chased from the territory of the Republic. The Vendée region is still in flames. Lyon, barely holding under siege, refuses to capitulate. Those who cannot be governed by justice will be governed by iron.

She could have read it in the newspapers.

What are you expecting me to tell you, Marie-Louise?

Secrecy then. A game two can play.

For there has been another letter from Jean-Louis, dropped at their doorstep when no one watched, the messenger no longer willing to knock on their door. *Strong gales, wind veering, porpoises crying like little infants when we catch them*, Jean-Louis writes. *You wouldn't recognize me now, Maman. I've hardened, grown strong.*

She pictures him on his journey to Boston on board of *Sea Otter*, his skin ruddy, sunburned, salty, like the sea breeze. Working in the ship's smithy to earn his keep, feeding on portable soup and hard biscuits that have to be softened before they can be chewed. Drinking sweet wort, which is both sugary and bitter and which—he assures her—will protect him from scurvy.

Now, in the Boston harbor, Jean-Louis waits for *Sea Otter* to set sail again. First south, past the Falkland Islands, around Cape Horn, then north. In the smithy he has learned how to refurbish old muskets for the Indian trade. When they reach the North West Coast he will barter them for otter pelts, which he will then take to China where the pelts will fetch sacks of tea, crates of porcelain and bales of silk.

It used to be two muskets for a good pelt, now it is six, he writes. *Some say that I've already come too late, but I'm of good thoughts. Please write to me here, at Cozy Cove Tavern, Boston Harbor, where a kind and friendly waitress, Annie, has vowed to keep your letters waiting for me until my return.*

Your loving son,

Jean-Louis.

Underneath, a post scriptum. *Has Father forgiven me? Will he ever? Is Hortense in good health? Suzette? Cecile? Jacques?*

The letter, read and reread, folded, lies hidden in her midwife's bag. She will not show it to Pierre. Not until she is sure he will read it without anger, without prejudice.

"Come sit here with me," her mother says in the mornings when Marie-Louise brings in her breakfast, patting the edge of the bed and grabbing her hand. She still needs to be fed but eats with appetite. Spoons licked clean end up under the pillow, which Véronique pats flat. "Because they'll steal it otherwise," she says.

The broken stories her mother tells loop and meander. The sedan chair is waiting. She has to dress up, for the count has sent for her. Lisette has eaten all the chocolate pastilles and now there are none. Francine was right, Lebel is a fuckwit. Her husband is calling her bad names. Mean. He is a hard man. He is a thief. He stole all her money. He didn't let her keep her baby.

The old notebook Marie-Louise has brought in hope to stir her memory elicits only passing interest. "I do not know what to do with it," her mother has confessed. "Do you?"

Sometimes Marie-Louise is still Adèle, but rarely. Mostly she has no name and she is her mother's beloved friend.

"You are so beautiful. So kind. You won't leave me again, will you?"

"I won't. I'm your daughter."

"How could it be? You are so much older than I am."

At the butcher stalls of Les Halles market cow and pig heads have replaced slabs of meat. Eggs, hidden somewhere in the back, can only be had for silver coins. In front of a bakery, women have been lining up behind a thick rope since dawn.

Denounce the crimes, denounce the criminals, the wall posters now demand. *Former servants must not forget that the Motherland is their sole mistress . . . relatives that it alone is their mother . . .*

On the twenty-fifth of Vendémiaire, the Widow Capet is taken to the guillotine in an open cart, dressed in a simple white shift, hair tucked into a bonnet. "I beg your forgiveness," she says, having stepped on the executioner's foot. "I didn't mean it."

One more thing Aunt Margot does not have to hear about.

Brumaire

BRUMAIRE IS THE MONTH OF FOG. The day is chilly, rainy. Marie-Louise is in the best room, trying on the walking shoes the cobbler has just delivered, resoled, brushed to a shine.

The loud banging on the front door sends La Grise, who has been chasing a ball of wool, under the ottoman. A midwife's summons, Marie-Louise thinks, as Suzette lets the caller inside. Marie-Louise is not the only midwife in Paris noting yet another surge of births. As if we were getting ready for more war, Madeleine has said.

Deputy Melville doesn't need a midwife. He has come with news.

"About my son?"

"About Citizen Pierre Vernault."

"But my husband is in Lyon."

"He has been called back."

Deputy Melville is in his early fifties. Dry, tired face, watery eyes. He calls himself Pierre's colleague. He smells of fear and speaks in short, broken sentences from which Marie-Louise plucks out one word, *arrested*.

Her face drains. Her heart flutters.

"When?"

"Last night at the city gates."

"How do you know?"

"News travels fast."

It is noon already, so it doesn't travel that fast.

"The guards from the Revolutionary Tribunal stopped the carriage. Took him to the Palais de Justice."

"Accused of what?"

"Corruption. Fomenting counterrevolution. Siding with dissenters."

"Impossible," she says, stepping forward; the resoled shoes squeak.

Deputy Melville looks at the floor. "It has happened."

"Has Danton been informed? Robespierre?" The innocent do not need to fear, she also says, firmly, a sentence she has heard many times. It sounds oddly petulant now, aggrieved.

Deputy Melville fumbles in his chest pocket for a handkerchief, wipes his forehead. He doesn't know who has been informed. Or when.

His fingers, Marie-Louise notes, are thick, stubby, stained with patches of inky black. Ugly, she thinks, which is uncharitable of her.

"Right . . . well . . . Nothing else to say . . . must be on my way," Deputy Melville stammers.

Outside the Palais de Justice a small crowd has gathered, mostly of women with children in tow. Babies wail; a boy of about three, dirty-faced, wants to pee. "Just now?" his pregnant mother asks. An older man, bald, a pristine white cravat around his neck, is sitting on a stone ledge, absorbed in a small leather-bound book. Two young women speak in low voices. "But who?" the one on the left asks. "How would I know?"

Murderers, Cannibals, someone scrawled on the wall.

"Citizeness Vernault, a sworn midwife," Marie-Louise tells the guard at the door.

The guard lets her in and motions toward a row of desks on the landing, where, a moment later, a pockmarked young clerk, a brown coat over his shoulders, eyes her with annoyance. He has made his voice stern, self-assured. Her husband, Citizen Vernault, has been arrested? Then he will be interrogated. Given a chance to prove his innocence just like everyone else. Justice must and will be served.

The vest underneath the brown coat, Marie-Louise notes, is blue, white and red.

What the clerk doesn't say she can read on his face. Wives, mothers, sisters are all a bloody nuisance. They do not listen. Or they listen and do not hear.

They insist on making irrelevant statements. If you believe them, there is no counterrevolution. No rising in the Vendée. No army of émigré traitors gathering in Spain, poised to attack their own motherland. No spies. No speculators. No royalists doing the dirty work of the émigrés. It is all malignant rumors. It is all personal vendettas.

"Your husband is in the Luxembourg Prison."

"May I see him?"

Her voice is measured, calm, but insistent. She is a sworn midwife after all. She will be hard to dismiss.

The clerk lowers his eyes, picks up a sheet of paper, pretends to read from it. Or maybe, Marie-Louise corrects herself, he does read from it. Perhaps someone has foreseen such questions, suggested the answers for him.

"Alas, Citizeness, that is not for me to decide."

❧

"Master said he is not home for anyone," Catherine, the maid, tells Marie-Louise at the Cour du Commerce apartment. "They are all leaving for Arcis in three days. By post coach, with the children."

They means George Danton and his wife of four months, Louise Gély, the very friend Gabrielle asked to take care of her two boys. Which is not much of a surprise. George Danton cannot stand living alone.

"I have to see him," Marie-Louise insists, stepping into the hall, which is even messier than when Gabrielle was alive. Two traveling trunks are standing in the middle of the hall, one on top of the other. Children's shoes are piled up in one corner. A red ball is lodged under the grandfather clock. A rocking horse, its mane torn out, lies on its side, one of its rockers snapped in half.

From the nursery Louise's voice warns, "Not so hard, Antoine. You'll break it." Inside, one of the boys blows a shrill whistle.

The maid rolls her eyes as she knocks on the nursery door. Who gives children such noisy toys? Eight months after their poor mother's death?

The new Madame Danton has her own crosses to bear.

"What is it now, Catherine?" Louise asks as she comes out, rosy-cheeked and smiling. Seeing Marie-Louise, she lifts a finger to her lips, biting on it like a schoolgirl. Gabrielle had feared she was too serious for her age, too buried in her books. I hope she won't forget to live, she had said.

"I need to see George," Marie-Louise says.

"But we are getting ready to leave," Louise says, but before she has time to say anything more, George Danton's booming voice comes from the room adjacent to the nursery: "Who is it now, Louise? Didn't I say I was not home to anyone?"

Louise, relieved, lifts her hands up in a gesture of surrender as he emerges in his dressing gown, a newspaper under his arm.

"Ah, it's you," he says, seeing Marie-Louise still in her overcoat. "Come in, come in."

A man like Danton can signal so much with his bulk alone. I could wring your neck. I could lift you and throw you to the ground. Or I can take you out of a burning building. Carry you through a rushing river.

"Has anything happened? Have they found your son?"

Does he not know then?

"It's Pierre," she says. "He has been arrested."

"Just now?"

"This morning."

Danton takes a heavy step toward her, calling for Catherine to come and take Madame's coat, right away. And bring coffee, and some brandy. Then he motions Marie-Louise to come inside. The bedroom where Gabrielle died is now a study, taken over by a table strewn with papers and blunted quills. Underneath them Marie-Louise can see patches of Gabrielle's favorite table-cloth. Yellow, embroidered with green stems, stained with ink.

"Sit . . . sit," he urges.

Marie-Louise shakes her head, but she does sit down slowly, feeling the thick folds of her skirt and her petticoats flatten underneath her.

Gabrielle is staring at her from atop a wooden column. Gabrielle made of bronze is a strong-looking woman. Determined, bold. On her plump face no trace of what she had gone through. No confusion. No blood. No shivers. No fear.

"Where is he now?" Danton asks.

Marie-Louise tells him what she knows. Which is so very little.

Catherine brings a cup of steaming coffee and two glasses with brandy. George Danton takes one, offers Marie-Louise the other. He tips his head back and empties his. She takes a sip, then puts her glass away. She wants to keep her wits sharp.

"Have you seen him?" he asks.

"They won't let me."

Danton's big scarred face colors slightly; the pockmarks take on an ashen hue.

"We have enemies," he says.

"The royalists?"

"The royalists are ancient history," he scoffs. "It's the former friends who are the real menace. Pierre didn't tell you much, did he?"

She shakes her head.

"The old struggle for power," Danton continues. "*Us* and *them*. It is quite simple. *They* dig up dirt on you and cry bloody shame. You wipe yourself off and cry foul."

"And then?" she asks.

"It used to be that one of the sides won."

"Used to?"

"There is no arguing now. It all happens behind closed doors. You say what you have to say. The jurors pass their judgment. There is no appeal."

"Robespierre?"

"He no longer listens to anyone."

"Does it mean you cannot help?"

"It means I can only try."

Marie-Louise knocks on many more doors that day, asking, imploring, calling on old debts of gratitude. Most of the deputies refuse to see her; those who do blame the royalists or some other vile enemies of the people. Or declare themselves powerless and send her on to someone else who supposedly still has Robespierre's ear. Every so often someone warns her to be cautious about whom she sees and what she says. Certain prejudices are far too easy to form. Or too tempting.

"What prejudices?"

"Well, perhaps I used that word too hastily."

It is already dark when George Danton comes to the house on rue du Cygne. He didn't see Pierre but managed to send him a note. And to see his dossier. Which was a giant favor.

Marie-Louise doesn't take her eyes off his face. In candlelight his scars look diminished, faded.

There have been denunciations, all anonymous. A "citizen who has no other ambition but to die for the freedom of his country" accused Pierre of "having criminal intelligence with scoundrels" and of "casting a prolonged vengeful look that is impossible to describe." A "concerned neighbor" heard Pierre refer to the people as "peasants and picklocks" and to the Republic as "a child in a cradle." A member of the military committee at the Commune Section accused him of buying food at the black market and failing to instill republican virtues in his son.

"And this was enough to arrest him?" she asks.

From the ottoman, Danton gives her a pained look. Does he really have to spell it out for her? Draw the bigger picture, connect political lines? Such accusations are all fluff. What really matters is much simpler. Pierre has been one of his, Danton's, men. His arrest is a message from Robespierre himself.

"A warning? Are you in danger, too, then?"

Danton shrugs his shoulders. One day he is in danger, another he is not. He has learned not to speculate on the future. When you sow in the field of the Republic, you must not count the cost of the sowing. Revolution always eats its children.

Marie-Louise clasps her hands, hard enough to feel the bones of her fingers.

"You can see him tomorrow," Danton says, standing up. "No guarantee, but it has been suggested that the Revolutionary Tribunal is not without a heart."

She walks after him to the hall, always chilly at this time, with the kitchen fire banked for the night. Not for long, as it turns out.

"Burn anything they shouldn't find," Danton says. He means the Section guards, if they come here sniffing.

The passageway on the ground floor of the Luxembourg Prison could've been an ordinary service corridor if it weren't for the three soldiers playing dice. One of them gives Marie-Louise a look of bewilderment, the others kiss the air and slap their knees.

The guard who is taking Marie-Louise to Pierre's cell tells them to cut it out for they are sullying the name of the revolution.

The soldiers laugh. The one who is still staring at Marie-Louise gives a loud belch and says, "Oh, do pardon me, I implore!"

The door is marked with the letter *V*, in chalk. The guard fumbles with the keys attached to a metal ring on his belt.

When the door opens Pierre is standing between a narrow folding bed and a small table. Marie-Louise has not seen him for a whole month, and it strikes her how haggard he looks. His black jacket is torn at the shoulder, the chemise underneath yellowed and crumpled. His hair is all mussed up, across his cheek a smudge of soot.

Her body sags, as if weighed with lead.

"This is not what you think," Pierre says, taking a step toward her. "I still do not despair of my fellow men nor of my release. Danton advised me to write to Robespierre."

"Did you?"

"Yes."

There is a crack in the wall. Someone on the other side of it groans.

"Don't cry," Pierre says.

Marie-Louise doesn't think she is crying, but of course she is.

In spite of what Marie-Louise believed to be a hefty bribe, the guard has positioned himself outside the door, which he has left open. No word can pass between them that he won't hear. How it changes everything, being aware that someone is listening. How hollow one's voice. How hesitant each word.

"Did something happen in Lyon?" she asks.

THE SCHOOL OF MIRRORS | 389

Pierre shakes his head. This is the wrong way to think. His arrest was a mistake, an overzealous response to some misguided denunciation. He is not the first one to whom this has happened, nor the last.

He won't tell her anything else, the tone of his voice says. Because he cannot? Because he doesn't know how? These are useless questions, Marie-Louise thinks. They mustn't waste the little time they have. Forgo what's possible right now.

The bed in Pierre's cell is covered with a thin, coarse blanket. There is no pillow. The room has a small fireplace but no fire. She can see their breaths, puff after puff of fog. His hands when he holds hers are ice cold. There is a bruise on his wrist.

He needs sheets for the bed, a thicker blanket and a pillow. He needs clean linen. He needs a pitcher of water. He needs a chamber pot, firewood, bellows, a coffeepot.

"What do they feed you?"

Some gruel he cannot bring himself to touch, let alone swallow.

She will send him soup.

Anything else?

Yes. His spectacles are broken. Could she buy him another pair? Not of silver, but of steel. Clear lenses, not green. Number fifteen. The merchant on rue Saint-Jacques will know what that means.

Marie-Louise straightens, energized by the very thought of being useful.

Pierre lifts her hand to his lips, kisses her knuckles. "This is all a ridiculous mistake," he says. "Tomorrow I'll be home."

By the time Marie-Louise returns later that day, most of the provisions have been delivered. Pierre has firewood, bellows, a pot of thick soup Hortense has cooked, a portable stove Madeleine managed to get from somewhere. To this Marie-Louise now adds a good supply of writing paper and quills.

This time she has bribed the guard enough to let them talk alone.

Still, they whisper.

He has not yet heard from Robespierre. He has given his testimony twice already. Answered all questions. Suggested lines of inquiry that he is sure are being followed right now. Those who denounced him, he argued, want revenge. Anyone who serves the revolution has angered many. Separate the wheat from the chaff.

She would like to tell him of the heaping pile of papers that went up in smoke. Speeches, letters, notebooks, statements. But what if someone is listening? So, she nods instead.

There is a rhythm to their conversation. Each toss served must be returned. There must be no pauses. Not a moment must be wasted.

"Are these the right ones?" she asks, handing him the spectacles she has brought.

They are. He can write now. The old ones, besides being broken, were too tight and gave him bad headaches. He is glad to be rid of them.

"Hortense also sends these," Marie-Louise says, extracting a small bundle of warming herbs. Angelica, garlic, rosemary, wild cherry, bay leaves. To sprinkle on his soup. Make tea with or even just to chew on. Bay leaves, Hortense still believes, avert ill luck.

"I'll smell like an apothecary."

"There are worse smells."

"True. Any more letters from Jean-Louis?"

"Not yet."

"He has been foolish."

She nods.

"Children are foolish."

She nods again.

"My father despaired of me, too."

"You never told me that."

"No. But you guessed anyway."

"Yes."

"Sometimes bigger forces make us do things we wouldn't have done otherwise," Pierre says.

"What do you mean?" she asks.

He shakes his head. He cannot say anything else.

When it is time for her to leave, Pierre asks for a twist of her hair. It must be a pretty common request, for the guard who has come to escort her back hands Marie-Louise a pair of tiny scissors. Blunt, as if they could've been a weapon.

"Sorry it is so thin," she says, snipping off the end of a curl. She feels as if she has aged in the past days, doubled in years, in heaviness. Just as her mother is getting younger in her mind, insisting they were playing together behind the house only the other day. Pretending to be kittens, jumping up and down until Maman told them to stop.

"It's enough."

"I will come back tomorrow. I will bring more soup."

~•~

The following day there is a new chalk mark on Pierre's door, X. Marie-Louise asks the guard what it means. He says that the verdict has been reached.

"Nothing ends up quite the way one imagines," Pierre says. "Which doesn't matter now, does it?"

He bites on his lower lip. His Adam's apple quivers when he swallows to clear his throat.

"What are you saying? What did they tell you?"

Pierre turns his head away.

"Please speak to me."

Pierre's voice is quiet, small. He regrets all that went wrong between them. "Please tell Jean-Louis when he returns that I don't blame him for running away. Tell him it had nothing to do with my arrest."

"And if he blames himself?"

"Tell him I said that a bird flapping its wings is not guilty of causing a storm."

Marie-Louise hopes for an exoneration. Some vile conspiracy will be revealed. Someone will see through this dirty, rigged game. Danton will storm the Revolutionary Tribunal, demanding explanations. Vernault is a true republican, he will say. I, Danton, can vouch for him. My name is on every document. You know me.

Pierre is taken from the Luxembourg Prison in a rumbling cart, without an overcoat. She runs behind it as fast as she can without falling.

This is what will keep coming back to her. That stumbling, slippery trot, the feel of her heavy skirt as she holds it up. Pierre's eyes locked on hers. A passerby wrapped in a black cape looking away out of what she wants to believe is kindness. The small crowd by the scaffold, the cart stopping. Pierre's hands being tied at the back, his hair shorn.

She is standing as close as the guards allow. Close enough that she can see a tiny quiver on her husband's lips as he forces what she will think of as a smile.

An hour may have one hundred minutes now, but time does not stretch. How many breaths left?

It's an easy death, people say. Quick when it matters.

Pierre Vernault makes no grand statements to posterity or history, no last appeal to justice. He does not claim innocence or warn others of what might happen to them if they let him die. Resigned, people will say about him later. Stoic. A mark of true greatness. Or something equally useless to her.

Firm steps all the way to the scaffold, she will write to Jean-Louis as soon as she knows where to send her letter. Steady. Your father died an honorable and brave man.

She hears the swish of the blade.

The world darkens and cracks.

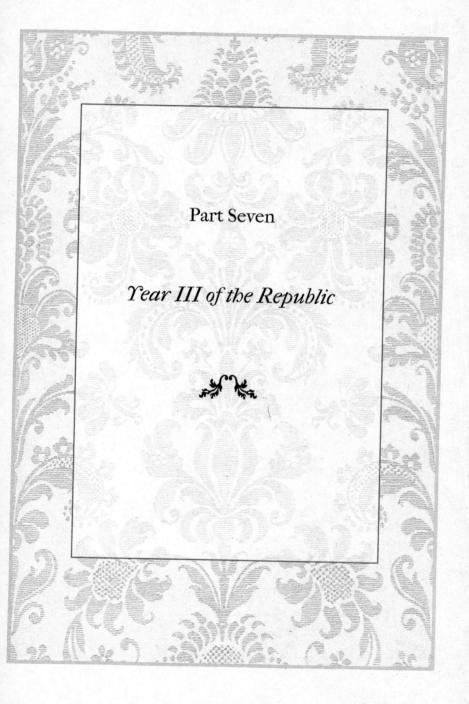

Part Seven

Year III of the Republic

Ventôse

THE HOUSE ON RUE DU CYGNE, still marked by the sign of a cradle and a messenger with a lantern, has a list of tenants pinned to the front door, a revolutionary requirement not yet rescinded: Marie-Louise Vernault, Véronique Clerantin, Hortense Roche.

The maids are gone, which is a blessing, since nowadays midwives are often paid in promises, debts incurred against the better times that cannot be far away. Suzette left first, packed and took off without even giving notice, as Hortense reminds Marie-Louise often. Cecile married her guard and moved out of Paris. Her husband is in the army now, fighting in Italy under General Buonaparte.

Shops trade in scraps and substitutes. Pear juice for wine, ashes for pepper, people say. If you want meat, eggs or butter, you have to turn to the street peddlers who raise their prices by the day. Outside a bakery Marie-Louise saw a woman yank a slice of bread from a child's hands and throw it into the gutter, screaming, "If I have to go hungry, so should everyone else."

The winter has been viciously cold. Even now, in the middle of March—Ventôse, that is—the upstairs rooms are closed off, the windows shuttered, to conserve heat. Marie-Louise and Véronique sleep in the best room on folding cots. In her mother's addled mind, they are still best friends. Sometimes they are "bad girls up to no good." Sometimes her mother puts her head on Marie-Louise's lap and mutters some silly words that make no sense. "Uppity, but lucky," she may say and then repeat it over and over again. Or purr like a cat when Marie-Louise's fingers caress her gray hair, what is left of it.

Just the other day Véronique slid her hand under the pillow. "Look what

I've found," she said, retrieving a spoon. Then, in a voice sparkling with mischievous laughter, she asked, "Why do I always find such ordinary things? Why can't I find a bottle of champagne!"

Hortense sleeps as always in her nook beside the kitchen, which smells even more like an apothecary. In her able hands, milkweed greens make a passable salad, stinging nettles are turned into a soup. Dry bunches of chamomile and mint hanging on strings above the fireplace are brewed for tea. So are the carrot peels drying on the stove.

"Why didn't you tell me she was your mother?" Hortense asked when Marie-Louise finally confessed her secret. She was hurt, yes, and angry, too. At not being trusted, she said, pursing her lips. A few hours later came the reproaches. "After everything I have done for you, Marie-Louise" was the hardest one to bear.

Forgiveness came without any words at all.

The Great Terror may have ended, but the midwives of Paris whisper of babies born with clenched fists, red marks on their necks or still like statues. Printer's boys hawk prints of Robespierre, the monster of the Revolution who, "after having killed all the French," stands alone amid a forest of guillotines. Or holds the bleeding Head of Liberty by the hair. Or, in hobbled boots, steps on a pile of bodies, George Danton's among them. Or, finally, is himself carried to the Celestial Guillotine, Protectress of Patriots.

Marie-Louise considers herself luckier than countless others. Pierre's remains were not thrown into a common grave and covered by quicklime, his clothes given to the gravediggers as payment. She buried him in the family grave, next to Aunt Margot and baby Angélique. The well-bribed guard passed on Pierre's last note to her.

Death is but a moment, one last beat of the heart. Please remember me for the best I have done, not the worst. Tell Jean-Louis that his father loved him as well as he could. Pay any debts I may have incurred, knowingly or not. My last thoughts will be of you.

—

Today the midday sun is strong enough to warm the air, tempt them to sit outside. At the back of the house where Hortense has dragged out three old chairs, Marie-Louise stretches her feet. Beside her, Véronique, wrapped up in the thickest of blankets, is holding a dry leaf, turning it in her fingers.

Her mother is slowly losing her sight, her right cheek twitches, she cannot stand up on her own. Not much longer on this earth, as Hortense puts it, though Véronique might still intone a wordless song and then when finished ask, "Was I marvelous?" Or grab Marie-Louise's hand to whisper, "He thinks he is my husband. But he is so fat, isn't he? And he stinks like a rutting bull."

Hortense bears the brunt of Véronique's much diminished mischief. She might find herself splashed with soapy water or have her apron strings undone. "I'm an awful girl," Véronique might say, slapping her own hand, while to Marie-Louise she will mouth: "I'm not sorry."

Hortense doesn't mind these antics. She says she would rather atone for her sins here on earth than waste time in Purgatory. Besides, she is sure Mistress Margot is watching them from above. Having a chuckle or wiping a tear.

What has been lost may never be fully recovered, and yet . . .

The leaf in her mother's gnarled fingers twirls back and forth. "Such a beautiful object. Where does it come from?"

"From a tree. The wind blew it in."

Véronique turns toward her with a puzzled half smile. "How is that possible?" she asks.

Marie-Louise takes the leaf, places it on her mother's open palm and blows until the leaf flies away.

"Just like that? Really?"

La Grise is meowing from behind the closed door, loudly protesting her exclusion or, more likely, demanding to be fed. Hortense, who insists on locking her in the house at all times, gets up and heads inside, muttering, "Have you seen any cats in the streets now, you dumb beast? Have you asked yourself why?"

Véronique covers her ears.

The gate at the back of the yard squeaks.

Marie-Louise holds her breath. Jean-Louis?

The man who has opened the gate is a stranger. Well off, judging by the care he has put into his appearance. The nankeen breeches, the brown coat, a tricorne hat over a wig. That he is not weary of such a display of old-fashioned elegance marks him as a foreigner.

"In need of a midwife?"

"No, Madame . . . Marie-Louise Vernault?"

"That's me."

Not quite a foreigner, it turns out, but a Frenchman who has just arrived from Boston. Entrusted with a letter from her son, to be delivered directly into her hands.

Dearest Maman,

Your letter has given me a lasting joy, in spite of the tragic news. I carry it in my breast pocket at all times, rereading what you wrote about Papa, his brave and honorable death, and his last words for me. I'm grateful for his forgiveness and yours.

I've not made my fortune in the Indian trade so I'm not sailing to China, but I'm not returning to France, either. My place is here in the New World, Boston for the next few months, and then Montréal, which is only a few days' journey from Boston by trade ship and more suitable for a Frenchman. I have already started looking for a good-quality printing press since I plan to open The Vernault Printshop there, which will publish books in English and French. There is, I've been assured by many knowledgeable people, a great hunger for stories about explorers, their adventures and confessions.

There is one more thing I need to tell you, regretting I have to do it so abruptly, and hoping to explain myself when I finally see you again. Annie, the friendly waitress who has kept your letters for me, has become my wife, and she is expecting our first child at the end of March, so by the time you are reading these words you may well be a grandmother. I pray for Annie's safe delivery, hoping that you and Hortense might come to live with us as soon as we settle. Experienced midwives are much needed in the New World so you would not find yourself idle. Please tell Hortense that she will have a proper kitchen garden and that I still miss her rabbit pie.

> *Your loving son,*
> *Jean-Louis.*

The world swims and blurs. Tears roll down her cheeks.

"Is he sorry for what he has done?" Véronique asks. Her head is tilted slightly, her eyes narrow.

"Yes, he is sorry."

"Has he sent for you?"

"Yes."

"Will you go?"

"Yes."

"Now?"

"No."

"Soon?"

"Yes."

In the end, Marie-Louise thinks, there is no end, just another beginning. Still blurry and blissfully unaware of its own origins, of everything that had happened before it was born.

Author's Note

I asked Madame, if the young lady knew that the King was the father of her child? "I do not think she does," replied she, "but, as he appeared fond of her, there is some reason to fear that those about her might be too ready to tell her; otherwise," said she, shrugging her shoulders, "she, and all the others are told, that he is a Polish nobleman, a relation of the Queen, who has apartments in the palace." This story was contrived on account of the cordon bleu, which the King has not always time to lay aside, because, to do that, he must change his coat, and in order to account for his having a lodging in the palace so near the King.

The above quote comes from *The Private Memoirs of Madame du Hausset, Lady's Maid to Madame de Pompadour,*[*] a lively account of court life at Versailles under Louis XV, first published in France in 1824. It is not certain that Madame du Hausset herself wrote these memoirs, some historians believe the author to be another courtier who "borrowed" her voice, but the book is nevertheless a fascinating source of eighteenth-century palace gossip, always fertile ground for a writer in search of an intriguing story to explore.

I came across the book some time ago when I was researching *Empress of the Night* and needed some context for the widespread international disapproval of Catherine the Great's love life. And since I was born in Poland, the words *a Polish nobleman, a relation of the Queen, who has apartments in the palace* caught my attention right away. Louis XV's queen, Maria Leszczyńska, was Polish, so a Polish nobleman who must disappear back to his homeland whenever it is expedient would have been the perfect disguise for a king bent

---

[*]   *The Private Memoirs of Madame du Hausset*, London, 1825.

on indulging his sexual fantasies. "She and the others" refers to the young residents of Deer Park, or Parc-aux-Cerfs, a house in the town of Versailles where the king's *valet de chambre*, Dominique Lebel, kept attractive lower-class girls who might entice his master's fancy.

Deer Park did exist. We know that the house was located on rue de Saint-Médéric and that it remained in the king's possession from around 1755 to 1771. We do not know how many girls resided there over the years, how many were sent to the king's bedroom, how many bore his children or what ultimately happened to them—or to those children. Some of the pamphleteers of the Revolution, bent on exaggerating the crimes of the ancien régime, write of hundreds of such girls, some as young as nine. Others, recording widely circulating anecdotes about Louis XV, Madame de Pompadour or Madame du Barry (Louis's final official mistress) mention two or three residents of Deer Park at one time, aged thirteen or fourteen, which still sounds outrageous to us, even if it seemed much less so at a time when fourteen-year-old brides were not uncommon, especially among upper classes. Some authors provide a few names: Mademoiselle Trusson, a daughter of one of the dauphine's maids; Mademoiselle Niquet, daughter of a magistrate from Toulouse. Others offer snippets of conversation, some brief scenes from their lives at Deer Park, and glimpses of the royal machinery of procurement, including Dominique Lebel's and Madame de Pompadour's involvement in it. Not much, perhaps, but enough to confirm that the mostly unrecorded stories of the Deer Park girls are part of a larger and unfortunately timeless story of how the powerful exert their sexual dominance over the powerless.

There is one more historical inspiration behind the novel, an extraordinary eighteenth-century French midwife who dedicated her life to improving natal care and to fighting infant mortality. Her name was Angélique Marguerite Le Boursier du Coudray and, as her American biographer, Nina Rattner Gelbart, documents so well in *The King's Midwife: A History and Mystery of Madame du Coudray*,* she singlehandedly revolutionized the practice and teaching of midwifery in France.

Madame du Coudray did present her formidable teaching machine at

---

*   Nina Rattner Gelbart, *The King's Midwife*, University of California Press, 1999.

Versailles, first to the king's surgeon-general Germain Pichault de La Martinière and then to Louis XV himself. (The royal presentation took place in October of 1759, a bit later than I place it in the novel.) Impressed, Louis XV granted Madame du Coudray not only the title of "the King's midwife" but also the funds to fulfill her mission. For over a quarter of a century afterward she traveled across France, teaching thousands of young peasant women the art of midwifery. She also raised and trained an orphaned peasant girl, Marguerite Guillaumanche, later Madame Coutanceau, her adoptive niece, who carried on her aunt's work well into the nineteenth century.

Out of over a hundred of Madame du Coudray's birthing machines in use, only one has survived, and can be viewed at the Museum of the History of Medicine in Rouen. Constructed out of wicker, fabric, leather, stuffing and sponges, the well-worn machine may have faded a bit with time, but it still looks impressive. It is displayed behind glass together with several soft model dolls which could be used to instruct an apprentice midwife to deliver a baby full-term, a premature one or twins, or simulate breech birth and a few other possible complications. Beside it hangs a map of Angélique du Coudray's extensive travels, a testimony to her mission to bring the art of midwifery to as many young women as she could manage, and thus give them a means of transforming their own lives as well as those of the women and children they cared for. Even if Madame du Coudray herself would not have claimed it, she gave them power over their own lives, a power the Deer Park girls were so heartlessly denied.

It was the spirit of the intrepid, indefatigable Madame du Coudray, and of her niece, which prompted me to imagine Aunt Margot and Marie-Louise.

Acknowledgments

I would like to express my gratitude to those who have given me time, help and encouragement in the years of writing *The School of Mirrors*: my agent, Helen Heller, always an early and most helpful reader of my drafts; my editor, Lara Hinchberger, a perfect midwife for this novel, both caring and firm when necessary; Amy Black and my wonderful Doubleday team, unwavering in their support.

Thank you, Maureen Scott Harris and Barbara Heathcote, for important conversations, and my husband, Zbyszek, for nudging my thoughts in directions I may have missed.

About the author

2 Meet Eva Stachniak

About the book

3 Behind the Book

6 Reading Group Guide

Insights,
Interviews
& More . . .

Meet Eva Stachniak

Marc Raynes Roberts

Eva Stachniak was born in Wrocław, Poland. She moved to Canada in 1981 and has worked for Radio Canada International and Sheridan College, where she taught English and humanities. Her first novel of Catherine the Great, *The Winter Palace*, was a #1 international bestseller and was followed by another Catherine the Great novel, *Empress of the Night*, also a bestseller. She lives in Toronto. ✑

Behind the Book

By Eva Stachniak

The writing of *The School of Mirrors* began with a secret house in the town of Versailles and a midwife with a mission.

The secret house was Deer Park, where Louis XV's *valet de chambre*, Dominique Lebel, kept attractive lower-class girls to satisfy his master's fleeting fancy. Not much is known about them. Deer Park girls—often referred to as "little birds" at the palace—were poor, pretty, and very young. Some eighteenth-century sources have preserved a name or two, fragments of conversations, a few details of their lives. We know that their parents were enticed with offers of money. We know that the girls were brought to Deer Park ostensibly to be trained as ladies' maids, and told that their master and benefactor was a Polish count, a cousin of the queen, who kept an apartment at Versailles. We know that they disappeared as swiftly as they appeared, married off or sent back home, their lives mostly lost to history.

The French midwife with a mission was Madame Angélique du Coudray. Not satisfied with being a certified midwife— already a well-respected and powerful position in her time—she believed in the power of education and in what we might now call socially conscious health policy. Bemoaning the fact that the superior training available to Parisian midwives required a lengthy and expensive stay in the capital, Angélique du Coudray came ▶

3

up with a revolutionary plan. She designed an intensive midwifery course she could take to her students, a course aided by a birthing machine of her own invention that was capable of simulating the stages of labor. In 1759, she presented that birthing machine at Versailles, appealing to Louis XV for funding. Then, for the next few decades, as the King's Midwife, she crisscrossed France with her course, empowering generations of young women and giving them opportunities they would not have had otherwise.

Véronique Roux, the heroine of *The School of Mirrors*, is a Deer Park girl. Her life, although imaginary, includes many of the details I've discovered through my research: the deceptive comforts of her gilded cage; the heady if brief attentions of a mysterious, powerful man; the illegitimate daughter she is not allowed to keep. By the time Véronique arrives at Deer Park, the house has become a well-functioning establishment. Dominique Lebel, the king's valet, oversees the procurement and grooming of the king's prospective mistresses. Madame de Pompadour, the official royal mistress, keeps a watchful eye on their "education" and—if any of them gets pregnant—manages their confinement and the placement of their children. Véronique may be a powerless "little bird," but her tale is also a wider and timeless story of the cage makers and the cage keepers.

Madame du Coudray and her indomitable spirit have offered me an entirely different insight into the lives of these eighteenth-century women, shaping the story of *The School of Mirrors* on many levels. The King's Midwife may appear in the novel only briefly, to make her legendary presentation at Versailles, but her influence reaches far and wide. The midwives in the novel, empowered by her teachings, improve the lives of women and children they care for. And, even more importantly, Marie-Louise, Véronique's illegitimate daughter, who outlives both the excesses of the ancien régime and the turmoil of the French Revolution, grows up to become a woman after Madame du Coudray's heart.

The School of Mirrors is a historical novel, but it is also a novel about women destined to live their lives during great historical upheavals. Monarchy falls and a revolution follows, while the heroines of my novel fall in and out of love, give birth and raise children, keep and reveal secrets, and bury and remember their dead. They do it with courage and fortitude, the best they can.

They are just like the women who raised me, and whom I loved and admired all my life.

I was born in Poland under a communist dictatorship, with the ruins of World War II still present. The women who raised me kept secrets big and small; secrets guarded from us, children, for fear of political reprisals; secrets which festered and poisoned those who had to keep them. I know well how trauma survives in families; how enforced silence reshapes the memories of the past. I know how important it is to reconstruct the forgotten voices and to learn from them. Voices like those of Véronique and Marie-Louise, a Deer Park girl confined by history and a midwife empowered by it. ∾

Reading Group Guide

1. At the start of the novel, we are told that the king's mistress, Madame de Pompadour, ". . . knows that the world is not run by those who trust but by those who foresee trouble well before it is conceived." Do you agree? Which other characters in this novel share that approach to life?

2. What did you make of King Louis and his circle of procurers? Does his exploitation of Deer Park's girls seem abhorrent to you? Or do they still benefit by obtaining a comfortable life that they would not have otherwise? Would you be willing to make that trade-off?

3. Why does King Louis create a royal patronage for Madame du Coudray? How will midwifery affect everyone in this novel?

4. Why is it so hard for Véronique to move on after the king spurns her, despite knowing that her future has been assured if she's willing to go along with the plan? Why does she continue to insist that the king is the father of her child? Would you have done the same?

5. Why does Marie-Louise become a midwife? What about her history may have made her uniquely qualified for this calling?

6. Marie-Louise reflects on the court at Versailles: "To overburden people with attention, to insist upon obligations that they do not desire, is not only to render yourself disagreeable, but contemptible." Do you agree? Was her life at Versailles "wasted," as she believes? What about the other denizens of contemptible Versailles, like Madame de Pompadour, Monsieur Lebel, and the Gourlons?

7. When Marie-Louise finds out the truth about her mother and father and Versailles, she thinks she hears her Aunt Margot whisper, "This is what I've been shielding you from . . . Burdens not of your own making." Did Mistress Leblanc do Marie-Louise a favor by keeping that secret all those years?

How might Marie-Louise's life be different had she known the truth?

8. Had you read other novels about the French Revolution prior to this one? How did you view the revolutionaries, including Pierre and Danton? What about the execution of Louis and Marie-Antoinette?

9. Consider the mothers and daughters in this book: Véronique and Marie-Louise; Véronique and her mother, Danielle; the queen and her daughters; even Madame de Pompadour and Alexandrine. What are the common threads in all those relationships? Which ones did you most identify with?

10. At the very end of the novel we read: "In the end, Marie-Louise thinks, there is no end, just another beginning. Still blurry and blissfully unaware of its own origins, of everything that had happened before it was born." What do you think becomes of Marie-Louise, Véronique, and Jean-Louis in the years after the novel ends? How do you envision their future? ∾